BISON
BOOKS

DATE DUE

8-16-16		
1-4-2020		

BISON FRONTIERS OF IMAGINATION

THE
Self-Propelled Island

~~~~~~~~~~~~~~~~~~~~~

JULES VERNE

Translated by Marie-Thérèse Noiset

Introduction by Volker Dehs

With editorial assistance by Robert Sandarg

University of Nebraska Press ≈ *Lincoln and London*

Publication of this book was made possible by a grant from The Florence Gould Foundation.

L'Île à hélice was originally published in French in 1895. Translation and critical apparatus © 2015 by the Board of Regents of the University of Nebraska.

Library of Congress Cataloging-in-Publication Data
Verne, Jules, 1828–1905.
[Île à hélice. English]
The self-propelled island / Jules Verne; translated by Marie-Thérèse Noiset; introduction by Volker Dehs; with editorial assistance by Robert Sandarg.
pages   cm. — (Bison frontiers of imagination)
"*L Île à hélice* was originally published in French in 1895" — Verso title page.
Includes bibliographical references.
ISBN 978-0-8032-4582-2 (cloth: alk. paper)
ISBN 978-0-8032-7671-0 (paperback: alk. paper)
ISBN 978-0-8032-7486-0 (epub)
ISBN 978-0-8032-7487-7 (mobi)
ISBN 978-0-8032-7488-4 (pdf)
1. Imaginary places—Fiction. 2. Voyages, Imaginary—Fiction. I. Noiset, Marie-Thérèse, translator. II. Dehs, Volker, 1964– writer of introduction. III. Sandarg, Robert, editor. IV. Title.
PQ2469.I4E5 2015   843'.8—dc23   2014044111

Set in Fournier MT Pro by M. Scheer.

CONTENTS

Introduction by Volker Dehs   vii

Translator's Note   xxi

PART ONE

I. The Concerting Quartet   3

II. The Power of a Cacophonous Sonata   12

III. A Chatty Mentor   24

IV. The Concerting Quartet Disconcerted   34

V. Standard Island and Milliard City   46

VI. Invitees . . . Inviti   57

VII. Heading West   70

VIII. Navigation   81

IX. The Hawaiian Archipelago   91

X. Crossing the Line   102

XI. The Marquesas Islands   114

XII. Three Weeks in the Tuamotus   127

XIII. Stopping at Tahiti   139

XIV. Parties and More Parties   150

PART TWO

I. In the Cook Islands   167

II. From Island to Island   179

III. Concert at the Court   191

IV. British Ultimatum   201

V. The Taboo at Tonga Tabu   212

VI. A Collection of Wild Animals   224

VII. The Hunt   234

VIII. The Fiji Islands and Their Inhabitants   240

IX. A Casus Belli   251

X. Change of Owners   264

XI. Offense and Defense   278

XII. Taking the Helm, Starboard or Larboard?   289

XIII. The Last Word by Pinchinat   302

XIV. Denouement   314

INTRODUCTION

THE MOST FAMOUS OF THE Extraordinary Voyages, a series of novels written by Jules Verne between 1868 and 1905, are "extraordinary" because of either the object being pursued or the means of transportation being utilized, or even both at the same time. *The Self-Propelled Island*, a novel written in two parts, published ten years before the death of its author, obviously belongs to the second category. The idea of a moving island, steered to follow a chosen course, ensuring perpetual spring weather and great tourist attractions for its fabulously rich inhabitants, is certainly one of Verne's most daring "technological inventions." This self-propelled island is much larger than the steamer *Great Eastern*, the largest vessel of Verne's time; it is infinitely more luxurious than the *Nautilus*, the legendary submarine that traveled the bottom of the oceans in *Twenty-Thousand Leagues under the Sea* (1869–70), or the bullet-shaped spacecraft circling the moon in *Around the Moon* (1870). Yet the self-propelled island Verne called Standard Island does not seem to have captivated readers to the same extent as inventions in his first novels. How can it be explained that *The Self-Propelled Island* remained relatively unknown? The answer to this question is a paradox, as will later be seen.

A Life Totally Devoted to Writing

Jules Verne's biographers have uniformly recognized the peculiar fact that it was on an island in the Loire (the river that crosses the Breton city of Nantes) that Jules Verne was born on February 8, 1828. Was this a harbinger of Verne's lifelong fascination with islands, floating or not, and of the bias he had for "Robinsonades"? (Indeed, several of his novels explore the fate of the castaway on a deserted island). The facts show that Verne's family left Feydeau Island less than a year after he was born and settled on the mainland across from the island not far from one of the most important ports of France at the time. Young Jules grew up with a brother and three sisters amid a well-to-do family, with the enviable prospect of one day replacing his father, Pierre, as one of the city's most reputable lawyers. However, this did not come to pass.

In November 1848 Jules arrived in Paris to complete his studies but showed little enthusiasm for studying law. He paid absolutely no attention to the revolutionary events of the time but instead directed all his efforts to being admitted into the literary circles of the city. He had already penned two unfinished novels and several historical dramas and comedies, as well as a good amount of poetry; all works that remained unpublished during his lifetime. He dreamed of becoming a famous writer, following in the footsteps of his literary idols: Honoré de Balzac, Alfred de Musset, and Victor Hugo. He was particularly encouraged to take this path by the Dumas father-and-son duo, the elder being the author of *The Three Musketeers* and his son of *The Lady of the Camellias*. The Dumases put on Verne's play *Les pailles rompues* (The broken straws) at the little Théâtre Historique in Paris, in 1850.

Although success was slow in coming, Jules Verne devoted himself entirely to a career in theater. What is perhaps most amazing is that Pierre Verne accepted with little objection his son's decision. Jules abandoned the conventional objective of becoming a lawyer and was supported by his father financially for a period of ten years.

Jules later became a stockbroker to support his family. In 1857 Verne married a young widow who had two daughters of her own, and in 1861 she bore him his only son, Michel. The young author continued writing in many genres: two travel novels, short stories, songs, poems, plays, and even art reviews. He would, however, have been a totally forgotten writer today had he not come in contact with the editor Pierre-Jules Hetzel in 1861 or 1862. Hetzel was a staunch Republican just back from a self-imposed ten-year exile in Belgium, where he lived after the coup d'état of President Louis-Napoléon, who had become Emperor Napoléon III. The editor rejected a story of travels in England and Scotland based on Verne's personal experience but encouraged the young writer to produce a novel that would be thoroughly innovative. His advice inspired

Verne to write about a balloon traversing the still mostly unexplored African continent. From the time of its publication in 1863, *Five Weeks in a Balloon* became an immediate success as well as a gold mine. Hetzel encouraged more novels of the same kind. In a much later interview Verne declared, "Although not wholly pleased with the idea, I complied with [his] request, and the result has been that since then, so far as my published works are concerned, I have completely discarded the old love and devoted all my energies and attention to the new."[1] The "old love" was the theater, which always remained Verne's secret interest.

From then on, his novels came in bursts of fortuitous inspiration: first *Journey to the Center of the Earth* in 1864, then *From the Earth to the Moon* in 1865; *The Voyages and Adventures of Captain Hatteras* (1867–68) and *The Children of Captain Grant* (1867–68) followed. These titles inaugurated Verne's series Extraordinary Voyages. The author created and explored the genre of "scientific novel" and, in doing so, proposed to construct, piece by piece, a picture of the earth. This was not about science fiction. In fact, the term "science fiction" appeared much later, in 1920, in the United States. The work was not about futuristic predictions either, since Verne rarely departed from the present. In 1863 Verne had proposed the novel *Paris in the 20th Century*, but Hetzel refused this work and it was not until 1994 that the book was published, posthumously.

Hetzel's rejections were few and far between, but the editor and his successor, Louis-Jules Hetzel, who was also his son, continually influenced the writing and the positive moral climate of the Extraordinary Voyages. Some critics even used the word "censored" after the correspondence between Verne and his editors was published.[2] The Hetzelian criticism often improved Verne's novels, a fact that the writer himself often acknowledged in his letters.

In 1873 Verne reached the height of his fame with the publication of *Around the World in Eighty Days*. An adaptation of the novel for the theater followed, as well as several other plays based on his most popular works. Verne had finally achieved the acclaim he had sought as a playwright. His plays were presented in the Théâtre du Châtelet, one of the greatest theaters in Paris, and throughout the world. After years of experimentation and relative poverty, Verne had finally attained success and financial freedom. Allowed at last to indulge his love of sea travels,

Verne bought three boats, one after the other, each more luxurious than the last. He took short trips as well as four longer cruises that helped fuel his imagination: he sailed the Mediterranean Sea in 1878 and 1884, the coasts of England and Scotland in 1879, and the Baltic Sea in 1881. Neither the political crises of the time, such as the Franco-Prussian War of 1870 or the Paris Commune of 1871, nor grave family problems, such as the declining health of his wife, the difficult character of his son, or the attack at gunpoint on his person by his mentally ill nephew, kept him from regularly writing two volumes a year. His works published after 1880 were less successful than his earlier publications, but his novels continued to be translated, into a dozen foreign languages, and in the public's mind he remains forever the father of Captain Nemo and the *Nautilus*. Verne pursued his literary work to the end of his life: "My object has been to depict the earth, and not the earth alone, but the universe, for I have sometimes taken my readers away from the earth, in the novel. And I have tried at the same time to realize a very high ideal of beauty of style. It is said that there can't be any style in a novel of adventure, but that isn't true; though I admit that it is very much more difficult to write such a novel in a good literary form than the studies of characters which are so in vogue to-day."[3]

Verne favored the quiet life and spurned worldly vanities. His humility astonished his contemporaries. In 1871 he settled in the provincial town of Amiens in Picardy, near his wife's family. In spite of his Royalist leanings, he was elected to the town council as a member of the opposing party, the Republicans, in 1888. He served on the council until 1903, when fatigue and ill health forced him to retire. When he died, on March 24, 1905, his son, Michel, the heir to his literary collection, discovered ten unpublished volumes of his work. Michel set about publishing the newfound volumes and worked at this task until 1919. He made considerable changes to the plots and even to the intended meanings of his father's stories, exacting the ultimate revenge in a relationship that had always been difficult.

Verne and the USA—An Ambiguous Relationship

The novels of Jules Verne owe a lot to two American writers: James Fenimore Cooper and Edgar Allan Poe. Since Verne lacked command of the English language, he read these authors' translated works: Cooper's when he was still a child, and Poe's around 1860. The poet Charles Baudelaire made Poe's works known to the people of France. He rendered Poe's name more famous and even more popular in France than it was in the United States. Poe's stories played a pivotal role in Verne's creation of the Extraordinary Voyages series, and Verne paid tribute to Poe in 1864 in an essay entitled "Edgard Poë et ses oeuvres" (Edgar Poe and his works; Verne adopted the French spelling of Poe's name). Verne preferred the logic of Poe's detective stories and travel novels to his macabre fantasy tales. He was particularly impressed by Poe's *The Narrative of Arthur Gordon Pym of Nantucket* and published a sequel teeming with geographical, maritime, and physical details, titled *An Antarctic Mystery; or, The Sphinx of the Ice Fields*, in 1897. Verne felt that, "leaving aside the obscure, what must be admired in Poe's works are the novel situations, the discussion of hardly known facts, the observation of human pathological states, the choice of topics, the forever strange personalities of his heroes with their sickly and nervous dispositions and their way of expressing themselves in bizarre interjections. And yet, among these impossible characteristics, sometimes is present a plausibility that engages the curiosity of the reader." This astute analysis of Poe's writings reads like a blueprint of Verne's novels.

Oddly enough, Verne expressed a certain reserve toward his model. That may surprise the reader but simply proves that Verne scrutinized Poe's stories through the particular lens used by Europeans, especially the French, looking at North America in the nineteenth century:

Allow me now to draw your attention to the more materialistic side of Poe's stories. Divine intervention plays no role in them and is not even acknowledged by Poe. In fact, he claims all things can be explained by physical laws, and so he even invents these laws when he needs them. The faith that would give him constant contemplation of the supernatural is not present in his works. His fantasy is "cold" fantasy, if I dare say, and, unfortunately, he is another follower of materialism. I believe this is less a result of his personal disposition than of the utterly practical and industrial influence of United States society. Poe wrote, thought and dreamed as an

American, a positive man; now, having recognized his bias, let us admire his works.[4]

This last quote is as important as the preceding one to define Verne's project. Verne did not embrace straight scientism. Neither did he eschew modern ideologies such as materialism or positivism, but he favored an *artistic* approach to the world. This has not been stressed enough. The United States is a constant presence in his novels from the very beginning, but it is seen through a lens of admiration mixed with skepticism. Verne's remarks sometimes border on the biting irony that Charles Dickens expressed in his novel *Martin Chuzzlewit* (1842–43). Dickens, one of Verne's favorite authors, had visited the United States in 1842, as had Verne in 1867. However, unlike his English counterpart, Verne did not embark on a cross-country lecture circuit of the United States:

I have even crossed the Atlantic on board the *Great-Eastern*, and set foot on American soil, where, I am ashamed to have to confess, I stayed only eight days. What was I to do? I had a ticket to go and come that was only good for a week!

After all, I saw New York, stopped at the Fifth Avenue Hotel, crossed the East River before the Brooklyn Bridge was built, sailed up the Hudson as far as Albany, visited Buffalo and Lake Erie, gazed on the Falls of Niagara from the top of the Terrapine Tower, while a lunar rainbow could be seen through the vapors of the mighty rapids, and finally, on the other side of the Suspension Bridge, sat down on the Canadian Shore, after which, I started back home. And one of my deepest regrets is to think that I shall never again see America—a country which I love, and which every Frenchman should love as a sister of France.[5]

In the 1880s Verne considered going back to America on a lecture tour, but he finally decided against it when he realized that lectures given in French were of little interest to the American public. Verne thus built his particular view of Americans without personal experience when he introduced American characters in his novels. With their practical business intuition, the American characters of Verne's novels are the prototype of modern man, the engineer. It is not by chance that Verne injected the idea of a trip to the moon in the head of an American: "The Yankees, these first mechanics of the world, are engineers in the same way that Italians are musicians and Germans, philosophers, by birth. Nothing is more natural, then, than seeing them bring their audacious ingenuity to ballistics. This is why they have massive cannons, much less useful than the sewing machines but as amazing, and even more admired."[6]

Verne wholly supported abolitionism. He devoted three works, two of them entirely, to the American Civil War: the short story "The Blockade Runners" (1865), the beginning of *The Mysterious Island* (1874–75) and the novel *Texar's Revenge; or, North against South* (1887). Other novels set in the United States could be added, but let us simply recall a rather unknown title, *The Will of an Eccentric*. In this novel, the United States is a giant game board in a game of Goose and the protagonists are the game pieces. In order to receive a fabulous inheritance, seven candidates must accept the roll of a die thrown by a lawyer, which sends them exploring the entire country.

Verne admired the Americans' ability to think big and act on the belief that bigger is better, but at the same time, he was critical of America's insatiable appetite and felt that immoderation and purely commercial endeavors end fatally in miserliness and false pride. The machines in the Extraordinary Voyages often serve as catalysts for these self-destructive tendencies, increasing the physical power of human beings while diminishing their moral qualities. Like the grandiloquent circus and show business man P. T. Barnum (1810–91) in real life, the impresario Phineas Taylor Barnum, a recurring and emblematic character in the works of Verne, embodies, in a humorous way, the two above-mentioned tendencies. This character reappears in *The Self-Propelled Island*, in the person of his own descendant, under the anagram of Calistus Munbar (meaning, in fact, "the most handsome Barnum" and playing at the same time on the word *calidus*: cunning). Barnum was already targeted in the short story "American Customs. The Humbug," probably written following Verne's return from the United States on the *Great Eastern*. Although lacking a regular plot, this satirical story offers the impressions of a Frenchman as he travels the United States. It makes fun of a self-made man as portrayed by the merchant Hopkins. Hopkins succeeds in deceiving people with his increasingly clever tricks.

The benevolent irony becomes grating in the novel *Sans dessus dessous*, published in English under the titles *Topsy-Turvy* and *The Purchase of the North Pole*. This novel is a sequel to the lunar novels, using the same characters. A group of American industrialists, wanting to reach some inaccessible coal resources, tries to displace the North Pole with an enormous cannon blast, and in so doing, they risk changing the conditions of the entire planet. It does not matter to them that the event will cause the demise of a part of humanity. They do not consider that their profits may be uncertain. In the end, the great disaster does not happen, thanks to a mistake made by the engineers. The novel ends in an ironic comment anticipating the conclusion of *The Self-Propelled Island*: "Now it seems that the inhabitants of our globe can sleep peacefully. Changing the way the Earth moves lays beyond the efforts allowed humanity. It does not belong to men to alter in any way the order established by the Creator in the system of the Universe."[7]

The American dream, as exciting as it is, risks deteriorating into a nightmare. According to Verne, this danger threatens not Americans alone, but the entire human race. Science cannot be used without conscience, with its only goal one of maximizing profits.

A Futuristic Novel

Toward the end of 1895, a journalist who ran into Verne strolling the streets of Amiens asked him how he came up with his idea, "even more impressive than all the preceding ones," to create *The Self-Propelled Island*. Verne replied,

> Don't laugh! This idea came to me on the *Pont des Arts*. It was suggested to me by Jean Macé, author of *La Bouchée de pain* [*The History of a Mouthful of Bread*] and founder of the *Ligue de l'Enseignement*, who died recently. . . .[8] Perhaps Macé, unknowingly my collaborator for a day, got this idea looking at a pleasure boat or simply at the running water. I kept his suggestion in mind, not giving it much thought or form. Thirty years later, I created Standard Island out of Macé's *bateau-mouche* (It may even have been a washhouse boat on the river). In the same way, I borrowed the theme of *A Floating City* from my travel to America aboard the prestigious *Great*

Eastern. All classical philosophy teachers teach their students that imagination merely transposes and juxtaposes elements taken from real life and daily observations. Their lectures show that the workings of the imagination resemble those of a child putting together a puzzle. An original frame of mind is required for these configurations. A specific ability is also needed, to choose, in the ordinary unfolding of life, the secondary details that will allow imagination to use them to its greatest advantage, overturning them, deforming them, amplifying them. . . . This is a rough analysis, albeit an accurate one, of the workings of the imagination.[9]

The Self-Propelled Island was first published as a series, then in two volumes, and finally in a large, illustrated octavo edition in 1895. It was not particularly well received by the French public: only nine thousand copies of the novel's second edition were sold by 1914, and fifteen thousand of the third. This was rather disappointing compared to the success of Verne's previous novels. In spite of this poor reception, translations of *The Self-Propelled Island* appeared in about twenty languages, but with the passages offensive to the British or Americans modified or omitted.

The reader learns almost incidentally that the action of *The Self-Propelled Island* takes place in an undisclosed year of the twentieth century, thus in the future. This renders plausible the invention of Standard Island and its luxurious amenities. The island is described, in the terms of its managers, as "this microcosm, the only one of its kind in the world," "the finest invention of the modern steel industry," "this masterpiece of human genius," "a piece of a superior planet fallen into the middle of the Pacific and a floating Eden." *The Self-Propelled Island* recycles parts of Verne's novel *Paris in the Twentieth Century*, which had not yet been published. Verne was probably convinced that *Paris in the Twentieth Century* would never be published, at least not in his lifetime. One key passage of that novel, written in 1863, helps the reader grasp what will happen thirty years later on *The Self-Propelled Island*:

What would our ancestors have thought, seeing these boulevards as bright as if they had been lit by the sun, these thousands of vehicles moving noiselessly on the quiet surface of the streets, these stores as opulent as palaces, pouring forth their light in a blaze of white. . . . They would no doubt have been very surprised; but the people of 1960 did no longer admire these marvels; they enjoyed them quietly, without being happier, though, because, in their quick gait and their American ardor, the demon of riches could be felt, pushing them ahead without any respite or pity.[10]

The narrator of *The Self-Propelled Island* puts aside the technological marvels of the island almost as soon as they are presented; they do not play a role in the development of the story. The billionaires of the island, living in a sort of Americanized Paris of the future, differ greatly from the rushed Parisians of *Paris in the Twentieth Century*. They no longer need to earn a living, as they possess all conceivable riches, ensuring them an ideal retirement far from the social inequalities of the Old and New Worlds. Their wishes are instantly fulfilled. With its particularly utopian characterization, this voluntary, chosen Robinsonade appears to be the exact opposite of *The Mysterious Island*. Published twenty years earlier, *The Mysterious Island* chronicles the adventure of five shipwrecked men who, possessing only their wisdom and their knowledge, must start anew, reinventing human civilization in record time, from the discovery of fire to the invention of the telegraph. Unfortunately, all their efforts are in vain, because a natural disaster, a volcanic eruption, destroys their island, annihilating all human ambition. It is worth noting that Verne, mostly in his manuscript for *The Mysterious Island* rather than in the published book, used real geographic names in order to make the initially happy island a sort of miniature North America. Standard Island, Verne's artificial island, was obviously built with the same intention, but here the conditions are inverted: first there exists superabundance, and the power of knowledge is replaced by the power of money. The results, however, are the same. A volcanic eruption also takes place in *The Self-Propelled Island* (part 2, chapter 4) and causes chaos, aggravated by the internal conflicts of the island's inhabitants. The skeptical narrator concludes, "Common sense never stands a chance of being adopted in this world" (part 2, chapter 12). Social utopia, even anchored in a sure economic foundation, will always prove very fragile.

As is often the case in utopian stories, the ideal world of *The Self-Propelled Island* is presented through the eyes of foreigners arriving from afar. Here the foreigners are members of a French string quartet who have been kidnapped and brought to the island to entertain its inhabitants. One might wonder why Verne chose a string quartet. The fact is that, due to an appreciation for the recent works of Haydn, Beethoven, and Schubert, the string quartet was considered the most refined expression of musical artistry of Verne's time. Its contemplative quality contrasted with the flamboyance of the symphony and the spectacle of the opera, which had deteriorated into a commercial enterprise even if it was still very much in vogue in the nineteenth century. Our four artists, displaying a fundamental contrast with the plutocrats of Standard Island, reinforce the romantic idea of an antagonism between art and business, even if they were attracted by very high wages. They comment on what is happening, like the ancient Greek chorus. Their remarks are the direct result of their four different temperaments, which can be individually defined as serious, admiring, fanciful, and angry. The disposition of one of them, the cellist Sébastien Zorn, is even revealed by his name, since "zorn" in German means "anger."

Verne makes ample use of onomastics in *The Self-Propelled Island*. This inclination has already been noted in the case of Munbar, the superintendent. The first name of Munbar's superior, the wise governor Cyrus Bikerstaff, refers to the American engineer Cyrus W. Field, who befriended Verne during his trip to the United States aboard the *Great Eastern*. Field is also the prototype for the engineer Cyrus Smith in *The Mysterious Island*. The last name of the governor comes from the pseudonym sometimes used by Jonathan Swift, the satirical Irish author of *Gulliver's Travels*. A secondary character, Barthelemy Ruge, alludes to Dickens's revolutionary novel *Barnaby Rudge* (1840–41). The pleasure Verne finds in punning can also be found in the names of the engineers of Standard Island's two harbors, Watson and Somwah. The fact that the two names are inversions of the two basic syllables ("wat/wah" and "son/som") suggests the fateful rotating movement that the island eventually experiences.

Following are two more examples of the inferences Verne sprinkles through the text of *The Self-Propelled Island*. At the end of 1894 he wrote to his longtime friend Alexandre Dumas, "Don't assume that I would ever forget you because I never see you anymore. . . . I only look at the maps now, and next year, if it pleases you, we will wander through the archipelagos of the Pacific on *The Self-Propelled Island*."[11] And indeed there is a hidden reference to A(lex)AN(dr)E DUM(a)S in the character of the French dance teacher, Athanase Dorémus A(th)AN(as)E D(oré)MUS, "an old man of seventy, thin, skinny, and short. He still had a sharp eye, all his teeth, and a full head of curly hair, white like his beard" (part 1, chapter 8). Dumas would have had the pleasure of recognizing himself in this description in the first volume, had he not died on November 27, 1895, at the age of seventy-one, only two weeks after the publication of the second volume.

Another secondary, but still important, character in *The Self-Propelled Island* is the philosophical king of Malécarlie who willingly gives up his throne. This king, a permanent resident of Standard Island, wants to improve his financial situation by becoming the main astronomer of the island. He resembles Dom Pedro II d'Alcantara (1825–91), the last king of Brazil, who was a member of both the Habsburg family and the family of the Count of Paris (pretender to the throne of France and well-known by Jules Verne). Dom Pedro was more interested in the arts and sciences than in governing. In November 1889 he refused to oppose his country's revolution, triggered by his decree to abolish slavery, and he emigrated to France. Since 1868, Dom Pedro had been, like Verne, a member of the Geographical Society of Paris and often attended its meetings. He was also a lover of astronomy. The allusion to Dom Pedro in the plot of *The Self-Propelled Island* amounts to a political stand by the writer. Although Verne no longer expected monarchy to make a comeback, he was not a firm believer in republicanism or in American-style democracy, as proved by notes and puns found in his unpublished papers, such as "Moinarchie," a word play combining "moi" (the French word for "me") and "monarchy," or his remark that "there is more freedom for citizens in the monarchy than in the republic." Further proof of Verne's skepticism can be found in his quote of Poe's famous words: "One would be safe in wagering that any given public idea is erroneous, for it has been yielded to the clamor of the majority."[12]

The Self-Propelled Island is a novel of progressive disillusion at every level. It is a farewell to the social utopia, a farewell to the illusion of man controlling nature's elements, a farewell to luxury and wealth, and finally a farewell to the ideal of the perfect machine, which proves defective in its very perfection and thus disappoints. While the submarine *Nautilus*, as unique as an artwork, arouses the reader's imagination, Standard Island is a mere industrial object that can be duplicated and loses its charm because of its sterility. This is a paradoxical result that probably explains why *The Self-Propelled Island* did not become very popular in its time. And yet the merciless unfolding of events reveals the undeniable nature of this novel that preserves love, extols musical art, and keeps a witty tone throughout the most harrowing experiences.

The critical commentary of the narrator of *The Self-Propelled Island* emphasizes the fictitious nature of the island, giving an artificial flavor to the story, which, in the French original, is strangely narrated in the present tense. In addition to expressions borrowed from the theater, metaphors reappear constantly in Verne's discourse, strengthening the impression that everything in this novel is man-made. These features increase the disillusion while at the same time making *The Self-Propelled Island* a very modern novel.

Floating islands and airships, most often intended for the wealthiest among us, were announced and later abandoned long before Jules Verne's novel was published. They still pervade the world news. Let us hope that if a construction similar to *The Self-Propelled Island* is ever built, it will be under more favorable auspices than those of Standard Island.

VOLKER DEHS

Translated by Marie-Thérèse Noiset

Notes

1. Gordon Jones, "Jules Verne at Home," *Temple Bar* (London), no. 129 (June 1904): 665.

2. *Correspondance inédite de Jules Verne et de Pierre-Jules Hetzel, 1863–1886*, ed. Olivier Dumas, Volker Dehs, and Piero Gondolo della Riva, 5 vols. (Geneva: Slatkine, 1999–2006).

3. Robert Harborough Sherard, "Jules Verne at Home: His Own Account of His Life and Work," *McClure's Magazine*, January 1894, 121.

4. J. Verne, "Edgard Poë et ses oeuvres," chapter 4, *Musée des Familles* 31 (April 1864): 208. (This quote and the preceding one are translated here from Verne's original text.)

5. J. Verne, "The Story of My Boyhood," *Boy's Companion*, April 9, 1891, 211, commons.wikimedia.org/wiki/File:Verne_Story_of_My_Boyhood.jpg.

6. J. Verne, *De la terre à la lune* (Paris: Hetzel, 1865), chapter 1 (translated from Verne's original).

7. J. Verne, *Sans dessus dessous* (Paris: Hetzel, 1889), chapter 21 (translated from Verne's original).

8. Jean Macé (1815–94), teacher and politician, was an old friend of the editor Hetzel, who published the greatest part of his works.

9. P[ierre] D[ubois], "A propos de *L'Île à hélice*: Interview-rencontre de M. Jules Verne," *Journal d'Amiens: Moniteur de la Somme*, December 28, 1895, 2 (translated from the original French).

10. Jules Verne, *Paris au XXe siècle* (Paris: Hachette, 1994), chapter 2 (translated from Verne's original).

11. A. Dumas fils, November 26, 1894, *Bulletin de la Société Jules Verne* 94 (1990): 33 (translated from the original French).

12. J. Verne, "Notes," Bibliothèques d'Amiens Métropole, Collection Jules Verne, MS JV 22, fol. 7, 6, and 24. (The quote by Verne here is in its original English.)

TRANSLATOR'S NOTE

IN ORDER FOR MY TRANSLATION to read smoothly, the Pacific Islands encountered in the novel have been given their present-day names, the measurements given by Verne have been converted from the metric system to the English system, and the narration has been translated into the past tense.

The Self-Propelled Island

PART ONE

I

~~~~~~~~~~~

The Concerting Quartet

WHEN A TRIP BEGINS BADLY, it rarely ends well. At least this is an opinion that the four musicians, whose instruments were lying on the ground, would surely have a right to maintain. Indeed, the carriage they had taken at the final station of the railroad had just tipped over onto the shoulder of the road.

"Anyone hurt?" asked the first musician who quickly stood up.

"All I have is a scratch," answered the second, wiping his cheek nicked by broken glass.

"Me, I was hardly grazed," said the third, who had a few drops of blood trickling from his calf.

"Where is my cello . . . ?" asked the fourth. "I hope nothing happened to my cello!"

Luckily, the instrument cases were intact. The cello, the two violins, and the viola had not been damaged by the jolting. They would hardly need tuning. Top-quality instruments they were.

"That damned railroad left us stranded halfway . . . ," said one.

"That damned carriage dumped us in the middle of this deserted land . . . !" replied the other.

"Right as night is falling . . . !" added the third.

"Luckily, our concert is only scheduled for the day after tomorrow!" observed the fourth.

Then several comical exchanges took place among these musicians, who accepted their misadventure cheerfully. One of them, following his ingrained habit of borrowing his jokes from musical terms, said,

"In the meantime, our carriage went 'out of tune'!"

"Pinchinat!" admonished one of his companions.

"And my opinion is," continued Pinchinat, "that too many of our adventures 'end up off key.'"

"Will you be quiet . . . ?"

"And that we would do well to 'transpose our pieces' to another carriage!" Pinchinat dared to add.

Yes, they had had a few dreadful adventures indeed, as the reader will soon find out.

This entire exchange took place in French, but it could as well have been carried out in English. The quartet spoke Walter Scott's and Cooper's language like their own, thanks to their many peregrinations through countries of Anglo-Saxon origin. Thus it was in this language that they addressed the driver of the carriage.

The good man was the worst off, since he had been thrown from his seat at the very moment the front axle broke. But he only received a few contusions that were more painful than serious. True, he could not walk because of a sprain. They would thus have to find a way of transporting him to the next village.

It was indeed a miracle that the accident did not cause any fatalities. The road meandered through a mountainous countryside, at times coming dangerously close to steep cliffs. In many places it ran alongside turbulent torrents and was cut by fords that were unfit for carriages. If the front axle had broken a few steps earlier, there is no doubt that the vehicle would have rolled down into these abysses and perhaps no one would have survived the disaster.

At any rate, the carriage was useless now. One of the two horses had hit its head on a stone and was groaning on the ground. The other had a deep cut on its hip. Thus, they had no carriage or horses left.

In short, bad luck had not spared them, these four musicians, in the territory of Southern California. They had suffered two accidents in twenty-four hours and, unless one is a philosopher, . . .

At that time, San Francisco, the capital of the state, was in direct communication by rail with San Diego, situated almost at the border of the old Californian province. It was toward this important city, where they were to give a much publicized and anticipated concert two days later, that the four travelers were heading. The train, having left San Francisco the day before, was only about fifty miles outside of San Diego when the first "contretemps" occurred.

Yes, the jolliest member of the gang called it a "contretemps" indeed, and we will ask you to tolerate this expression from the former student of musical notation.

If there had been an unavoidable stop at the Paschal station, it was because the tracks had been swept away by a flash flood for a distance of three to four miles. It had been impossible to catch the train two miles farther on, because a transfer had not yet been organized, the train accident having happened only a few hours earlier.

The passengers had to make a choice: either wait for the track to reopen or, at the next village, take any carriage they could find for San Diego.

The quartet decided on this last option. In a neighboring village, they found a rickety, old, moth-eaten carriage that was not in the least comfortable. They haggled over the price with the owner and lured the driver with the promise of a generous tip. They left with their instruments but not with their luggage. It was about two in the afternoon and, until seven, the trip continued without too much trouble or fatigue. But then a second "contretemps" occurred: the carriage toppled over in such an unfortunate way that they could not use it to go on.

And the quartet was still a good twenty miles from San Diego!

But why would four musicians, of French nationality and born in Paris moreover, venture through this incredible region of Southern California?

Why . . . ? We are going to briefly explain this and paint, with a few strokes, the four virtuosos whom fate, that whimsical distributor of roles, was going to put in contact with the characters of this astonishing story.

During that year—we cannot precisely tell you what year this was, give or take thirty years—the United States had doubled the number of stars on its federal flag. Its industrial and commercial powers were in full bloom after annexing the Canadian Dominion to the farthest border of the Polar Sea and the Mexican, Guatemalan, Honduran, Nicaraguan, and Costa Rican provinces up to the Panama Canal. At the same time, the aesthetic sense of these Yankee invaders had developed. Though their production was still very limited in the field of fine arts, and their national genius rather closed to painting, sculpture, and music, the taste for beautiful artwork had become widespread among them. By regularly buying the paintings of the Old Masters for outrageous prices in order to build up their private or public collections, by hiring famous singers and actors as well as the most talented musicians for exorbitant fees, they had finally acquired an appreciation for beautiful, noble things that had escaped them for so long.

In music, it was the famous composers of the second half of the nineteenth century, Meyerbeer, Halévy, Gounod, Berlioz, Wagner, Verdi, Massé, Saint-Saëns, Reyer, Massenet, Delibes, who had first fascinated the dilettantes of the New World. Later, little by little, they began to understand the more profound works of Mozart, Haydn, and Beethoven, going back to the source of this sublime art that had started pouring out during the eighteenth century. After the operas came the operettas, the dramas, the symphonies, the sonatas, the orchestral suites. And now the sonata was extremely popular in the various states of the Union. The people would gladly have paid for one, musical note by musical note, twenty dollars for a full note, ten for a half, and five for an eighth.

It was at this very moment that, aware of this extreme craze, four very talented musicians decided to seek success and fortune in the United States of America. They were four close friends, all former students at the Conservatory, well-known in Paris and much appreciated in the world of what we call "chamber music," which, until then, was not widespread in North America. It was with rare perfection, marvelous unity, and deep feelings that they interpreted the works for four string instruments, a first and second violin, a viola, and a cello, written by Mozart, Beethoven, Mendelssohn, Haydn, and Chopin. We will add that their music was not in the least raucous and not performed to show off their expertise but had such an impeccable interpretation and incomparable virtuosity! The success of this quartet can better be understood if we recall that at that time people were starting to tire of the formidable harmonic and symphonic orchestras. Music may be nothing but a shaking of artistically combined sound waves, but there is no need to unleash these waves in earsplitting storms.

In short, our four musicians had decided to initiate the Americans into the fine and ineffable enjoyment of chamber music. They left together for the New World and, in the last two years, the Yankee music lovers had not begrudged them their hurrahs or their dollars. Their musical matinees and evenings attracted large audiences. The Concerting Quartet—as they were called—could hardly manage to accept all the private invitations of the rich. Without them, no party, gathering, reception, five o'clock, or garden party attracted the attention of the public. Thanks to this infatuation, the quartet had pocketed large sums of money, which would already have amounted to a nice bundle if it had been deposited in the Bank of New York. But why not admit it? They were big spenders, our Americanized Parisians! They did not give much thought to saving, these princes of the bow, these kings of the four strings! They had acquired a taste for this adventurous life, certain as they were to be welcomed and rewarded accordingly, while running from New York to San Francisco, from Quebec to New Orleans, and from Nova Scotia to Texas. In a word, they were rather Bohemian—they belonged to the Bohemia of youth, which is the oldest, the most charming, the most enviable, and the best-liked province of our old France!

Unless we are seriously mistaken, it now seems time to introduce them to you one by one, especially to those among our readers who have never had and who will never have the pleasure of hearing them.

Yvernès, the first violin, was thirty-two years old and taller than average. He had had the good sense to stay skinny; his hair was blond and curly at the ends, and his face was clean-shaven. He had big brown eyes and long fingers constructed to deploy lavishly at the touch of his Guarnerius. He looked elegant and enjoyed draping himself in a dark-colored cloak topped by a silk stovepipe hat. He was a bit of a showoff, perhaps, and certainly the most carefree of the group, the least preoccupied with financial questions, a prodigious musician, an admirer of beautiful things, and a virtuoso of great talent with a promising future.

Frascolin, the second violin, was thirty and short with a tendency toward obesity that made him fume. His hair was dark as well as his beard. He had a big head, brown eyes, a long nose with quivering nostrils, and a red spot where his gold, forever-present pince-nez—he was hopelessly nearsighted—left its mark. He was a fine fellow, kind and helpful, taking on chores to relieve his companions. He kept the books for the quartet, preaching thrift, but was never listened to. He did not at all envy the success of his friend Yvernès, since he was not ambitious enough to climb to the heights of first violinist. He was an excellent musician, though, and, at that moment, was wearing an enormous smock over his travel clothes.

Pinchinat was the alto; they usually called him "Your Highness." At twenty-seven, he was the youngest of the troupe, the most playful also, one of those incorrigible types who remain children their entire lives. He had fine features and witty, alert eyes. His hair was rather red and he sported a pointy mustache. His tongue was constantly darting between his sharp white teeth. He was an inveterate lover of jokes and puns and was always ready for an attack or a retort. His mind was in perpetual motion, a fact that he attributed to his reading of the many C keys that his instrument required: "It's a real assortment of housewifely tasks," he used to say. He was always in a good mood, enjoying his pranks without thinking of the trouble they could bring to his comrades, and for this he was many times scolded, rebuked, and "caught" by the head of the Concerting Quartet.

Indeed, the quartet had a leader; he was Sébastien Zorn, the cellist, who was their boss because of his talent and also because of his age. He was fifty-five, short, and round. His heavy hair, still blond, formed spit curls at his temples. His bristling mustache blended with his untidy sideburns that ended in points. He had a brick-red complexion; his eyes shone through the lenses of glasses, to which he added a pince-nez when he read music. His hands were chubby; the right one, accustomed to the undulating movements of the bow, was adorned with large rings on the third and little fingers.

We believe that this brief sketch will suffice to present the man and the artist. But a fellow does not hold a sound box between his legs for over forty years without being affected by it. It transforms his life, alters his character. Most cellists are loquacious and ill-tempered; they speak in high-and-mighty tones and are witty to boot. And so was Sébastien Zorn, to whom Yvernès, Frascolin, and Pinchinat gladly left the leadership of their musical tours. They let him speak and act as he saw fit because he knew what he was doing. Accustomed to his haughty ways, they laughed when his outbursts went "over the bar," which was unfortunate for a musical performer, remarked the disrespectful Pinchinat.

The arrangement of their programs, the decisions regarding their itineraries, and the correspondence with their impresarios were among Zorn's numerous responsibilities that often caused his fiery temper to flare up. But he did not intervene in the fees they received and the money they spent. These items were entrusted to their second violin and first accountant, the meticulous and fastidious Frascolin.

Now the quartet has been presented to you as it would have been onstage. The very different if not highly original characters who made it up are known to the reader. We now ask him to let the incidents of this strange story unfold. He will see what role these four Parisians were called to play, how, after receiving so many bravos throughout the states of the American Confederation, they were going to be transported . . . But let's not anticipate, "let's not accelerate the beat," as His Highness would say; let's be patient.

The four Parisians thus found themselves on a deserted road in Southern California at eight o'clock at night, next to the pieces of their "Upturned Carriage"—music by Boieldieu—said Pinchinat. If he, Frascolin, and Yvernès philosophically accepted their misadventure, if it even inspired them to turn out a few professional jokes, you will understand that for the quartet's leader it was the occasion to indulge in a fit of rage. What do you expect? The cellist was irritable; he was, as they say, hot-tempered. That is why Yvernès advanced that he was a descendant of Ajax and Achilles, those two ferocious heroes of antiquity.

So that we will not forget, let us mention once again that Zorn was irascible, Yvernès phlegmatic, Frascolin calm, and Pinchinat overflowing with joviality. They were all excellent friends, as close as brothers. They felt bound by ties that no discussion of interest or self-esteem could break, by common tastes all drawn from the same source. Their hearts, like their well-crafted instruments, were always in tune.

While Sébastien Zorn was cursing and examining the case of his cello to make sure it was not damaged, Frascolin went up to the driver:

"Well, my friend," he asked, "tell me what we are going to do."

"What people do when they have no carriage or horses left . . . wait . . ."

"Wait for one to show up!" cried Pinchinat.

"And what if none showed up . . ."

"Then you look for one," observed Frascolin, who never abandoned his practical bent.

"Where . . . ?" demanded Sébastien Zorn, still struggling with his case on the road, in a frenzy.

"Where there is one!" replied the driver.

"Hey! Just a minute, mister driver," continued the cellist, gradually raising his voice, "is that an answer? What? Here is a clumsy fellow who tips us over, smashes his carriage, and maims his horses, and then he simply says, 'Get out of this mess on your own' . . . !"

Carried away by his natural verbosity, Sébastien Zorn was starting to pour out an endless series of completely useless arguments when Frascolin interrupted him with the following words:

"Let me take care of this, my dear Zorn."

Then, again addressing the driver, he asked, "Where are we, my friend . . . ?"

"Five miles away from Freschal."

"Is that a railway station . . . ?"

"No . . . It's a village near the coast."

"Will we be able to find another carriage there?"

"A carriage . . . no . . . but maybe a cart . . ."

"A cart pulled by oxen as in the time of the Merovingian kings!" exclaimed Pinchinat.

"It does not matter!" said Frascolin.

"Well!" snorted Sébastien Zorn, "you should rather ask him if there is an inn in this dump called Freschal . . . I am fed up with traveling at night . . ."

"My friend," asked Frascolin, "is there any sort of an inn in Freschal?"

"Yes, the inn where we were supposed to change horses."

"And to find this village, all we have to do is follow the main road . . . ?"

"Yes, straight ahead."

"Let's go!" shouted the cellist.

"But it would be cruel to abandon this poor man here . . . in distress," observed Pinchinat.

"Let's see, my friend, couldn't you . . . if we helped you . . . ?"

"That's impossible!" answered the driver. "Anyway, I prefer to stay here . . . with my carriage . . . When daylight comes, I will find a way to get out of this mess . . ."

"Once we are in Freschal," continued Frascolin, "we could send you some help . . ."

"Yes . . . the innkeeper knows me well and he will not leave me in this predicament . . ."

"Are we leaving or not . . . ?" shouted the cellist, who had already picked up his instrument case.

"In a second," replied Pinchinat. "But first give me a hand setting down our driver against the embankment . . ."

Indeed, they had to pull him from the middle of the road since he could not use his badly injured legs. Pinchinat and Frascolin picked him up, carried him, and placed him against the roots of a big tree whose low branches formed a sort of bower.

"Are we leaving or not . . . ?" roared Sébastien for a third time after securing the case to his back with the double strap used for that purpose.

"Mission accomplished," said Frascolin. Then, addressing the man, "So, it's a done deal . . . the innkeeper from Freschal will send you help . . . Until then, do you need anything, my friend . . . ?"

"Yes . . ." answered the driver. "I could use a good swig of gin, if you have any left in your flasks."

Pinchinat's flask was still full and His Highness gladly handed it to him.

"With this, old chap," he said, "you will stay warm tonight . . . on the inside!"

A last call from the cellist convinced his companions to start on their way. It was a good thing that their luggage was on a train instead of with them in the carriage. If it were to arrive in San Diego a bit late, at least they would not have the trouble of carrying it to the village of Freschal. The violin cases were enough to carry, and the cello case was even too much. But of course, a musician worthy of the name never parts with his instrument—no more than a soldier with his rifle or a snail with his shell.

II

~~~~~~~~~~

The Power of a Cacophonous Sonata

TRAVELING AT NIGHT ON FOOT, on a road you do not know, in the midst of an almost deserted region where regular travelers are generally in shorter supply than criminals has to be a little disconcerting. This is the situation the quartet faced. As everyone knows, the French are brave, and these four were as brave as they come. However, between bravery and temerity there exists a line that common sense should not cross. After all, if the train had not run into a plain flooded by a swollen river and their carriage had not tipped over five miles from Freschal, our musicians would not have been forced to venture at night onto this hazardous path. Let's hope, however, that no harm will come to them.

It was around eight o'clock in the evening when Sébastien Zorn and his companions started toward the coast, following the instructions of their driver. Since they had only their leather violin cases, light and not bulky, they would have been wrong to complain, and none of them did, neither the wise Frascolin, nor the merry Pinchinat, nor the idealistic Yvernès. But the cellist with his cello case, like an armoire attached to his back! We can understand, especially considering his difficult disposition, that he found cause for fuming. And so, grunts and moans came out in onomatopoeic *oohs*, *ahs*, and *oufs*.

It was already very dark. Thick clouds were chasing each other through the sky, sometimes split by narrow tears through which a mocking moon would appear, almost in its first quarter. We do not know why the blonde Phoebe did not appeal to Sébastien Zorn. Was it, perhaps, because he was angry and irritable? He shook his fist at her, screaming,

"Well, what are you doing there, with your stupid profile ...! I really don't know of anything more idiotic than this kind of an unripe melon slice strolling across the sky!"

"It would be better if the moon looked us in the face," said Frascolin.

"And why is that . . . ?" asked Pinchinat.

"Because we would have more light."

"Oh! chaste Diana," Yvernès declaimed. "Oh peaceful messenger of the night, oh pale satellite of the earth, oh adored idol of the adorable Endymion . . ."

"Are you through with your ballad?" yelled the cellist. "When these first violinists start playing hearts and flowers . . ."

"Let's walk faster," said Frascolin, "or we risk having to sleep under the stars . . ."

"If there were any . . . and miss our concert in San Diego!" observed Pinchinat.

"That's a pretty thought indeed!" exclaimed Sébastien Zorn, shaking his case, which emitted a plaintive sound.

"But this came from you, my old friend, it was your idea . . ." said Pinchinat.

"My idea . . . ?"

"Indeed! If only we had stayed in San Francisco, where there was an entire collection of Californian ears to charm!"

"Let me ask you once more," said the cellist, "why did we leave . . . ?"

"Because you wanted to."

"Well then, I must admit that I had an unfortunate inspiration, and if . . ."

"Ah . . . ! My friends!" interrupted Yvernès, pointing to a certain spot in the sky where a narrow ray of moonlight bordered a cloud with a white edge.

"What's the matter, Yvernès . . . ?"

"Look at that cloud shaped like a dragon, its wings spread out like the tail of a peacock adorned with the hundred eyes of Argus!"

It is likely that Sébastien Zorn did not have the extreme power of hundredfold vision that the guardian of Inachus's daughter possessed, for he did not notice a deep rut in which he inadvertently stepped. He fell on his belly in such a way that, with his case on his back, he looked like a fat beetle crawling on the ground.

The musician was furious and had good reason to be so. He berated the first violinist, who was admiring his aerial monster.

"It's Yvernès's fault!" asserted Sébastien Zorn. "If I had not tried to look at his damned dragon . . ."

"It's no longer a dragon, it's an amphora now! Even with a feeble imagination, you can see it in the hands of Hebe pouring out the nectar."

"Watch out, there may be a lot of water in this nectar," exclaimed Pinchinat, "and your charming goddess of youth could get us thoroughly drenched."

This would have complicated matters and, indeed, it started to look like rain. Thus it seemed advisable to walk faster and look for shelter in Freschal.

They picked up the very annoyed and grumpy cellist and helped him to his feet. The kind Frascolin offered to carry his case, but Sébastien Zorn refused his help at first . . . To part with his instrument . . . a Gand and Bernardel cello that you might as well have called his other half . . . But he finally had to give in and his precious other half passed to the back of the helpful Frascolin, who entrusted his own lighter case to Zorn.

They started back on the road. They walked at a good pace for the next two miles. No incident worth noting. The night was getting darker and darker with the threat of rain. A few very large drops started to fall, proving that they came from high, stormy clouds. But the amphora of pretty Hebe did not pour forth any more water and our four night birds hoped to reach Freschal perfectly dry.

There were still serious precautions to be taken to avoid falls on this dark road, deeply gullied and sometimes breaking at sharp angles, bordered with wide crevices alongside somber chasms where one could hear the trumpets of roaring torrents. If Yvernès, with his temperament, found the situation poetic, Frascolin thought it frightening.

There were also grounds for fearing unfortunate encounters that rendered the safety of travelers on these roads of Southern California rather problematic. The only weapons the quartet possessed were the bows of three violins and a cello, and those might have seemed inadequate in a country where the Colt revolver was invented and perfected. If Sébastien Zorn and his friends had been American, they would have armed themselves with one of these pistols encased in a special gusset of their trousers. Even on the train from San Francisco to San Diego, a true Yankee would not have started his trip without his precious six-shooter. But our Frenchmen had not thought this necessary. We can even say that they had not thought of it at all and that maybe they would regret it.

Pinchinat walked in front, peering into the embankments. Where the road was really hemmed in on the left and right, there was less fear of being surprised by a sudden aggressor. Always the joker, His Highness felt a vague impulse to play a trick on his friends, a strong desire to scare them, to stop in his tracks and utter in a voice trembling with terror,

"What's that . . . ? Over there . . . What do I see . . . ? Get ready to shoot . . ."

But when the road ran through a deep forest, in the middle of those mammoth trees, those sequoias that reach a hundred fifty feet, those giants of the California regions, his longing for banter left him. Ten men could have been waiting in ambush behind each of those enormous trunks . . . A bright flash followed by a sharp bang . . . the quick hissing of a bullet . . . were they going to see it . . . were they going to hear it . . . ? In such places, obviously perfect for a night attack, an ambush was to be expected. If you were lucky enough not to come into contact with bandits, it was because these estimable people had completely disappeared from the American West or were working in financial operations in the markets of the old and new continents . . . ! What an end for the great-grandsons of the Karl Moors and Jean Sbogars! Who could have been having such thoughts? Who but Yvernès? Indeed, he was thinking, "The play does not deserve this set."

Suddenly, Pinchinat froze.

Frascolin, who was following him, did the same. Sébastien Zorn and Yvernès soon caught up with them.

"What's the matter?" asked the second violin.

"I thought I saw something . . . ," answered the alto.

And this time, he was not joking. A shape had just moved between the trees.

"Is it a man or a beast . . . ?" questioned Frascolin.

"I don't know."

Which one would have been more desirable, nobody could have ventured to say. They all looked around, keeping close together, not moving or uttering a single word. Through a break in the clouds, moonbeams suddenly flooded the dome of this dark forest and filtered to the ground through the branches of the sequoias. Now one could see a hundred feet in every direction.

Pinchinat had not been fooled by his imagination. The mass they saw was too big to be a man; it could only be an enormous quadruped. What kind of quadruped . . . ? A wild beast . . . ? Yes, certainly a wild beast . . . But what kind of wild beast . . . ?

"A plantigrade!" Yvernès said.

"To hell with the animal," murmured Sébastien Zorn in a low but impatient voice, "and when I say animal, I mean you, Yvernès . . . ! Can't you speak like everyone else . . . ? What on earth is a plantigrade?"

"It's an animal that walks upright!" explained Pinchinat.

"A bear!" answered Frascolin.

It was a bear indeed, and a big one. You don't meet lions, tigers, or panthers in the forests of Southern California. Bears are common dwellers there and encounters with them are usually unpleasant.

We should not be surprised, then, that our Parisians decided, as one man, to walk away from this plantigrade. After all, wasn't he in his own territory . . . ? So the group got tighter and they walked backward while facing the beast, slowly, pretending they were not ready to run away.

The bear followed them with small steps, flapping his front paws like a semaphore and swaying his haunches like a Spanish maid. He was gradually gaining ground and his behavior became hostile: raucous cries, flapping of jaws that were very disturbing.

"What if we all buzzed off in different directions . . . ?" proposed His Highness.

"Certainly not!" answered Frascolin. "One of us would be caught and would pay for the others!"

They did not take the unsound advice that could have obviously produced regrettable consequences.

So the quartet arrived, as a body, at the edge of a brighter clearing. The bear had come closer and was only ten steps away. Did the place seem right for him to attack them . . . ? Probably so, for his roaring got louder and he walked more quickly.

The group stepped back faster and the second violin gave a more pressing recommendation:

"Stay calm, my friends . . . stay calm!"

They crossed the clearing and found the shelter of trees again, but they were in no less danger there. Moving from one tree to the next, the animal could pounce on them without warning, and this was exactly what he was going to do when he slowed down and his growling abruptly stopped . . .

The heavy darkness was suddenly filled with overpowering music, an expressive largo unveiling the very soul of the artist.

It was Yvernès, who had taken his violin out of its case and was making it vibrate under the powerful caresses of his bow. How brilliant! But indeed, why wouldn't musicians have expected music to save them? Didn't the stones moved by Amphion's melody arrange themselves of their own accord around Thebes? Didn't the wild beasts tamed by Orpheus's lyrical inspirations run to him? Well, we must believe that this Californian bear, given his atavistic dispositions, was as artistically gifted as his peers from the fable, for he lost his ferocity and his music lover's instincts took over. Letting out admiring whimpers, he followed the quartet that was backing up as one man. He did just about everything to show his pleasure but shout "Bravo . . . !"

Fifteen minutes later, Sébastien Zorn and his companions were at the edge of the woods. They got out with Yvernès still playing his violin . . .

The animal had stopped. He did not seem to want to go farther. He clapped with his big paws.

And then Pinchinat grabbed his instrument and yelled, "The Bear Dance, and with panache!"

Then, while the first violin furiously scraped away at the well-known tune in the major mode, the alto accompanied him with a shrill, false bass in the minor one . . .

The animal began to dance, lifting his right foot, then his left, thrashing and twisting about, as he let the group move away down the road.

"Humph!" observed Pinchinat. "It was just a circus bear!"

"No matter!" answered Frascolin. "Our friend Yvernès had a truly great idea!"

"Let's get out of here . . . *allegretto*," replied the cellist, "and without looking back!"

It was about nine o'clock when the four disciples of Apollo arrived safe and sound in Freschal. They had walked at a good pace during this last stage of their trip even though they were no longer followed by the plantigrade.

A cluster of about forty houses, or rather wooden huts, surrounding an area planted with beech trees . . . that was Freschal, an isolated village two miles from the coast.

Our musicians slipped between a few dwellings shaded by large trees. They emerged in the square and caught sight of the humble tower of a small church in the background. They formed a circle, as if they were going to play for a special occasion, but instead exchanged their thoughts.

"You call this a village . . . ?" said Pinchinat.

"Did you expect to find a city like Philadelphia or New York?" replied Frascolin.

"But your village is asleep!" retorted Sébastien Zorn, shrugging his shoulders.

"Let's not wake up a sleeping village!" Yvernès melodiously sighed.

"*Au contraire*, let's wake them up!" cried Pinchinat.

Indeed, unless they wanted to spend the night in the open, they had no choice. At any rate, the square was totally deserted and there was complete silence. There was not a shutter half-open or a single light in the windows. The palace of Sleeping Beauty could have stood there in absolute peace and quiet.

"Well, where is that inn . . . ?" asked Frascolin.

Yes . . . the inn the driver had mentioned, where his travelers in distress were to be welcomed and given suitable accommodations . . . And the innkeeper who was to send help to the unfortunate driver, where was he . . . ? Had the poor man dreamed these things . . . ? Or was there another explanation? Had Sébastien Zorn and his companions gotten lost? Were they in Freschal after all?

These various questions needed straight answers. They had to be put to the natives, and to do that our travelers would have to knock on the door of one of the houses, preferably the inn, if they could, perchance, discover which one it was.

The four musicians went searching around the gloomy place, walking around the dwellings, hoping to catch sight of a sign hanging at the front of a house, but they found no trace of an inn.

Well, if there was no inn, there could still be a friendly place, and since they were not in Scotland, they decided to act like Americans. Would a native of Freschal turn down a dollar or even two per person in exchange for supper and a place to sleep?

"Let's knock," said Frascolin.

"In time," added Pinchinat, "in six-eight time!"

If they had knocked in three-four time, the result would have been the same. Not one door or window opened, even though the Concerting Quartet knocked at a dozen houses.

"We made a mistake," said Yvernès. "This is not a village, it is a cemetery, where, if people are sleeping, they are sleeping the eternal sleep . . . *Vox clamantis in deserto*."

"*Amen!* . . ." responded His Highness in the deep voice of a cathedral singer. What could they do, since the inhabitants persisted in this complete silence? Should they push on toward San Diego . . . ? They were literally dying of hunger and fatigue . . . and then, what road could they follow without a guide in the middle of this dark night . . . ? Should they try to find another village . . . ? But which one . . . ? If they believed what the driver had said, there was no other village on this part of the coast . . . They would only get more lost . . . It was best to wait for dawn . . . ! However, spending half a dozen hours without shelter, under a sky starting to fill with big, low clouds threatening to change into rain, was not a viable solution, not even for musicians. Then Pinchinat had an idea. His ideas were not always excellent, but his head was always full of them. Anyway, the wise Frascolin approved of this one.

"My friends," said Pinchinat, "what made us succeed with a bear could maybe help us with a Californian village . . . We tamed that plantigrade with a little music . . . Let's awaken these peasants with a spirited concert full of *forte* and *allegro* . . ."

"It's worth a try," answered Frascolin.

Sébastien Zorn did not even let Pinchinat finish his sentence. With his cello out of its case and resting on its steel point, Zorn, who had no place to sit, stood, bow in hand, ready to release all the voices stored in the instrument's sonorous shell. Almost immediately, his comrades were ready to follow him to the limits of their art.

"Onslow's quartet in B-flat," he said. "One measure to get us warmed up."

This Onslow quartet, they knew it by heart. Excellent musicians do not need to see in order to walk their skilled fingers across the strings of a cello, two violins, and a viola.

They simply followed their inspiration. They had perhaps never played with more talent and spirit in the concert halls and theaters of America. The air became filled with a sublime harmony and, unless they were deaf, how could human beings have remained indifferent? Even if they had been in a cemetery, as Yvernès had suggested, the tombs would have opened and, charmed by the music, the dead would have risen and their skeletons would have clapped their bony hands.

And yet the houses remained closed, the sleepers did not wake up. The piece ended in the burst of its powerful finale, yet Freschal gave no sign of life.

"So! That's how it is!" cried Sébastien Zorn in a paroxysm of anger. "Do they need a hullaballoo like their bears for their peasant ears . . . ? So be it! Let's do it again, but you, Yvernès, play in D, you, Frascolin, in E, you, Pinchinat, in G. I will remain in B-flat, and now, with all our might!"

What a cacophony they made! What a tearing of eardrums! It reminded them of that makeshift orchestra directed by the Prince de Joinville in an unknown village in Brazil! It was a horrible symphony, as if they were playing Wagner backward on cheap instruments.

In the end, Pinchinat's idea proved excellent. This awful performance accomplished what their splendid rendition had been unable to do. Freschal started waking up. The musicians saw lights here and there. A few windows opened. The people of the village were not dead, since they were showing signs of life. They were not deaf, either, since they heard and listened . . .

"They are going to throw tomatoes at us!" said Pinchinat during a pause, for if the quartet had carefully kept the *tempo* of the piece, they had not respected its tonality.

"That's all right . . . we'll eat them!" answered the practical Frascolin.

And at Sébastien Zorn's command, they went on with their concert, with even more gusto. When the piece ended with perfect timing in four different keys, the four musicians put down their instruments.

No! There were no tomatoes flying out of the twenty or thirty wide-open windows, but there were applause, hurrahs, and hip-hip-hoorays. Never had Freschalian ears been filled with such musical pleasure. And without a doubt, every house would now be ready to welcome such brilliant virtuosos as their guests.

But while they were engaged in their musical fury, a new spectator had come toward them without their noticing him. This individual had come out of some sort of electric carriage and was standing in one corner of the square. He was a tall, portly man, as far as they could judge on this dark night.

And while our Parisians were wondering if, after the windows, the doors of the houses would open to welcome them—which now seemed very doubtful, to say the least—the newcomer came toward them and, in a pleasant voice, said in perfect French,

"Gentlemen, I am a music lover and I have just had the pleasure of applauding you . . ."

"For our last piece . . . ?" asked Pinchinat, ironically.

"No, gentlemen . . . for the first one. I have rarely heard this Onslow quartet played with more talent!"

Without a doubt, this character was an expert.

"Sir," answered Sébastien Zorn on behalf of his comrades, "we much appreciate your compliments . . . If our second interpretation hurt your ears, it is because . . ."

"Sir," replied the stranger, interrupting Zorn, who would have been long-winded, "I never heard anyone play so off-key with such perfection. But I understood why you were doing it. It was to wake up the good people of Freschal, who have already gone back to sleep . . . Well, gentlemen, what you were trying to get from them by this desperate attempt, please allow me to offer it to you . . ."

"Hospitality . . . ?" asked Frascolin.

"Yes, hospitality, Scottish hospitality of the best kind. If I am not mistaken, I have before me the Concerting Quartet, renowned throughout our beautiful America, which has received them with open arms."

"Sir," Frascolin felt compelled to add, "we are truly flattered . . . And . . . this hospitality, where could we find it with your help . . . ?"

"Two miles from here."

"In another village?"

"No . . . in a city."

"An important city . . . ?"

"Certainly."

"Excuse me," observed Pinchinat. "But we were told that there were no other cities until San Diego . . ."

"This is an error that I cannot understand."

"An error . . . ?" repeated Frascolin.

"Yes, gentlemen, and if you will accompany me, I promise you a welcome that great musicians like you have a right to expect."

"I think we should accept," said Yvernès.

"I agree with you," declared Pinchinat.

"Wait a minute . . . wait a minute," shouted Sébastien Zorn. "Let's not go faster than the orchestra leader!"

"What do you mean . . . ?" asked the American.

"That we are expected in San Diego," answered Frascolin.

"In San Diego, where the city booked us for a series of musical matinees, the first of which will take place Sunday, the day after tomorrow . . ." added the cellist.

"Harrumph!" retorted the man in a tone of extreme annoyance. But then he added, "That's all right, gentlemen. One day will give you enough time to visit a city that is very much worth seeing, and I will make sure that you are brought to the nearest station in order to be in San Diego at the appointed time!"

Well, the offer was appealing and so was the welcome. The quartet was assured of finding a good room in a good hotel, in addition to the warm welcome that this kind man was promising them.

"Do you accept, gentlemen . . . ?"

"We do," answered Sébastien Zorn, who, being hungry and tired, did welcome the invitation.

"All right," replied the American. "We are going to leave immediately . . . We will be there in twenty minutes and I am sure that you will thank me!"

Needless to say, after the last hurrahs brought about by their chaotic concert, the windows of the houses were shut again. With its lights out, the village of Freschal plunged back into its deep sleep.

The American and the four musicians walked to the carriage. The musicians laid down their instruments and sat in the back while the American took a seat in front, next to the driver. A lever was pushed, the batteries kicked in, the vehicle set off and soon picked up speed, going toward the west.

Fifteen minutes later, a whitish glow appeared like a dazzling diffusion of moonlight. It was a city that our Parisians could never have imagined.

The vehicle stopped and Frascolin said,

"Well, we have finally reached the shore."

"This is not the shore . . . ," answered the American. "It is just a river that we must cross . . ."

"How are we going to do that . . . ?" asked Pinchinat.

"On that ferryboat, which will carry us and our vehicle."

Indeed, there was in front of them one of the ferryboats that are so common in the United States. The vehicle went on board with its passengers. This ferryboat must have run on electricity because it did not let out any steam and in a few minutes it reached a harbor on the other side of the river.

The vehicle took to the road again and traveled through the countryside. It entered a park where aerial devices were pouring out intense light.

The gate of this park opened up on a long street paved with stones. Five minutes later, the musicians found themselves on the front steps of a comfortable hotel, where they received an auspicious welcome thanks to a word from the American. They were quickly ushered to a table loaded with delicious food and they ate heartily, as you can imagine.

When they were done eating, the hotel manager led them to a vast bedroom lit with incandescent lights with dimmer switches. As soon as they were there, they fell asleep in the four beds arranged in the four corners of the room, putting off until the next day the explanation for these marvels; and they snored with the rare harmony that had given the Concerting Quartet its fame.

III

~~~~~~~~~~~~~

A Chatty Mentor

THE NEXT MORNING AT SEVEN, the following words, or rather shouts, were heard in the shared bedroom of the quartet after the booming imitation of a trumpet. It sounded like the reveille.

"Up and at 'em! On your feet . . . double time!" yelled Pinchinat.

Yvernès, the most laid-back of the musicians, would have preferred to emerge from the warm blankets of his bed in triple time or even quadruple time. But he had to follow the example of his comrades and quickly go from lying down to standing up.

"We do not have a single minute to waste, not one . . . !" observed His Highness.

"True!" answered Sébastien Zorn. "We have to be in San Diego tomorrow."

"Well," retorted Yvernès, "half a day will be enough to visit an American town of this kind."

"What surprises me," added Frascolin, "is that there is an important city close to Freschal . . . ! How could our driver have forgotten to tell us about it?"

"The most crucial thing was to find it, my old treble key, and we did!" Light was pouring through the two wide windows of their room, which overlooked a magnificent mile-long street bordered by trees.

The four friends got ready in a comfortable bathroom. It was a quick and easy task because the place was equipped with the latest modern refinements: faucets thermometrically programmed for hot and cold water, basins emptying automatically, water heaters, curling irons, sprayers of fragrant essences dispensing on demand, rotating fans running on electricity, mechanically activated brushes, some of them for their hair, others for their clothes and boots, so as to get a complete cleaning and polishing.

And, in several places, in addition to the clock and the electric lamps that were all within easy reach, there were also the buttons of bells and telephones allowing instant communication with the diverse services of the hotel.

Sébastien Zorn and his companions could contact not just the hotel personnel, but various areas of the city and perhaps—this was Pinchinat's opinion—any city in the United States of America.

"Or even in Europe," added Yvernès.

Before they could try this, the following message was sent to them in English by telephone at seven forty-seven:

"Calistus Munbar sends his morning greetings to each of the honorable members of the Concerting Quartet and invites them to come down, when they are ready, to the dining room of the Excelsior Hotel, where breakfast is waiting for them."

"The Excelsior Hotel!" said Yvernès. "The very name of this resort is superb."

"Calistus Munbar, that's our kind American," retorted Pinchinat, "and his name is splendid also!"

"My friends," said the cellist, whose stomach was as demanding as its owner, "let's go and eat, since breakfast is served, and after that . . ."

"And after that . . . let's explore the city," added Frascolin, "but which city can it be?"

When our Parisians were dressed or just about, Pinchinat answered by phone that they would honor Mr. Calistus Munbar's invitation in less than five minutes.

Indeed, as soon as they were ready, they entered an elevator that started moving and brought them to the monumental hall of the hotel. At the end of this hall, they noticed the door of the spacious dining room gleaming with gold.

"I am at your disposition, gentlemen, completely at your disposition!"

It was the man they had encountered the day before who had just uttered this ten-word sentence. He belonged to that category of people who do not need an introduction. It seems that you have known them for a long time or, to use an even better expression, forever.

Calistus Munbar must have been between fifty and sixty years old but he did not look any older than forty-five. He was taller than most, had a slight paunch and thick, strong arms and legs. He was energetic and robust and had manly gestures. In a word, he was the picture of health.

Sébastien Zorn and his friends had often met this type of man, which is common in the United States. Calistus Munbar's head was enormous, a ball with hair still blond and curly, moving like foliage in the wind. He had a ruddy complexion. His beard, yellowish and rather long, was parted in two points. His mustache was shaven. His mouth turned upward at the corners in a mocking smile and his teeth were of sparkling ivory. His nose, a bit thick at the end and with palpitating nostrils, was solidly planted at the base of a forehead showing two vertical folds. It supported a pince-nez held by a silver thread as thin and supple as silk. Behind the lenses of this pince-nez shone constantly moving eyes with greenish irises and pupils burning with fire. The head of Calistus Munbar was attached to his shoulders by a bullish neck. His trunk rested squarely on fleshy thighs, solid legs, and feet pointing a bit outward.

Calistus Munbar wore a big brown jacket. A decorated handkerchief showed at the top of his breast pocket. His vest was white and low cut, with three gold buttons. It was joined from one side to the other by a massive chain, carrying a chronometer at one end and a pedometer at the other, with various amulets jingling in the center. Several rings on his fat pinkish fingers complemented this adornment. His shirt was immaculately white, shiny and stiff with starch. It was studded with three diamonds and had a wide, turned-down collar harboring a diminutive tie made of gold braid. He wore striped trousers falling in deep pleats that became narrower as they reached the aluminum hooks of his laced boots.

The face of this Yankee was extremely expressive and open; it was the face of a man absolutely sure of himself, the face of a seasoned man. This fellow was obviously resourceful and also energetic, as could be surmised by the tone of his muscles and the continual tensing of his eyebrows and his jaw. He had an easy, loud laugh, more nasal than oral, a sort of jittery giggle, what physiologists call *hennitus*.

This was Calistus Munbar. When the quartet came in, he raised his big hat, on which a feather à la Louis XIII would not have been out of place, and he shook hands with the musicians. He led them to a table where a simmering pot of tea and toasted bread awaited them. Munbar talked incessantly; he did not allow a single question—maybe to avoid having to answer it—as he extolled the splendors of his city and the extraordinary creation that it was. He talked without cease and when breakfast was over he ended his monologue with these words:

"Gentlemen, follow me, please. But first, let me give you one word of advice . . ."

"And what would that be?" asked Frascolin.

"It is expressly forbidden to spit in our streets . . ."

"Oh! But we don't do that . . . ," protested Yvernès.

"Good! That will keep you from getting fined!"

"Not spit . . . in America!" murmured Pinchinat with a mixture of surprise and disbelief.

It would have been difficult to find a more knowledgeable guide than Calistus Munbar. He knew this city in and out. He could name the owner of every hotel, the residents of every house. Passers-by greeted him with kind familiarity.

The city was built on a regular pattern. The avenues and streets intersected at right angles and resembled a chessboard. Verandas jutted above the sidewalks. There was a unity in the city's geometrical plan, but there was also variety in the style of the houses and their inside arrangement. The houses were built according to the fancy of their architects. Except for a few commercial streets, these houses looked like palaces with their main courtyards flanked by elegant pavilions, the architectural design of their fronts, the luxury that one could picture inside their apartments, the gardens, not to say the parks, in their backyards. We should point out, however, that the trees, probably recently planted, were not yet fully grown. It was the same for the squares created at the intersections of the main arteries, covered with lawns in the refreshing English fashion. There, the clumps of bushes, species from the temperate zones mixed with some from the tropics, had not drawn enough vegetative sustenance from the depths of the ground. This natural feature was in striking contrast to the region of western America where there were many giant forests in the vicinity of the great Californian cities.

The quartet walked ahead, scrutinizing this section of the city, each one according to his particular interests—Yvernès attracted by what did not attract Frascolin, Sébastien Zorn enticed by what did not entice Pinchinat—but all very curious about the mystery surrounding this unknown city. From their diversity of views would probably come an assortment of appropriate comments. Anyway, Calistus Munbar was with them and could answer all their questions. But what answers did they need . . . ? Munbar did not wait for questions; he talked and talked and they simply let him talk. His windmill of words constantly turned at the slightest wind.

Fifteen minutes after they left the Excelsior Hotel, Calistus Munbar said, "Here we are on Third Avenue and there are about thirty avenues in the city. This one is the most commercial one; it is our Broadway, our Regent Street, our Boulevard des Italiens. In the stores and bazaars, you'll find the basic and the superfluous, everything needed for well-being and modern comfort."

"I see the stores," said Pinchinat, "but I don't see the customers."

"Perhaps it is too early in the morning," added Yvernès.

"No," answered Calistus Munbar, "it is because most orders are sent by telephone or telautograph."

"What does that mean?" asked Frascolin.

"It means that we usually use the telautograph, a revolutionary device that sends the written word the same way the telephone sends the spoken word; and let's not forget the kinetograph, which records movements and does for the eye what the phonograph does for the ear. We also have the telephote, which records images. Our telautograph gives serious assurance that a simple message cannot be falsified by anyone. We can sign orders and drafts electronically."

"Even marriage certificates . . . ?" asked Pinchinat in an ironical tone.

"Of course, my dear alto. Why wouldn't people marry via telegraphic wire?"

"And what about divorce . . . ?"

"Divorce too . . . ! This is what wears out our devices!"

And with this remark, the guide burst into loud laughter that made all the trinkets on his vest jingle.

"You are so cheerful, Mr. Munbar," said Pinchinat, sharing in the gaiety of the American.

"Yes . . . like a flock of finches on a sunny day!"

At this point, they reached an intersecting street. It was Nineteenth Avenue, from which all trade was banned. Tramlines ran down it as well as down the other avenue. Vehicles went by rapidly without raising a speck of dust because the road surface, covered with rot-resistant flooring made of Australian *karry* or jarrah—it might as well have been Brazilian mahogany—was as clean as if it had been scrubbed with steel wool. It was then that Frascolin, who always detected physical phenomena, noticed that the ground resounded under his feet like a metallic surface.

"What great ironworkers!" he said to himself. "They now make streets of sheet metal."

And he was about to ask questions of Calistus Munbar when the latter exclaimed,

"Gentlemen, look at this mansion!"

And he pointed to a huge, gorgeous building where the pavilions built on each side of the main courtyard were enclosed by an aluminum gate.

"This mansion—I should say this palace—is the residence of the family of one of the main notables of the town. This is Jem Tankerdon, the owner of bottomless oil wells in Illinois, the richest, perhaps, and consequently, the most honorable and honored of all our citizens . . ."

"Is he a millionaire?" asked Sébastien Zorn.

"Humph!" went Calistus Munbar. "A million for us is like a dollar for everyone else; here we count by the billions. In this city, there are only extremely rich nabobs. This explains how the merchants from the commercial quarters make a fortune in a few years—I mean the retail merchants—for wholesalers do not exist in this microcosm, the only one of its kind in the world . . ."

"Are there any manufacturers . . . ?" asked Pinchinat.

"No, no manufacturers!"

"And shipowners . . . ?" asked Frascolin.

"None either."

"Independently wealthy people then . . . ?" asked Sébastien Zorn.

"Only independently wealthy people and merchants on their way to being independently wealthy."

"Well . . . and what about workmen . . . ?" remarked Yvernès.

"When we need workmen, we bring them from outside, gentlemen, and when their work is done, they go home . . . with a hefty bundle . . . !"

"Come on, Mr. Munbar," said Frascolin, "you must still have a few poor in your town, at least to make sure their species does not disappear . . ."

"Poor people, my dear second violin . . . ? You will not find a single one!"

"Then begging is forbidden . . . ?"

"There was never any reason to forbid it, for the city was never open to beggars. That is all very well for the cities of the Union with their asylums, their workhouses . . . and the penitentiaries that complete them . . . but not for us."

"Are you going to declare that you have no prisons . . . ?"

"Not any more than we have prisoners."

"But what about criminals . . . ?"

"We ask them to stay in the old and the new continents, where they can practice their vocation under more advantageous conditions."

"Well, Mr. Munbar," said Sébastien Zorn, "listening to you, we'd believe we're not in America anymore."

"You were there yesterday, my dear cellist," answered their amazing mentor.

"Yesterday . . . ?" retorted Frascolin, who wondered what this strange sentence could mean.

"Yes, indeed . . . ! Today you are in an independent city, a free city that is its own master and where the Union has no rights . . ."

"And what is its name . . . ?" asked Sébastien Zorn, whose naturally quick temper was starting to show through.

"Its name . . . ?" answered Calistus Munbar. "I don't wish to reveal it yet . . ."

"And when shall we learn it . . . ?"

"When your visit, which will greatly honor it, is over."

The reticence of the American was peculiar to say the least. But after all, it did not matter. Before noon, the quartet would be done with their strange walk and even if they learned the name of this city only when they were about to leave it, that would be enough for them, right? The only lingering question was this: how could such an important city be located on the California coast without belonging to the Federal Republic of the United States and, moreover, how could one explain that the driver of the carriage never thought of mentioning it? The most important thing for the musicians was, after all, to reach San Diego within twenty-four hours; there they would learn the answer to this enigma even if Calistus Munbar decided not to reveal it.

This strange character just went on with his smooth talk, but not without showing that he did not wish to give a clearer answer.

"Gentlemen," he said, "we are entering Thirty-Seventh Avenue. Look at this admirable perspective! In this area there are no stores or markets, either; there is none of that street traffic that signals commercial activity. Only mansions and private homes, but they are not as expensive as on Nineteenth Avenue. Here the fortunes do not exceed ten to twelve million . . ."

"They're practically beggars!" answered Pinchinat, screwing up his face with contempt.

"Hey! My dear alto," retorted Calistus Munbar, "you can always be someone else's beggar. A millionaire is rich compared to a man who only has a hundred thousand dollars! He is not rich compared to the one who has a hundred million!"

Many times already our musicians had noticed that of all the words used by their mentor, the word "million" recurred most frequently, a prestigious word if there ever was one! He enunciated it with a metallic resonance, puffing out his cheeks. He seemed to be minting coins while talking. If it were not diamonds that fell from his lips like the pearls and emeralds that fell from the mouth of the fairies' godchild, it was gold coins.

Sébastien Zorn, Pinchinat, Frascolin, and Yvernès kept on strolling through this extraordinary city whose geographic designation was still unknown to them. The streets were animated by the comings and goings of passers-by, all comfortably dressed; they were never bothered by the sight of poor people in rags. Everywhere there were trams, carriages, and trucks running on electricity. Some of the long arteries were equipped with moving sidewalks activated by an endless belt on which people swiftly walked as they would on a moving train.

There were also electric carriages traveling on the roads as smoothly as a cue ball on a pool table. As for carriages in the true sense of the word, that is, vehicles pulled by horses, they were found only in the affluent areas.

"Ah! There is a church," said Frascolin.

And he pointed to a rather heavy structure without any architectural style, a huge block in the middle of a square covered with lush lawns.

"It is the Protestant church," answered Calistus Munbar, stopping in front of the building.

"Are there any Catholic churches in your city . . . ?" asked Yvernès.

"Yes, sir. Besides, I must mention to you that although there are about one thousand different religions on our globe, here we confine ourselves to Catholicism and Protestantism. It is not like the United States, divided by religion if not by politics, where there are as many sects as there are families, be they Methodists, Anglicans, Presbyterians, Anabaptists, Wesleyans, etc. Here we only have Protestants faithful to the Calvinist doctrine and Roman Catholics."

"And what is their language?"

"English and French are commonly used . . ."

"We congratulate you for that," said Pinchinat.

"The city is thus divided into two sections that are about equal," retorted Calistus Munbar. "Here we are in the section . . ."

"The west section, I believe . . . ," observed Frascolin, looking at the position of the sun.

"West . . . if you wish . . ."

"What do you mean . . . if I wish . . . ?" retorted the second violin, rather surprised by this answer. "Do the cardinal points of this city vary as anyone pleases . . . ?"

"Yes . . . and no . . . ," said Calistus Munbar. "I will explain this to you later . . . Now let me return to this . . . west section . . . if that's what you want to call it. It is inhabited only by Protestants, who remained, even here, very practical people, while the Catholics, more intellectual and refined, live in the . . . east section. That tells you it's the Protestant church."

"It sure looks like it," observed Yvernès. "With all that heavy architecture, prayers will never rise toward the heavens but will fall instead."

"A beautiful sentence!" exclaimed Pinchinat. "Mr. Munbar, in a city with such modern inventions, one can probably hear the sermon or mass by telephone . . . ?"

"Certainly."

"And also go to confession . . . ?"

"Yes, just as one can get married by telautograph, and you will admit that it is convenient . . ."

"That's hard to believe, Mr. Munbar," answered Pinchinat, "very hard to believe."

IV

~~~~~~~~

The Concerting Quartet Disconcerted

AT ELEVEN O'CLOCK, AFTER SUCH a long walk, they had a right to be hungry. And our musicians took advantage of their right. Their stomachs were crying for food in unison and they agreed that they absolutely had to have lunch.

This was also the opinion of Calistus Munbar, who was, as much as his guests, subject to the need for daily nourishment. But would he take them back to the Excelsior Hotel?

He did indeed, because it seemed that there were not many restaurants in this town, where everyone probably preferred to hole up at home and which tourists from both worlds did not seem to visit much.

In a matter of minutes, a tram brought the famished people to their hotel and they sat down at a table covered with copious dishes. This was in striking contrast to the typical American meal, where the abundance of dishes does not make up for their meagerness. The beef and lamb were excellent, the poultry tender and flavorful, the fish tantalizingly fresh. Moreover, instead of the iced water served in the restaurants of the Union, there were various beers and wines that the French sun had distilled ten years before upon the hills of Medoc and Burgundy.

Pinchinat and Frascolin did justice to this lunch at least as much as did Sébastien Zorn and Yvernès . . . It goes without saying that Calistus Munbar had invited them and that they would have been impolite not to accept.

What's more, the loquacious Yankee was in excellent humor. He talked about everything that had to do with the city, with the exception of the one thing that his guests really wanted to know: the name of this independent city, which he hesitated to disclose. They needed to be patient.

He would reveal it at the end of their explorations. Had he intended to get the quartet drunk to make them miss their train for San Diego . . . ? Probably not, but they drank hard after eating well and they were finishing their dessert with tea, coffee, and liqueurs when the sound of a shot shook the windows of the hotel.

"What's that?" asked Yvernès with a start.

"Don't worry, gentlemen," answered Calistus Munbar. "It's the cannon of the observatory."

"If it's striking twelve," replied Frascolin, looking at his watch, "I'd say it's late."

"No, my dear alto, no! The sun isn't any later here than anywhere else." And a strange smile passed on the lips of the American; his eyes sparkled behind his pince-nez and he rubbed his hands together. You would almost be tempted to believe that he was pleased to have played a trick on the group.

But Frascolin, who was not as keyed up by the good meal as his companions, looked at him suspiciously, not knowing what to believe.

"Let's go, my friends, allow me to call you my friends," Munbar added very cordially, "we now must visit the second part of town. I would die of disappointment if you did not see every single detail of it. We don't have a minute to waste . . ."

"At what time does the train for San Diego leave . . . ?" asked Sébastien Zorn, always worried about the musicians missing their commitments if they arrived late.

"Yes . . . At what time . . . ?" repeated Frascolin.

"Oh . . . ! In the evening," answered Calistus Munbar with a wink of his left eye. "Come on, my guests, come on . . . You will not regret having taken me as your guide!"

How could they say no to such an obliging chap? The four musicians left the dining room of the Excelsior Hotel and strolled alongside the road. To tell the truth, the wine had probably made them a bit drunk, since they felt some sort of tingling running through their legs. The ground seemed to have a slight tendency to disappear under their steps. And yet, they were not walking on one of those mobile sidewalks.

"Hey! Hey . . . ! Let's help each other, by Jove!" yelled His Highness, staggering.

"I think we drank a bit too much!" retorted Yvernès, wiping his forehead.

"Well, my dear Parisians," observed the American, "one time is all right. We had to drink to welcome you . . ."

"And we drained the barrel!" replied Pinchinat, who had done his part and had never felt in a better mood.

With Calistus Munbar leading them, they took a street that brought them to one of the districts of the second part of town. This section was more animated than the first and looked less puritanical. They felt as if they had suddenly been transported from the northern states of the Union to the southern, from Chicago to New Orleans, from Illinois to Louisiana. The stores offered better merchandise, the houses were more elegantly adorned, and the family estates more comfortable. The mansions were as magnificent as those in the Protestant section, but they were also more pleasant to look at. The people were different in the way they appeared, walked, and carried themselves. The city began to look double, like certain stars, except that its sections did not revolve around each other; it was two cities standing side by side.

When they were almost in the center of the section, the group stopped at about the middle of Fifteenth Street and Yvernès exclaimed,

"My word, this is a palace . . ."

"The palace of the Coverley family," answered Calistus Munbar. "Nat Coverley is the equal of Jem Tankerdon . . ."

"Is he richer than him . . . ?" asked Pinchinat.

"Just as rich," said the American. "He is a former banker from New Orleans who has more hundreds of millions than he has fingers on both hands!"

"A nice pair of gloves, my dear Mr. Munbar!"

"Indeed."

"And these two notables, Jem Tankerdon and Nat Coverley, are enemies . . . of course?"

"Rivals, at least, who try to establish their supremacy in the city's affairs and are jealous of each other . . ."

"Will they end up eating each other . . . ?" asked Sébastien Zorn.

"Maybe . . . and if one devours the other . . ."

"What indigestion that will bring!" answered His Highness.

And Calistus Munbar found this retort so hilarious that he laughed until his belly shook.

The Catholic church stood on a spacious square that helped one admire its pleasant proportions. It was built in the Gothic style, the style that can be appreciated up close because the vertical lines that render it so beautiful lose their character when seen from afar. Saint Mary's Church deserved to be admired for its slender pinnacles, its delicate rosaces, its elegant ogives in flamboyant Gothic and its graceful windows that looked like praying hands.

"This is an excellent example of Anglo-Saxon Gothic!" said Yvernès, who was a connoisseur of architecture. "You were right, Mr. Munbar; the two sections of your city do not have more in common than the church of the first one and the cathedral of the second."

"And yet, Mr. Yvernès, they were born of the same mother."

"But probably not of the same father . . . ," observed Pinchinat.

"Oh! Yes, from the same father also, my dear friends! But they were raised differently. They were designed to fulfill the needs of those who came here to find a quiet, happy life free from all care . . . a life that no city in the old or new continent can offer."

"By Jove, Mr. Munbar," answered Yvernès, "be careful not to arouse our curiosity too much! It's as if you were singing one of these musical phrases that makes one yearn for the keynote . . ."

"And that ends up tiring your ear!" added Sébastien Zorn. "Now, isn't it time for you to reveal the name of this extraordinary city . . . ?"

"Not yet, my honored guests," answered the American, readjusting his gold pince-nez on his nasal appendage. "Wait for the end of our walk; let's go on . . ."

"Before we go on," said Frascolin, who felt vague pangs of anxiety pervade his curiosity, "I have something to propose."

"What is it . . . ?"

"Why don't we climb to the top of Saint Mary's Church. From there, we could see . . ."

"Oh no!" exclaimed Calistus Munbar, shaking his big tousled head. "Not now . . . later . . ."

"When, then . . . ?" asked the cellist, who was getting annoyed by so many mysterious and evasive answers.

"At the end of our excursion, Mr. Zorn."

"Will we come back to this church, then?"

"No, my friends, but our walk will end with a visit to the observatory, whose tower is one-third higher than the spire of Saint Mary's Church."

"But after all," retorted Frascolin, "why not take advantage of this now . . . ?"

"Because . . . it would ruin the effect!"

And they were unable to draw a clearer answer from this enigmatic character. It was best to give in, and so they walked conscientiously through the various avenues of the second section of town. After that they visited the commercial districts of the tailors, the boot makers, the hat makers, the butchers, the grocers, the bakers, the fruit sellers, etc. Calistus Munbar was greeted by most people he met and he returned their greetings with a complacent satisfaction. He was full of anecdotes, like a barker at a sideshow, and his tongue rattled incessantly like a bell during the holidays.

Around two o'clock the quartet reached the edge of this side of the city. It was bordered by a magnificent gate adorned with flowers and climbing plants. Beyond that, the countryside stretched in a circular line that blended in with the horizon.

And there Frascolin noticed something that he did not judge necessary to share with his companions. It would probably all be explained once they reached the top of the observatory tower. What he had observed was that the sun, instead of being in the southwest, as it should be at two o'clock, was now in the southeast.

This would, of course, surprise a mind as reflective as Frascolin's and he was starting to rack his brain when his musings were interrupted by Calistus Munbar, who exclaimed,

"Gentlemen, the tram is leaving in a few minutes. En route to the harbor . . ."

"The harbor . . . ?" retorted Sébastien Zorn.

"Oh! It's a mile trip at the most and it will allow you to admire our park!"

If there was a harbor, it must have been located a little above or a little below the town on the coast of Southern California . . . In fact, where could it have been but on some point of this shore?

A bit perplexed, the musicians sat down in an elegant tram where several travelers were already seated. These passengers shook hands with Calistus Munbar—everyone knew this amazing fellow—and the engines started the tram rolling.

Calistus Munbar had been right to call the countryside around the city a park. There were roads extending as far as the eye could see, green lawns, and painted barriers, straight or zigzagging, that they called fences. There were fields surrounded by clumps of trees of all kinds: oaks, maples, beech trees, chestnut trees, nettle trees, elms, cedars, all still young and animated by thousands of species of birds. It resembled a real English garden, with gushing fountains, baskets of flowers blooming in their spring freshness, and clusters of shrubs of the most diversified kinds: giant geraniums as in Monte Carlo, orange and lemon trees, olive trees, oleanders, lentisks, aloes, camellias, dahlias, rosebushes from Alexandria with their white flowers, hydrangeas, white and pink lotuses. There were South American passionflowers, rich collections of fuchsias, salvias, begonias, hyacinths, tulips, crocuses, narcissi, anemones, Persian buttercups, irises, cyclamens, orchids, calceolarias, tree ferns, and also those species found in tropical zones, such as cannas, palm trees, date trees, fig trees, eucalyptuses, mimosas, banana trees, guava trees, baobabs, coconut trees, in short, everything that a true gardener could expect from the richest botanic field.

With his tendency to evoke the memories of ancient poetry, Yvernès must have felt transported to the bucolic landscapes of *The Astrée*. But if there were plenty of sheep in these fresh pastures, if red cows were grazing behind the fences, if deer, does and fawns, and other graceful quadrupeds of the forest were bounding among the clumps of trees, the shepherds and the charming shepherdesses of d'Urfé were sorely absent. As for the Lignon River, it was represented by a serpentine stream that flowed boldly through the hilly terrain of the countryside.

Yet everything there seemed artificial.

This provoked Pinchinat, always ironical, to ask,

"Is that all you have for a river . . . ?"

And Calistus Munbar answered,

"Why have rivers . . . ? What are they good for . . . ?"

"To have water, of course!"

"Water . . . You mean that generally unsanitary substance harboring microbes and typhoid fever . . . ?"

"I know, but it can be purified . . ."

"Why would we go through all that trouble when it's so easy to make hygienic water, free from all impurities, and as sparkling or ferruginous as you wish?"

"You make your own water . . . ?" asked Frascolin.

"Yes, indeed, and we distribute it hot and cold to every house the same way we distribute light, sound, the time of day, warm air, cool air, energy, antiseptics, and electrification by auto-conduction . . ."

"Would you have me believe, then," asked Yvernès, "that you also make the rain to water your lawns and your flowers . . . ?"

"Certainly, my dear sir," replied the American, causing the jewels on his fingers to sparkle through the thick tufts of his beard.

"Rain on demand!" exclaimed Sébastien Zorn.

"Yes, my dear friends, rain that underground ducts bring in a regular, timely, and practical fashion. Isn't this better than waiting for nature's whimsy and being subject to the fickleness of climates; better than complaining about bad weather, be it too much rain or too long a dry spell, without being able to change it?"

"Let me stop you right there, Mr. Munbar," said Frascolin. "I'm willing to believe that you can produce rain at will, but how would you keep it from falling from the sky?"

"The sky . . . ? What does the sky have to do with this . . . ?"

"The sky, or if you prefer, the clouds that burst, the atmospheric currents with their accompanying cyclones, tornadoes, storms, squalls, and hurricanes . . . During the bad season, for example . . ."

"The bad season . . . ?" repeated Calistus Munbar.

"Yes . . . winter . . ."

"Winter . . . ? What's that . . . ?"

"We're telling you winter, with deep freezes, snow, and ice!" exclaimed Sébastien Zorn, infuriated by the Yankee's ironic answers.

"We don't have those!" answered Calistus Munbar calmly.

The four Parisians exchanged glances. Were they dealing with a madman or a trickster? If it was the first, they should have him locked up; if it was the second, they should give him a good thrashing.

Meanwhile, the tram was traveling at a slow speed in the midst of these enchanted gardens. To Sébastien Zorn and his companions, it looked as if beyond the borders of this huge park, carefully cultivated fields were spreading their various colors. They resembled those swatches of material displayed outside the tailors' shops of the past. They were probably fields of vegetables, potatoes, cabbages, carrots, turnips, leeks, in short, everything needed to make a perfect stew.

The musicians could not wait to be out in the countryside to find out what this strange region produced in wheat, oats, corn, barley, buckwheat, and other cereals.

But a factory suddenly appeared, its metal chimneys towering above its low, frosted-glass roofs. These chimneys, reinforced by iron supports, looked like those of a moving steamer, a *Great Eastern* whose hundred thousand horsepower activated its sturdy propellers. But there was a difference: instead of black smoke, the chimneys emitted only a light vapor that did not pollute the atmosphere.

This factory covered about ten thousand square yards. It was the first industrial structure the quartet had seen since they started "touring"— pardon the expression—the city under the guidance of the American.

"Hey, what's this building . . . ?" asked Pinchinat.

"It's a factory running on petroleum," answered Calistus Munbar, whose sharp glance threatened to pierce the lenses of his pince-nez.

"And what does your factory make . . . ?" asked Pinchinat.

"Electrical energy, which is distributed throughout the entire city, the park, and the countryside, producing power and light. At the same time, this factory feeds our telegraphs, our telautographs, our telephones, our telephotes, our bells, our kitchen stoves, our machines, our arc lights, our incandescent lights, our aluminum moons, our underwater cables . . ."

"Your underwater cables . . . ?" asked Frascolin, greatly interested.

"Yes . . . ! The ones that connect the city to various points on the American coast . . ."

"And you needed such an enormous factory . . . ?"

"You'd better believe it . . . We use a tremendous amount of electricity . . . and of moral energy too!" replied Calistus Munbar. "Believe me, gentlemen, we needed an incalculable amount of both to found this incomparable city, unrivalled in the entire world!"

They could hear the deafening rumblings of the gigantic factory, the powerful belchings of its steam, the violent jolts of its machines, and their repercussions on the ground. All this attested to a mechanical effort superior to anything modern industry had yet produced. Who could have imagined that so much power was needed to activate generators or charge batteries?

The tram went on and came to a stop a quarter of a mile farther, at the harbor station.

The travelers got out and their guide, still overflowing with laudatory comments, led them to the banks alongside the warehouses and docks. The oval basin of this harbor could shelter no more than a dozen ships. It was an anchorage rather than a port, ending in jetties; two piers, supported by iron frames and lit by lanterns, allowed ships to enter easily from the sea.

On that day there were only half a dozen steamers at the wharves: some of them transporting fuel, others the necessities of daily consumption. There were also a few boats equipped with electrical devices and used for deep-sea fishing.

Frascolin noted that the entrance of the harbor faced north and he concluded that it was located in the northern part of Southern California, where, in several places, the coast juts out into the Pacific. He also noticed that the ocean current ran strongly eastward, since it flowed against the pier heads like sheets of water alongside a moving ship. This was probably due to the rising tide, although tides are very mild on America's west coast.

"Where's the river we crossed by ferry last night?" asked Frascolin.

"At our back," simply replied the Yankee.

But they had no time to linger if they wanted to be back in town to catch the evening train for San Diego.

Sébastien Zorn reminded Calistus Munbar of their agreement and he responded,

"Don't worry, my dear, good friends . . . we have plenty of time . . . A tram will bring us back to town after following the coast . . . You wanted to have an overall view of the region and I can assure you that you'll have it in less than an hour, from the top of the observatory tower."

"Can we be sure of that . . . ?" insisted the cellist.

"I assure you that tomorrow at sunrise, you will no longer be where you are now!"

They had no choice but to accept this rather ambiguous answer. Anyway, Frascolin's curiosity was extremely aroused, even more than that of his comrades! He could not wait to stand at the top of this tower from where the American claimed you could see for at least one hundred miles. If after that they still did not know the geographic location of this incredible city, they could not expect to ever know it.

At the back of the anchorage was a second tramline that ran along the shore. The tram had six cars and many travelers had already settled in. These cars were pulled by an electric locomotive with batteries of two hundred amps and could cover ten to twelve miles in an hour.

Calistus Munbar helped the quartet board the train and it seemed to our Parisians that it had been waiting for them before starting on its way.

What they saw of the open country did not differ much from the park between the town and the port. It was the same manicured, flat land. Green pastures and fields instead of lawns, that was all; fields of vegetables but none of grains. At this moment, an artificial rain sent out by the underground ducts was falling in a beneficent shower on long rectangles made perfectly straight by gardener's lines.

The sky could not have measured and distributed this rain in a more mathematical and appropriate way.

The tramline followed the coast, with the sea on one side and the fields on the other. The tram traveled that way for four miles. Then it stopped in front of a battery of twelve large-caliber artillery pieces. The entrance bore this name: "Prow Battery."

"Cannons that are breech loaded but do not fire that way . . . like so many in old Europe!" observed Calistus Munbar.

At this point, the coast was deeply indented. A sort of cape jutted out very sharply, like the prow of a ship or even the ram of a battleship on which the waters divided, showering it with their white foam. This was probably due to the current, because the swell of the sea produced only long waves, which became smaller and smaller with the setting of the sun.

From this point, another tramline went down toward the center while the first one followed the curves of the coast.

Calistus Munbar made his guests change lines, telling them that they were going back directly to the city.

They had toured enough. Calistus Munbar pulled out his watch, a masterpiece by Sivan of Geneva, a talking, phonographic watch. He pressed a button and these words could distinctly be heard: "Thirteen past four."

"Don't forget that we must climb to the observatory," Frascolin reminded him.

"Forget it, my dear and already old friends . . . ! I'd rather forget my own name, which is pretty well-known, if I may say so! Four more miles and we'll be in front of the magnificent building rising at the end of First Avenue, the street that divides our city into two sections."

The tram started. Beyond the fields on which fell the afternoon rain— that's what the American called it—they went back to the park enclosed by fences, with its lawns, its flower beds, and its clumps of bushes.

A clock struck four thirty. Two hands on a huge dial resembling the one of the Parliament House in London told the time on the face of a four-sided tower.

At the bottom of this tower rose the buildings of the observatory, used for diverse activities. A few of them, topped by metallic rotundas with glass slits, allowed the astronomers to follow the course of the stars. These buildings surrounded a central courtyard, in the middle of which stood a tower one hundred fifty feet tall. From its upper gallery, the eye could see as far as fourteen miles ahead, since the horizon was not obstructed by any rise in the terrain, hill or mountain.

Calistus Munbar, walking ahead of his guests, entered a door opened for him by a man in superb livery. At the end of the hall there was an electric elevator. The quartet entered it with their guide. The elevator went up with a smooth and regular movement. Forty-five seconds later, it stopped at the level of the upper platform of the tower.

From this platform flew a gigantic flag that floated in the northern breeze.

What was the nationality of this flag? None of our Parisians could tell. It seemed to be the American flag with its red and white stripes, but its left-hand corner, instead of the sixty-seven stars that shone in the sky of the Confederation at the time, bore only a single star; a star or rather a golden sun spread out on a blue background, and whose brightness seemed to rival that of the sun itself.

"This is our flag, gentlemen," said Calistus Munbar, respectfully taking off his hat.

Sébastien Zorn and his comrades felt obliged to do the same. Then they moved forward to the parapet and, leaning over . . .

What screams, first of surprise and then of anger, came out of their mouths!

The entire countryside extended beneath their eyes. It formed a regular oval surrounded by the horizon of the ocean and, as far as they could see, there was no land in sight.

And yet, the night before, after leaving the village of Freschal in the carriage of the American, Sébastien Zorn, Frascolin, Yvernès, and Pinchinat had continuously followed a dirt road for a distance of two miles. Then they took their carriage on a ferryboat to cross the river and found dry land again . . . For sure, if they had left the California coast for any sea voyage, they would certainly have noticed it.

Frascolin turned toward Calistus Munbar and asked, "Are we on an island?"

"As you can see!" answered the Yankee, with the kindest smile.

"And what's the name of this island . . . ?"

"Standard Island."

"And of this city . . . ?"

"Milliard City."

V

~~~~~~~~

Standard Island and Milliard City

AT THAT TIME, THE WORLD was still waiting for a bold geographer-statistician to reveal the exact number of islands scattered across the surface of the globe. It would not be rash to claim that there are several thousands. Was it possible then, that of all these islands, not one met the requirements of the founders of Standard Island and the demands of its future inhabitants? Indeed, not a single one could satisfy them. This is how the practical "americomechanical" idea of creating an out-and-out artificial island that would be the finest invention of the modern steel industry came into being.

Standard Island—which we might call "the prototypical island"—was self-propelled. Milliard City was her capital. Why was it given this name? Evidently because it was the city of billionaires, a Gouldian, Vanderbiltian, Rothschildian city. But you will object that the word "milliard" does not exist in English . . . , the Anglo-Saxons of the old and the new continents have always used the expression "a thousand million"; "milliard" is a French word. That is correct, and yet, a few years before, the word had entered the language of Great Britain and the United States. It was thus only right to call the capital of Standard Island Milliard City.

The idea of creating an artificial island was not extraordinary in itself. With a sufficient mass of materials submerged in a river, a lake, or a sea, the building of an island is not beyond man's capacity. But this did not suffice. In view of its purpose and the demands it had to meet, this island needed to be able to move and therefore it had to float. That was the problem, but it was not an insoluble one, for the steel mills had machinery with practically unlimited power.

By the end of the nineteenth century, the Americans, with their instinct for everything "big," had developed a plan for installing a gigantic raft a few hundred miles off the coast and held in place by anchors. It was not to be a real city, but a station on the Atlantic with restaurants, clubs, theaters, etc., where tourists could find all the amenities of the most fashionable spas. It is this project that was now being realized and completed. However, instead of the stationary raft, they created the moving island.

Six years before this story began, an American company, under the name of Standard Island Company Incorporated, was created with a capital of five hundred million dollars divided into five hundred shares, to construct an artificial island that would offer the American nabobs various advantages that the sedentary regions of our earthly globe did not possess. The shares were sold rapidly since there were, at that time, so many immense fortunes in America, coming from the railways, the banking industry, from oil wells, and even the sale of salt pork.

It took four years to build this island. Let us now reveal her main dimensions, interior layouts, and the means of locomotion that allowed her to cruise through the most beautiful parts of the immense Pacific Ocean.

Floating villages do exist, in China on the Yang-Tse-Kiang River, in Brazil on the Amazon, and in Europe on the Danube. But they are ephemeral constructions: a few small houses set atop long wooden rafts. When they reach their destination, the rafts are taken apart, the houses are dismantled, and the villages no longer exist.

But the island we are talking about was something entirely different: she was to be launched upon the sea, and she was built to last . . . as long as man-made works can last.

And besides, who knows if the earth will not, one day, be too small for its inhabitants, who will number close to six billion in 2072, as the scientists who are disciples of Ravenstein affirm with astonishing precision? Will men not be forced to build on the sea when the continents become overcrowded?

Standard Island was an island made of steel. The strength of her hull was calculated to support the enormous weight that it had to bear. It was made up of two hundred seventy thousand caissons, each of them fifty-four feet high, thirty feet long, and thirty feet wide. Thus each caisson had a horizontal surface of nine hundred square feet. All these caissons, bolted and riveted together, gave the island a surface area of about ten and a half square miles. In the oval shape that her builders gave her, the island was four and a half miles long by three miles wide and her circumference was roughly eleven miles.

The submerged part of the hull measured thirty feet, its freeboard twenty. The vessel drew thirty feet of water. Her volume was about five hundred sixty-five million cubic yards and her displacement, being three-fifths of this volume, was three hundred thirty-nine million cubic yards.

The portion of the caissons below water was covered with a product discovered only recently—its inventor became a billionaire—which kept barnacles and shells from adhering to the parts in contact with seawater.

There was no danger of the base of the new island getting out of shape or breaking since the metal sheets of her hull were secured by crosspieces solidly bolted and riveted onsite.

Special shipyards were needed for the fabrication of this enormous naval construction. The Standard Island Company built her after acquiring Madeleine Bay and its coast at the extremity of the long peninsula of old California, almost at the limit of the Tropic of Cancer. It was in this bay that all the work was done under the direction of the Standard Island Company engineers, whose leader, the famous William Tersen, died a few months after completing the work, just like Brunnel after the unsuccessful launching of his ship the *Great Eastern*. And this Standard Island was indeed a modernized version of the *Great Eastern*, but a thousand times larger.

Obviously, they could not build the island in the ocean. They had to build her in sections, in compartments placed side by side on the waters of Madeleine Bay. This part of the American coast became the home base of the moving island, which could return there if she needed repairs.

The frame or hull of the island, made up of these two hundred seventy thousand compartments, was covered with a layer of fertile soil, except in the part reserved for the center of town, which was solidly reinforced. This humus was adequate to support vegetation limited to lawns, flower beds and bushes, clumps of trees, meadows, and vegetables. It would have been impractical to expect this artificial soil to produce grains and to provide the feed for cattle, which were regularly imported anyway.

But they thought it useful to create the necessary installations to produce milk and poultry independently of importation.

Three-quarters of the ground of Standard Island was reserved for vegetation, that is to say, about eight square miles where the lawns of the parks offered permanent greenery, where the fields used for intensive cultivation produced an abundance of vegetables and fruit, and where the artificial meadows served as pasture for sheep. And here electroculture was largely used, that is to say, the introduction of a continuous current, which greatly accelerated the maturation process and produced vegetables of incredible size, such as radishes one and a half feet long and carrots weighing six pounds each. These vegetable gardens and orchards could compete with the most beautiful ones in Virginia and Louisiana, and this should be no surprise because, on this island so aptly called "the Jewel of the Pacific," they never spared any expense.

Her capital, Milliard City, covered about one-fifth of the island, the portion of ten and a half square miles that had been reserved for it and had a perimeter of five and a half miles. Those of our readers who were so considerate as to accompany Sébastien Zorn and his comrades on their tour of the city know the area well enough not to get lost in it. Besides, one never gets lost in American cities, which are both fortunate and unfortunate enough to be modern: fortunate because of the simplicity of their layout and unfortunate because they entirely lack an artistic and whimsical side. We know that Milliard City had an oval shape and was divided into two sections separated by a central artery, First Avenue, which was about two miles long. The observatory that rose at one end had as its counterpart the town hall, whose imposing mass stood out at the other end. All public services were centralized there: the civil registry, water and sanitation, plantations and parks, municipal police, the customshouse, open-air markets, cemeteries and hospitals, places of worship, schools, and museums.

And now, what was the population living within this eleven-mile circumference like?

It is said that the world today contains twelve cities that have more than one million residents; four of these are in China. Well, our self-propelled island only had about ten thousand inhabitants and they were all from the United States. The Standard Island Company had not wanted any potential international controversy to arise between the citizens who came to this modern construction in quest of peace and quiet. It was enough and even too much that as far as religion was concerned, they were not all of the same persuasion. But it would have been difficult to reserve the exclusive right to establish residence on the island to the northern Yankees who were living on the port side of Standard Island or, inversely, to the Americans from the south who were on her starboard side. Moreover, the interests of the Standard Island Company would have suffered from such exclusivity.

When the steel base was completed and the area intended for the city ready for construction, when the layout of the streets and avenues was agreed on, the buildings began to rise. There were magnificent hotels and more modest dwellings intended for shops, public edifices, and churches, but there were no buildings twenty-seven floors high resembling those Chicago skyscrapers that literally scrape the clouds. The materials used in these constructions were light but sturdy. Aluminum was the metal of choice. It is seven times lighter than iron for an equal volume. It is truly the metal of the future, as Sainte-Claire Deville called it, and it met all the requirements for erecting sturdy structures. To this they added artificial stones, which are cement cubes that are very easily laid out. They even used glass bricks, hollowed out, blown, molded like bottles, and held together by a thin layer of mortar. These were transparent bricks that could build, if one so desired, the ideal glass house. But as a rule, it was the metal framework that was mostly used and that can now be found in various examples of naval architecture. After all, what was Standard Island but a gigantic ship?

All these properties belonged to the Standard Island Company. The people who lived there were only tenants, no matter how rich they were. But every care was taken to fulfill all the requirements for comfort and preferences coming from these incredibly wealthy Americans, so rich that the European kings and the nabobs of India would cut a sad figure next to them.

Indeed, if according to statistics the gold accumulated throughout the entire world is worth eighteen trillion dollars and the silver, twenty trillion, the inhabitants of this Jewel of the Pacific possessed a high percentage of it.

Besides, from the start the financial aspects of the project ran smoothly. The hotels and private residences were rented at fabulous prices. Some of these rentals amounted to more than several million dollars, and many families could afford to spend such enormous amounts on their annual rent without batting an eye. So, for that reason alone, the company earned a considerable income. You will agree that the capital of Standard Island deserved the name that it bears in the geographical nomenclature.

Besides these affluent families, there were a few hundred whose leases amounted to between one and two hundred thousand dollars and who were satisfied with their modest situation. The rest of the population was made up of professors, retailers, employees, servants, and foreigners, who were not very numerous and who were not authorized to settle in Milliard City or on any other part of the island. There were very few lawyers, which accounted for the paucity of lawsuits, and even fewer doctors; as a result, the mortality rate was ridiculously low. Besides, every resident was completely aware of his physical condition, his muscular strength being measured by the dynamometer, his pulmonary capacity by the spirometer, the contracting power of his heart by the sphygmometer, and finally, his degree of energy indicated by the magnetometer. Furthermore, within the city there were no bars, no cafés, no taverns, nothing that could lead to alcoholism. There was never a case of dipsomania, or should I say drunkenness, to be understood by people who do not know Greek. Moreover, let us not forget that the city services distributed electric energy, light, mechanical power, heat, compressed air, rarefied air, cold air, and water under pressure, as well as pneumatic telegrams and phone messages. If people died in this self-propelled island, methodically exempt from extreme weather and sheltered from the influence of microbes, it was because everyone had to die, but only as centenarians, after the springs of life had been dried up by old age.

Were there soldiers on Standard Island? Yes, there was a battalion of five hundred men under the command of Colonel Stewart; the creators of the island had anticipated that the waters of the Pacific would not always be safe. When approaching certain groups of islands, it was wise to be on guard against attacks by pirates. The militia was generously paid; each man earned a higher salary than the best generals in old Europe, a fact that should not surprise you. The recruiting of these soldiers, who were housed, clothed, and fed at the expense of the administration, was done under excellent conditions controlled by supervisors as rich as Croesus.

Was there a police force on Standard Island? Yes, just a few squads, but that was enough to ensure the security of a city that had no reason to expect trouble. After all, one needed authorization to live there. The coast was guarded by a group of customs officers who were on the lookout day and night. Standard Island could be entered only by her harbors. How could criminals penetrate her? As for those few who did become crooks while already living there, they were arrested immediately, inevitably convicted, and deported to the east or west of the Pacific, to a corner of the new or old continent, and were never allowed to return to Standard Island.

We mentioned the harbors of Standard Island. Were there several of them? Yes, two, each one located at one of the extremities of the small diameter of the oval that formed the general shape of the island. One of these harbors was called Starboard Harbor and the other Larboard Harbor, following the designations used in the French navy.

There was never any fear that the regular importations might be interrupted. Indeed, they could not be, thanks to the creation of these two harbors facing opposing directions. If, because of bad weather, one of the harbors could not be used, the other was open to vessels, whose service was thus guaranteed in any kind of weather. It was through Larboard Harbor and Starboard Harbor that the island was supplied with various necessities: fuel brought by special steamers; flour and grain; beer, wine, and other drinks such as tea, coffee, and chocolate; plus groceries, canned goods, etc. It was there, too, that the beef, lamb, and pork from the best American markets arrived, ensuring the consumption of fresh meat. In a word, the island offered every edible delicacy that the most discriminating gourmet could wish for. It was there, also, that were imported the clothing material, the lingerie, and the fashions that would satisfy the most refined dandy or the most elegant woman. All this merchandise could be bought at the retail stores of Milliard City; we would not dare reveal at what price for fear of arousing the incredulity of our readers.

All this being understood, one will still wonder how the regular service of steamers was established between the American shore and a self-propelled island, which was of course moving, being one day in one place and the next a few miles away.

The answer is very simple. Standard Island did not travel haphazardly. She followed a route mapped out by the administration on the advice of the observatory meteorologists. Her journeys through this area of the Pacific, which contains the most beautiful archipelagos, sometimes incurred a few modifications. As much as possible, they avoided the spells of hot and cold weather that cause so many pulmonary illnesses. This is what allowed Calistus Munbar to say about the winter, "What's that?" Standard Island traveled only between the thirty-fifth degree north and the thirty-fifth degree south of latitude. She covered a distance of seventy degrees, or about fourteen hundred knots, an excellent area to navigate! Other ships always knew where to find this Jewel of the Pacific since her course was set beforehand between various groups of delightful islands that formed as many oases on the desert of this huge ocean.

Well, even if it had not been the case, the ships would not have been reduced to search at random for the location of Standard Island. The company could have taken advantage of the twenty-five cables, each sixteen thousand miles long, owned by the Eastern Extension Australasia and China Co. But the self-propelled island did not want to depend on anyone. So a few hundred buoys supporting the ends of electric cables connected to Madeleine Bay were scattered on the surface of the sea. When the moving island came across one of these buoys, technicians would connect her cable to the instruments in their observatory and send dispatches to their agents on the bay, who were thus always informed of the longitudinal and latitudinal position of Standard Island. Consequently, the service of the supply ships was as regular as if done by railroad.

There is still, however, one important point that needs to be clarified.

How did they supply the island with fresh water?

Water . . . ? It was made by distillation in two special factories located near the harbors. It was brought by pipes to the residences or channeled under the soil in the countryside. Thus it was available for all domestic and public uses and fell in beneficent showers on the fields and lawns, which were no longer subject to the whims of the sky. This water was not simply fresh; it was distilled, electrolyzed, more hygienic than the purest springs of the continents, a drop of which, no bigger than a pin-head, contained fifteen billion microbes.

We still have to explain how this marvelous construction moved. She did not need to go at high speed since, over a period of six months, she was not supposed to venture out of the tropical area enclosed between the tropics on one side and the one hundred thirtieth and one hundred eightieth meridians on the other. Standard Island had to cover no more than fifteen to twenty miles in a period of twenty-four hours. This distance could have been easily covered by towing. They could have used a cable made of an Indian plant called "bastin," which is at the same time strong and light and could have floated near the surface of the water without risk of being damaged in the deep sea. This cable could have been rolled up on steam-activated cylinders at both extremities of the island and Standard Island would have been towed forward and backward like the boats going up and down certain rivers. But this cable would have had to be of incredible thickness to pull such an enormous mass and it would have been subjected to much wear and tear. Standard Island would have been an island in chains. She would have been forced to follow the implacable tow line, and when their liberty is at stake, the citizens of free America are superbly uncompromising.

Luckily, at that time the electrical engineers had made so much progress that you could ask anything of this electricity, soul of the world. It is therefore to electricity that the locomotion of the island was entrusted. Two factories sufficed to run generators of practically infinite power that supplied continuous energy of a moderate two thousand volts. These generators set in motion a powerful system of propellers placed near the two harbors. They produced five million horsepower each through their hundreds of boilers heated with oil briquettes, which were less cumbersome and dirty than coal and had more heating power. These factories were managed by two chief engineers, Mr. Watson and Mr. Somwah, with the help of a considerable staff of engineers and stokers under the higher command of Commodore Ethel Simcoë. From his residence at the observatory, the commodore communicated by telephone with the factories situated near the two harbors. It is from him that originated the instructions to advance or retreat according to plan. It is from there that, during the night of the twenty-fifth to the twenty-sixth, Standard Island, which was waiting near the coast of California at the beginning of her annual voyage, received the order to proceed.

Those of our readers who feel confident enough to let their thoughts go on board Standard Island will take part in the various episodes of this journey on the waters of the Pacific, and hopefully they will find no cause to regret their decision.

The maximum speed of Standard Island, when her engines took full advantage of their twelve million horsepower, could reach eight knots per hour. The most powerful waves, when lifted by a storm, would have no effect on her. Her size made her impervious to rough seas. Neither was seasickness to be feared. On their first days aboard, passengers hardly felt the slight vibrations that the rotation of her propellers imparted to her foundation. With sixty-five-foot-long rams extending from her front and back, she parted the waters effortlessly and was able to travel the vast liquid field opened to her voyages without a jolt.

It goes without saying that the electricity produced by the two factories served other purposes beside the locomotion of Standard Island. It lit the countryside, the park, and the city. It furnished an intense source of energy to the lighthouses whose beams, illuminating the sea, revealed the presence of the self-propelled island from afar and prevented all danger of collision. It delivered the various currents used by the telegraphic, telephotic, telautographic, and telephonic services to satisfy the needs of private houses and commercial neighborhoods. It also supplied the artificial moons with five thousand candlepower, which could light an area of six hundred square yards.

At that time, this extraordinary naval construction was taking her second tour of the Pacific Ocean. One month earlier she had left Madeleine Bay, going up toward the thirty-fifth parallel to start her excursion at the latitude of the Hawaiian Islands. She was just traveling alongside the coast of Southern California when Calistus Munbar, having learned by phone that the Concerting Quartet had left San Francisco and was heading toward San Diego, decided to secure the collaboration of these distinguished musicians. We know how he treated them, leading them aboard the self-propelled island, which was moored a few cables away from the shore, and how, thanks to his trickery, chamber music would charm the music lovers of Milliard City.

Such was this ninth wonder of the world, this masterpiece of human genius, worthy of the twentieth century, on which two violinists, one alto, and one cellist were now the guests and which was taking them away to the western areas of the vast Pacific Ocean.

VI

~~~~~~~~~~~~

Invitees . . . Inviti

EVEN SUPPOSING THAT SÉBASTIEN ZORN, Frascolin, Yvernès, and Pinchinat were individuals who took everything in stride, it would have been difficult for them to resist a legitimate fit of anger that would make them want to jump down Calistus Munbar's throat. They had every reason to believe they were walking on American soil, and yet they had been spirited away to the high seas. They thought they were some twenty miles away from San Diego, where they were expected to give a concert the next day, but they suddenly learned that they were drifting away on an artificial, floating and moving island. In truth, an outburst from them would have been entirely understandable.

Fortunately for the American, he shielded himself from this first attack. He took advantage of the surprise, or more exactly the bewilderment of the quartet; he left the tower's platform, went down the elevator, and, for the moment at least, was out of reach of the protests and insults of the four Parisians.

"What a scoundrel!" exclaimed the alto.

"What an animal!" bellowed the cellist.

"Wait a minute, what if, thanks to him, we are on our way to see marvels . . . ?" the first violin calmly asked.

"Are you going to make excuses for him?" asked the second violin.

"He has no excuses," said Pinchinat, "and if Standard Island has a court of law, we'll send him to prison, that Yankee trickster!"

"And if it has an executioner," howled Sébastien Zorn, "we'll have him hanged."

But before they could impose these various punishments, they had to descend to the level of the Milliard City residents, since there were no police one hundred fifty feet in the air. This would have been done in an instant if they had been able to come down. But the elevator did not come back up and there were no stairs in sight. Stuck at the top of the tower, the quartet had no means of communication with the rest of humanity.

After their first outpouring of spite and indignation, Sébastien Zorn, Pinchinat, and Frascolin, leaving Yvernès to his own contemplations, remained silent and still for a while. Above them the flag floated atop its staff. Sébastien Zorn felt a ferocious desire to cut its rope and bring it down like a ship dipping its colors. But his comrades did not want to get into any more trouble and they stayed his hand as he was wielding his sharpened bowie knife.

"Let's not put ourselves in the wrong," observed the wise Frascolin.

"Then . . . you're accepting the situation . . . ?" asked Pinchinat.

"No . . . but let's not make it more difficult!"

"But our luggage is on its way to San Diego . . . ," said His Highness, crossing his arms.

"And what about our concert tomorrow . . . !" exclaimed Sébastien Zorn.

"We'll give it by telephone!" answered the first violin, whose joke did not help calm down the irascible cellist.

The observatory, we should recall, occupied the middle of a vast square where First Avenue ended. At the other end of this two-mile-long artery that divided the two sections of Milliard City, the musicians caught sight of a sort of monumental palace crowned by a very airy and elegant belfry. They thought that it was probably the seat of government of the island, the residence of the municipality, if indeed Milliard City had a mayor and deputies. They were right. At that very moment, the clock of the belfry let out its joyous carillon, whose notes reached the tower with the last undulations of the breeze.

"Listen . . . ! It's in D major," said Yvernès.

"And in two-four time," said Pinchinat.

The belfry struck five.

"And where are we going to eat," cried Sébastien Zorn, "and sleep . . . ? Are we going to spend the night on this platform, one hundred fifty feet in the air, thanks to this miserable Munbar?"

This was to be feared, unless the elevator came back and offered the prisoners a means of leaving their prison.

Indeed, dusk is short in these low latitudes and the sun falls like a missile in the sky. Turning their eyes to the extreme limit of the horizon, the quartet saw nothing but a deserted sea without a single sail or trace of smoke. Throughout the countryside, trams were following the coastline or going toward the two harbors. At that time, the park was still very much alive. From atop the tower, it looked like an enormous basket of flowers where azaleas, clematis, jasmine, wisterias, passionflowers, begonias, salvias, hyacinths, dahlias, camellias, and roses of a hundred different varieties were blooming. There were plenty of people out walking, grown men, young men, not at all like those little dandies who are the shame of the large European cities, but vigorous men with muscular bodies. Women and girls, most of them dressed in pale yellow, the preferred color of those torrid regions, were walking pretty little dogs wearing silk coats with golden ties. Here and there, people were following the sandy paths that wound between the lawns. Some were reclining on the cushions of the electric cars, others were sitting on the benches sheltered by the shade trees. Farther down, young gentlemen were playing tennis, croquet, golf, football, and polo too, mounted on nervous ponies. Groups of children—those American children who are so amazingly vivacious and independent at such a young age, the little girls especially—were playing on the grass. A few horseback riders were trotting down meticulously kept lanes, others were stopping at lively garden parties.

The commercial quarters of the city were still busy at this time of day.

The moving sidewalks progressed with their charge of people along the main arteries. At the bottom of the tower, there was a constant stream of men and women whose attention the prisoners would have been pleased to attract. Several times Pinchinat and Frascolin called out to them. And they were heard: people stretched out their arms, they even shouted greetings, but they showed no surprise. They did not seem shocked to see this pleasant group waving and calling from the platform. The words they sent were just expressions of kindness and courtesy: hellos, good-byes, and how-do-you-dos. The population of Milliard City, where Calistus Munbar had previously taken the four Parisians, seemed informed of their arrival.

"Eh . . . ! They're making fun of us!" said Pinchinat.

"Looks like that to me!" answered Yvernès.

An hour went by, an hour during which their calls for help went unanswered. The urgent supplications of Frascolin did not meet with any more success than the repeated insults of Sébastien Zorn. It was approaching dinnertime; the park started to empty and the streets became deserted. It was infuriating!

"We are probably like those uninitiated whom an evil genius lures inside a sacred enclosure and who are condemned to perish for having seen what their eyes were not supposed to see . . . ," said Yvernès, evoking romantic memories.

"And they would let us perish, tortured by hunger!" added Pinchinat.

"But this won't happen before we have exhausted all means of prolonging our existence!" cried Sébastien Zorn.

"And if we get to the point where we have to eat each other . . . Yvernès will be first!" said Pinchinat.

"Whenever you deem it necessary!" said the first violin in a teary voice, bowing his head to receive the fatal blow.

At that moment a noise came from the depths of the tower. The elevator returned and stopped at the level of the platform. Expecting Calistus Munbar to appear, the prisoners got ready to receive him as he deserved . . .

But the elevator was empty.

Fine! They might have to wait, but the deceived would still find the deceiver. The first thing to do was to get down to his level, and the way to do this was to step inside the elevator, which they did.

As soon as the cellist and his companions were inside, it started down and in less than one minute reached the bottom of the tower.

"And to think," cried Pinchinat, stamping his foot on the ground, "that we are not even on natural soil."

It was not the right moment to come up with such stupid nonsense. No one answered him. The door opened. The four of them got out. The interior courtyard was deserted. They walked across it and took one of the paths along the square.

There, a few people were going back and forth, paying no attention to the strangers. Following a remark of Frascolin warning them to be careful, Sébastien Zorn abandoned his ill-timed recriminations. It was from the authorities that they had to demand justice. Theirs was not a life-and-death situation. The quartet thus decided to go back to the Excelsior Hotel and to wait until the next day to insist on their rights as free men, and they started walking along First Avenue.

Did these Parisians at least attract some public attention . . . ? Yes and no. People looked at them, but without much interest, perhaps thinking that they were some of those rare tourists who sometimes paid a visit to Milliard City. But the quartet, on their part, did not feel very much at ease in their rather extraordinary circumstances. They felt that people were staring at them far more than they really were. On the other hand, the island residents, those people who had willingly left behind their ilk and were wandering on the waters of the largest ocean of our world, seemed bizarre to our Parisians. With a bit of imagination, one could have fancied that they belonged to another planet of the solar system. And that was indeed Yvernès's opinion, drawn as he was by his excitable mind toward imaginary worlds. As for Pinchinat, he simply said,

"All these passers-by look like millionaires to me, and I have the impression that each one is sporting a small propeller on his back, just like this island."

But the musicians were becoming more and more hungry. They had eaten lunch a good while ago and their stomachs were clamoring for food. So they returned to the Excelsior Hotel as quickly as possible. They would wait until the next day to take the steps they had agreed on: after receiving an indemnity that Calistus Munbar would of course have to pay out of his own pocket, they would demand to be brought to San Diego aboard one of the Standard Island steamers.

But as they were following First Avenue, Frascolin stopped before a magnificent building, the front of which bore the following inscription in large gold letters: CASINO. To the right of the superb arch atop the main door was a restaurant and through its windows, decorated with arabesques, they could see a series of tables, some of them occupied by diners, where numerous waiters attended to their needs.

"We can eat here . . . !" said the second violin, looking at his famished comrades.

"Let's go in!" responded Pinchinat laconically.

They entered the restaurant one by one. People did not seem to pay much attention to them; it was an eating establishment popular with strangers. Five minutes later, our starving friends were working their way through the first course of their meal, the menu of which had been drawn up by Pinchinat, who was an expert at this sort of thing. Fortunately, the quartet had a lot of money, and if they had to part with it on Standard Island, they would soon be affluent again after giving a few concerts in San Diego.

The cuisine was excellent, much better than in the hotels of New York and San Francisco. The cooking was done on electric stoves that functioned as well on low heat as on high. After the canned oyster soup, the creamed corn, the raw celery, the rhubarb cakes—all traditional foods— they were served fresh fish, superbly tender steaks, game probably coming from the California forests, and vegetables from the intensive farming of the island. As for drinks, they were not offered ice water, as is the custom in America, but various beers and wines that the vineyards of Burgundy, Bordeaux, and the Rhine had poured into the cellars of Milliard City at a very high price, you better believe it!

This bill of fare cheered up our Parisians. Their thoughts took another turn. Perhaps they started to see their adventure in a brighter light. Everyone knows that orchestra musicians are heavy drinkers. This is normal for people who must chase the sound waves through wind instruments. It is less excusable in those who play the strings. But what does it matter? Yvernès, Pinchinat, and even Frascolin were starting to see life through rose-colored glasses, and we might even say through golden glasses in this city of billionaires. Only Sébastien Zorn, unlike his comrades, did not let his anger drown in the vintages of France.

In short, the quartet was, as they say, completely "plastered" when the time came to ask for the check. It was handed to Frascolin, their treasurer, by the headwaiter, all dressed in black.

The second violin glanced at the total; he got up, sat down, got up again, rubbed his eyes, and stared at the ceiling.

"What's the matter with you . . . ?" asked Yvernès.

"I am shivering from head to toe!" answered Frascolin.

"Expensive, eh . . . ?"

"Outrageous . . . Two hundred francs . . ."

"For the four of us . . . ?"

"No . . . for each."

In fact, it was one hundred sixty dollars, no more and no less. The wild fowl were fifteen dollars apiece, the fish twenty, the steaks twenty-five, the Medoc and Burgundy thirty dollars a bottle, and the rest just as expensive.

"Good Lord!" exclaimed His Highness.

"What crooks!" cried Sébastien Zorn.

These words, exchanged in French, were not understood by the head-waiter, although he could more or less figure out what was happening. But if a slight smile appeared on his lips, it was a smile of surprise, not of contempt. It seemed absolutely normal to him that a meal would cost one hundred sixty dollars. Such were the prices on Standard Island.

"Let's not make a scene!" said Pinchinat "The honor of France is at stake! Let's pay . . ."

"And then let's be on our way to San Diego, by any means," replied Frascolin. "After tomorrow, we won't have enough money left to buy a sandwich!"

Having said this, he took out his wallet and drew from it a considerable amount of paper dollars that luckily were legal tender in Milliard City. He was about to hand them to the waiter when they heard a voice proclaiming,

"These gentlemen don't owe a thing."

It was Calistus Munbar. The Yankee had just entered the room. He was in an excellent mood, smiling and beaming as always.

"It's him!" cried Sébastien Zorn, who felt like grabbing Munbar by his throat and squeezing it the way he squeezed his cello in the forte parts . . .

"Calm down, my dear Zorn," said the American. "Let's go into the living room, where coffee is waiting for us. There we'll talk at leisure, and at the end of our conversation . . ."

"I will strangle you!" retorted Sébastien Zorn.

"No . . . You will kiss my hands . . ."

"I will kiss nothing!" roared the cellist, both red and pale with anger.

A moment later, Calistus Munbar's guests were reclining on comfortable couches while the Yankee was swaying back and forth on a rocking chair.

And, introducing himself to his guests, here is what he said:

"I am Calistus Munbar, a New York native, fifty years of age, great-grandnephew of the famous Barnum, currently superintendent of the arts on Standard Island, in charge of all that relates to painting, sculpture, and music, and more generally, of all the entertainment in Milliard City. And now that you know me, gentlemen . . ."

"Would you, by any chance, also be a police officer charged to lure people into traps and keep them there against their will . . . ? asked Sébastien Zorn.

"Don't be too quick to judge me, my irritable cellist, and wait for the end."

"We will wait," retorted Frascolin in a solemn tone, "and we are listening to you."

"Gentlemen," Calistus Munbar went on in a pleasant tone, "during this discussion, I only want to talk to you about music as it now exists on our self-propelled island. Milliard City does not have theaters yet, but when we decide to have them, they will rise from the ground as if by magic. Up until now, our citizens have indulged their musical tastes by using a sophisticated apparatus to keep them abreast of musical masterpieces. We listen to the ancient and modern composers, to the great vocalists and instrumentalists of today at our leisure, through the phonograph."

"A joke, your phonograph," exclaimed Yvernès scornfully.

"Not true, my dear first violin," answered the superintendent. "We possess devices that more than once were indiscreet enough to listen to you when you were playing in Boston or Philadelphia. And if you so desire, you will be able to give yourselves an ovation."

At this time, the inventions of the famous Edison had attained the ultimate degree of perfection. The phonograph was no longer the simple music box it had resembled at its beginnings. Thanks to its admirable inventor, the ephemeral talent of the players, the instrumentalists, and the singers could be preserved for the appreciation of future generations with as much fidelity as the works of painters and sculptors. It was an echo, if you wish to call it that, but an echo as faithful as a photograph, reproducing the nuances and subtleties of the songs or the performances in their unalterable purity.

Calistus Munbar had talked with so much enthusiasm that the four musicians were tremendously impressed. He spoke of Saint-Saëns, Reyer, Ambroise Thomas, Gounod, Massenet, and Verdi, as well as of the immortal masterpieces of Berlioz, Meyerbeer, Halévy, Rossini, Beethoven, Haydn, and Mozart, as one who knew them thoroughly, who appreciated them and had devoted his already long life as an impresario to making them known. The quartet enjoyed listening to him. Besides, Munbar did not seem to have been affected by the Wagnerian craze, which was already waning at the time.

When Munbar stopped to catch his breath, Pinchinat, taking advantage of the lull, said,

"All this is very nice, but as I see it, your Milliard City never heard anything but canned music and preserved melodies sent to you just like sardines and salt beef."

"Forgive me, my dear alto."

"I forgive you, but I still insist on this point: your phonographs carry only the past and a musician can never be heard in Milliard City at the moment he is playing . . ."

"Forgive me once again."

"Our friend Pinchinat will forgive you as much as you want, Mr. Munbar," said Frascolin. "He is full of forgiveness. But his observation is entirely correct. If only you could communicate with the theaters of Europe and America . . ."

"Do you see this as impossible, my dear Frascolin?" asked the superintendent as he ceased rocking.

"What do you mean . . . ?"

"I mean that it is simply a question of money, and since our city is wealthy enough to satisfy all its whims, all its musical yearnings, it has already been done."

"How . . . ?"

"'With our theatrophones, installed in the concert room of this casino. As you know, our company owns, submerged in the waters of the Pacific Ocean, many cables attached to Madeleine Bay on one end and tied to powerful buoys on the other. So, when one of our citizens wants to hear a singer of the Old or the New World, we pick up one of the cables and send a telephone order to our agents at Madeleine Bay. These agents establish communication with America or Europe. The cables are then connected with the theater or the concert hall requested by our music lovers, who, seated in the casino, actually attend the distant performances and shower them with applause . . ."

"But over there, the musicians cannot hear the applause . . . ," cried Yvernès.

"I beg your pardon, my dear Mr. Yvernès, they hear it by the return cable."

And then Calistus Munbar launched into transcendental considerations on music, recognized not just as one of the manifestations of art but as a therapeutic agent. Following the method of J. Harford from Westminster Abbey, the residents of Milliard City had had the opportunity to experience the extraordinary advantages that this use of music could bring them. It was a method that kept them in perfect health. Music directly influences the nervous system: harmonic vibrations dilate the arteries, affect the circulation of blood, making it move faster or slower according to the needs of the body. It also causes an acceleration in heart rate and breathing by virtue of the tonality and intensity of the sounds, and, at the same time, it helps maintain healthy tissues. Therefore, throughout Milliard City, musical energy outlets existed that transmitted audio waves by telephone to the residences.

The quartet listened, flabbergasted. They had never heard their art discussed from a medical point of view and they were probably none too happy about this. However, our eccentric Yvernès was carried away by those theories that go back to King Saul, in accordance with the prescriptions and methods of the famous harpist David.

"Yes . . . ! Yes, indeed . . . !" exclaimed Yvernès after the last tirade of the superintendent. "It is obvious. You just have to select the music that fits the diagnosis! Wagner or Berlioz for a weak constitution . . ."

"And for fiery dispositions, Mendelssohn or Mozart, who advantageously replace strontium bromide!" answered Calistus Munbar.

At this point Sébastien Zorn harshly interrupted all this high-flown chat.

"This is totally out of place," he said. "Why did you bring us here?"

"Because string instruments are those that have the strongest effect . . ."

"Really, my dear sir! So it is to treat the neuroses of your people that you interrupted our travel and kept us from getting to San Diego, where we were to give a concert tomorrow . . ."

"Yes, indeed, my dear friends."

"And you simply saw us as some sort of musical medical men or apothecaries . . . ?" cried Pinchinat.

"Certainly not, gentlemen," answered Calistus Munbar, getting up. "I saw you only as artists of great talent and renown. The hurrahs that welcomed the Concerting Quartet on their tour of America were also heard on our island. So the Standard Island Company felt that it was time to replace our phonographs and theatrophones with tangible virtuosos made of flesh and blood and to give our fellow citizens the inexpressible joy of a live performance of musical masterpieces. We wanted to start with chamber music before organizing orchestras. We immediately thought of you, who are the chosen representatives of this kind of music. I was given the mission of bringing you to us at any price, even by kidnapping you if I had to! You will be the very first musicians performing live on Standard Island, and you can imagine the welcome you are going to receive!"

Yvernès and Pinchinat felt very much shaken by the superintendent's enthusiastic spiel. They did not even entertain the thought that it might be nothing more than a hoax. But Frascolin, always the reflective one, wondered if their adventure should be taken seriously. After all, on such an extraordinary island, how could things not appear extraordinary? As for Sébastien Zorn, he was determined not to surrender.

"No, sir," he exclaimed, "you do not spirit people away like this against their will . . . ! We will file a complaint against you . . . !

"A complaint . . . ! You should shower me with thanks, ingrates that you are!" replied the superintendent.

"We'll make sure to sue for damages, my dear sir . . ."

"Damages . . . ! I will offer you a hundred times more than you could imagine . . ."

"How much would that be?" asked the practical Frascolin.

Calistus Munbar took out his wallet and produced a paper bearing the name of the Standard Island Company. He handed it to the musicians, saying, "Put your four signatures at the bottom of this contract and we'll be in business."

"Sign a document without reading it first . . . ?" asked the second violin. "This is simply not done!"

"You would have nothing to regret, though!" retorted Calistus Munbar, shaking with laughter. "But let's do this according to the rules. This is an agreement proposed to you by our company; a one-year agreement starting today. It states that you will play chamber music for us, following the program you set up for America. In twelve months Standard Island will be back in Madeleine Bay and you will be on time . . ."

"For our concert in San Diego, right?" cried Sébastien Zorn. "In San Diego where they will welcome us with hisses and boos . . ."

"No, gentlemen, with hurrahs! Musicians such as you, the music lovers are always too honored and happy to have a chance to listen to them . . . even one year late!"

How could you hold a grudge against such a man?

Frascolin took the contract and read it with great attention.

"What guarantees will we have . . . ?" he asked.

"The guarantee of the Standard Island Company with the signature of our governor, Mr. Cyrus Bikerstaff."

"And the salary will be as indicated in this contract . . . ?"

"Yes, one million francs . . ."

"Just for the four of us . . . ?" exclaimed Pinchinat.

"No, for each," answered Calistus Munbar, smiling, "and these figures do not even take into account your worth, which is beyond compare!"

It would have been difficult to be kinder. And yet Sébastien Zorn still protested. He did not want to accept the offer at any price. He wanted to leave for San Diego, and it was not an easy task for Frascolin to assuage his anger.

Besides, it was understandable that the superintendent's proposal could make anyone a bit suspicious. A one-year contract, at one million francs for each musician, could this be serious . . . ? Absolutely serious, as Frascolin realized when he asked,

"How will this salary be paid . . . ?"

"Every three months," answered the superintendent, "and here is the money for the first trimester."

And with that, he made four piles from the banknotes stuffed in his wallet, four piles of fifty thousand dollars, or two hundred fifty thousand francs, that he handed to Frascolin and his friends.

This is one way of doing business, the American way.

Sébastien Zorn could not help being a little shaken, but since his bad mood always took precedence over everything else, he blurted out,

"After all, with the high price you pay for everything on your island, if a partridge costs twenty-five francs, I bet that a pair of gloves costs a hundred and a pair of boots five hundred . . . ?"

"Oh! Mr. Zorn," exclaimed Calistus Munbar, "our company isn't concerned with such trifles, and it wants the musicians of the Concerting Quartet to be supplied with everything they need during their stay on its property!"

How could they have responded to such a generous offer except by signing the agreement?

So this is exactly what Frascolin, Pinchinat, and Yvernès did. Sébastien Zorn still grumbled that all this was absurd . . . that to embark on a self-propelled island made no sense . . . that they would see how it would all end up . . . , but, finally, he signed, too.

Once these formalities were done with, Frascolin, Pinchinat, and Yvernès did not kiss the hand of Calistus Munbar, but each gave him a friendly handshake. Four handshakes worth one million each.

VII

<center>~~~~~~~~~~</center>

Heading West

STANDARD ISLAND PROCEEDED SLOWLY THROUGH the waters of the Pacific Ocean, whose name is justified at this time of the year. Accustomed to the even motion of the past twenty-four hours, Sébastien Zorn and his companions no longer noticed that they were traveling by sea. Despite the ten-million horsepower activating its hundreds of propellers, the steel hull of Standard Island hardly vibrated. Milliard City was not shaking on its base. They could not feel the rolling that affects even the most powerful battleships. In the houses, there were no tables or lamps fastened to the floor. There was no need for that. The houses in Paris, London, or New York were not more firmly secured to their foundations.

After a few weeks' stay at Madeleine Bay, the council of notables of Standard Island met at the request of the president of the company and mapped out the itinerary of their annual voyage. The self-propelled island was going to visit the main archipelagos of the eastern Pacific, with their hygienic atmosphere so rich in ozone and condensed, electrified oxygen that it contained active particles absent from oxygen in its usual state. They took advantage of the fact that their island could move freely: they could choose to go east or west, approach the shores of America or the eastern coast of Asia at their pleasure. Standard Island went where her residents wanted her to go in order to enjoy the diversions of a varied excursion. And even if they had wanted to leave the Pacific for the Indian or Atlantic Oceans, and circle Cape Horn or the Cape of Good Hope, they would simply have proceeded in that direction and neither currents nor storms could have kept them from reaching their destination.

But they did not wish to explore these distant seas where the Jewel of the Pacific could not have found what this ocean offered them with its endless arrays of archipelagos. This was an area wide enough for multiple excursions. The self-propelled island could explore it one archipelago at a time. Standard Island was not endowed with the special instinct of animals, that sixth sense of orientation that drives them where their needs call them, but was led by a firm hand following a program that had been discussed at length and unanimously approved. Until then, the Starboardites and the Larboardites had never disagreed on the plan. And at that moment, it was according to their joint decision that they were advancing westward toward the Hawaiian Islands. The distance of about twelve thousand leagues between this archipelago and the place where the quartet had come on board would be covered in about a month's time, proceeding at a moderate speed, and Standard Island would remain in this archipelago until her residents decided to travel to another group in the Southern Hemisphere.

The day after their memorable encounter with Calistus Munbar, the quartet left the Excelsior Hotel and settled in an apartment that was placed at their disposal in the casino. It was a very comfortable and richly furnished place. First Avenue stretched in front of their windows. Sébastien Zorn, Frascolin, Pinchinat, and Yvernès each had their own bedroom opening on a common living room. The central courtyard of the building offered them the shade of its trees in full bloom and the coolness of its gushing fountains. On one side of this courtyard stood the museum of Milliard City and on the other, the concert hall where the Parisian musicians were going to replace so advantageously the echoes of the phonographs and the transmissions of the theatrophones. Twice a day, three times a day, as many times a day as they wished, the table would be set for them by the headwaiter, who would no longer hand them incredible bills.

That morning, as they met in the living room a few minutes before going down to breakfast, Pinchinat said,

"Well, my dear music makers, what do you think about what's happening to us?"

"It's a dream," answered Yvernès, "a dream in which we are hired at a million francs a year . . ."

"But it is also reality," added Frascolin. "Reach into your pockets and you will find that first quarter of a million . . ."

"We still have to see how it will all end up . . . ! Very badly, I presume!" cried Sébastien Zorn, who wanted to find fault with the deal he was engaged in against his will.

"Besides, where is our luggage . . . ?" he asked.

Indeed, by now their luggage was probably in San Diego, from where it would not come back and where its owners could not go to fetch it. Anyway, it consisted of very rudimentary items: a few suitcases with their linens, toiletries, a change of clothes, and the official costumes of musicians who will perform before an audience.

They had no need to worry about this. In the next forty-eight hours, their well-worn wardrobes would be replaced by new ones that were presented to them, and for which they did not have to pay fifteen hundred francs for a suit of clothes and five hundred for a pair of boots.

Besides, Calistus Munbar was so pleased with the way he had handled this delicate business that he made sure that the quartet lacked nothing. They could not have imagined a more thoroughly obliging superintendent. Munbar lived in one of the apartments of the casino that he managed, and the company paid him a salary worthy of his lavishness and prodigality . . . We prefer not to reveal its amount.

The casino contained reading rooms and game rooms but baccarat, *trente et quarante*, roulette, poker, and other games of chance were strictly prohibited. It also housed a smoking room, from which tobacco smoke, prepared by a recently founded company, was sent directly to the residences. The tobacco burned in the furnaces of this central area produced purified smoke, free of nicotine, that was distributed to each user through individual pipes equipped with amber end pieces. The customers simply put their lips to these amber mouthpieces and a meter would register their daily consumption.

Inside this casino, where music lovers could listen to the distant sounds that the quartet would soon add to, were also stored the art collections of Milliard City. To art lovers, the museum, rich in ancient and modern paintings, offered numerous masterpieces acquired at exorbitant prices: canvases of the Italian, Dutch, German, and French schools, which the collections of Paris, London, Munich, Rome, and Florence would envy. It contained works by Raphael, da Vinci, Giorgione, Correggio, Domenichino, Ribeira, Murillo, Ruysdael, Rembrandt, Rubens, Cuyp,

Frans Hal, Hobbema, Van Dyck, Holbein, etc. It also housed many modern paintings by Fragonard, Ingres, Delacroix, Scheffer, Cabat, Delaroche, Régnant, Couture, Meissonier, Millet, Rousseau, Jules Dupré, Brascassat, Mackart, Turner, Troyon, Corot, Daubigny, Baudry, Bonnat, Carolus Duran, Jules Lefebvre, Vollon, Breton, Binet, Yon, Cabanel, etc. In order to ensure that these pictures would last forever, they were placed inside glass cases in which a vacuum had been created. It should be noted that the impressionists and the futurists had not yet cluttered this museum; but this omission would probably not last and Standard Island would not escape the invasion of this decadent plague. The museum also possessed very valuable marble statues, by renowned ancient and modern sculptors, placed in the casino's courtyards. Thanks to the climate of Standard Island, which was devoid of rain and fog, statues and busts could well withstand the affronts of time.

It would be presumptuous to claim that all these marvels were often admired, that the nabobs of Milliard City had a highly cultivated taste for these artful creations, and that their artistic sensitivity was extremely developed. We must note, however, that the Starboard section counted more art lovers than the Larboard one. But when the acquisition of any masterpiece was proposed, they generally all agreed and their incredible offers took the work of art away from all the Dukes of Aumale and all the Chauchards of the old and new continents.

The most popular areas of the casino were the reading rooms stacked with magazines and European and American newspapers brought by the regular service of the Standard Island steamers to Madeleine Bay. After being leafed through, read, and reread, this printed material was placed on the shelves of the library along with several thousand works waiting to be filed. It required the presence of a librarian, who was paid twenty-five thousand dollars and may have been the least busy of all the island employees. This library also contained a good amount of phonographic books that people did not even need to read. They could simply press a button in order to hear the voice of a talented speaker read the book aloud, much like Mr. Legouvé would read Racine's *Phèdre*.

The two local newspapers were written, edited, and printed in the casino's printing shops under the direction of two chief editors. One was the *Starboard Chronicle*, the Starboardites' newspaper, and the other the *New Herald*, the Larboardites' one. Their news included stories of human interest, the arrivals of steamers, maritime news, naval encounters, the market prices for the commercial quarters, the daily latitudinal and longitudinal positions of the island, the decisions of the notables, the orders of the governor, wedding, birth, and death announcements, the latter being very rare. However, never any thefts or murders. The courts heard only civil complaints and disputes between citizens. There were never articles about centenarians, since living a long life was no longer the privilege of a lucky few.

Information on international politics came to the island through phone communication with Madeleine Bay, where the cables submerged in the depths of the Pacific were linked. The billionaires were thus informed of anything of interest happening throughout the world. We should add that the *Starboard Chronicle* and the *New Herald* did not disparage each other. Until then, they had coexisted on rather good terms, but their courteous exchange would not necessarily last forever. Very tolerant and conciliatory in all religious matters, both Protestants and Catholics cooperated closely on Standard Island. But who could predict the future? Politics could rear its ugly head, business rivalries could take over, questions of personal interest or pride could come into play . . .

In addition to their two daily newspapers, the islanders had weeklies and monthlies reprinting the articles of foreign newspapers, the writings of the successors of Sarcey, Lemaître, Charmes, Fournel, Deschamps, Fouquier, France, and other excellent critics. There were illustrated magazines also, plus a dozen scandal sheets covering social events. These were strictly published to titillate the mind . . . and even the stomach, for a few minutes. Indeed, a few of them were printed on edible sheets with chocolate ink. When the islanders were through reading them, they ate them for breakfast. Some of them were astringent and others had a slightly purgative effect, and they were all very digestible. The quartet found this invention as amusing as it was practical.

"These make for easily digested readings!" Yvernès judiciously exclaimed.

"And it's nourishing literature, too!" retorted Pinchinat. "Edible literature goes very well with hygienic music!"

Now, it is time to wonder which resources the self-propelled island possessed that could offer her residents a standard of living superior to that of any other city in the world. Her revenues had to be astronomically high, considering the money going out to the various services and the high salaries paid to all her employees.

When the quartet questioned the superintendent about this, he replied,

"Here, we don't bother with business. We have no Board of Trade, no stock market, and no industry. The only commerce we engage in is to satisfy the needs of the islanders and we will never offer foreigners the equivalent of the Chicago World's Fair of 1893 or the Paris Exposition of 1900. No! The powerful religion of business has no place here and we never shout 'go ahead' except to tell the Jewel of the Pacific to proceed forward. So it is not from business that we expect the necessary resources to maintain Standard Island, it is from customs duties. Yes! The customs duties are high enough to meet all the needs of our budget."

"And what is your budget . . . ?" asked Frascolin.

"Twenty million dollars, my dear friends!"

"That's one hundred million francs," exclaimed the second violin, "and for a city of ten thousand people . . . !"

"Correct, my dear Frascolin, and this sum comes entirely from customs duties. We have no tax revenues since our local production is almost insignificant. No! We simply have the monies levied at Starboard and Larboard Harbors. This explains why consumer products are so expensive, but these relatively high prices are acceptable because, as exaggerated as they may seem to you, they are in keeping with everyone else's means."

And here Calistus Munbar got carried away again. He praised his city and his island, calling them a piece of a superior planet fallen into the middle of the Pacific and a floating Eden where wise people took refuge. He asserted that if happiness could not be found here, it did not exist! He made a true sales pitch! It was as if he were saying, "Come in, ladies, come in, gentlemen . . . Get your tickets . . . There are very few seats left . . . The show is about to begin . . . Who still needs a ticket . . . ? Etc., etc."

It was true that the seats were few and the tickets expensive! Well! The superintendent juggled these millions that were nothing but numbers in this city of billionaires!

It was during this tirade, in which Munbar's sentences gushed forth like a waterfall and his gestures acquired a semaphoric frenzy, that the quartet learned about the diverse branches of the island's administration. The schools were free and mandatory, and the teachers were paid abundantly. The children learned the dead and living languages, history and geography, the physical sciences, mathematics, and the arts. According to Calistus Munbar, they learned all this better than in any university or academy of the Old World. The truth was that the students did not work very hard in the public school and that, if the current generation still had a sprinkling of the subjects taught in the colleges of the United States, the next one would have less education than income. That was their weak point, and perhaps human beings can only lose by cutting themselves off from the rest of humanity.

Well, did they not travel to foreign nations of the world, the residents of this artificial island? Did they not visit the lands beyond the seas and the great capitals of Europe? Did they not explore the countries whose pasts provided so many masterpieces of all sorts? Admittedly, there were a few who journeyed to distant regions, driven by certain feelings of curiosity. But it made them tired. Most of them became bored. They did not find anything there resembling their uniform existence on Standard Island. They suffered from the heat; they suffered from the cold; they became ill, and people did not become ill on Standard Island. So they could not wait to go back to their island, those foolish people who had had the unfortunate idea of leaving it. What did they gain from their travels? Nothing. "Empty they went, and empty they returned," as the ancient Greek proverb says, and we will add, "and empty they remained."

As for the foreigners that the celebrity of Standard Island—this ninth wonder of the world, since the Eiffel Tower was now the eighth, at least that is what people said—might have attracted, Calistus Munbar thought there would never be many. The islanders did not wish it otherwise, anyway, even if the turnstiles of the two harbors would have taken in even more money. Most of the foreigners who had come the year before were American. Very few from other countries. There were several English citizens, though. You could recognize them at their invariably rolled-up pant legs, because it always rains in London. Besides, Great Britain viewed the creation of Standard Island very critically. The English believed that the island hindered sea travel and they would have liked to see her disappear. The Germans, for their part, were not welcome. It was felt that if they were allowed to settle in Milliard City, they would transform it into a new Chicago. Of all the foreigners, the French were the ones whom the company admitted with most kindness and consideration, since they did not belong to the invading races of Europe. But had a Frenchman ever appeared on Standard Island until then?

"Probably not," observed Pinchinat.

"We're not rich enough," added Frascolin.

"Not rich enough to be one of the nabobs maybe, but rich enough to be an employee."

"Do any of our compatriots live in Milliard City . . . ?" asked Yvernès.

"There is one . . ."

"And who is this lucky man . . . ?"

"Monsieur Athanase Dorémus."

"And what does he do here, this Athanase Dorémus?" exclaimed Pinchinat.

"He is a professor of dance, charm, and good manners, paid handsomely by the government, to say nothing of the income he receives from private lessons."

"Lessons that only a Frenchman can give . . . !" added His Highness.

Now that the quartet was well informed about the organization of Standard Island's administrative life, they could simply enjoy the pleasures of the voyage that was carrying them westward. Had it not been for the sun rising on one part on the island one day and on another the next, according to the direction chosen by Commodore Simcoë, Sébastien Zorn and his companions would have believed that they were on terra firma. Twice during the next two weeks, thunderstorms erupted with violent squalls, for there are still a few in the Pacific regardless of its name. Sea swells came to break on the metallic hull of Standard Island; they covered it with foam as if it were an ordinary shore. But the vessel did not even quiver under the assaults of the angry sea. The fury of the ocean was powerless against her. The genius of man had prevailed over nature.

Two weeks later, on June 11, the first chamber music concert took place. It was advertised in electric letters along the larger avenues. Needless to say that the musicians had already been introduced to the governor and the city officials. Cyrus Bikerstaff had welcomed them most warmly. The newspapers had mentioned the success of the Concerting Quartet in the United States and congratulated the super-intendent for bringing them to the island in a rather strange manner, as we know. What a pleasure it was to hear and see at the same time these musicians performing the works of the masters. What a treat for connoisseurs!

That the Parisians were hired by the casino of Milliard City at fab-ulous salaries did not make their concerts free to the public. Far from it. The administration expected a large profit from these concerts, like the American impresarios whose female singers cost them a dollar a measure, and even a dollar a note. It was customary for the residents of the island to pay for the theatrophonic and phonographic concerts of the casino and, on that day, they would pay significantly more. The seats were all at the same price, two hundred dollars each or a thousand francs in French currency, but Calistus Munbar was sure that he would have a full house.

And he was not disappointed. Every seat was taken. The elegant and comfortable hall of the casino contained only about a hundred seats, it is true, and if they had been sold at auction, no one knows what profit they might have brought. But this would have been contrary to Stan-dard Island's usage. Indeed, anything that had market value, the super-fluous as well as the necessary, was recorded ahead of time on the price lists. Without this precaution, and considering the immense fortunes of some of the residents, one man could have reserved the entire room for himself, and this was to be avoided. In truth, if the rich Starboardites went to the concert out of their love of music, it was certainly possible that the Larboardites went because it was the thing to do.

When Sébastien Zorn, Pinchinat, Yvernès, and Frascolin appeared before the spectators of New York, Chicago, Philadelphia, and Balti-more, they were not exaggerating when they said, "Here is an audience worth millions." But on this particular evening, they would have been far from the truth if they had not counted in the billions. Just think about it! Jem Tankerdon, Nat Coverley, and their families sat prominently in the first row. In the other rows, there were many music lovers who were not true billionaires but still had "big bags," as Pinchinat remarked.

"Let's go!" said the leader of the quartet when the time came to step onto the stage.

And they went, no more nervous and perhaps even less so than they would have been in front of a Parisian audience, which may have had less money in their pockets but more artistic sense in their heads.

We must add that, although they had not yet taken lessons from their compatriot Dorémus, Sébastien Zorn, Yvernès, Frascolin, and Pinchinat wore very correct outfits: white ties at twenty-five francs each, pearl-gray gloves at fifty francs, shirts at seventy francs, boots at a hundred eighty francs a pair, vests at two hundred francs, black trousers at five hundred francs, black coats at fifteen hundred francs, and all this paid for by the administration, of course. They were applauded very warmly by the Starboardites, and a little more discreetly by the Larboardites; this was just a difference in temperament.

The concert program consisted of four pieces furnished them by the casino library, which had been richly stocked under the care of Calistus Munbar:

First Quartet in E-flat, op. 12, by Mendelssohn;
Second Quartet in F major, op. 16, by Haydn;
Tenth Quartet in E-flat, op. 74, by Beethoven;
Fifth Quartet in A major, op. 10, by Mozart.

The musicians performed exquisitely in this billionaired hall aboard this floating island, on the surface of an abyss more than three miles deep in this area of the Pacific. They received the considerable success they deserved, especially from the audience of the Starboardite section. The superintendent was worth watching during this memorable evening: he was jubilant. He looked as if he was the one who had just played two violins, a viola, and a cello, and all at the same time. What a wonderful start for the champions of the concerting music . . . and for their impresario!

It is worth noticing that, if the hall was at full capacity, the casino was also crowded. Indeed, there were many who had not been able to get a seat and others that the high prices kept out. These outside listeners could only receive a few crumbs. They could only hear from a distance, as if the music came out of a phonograph box or the receiver of a telephone. But their applause was just as loud.

And it became positively thunderous when, after the concert, Sébastien Zorn, Yvernès, Pinchinat, and Frascolin appeared on the terrace at the left of the pavilion. First Avenue was flooded with light. From high up in space, the electric moons sent rays that would have made the moon jealous.

Across from the casino, on the sidewalk, apart from the crowd, a couple attracted Yvernès's attention. A man was standing there with a woman on his arm. The man, taller than most, with a noble, severe, and even sad face, was about fifty years old. The woman, a few years younger, was tall with a proud bearing. A few strands of white hair showed under her hat.

Yvernès, impressed by their reserved composure, pointed them out to Calistus Munbar:

"Who are those people?" he asked.

"Those people . . . ?" answered the superintendent, screwing up his face in contempt. "Oh . . . ! They are music fanatics."

"And why didn't they buy seats in the casino hall?"

"Probably because it was too expensive for them."

"So, what are they worth . . . ?"

"They barely have two hundred thousand francs of income."

"Harrumph!" said Pinchinat. "And who are these poor wretches?"

"The king and queen of Malécarlie."

VIII

~~~~~~~~~

Navigation

AFTER BUILDING THIS AMAZING NAVIGATING machine, the Standard Island Company had to deal not only with her maritime organization but also with her administration.

As we already know, the maritime organization had as director, or rather as captain, Commodore Ethel Simcoë of the U.S. Navy. Fifty years old, he was an experienced sailor, thoroughly familiar with every area of the Pacific, its currents, its storms, its reefs, its underwater corals. He was therefore perfectly capable of leading with a firm hand both the self-propelled island entrusted to his care and the wealthy people for whom he was responsible before God and the society's stockholders.

The administration, with its various regulatory services, was in the hands of the governor of the island. Mr. Cyrus Bikerstaff was a Yankee from Maine, one of the Federal States that took a minimal part in the fratricidal battles of the American Confederation during the American Civil War. Cyrus Bikerstaff was therefore a good choice to maintain a happy medium between the two sections of the island.

The governor, in his late sixties, was a bachelor. He was a cold individual with excellent self-control. He was very energetic in spite of his phlegmatic appearance, very English in his reserved attitude, his gentlemanly manners, and the diplomatic discretion that characterized his words and actions. In any country other than Standard Island, he would have been a very important, highly respected man. But there he was, after all, only the main agent of the company. Moreover, although his salary was as high as the revenue of a small European king, he was not truly rich and thus could not cut an impressive figure among the nabobs of Milliard City.

Cyrus Bikerstaff was at the same time governor of the island and mayor of her capital city. He lived in the mansion on the opposite end of First Avenue from the observatory where Commodore Ethel Simcoë resided. It was also there that his offices were located and that all official documents were kept: registrations of births—sufficient to ensure the future of the island—of deaths—the deceased were transported to the cemetery of Madeleine Bay—and of marriages, which had to be legalized by the authorities prior to the religious ceremony, in keeping with the rules of Standard Island. The many services of the administration also functioned there without any complaints from the administered, which did credit to the mayor and his deputies. When Sébastien Zorn, Pinchinat, Yvernès, and Frascolin were introduced to Cyrus Bikerstaff by the superintendent, he gave the very favorable impression of a good and just man with a practical mind, who did not give way to prejudice or delusions.

"Gentlemen," he said to them, "we are very lucky to have you. The means used by our superintendent were perhaps not quite correct, but I am sure that you'll forgive him. Besides, you will have no cause to complain about the treatment our island will give you. We will require only two concerts per month, so you will be free to accept the private invitations that you will surely receive. We welcome you as musicians of great talent and we will never forget that you were the first artists whom we had the honor of welcoming to our island!"

The quartet was delighted by this welcome and did not conceal their satisfaction from Calistus Munbar.

"Yes, Mr. Cyrus Bikerstaff is a fine man," answered the superintendent with a slight shrug of his shoulders. "It's a pity that he does not possess a billion or two . . ."

"No one is perfect!" replied Pinchinat.

The governor-mayor of Milliard City had two deputies who helped him in the very simple administration of the self-propelled island. Under their command, a few employees, well paid, as would be expected, worked in the various services. There was no municipal council. It would have been useless. In its place, they had a council of notables, a group of about thirty people extremely well qualified by their intelligence and their fortune. They met when there were important decisions to make, for example, the choice of the itinerary best suited to everyone's well-being. As our Parisians could see, this subject sometimes needed to be discussed and problems could arise before a consensus was reached. But until then, thanks to his skillful and wise mediation, Cyrus Bikerstaff had always been able to reconcile conflicting interests while respecting the self-esteem of his constituents. Appropriately, of his two deputies, one—Barthelemy Ruge—was Protestant and the other—Hubley Harcourt—Catholic. They were both chosen from the high-ranking officials of the Standard Island Company and they zealously assisted Cyrus Bikerstaff.

The island where the quartet would spend an entire year had already roamed the ocean for eighteen months, enjoying complete independence even from diplomatic relations, free on this vast sea of the Pacific, sheltered from unpleasant weather and navigating beneath the skies of her choice. In spite of what the cellist said, the musicians could neither imagine nor fear encountering certain adventures or facing unexpected situations in the future, since everything was settled ahead of time and occurred in an orderly and regular fashion. And yet, in creating this artificial island, launched onto the surface of a vast ocean, did human genius not perhaps reach beyond the limits assigned to it by its Creator . . . ?

The island proceeded westward. Every day, when the sun crossed the meridian at noon, the event was recorded by the observatory officers under the command of Commodore Ethel Simcoë. A four-faced dial set on each side of the city hall belfry registered the exact longitudinal and latitudinal positions of the island, and this information was simultaneously relayed by telegraph to every corner, hotel, public building, and private residence, along with the time of day, which varied as they traveled east or west. The billionaires could therefore know at any given time exactly what point of her itinerary Standard Island had reached.

Except for its imperceptible motion on the surface of the ocean, Milliard City was not unlike the great capitals of the old and new continents. Life in the city was the same. Public and private existences were organized in the same way. Since they were not very busy, after all, our musicians used their first free hours to visit everything on this strange Jewel of the Pacific. Trams brought them to every point of the island. They particularly admired the two electric plants for the simple organization of their equipment, the power of their engines activating a double string of propellers, and the admirable discipline of their personnel. Engineer Watson ran one of the plants and engineer Somwah was in charge of the other. At regular intervals, the steamers servicing the island docked at Starboard Harbor or at Larboard Harbor, depending on the best position for making land.

If the stubborn Sébastien Zorn refused to admire these marvels, if Frascolin showed a certain admiration, the enthusiastic Yvernès lived in continual rapture. According to him, by the end of the twentieth century every area of the sea would be traversed by floating cities. This would be state-of-the-art progress and comfort in the future. What a superb spectacle was this moving island that went to visit her sisters in Oceania! As for Pinchinat, he felt particularly elated in this wealthy environment where they talked about millions the way that others talk about twenty-dollar gold pieces. Banknotes were the everyday currency. People usually had two or three thousand dollars in their wallets. And more than once, His Highness would say to Frascolin: "Hey, buddy, would you have change for fifty thousand francs . . . ?"

In the meantime, the Concerting Quartet had met a few people and was certain to be welcomed anywhere. Besides, who would not have been eager to welcome them, recommended as they were by the amazing Calistus Munbar?

First they paid a visit to their compatriot, Athanase Dorémus, professor of dance, charm, and good manners.

This good man resided in the Starboard section, in a modest house on Twenty-Fifth Avenue, with a rent of three thousand dollars. He had as a servant an old black woman to whom he paid a monthly salary of one hundred dollars. He was delighted to meet other Frenchmen . . . Frenchmen who were an honor to France.

Dorémus was an old man of seventy, thin, skinny, and short. He still had a sharp eye, all his teeth, and a full head of curly hair, white like his beard. He walked steadily, with a certain rhythm, his chest out and his back straight. He kept his arms at his sides and his feet, which were exquisitely shod, pointed slightly outward. Our musicians took great pleasure in chatting with him and he gladly responded, because he was as talkative as he was charming.

"I am so happy, my dear compatriots, I am so happy," he repeated twenty times during the first visit of the quartet, "I am so happy to meet you! What a wonderful idea you had to come and settle in this town! You will not regret it, for now that I am used to it, I would find it impossible to live in any other place!"

"And how long have you lived here, Monsieur Dorémus?" asked Yvernès.

"Eighteen months," answered the professor, planting his feet firmly on the ground, "I go back to the very beginnings of Standard Island. Thanks to the excellent references I had from New Orleans, where I was living, my services were accepted by Mr. Cyrus Bikerstaff, our beloved governor. Since that blessed day, the salary I have been paid to direct the conservatory of dance, charm, and good manners has allowed me to live . . ."

"As a millionaire!" cried Pinchinat.

"Oh! The millionaires here . . ."

"I know . . . I know . . . my dear compatriot. But according to what the superintendent told us, your classes at the conservatory are not very popular."

"True. I only have students in town, and they are all young men. The young American ladies believe that they are naturally charming; the young men prefer to take their lessons in private, and I secretly teach them good French manners!"

He smiled while speaking, simpered like an old coquette, and struck artistic poses.

Athanase Dorémus was from Santerre in Picardy. He had left France at a very young age and settled in the United States, in New Orleans. There, among the population of French origin of our regretted Louisiana, he had many occasions to put his talents to use. Well received by the most prominent families, he achieved success and was able to save money, but a typical American business failure wiped out all that he had. This was right at the time when the Standard Island Company was launching its project, printing pamphlets, sending out advertisements, calling on all the super-rich people who had made enormous fortunes in the railroads, oil wells, and pork sales, salted and not. Athanase Dorémus thought of seeking employment with the governor of this new city, where there would not be many professors of his sort. Well acquainted with the Coverley family of New Orleans, and thanks to the recommendation of this family's patriarch, who was to become one of the best-known Starboardites of Milliard City, he was hired; and this is how a Frenchman, and from Picardy to boot, became one of the officials of Standard Island. Dorémus's lessons were given only in his home, it is true, and the classroom of the casino never saw anyone but the professor reflected in its mirrors. But why would this have mattered, since his salary remained the same?

All in all, the professor was a good chap, a bit peculiar and fussy, rather conceited, and convinced that he possessed the legacy of the Vestrises and the Saint-Leons combined with the traditions of the Brummels and the Lord Seymours. But, in the eyes of the quartet, he was a compatriot, a quality always appreciated when you are thousands of miles from France.

The four Parisians had to tell him about their latest adventures, under what circumstances they came to Standard Island, how they had been lured aboard, yes, "lured" was the correct word, and how the vessel had weighed anchor a few hours after they boarded.

"Knowing our superintendent, this does not surprise me," answered the old professor. "It's another one of his tricks . . . He has played some before and will play many more . . . ! He is a true descendant of Barnum, who will end up jeopardizing the company . . . an inconsiderate fellow who could use a few lessons in good manners . . . one of those Yankees who ensconce themselves in an armchair with their feet on the window-sill . . . ! He's not a bad sort at heart, but he thinks he can do anything he wants . . . ! Anyway, my dear compatriots, don't hold that against him, and except for your missed concert in San Diego, you will surely congratulate yourselves on your stay in Milliard City. People will treat you with great consideration . . . which will make you feel good . . ."

"Especially at the end of each trimester!" answered Frascolin, whose function as treasurer of the group was becoming very important.

Responding to the question of the quartet about the rivalry between the two sections of the island, Athanase Dorémus confirmed what Calistus Munbar had told them. According to Dorémus, there was a dark cloud on the horizon and even the threat of an approaching storm. A conflict of interest and self-respect was feared between the Starboardites and the Larboardites. The wealthiest families in town showed a growing jealousy toward each other and, unless some wise proposal succeeded in bringing them together, an explosion could be expected . . . Yes . . . an explosion . . . !

"As long as it does not make the island explode, we don't have to worry about it . . ." observed Pinchinat.

"At least as long as we are on it!" added the cellist.

"Oh . . . ! The island is solid, my dear compatriots!" answered Athanase Dorémus. "For eighteen months now she has been roaming the seas without incurring any serious accident. Only three insignificant repairs were needed, and they did not even require a trip back to Madeleine Bay! Remember, this island is made of sheets of steel . . . !"

This settled the matter. Indeed, if sheets of steel did not guarantee their safety, what other metal could be trusted? Steel is made of iron and our globe itself, almost in its entirety, is nothing else than an enormous mass of carbide. Standard Island, then, is simply a miniature replica of the earth.

Next Pinchinat wanted to know what the professor thought of Governor Cyrus Bikerstaff:

"Is he made of steel also?"

"Yes, Monsieur Pinchinat," answered Athanase Dorémus, "he has great energy and is a skilled administrator. But in Milliard City, it's not enough to be made of steel . . ."

"One must be made of gold," retorted Yvernès.

"Exactly, or else you are not valued."

This was the truth. Cyrus Bikerstaff, in spite of his high position, was only an agent of the company. He directed the various proceedings of the administration: he was in charge of collecting customs moneys, looking after public health, overseeing the sweeping of the streets and the upkeep of the park grounds, hearing the taxpayers' complaints; in a word, of making enemies of most of his constituents, but that was all. On Standard Island, one had to be valued and, as the professor said, Cyrus Bikerstaff was not valued.

Besides, his functions forced him to maintain a balance between the two parties, to keep a conciliatory attitude, to not risk anything that would please one side but not the other. This was not easy politics.

Indeed, ideas already circulated that could bring a conflict between the two sections. If the Starboardites had settled on Standard Island simply to enjoy their wealth in peace, the Larboardites were starting to miss their commerce. They were thinking about using the self-propelled island as a huge trading ship to transport cargos to the diverse markets of Oceania and wondered why all business was banished from Standard Island . . . In short, although they had been on the island for less than two years, these Yankees, with Tankerdon as their leader, were yearning for their former businesses. And even if until then they had only talked about this, it still worried Governor Cyrus Bikerstaff. He hoped, however, that the future would not get worse and that these inner differences would not disturb a place expressly constructed for the peace and quiet of its residents.

Taking leave of Athanase Dorémus, the quartet promised to visit him again. Usually, the professor went to the casino in the afternoon, although no students showed up. And there, because he did not want to be accused of lacking punctuality, he waited, preparing his lesson in front of the unused mirrors of the room.

Meanwhile, the self-propelled island proceeded daily westward and slightly south, so as to rejoin the Hawaiian Archipelago. In these latitudes, close to the torrid zone, the temperature was already high. The billionaires could not have stood the heat if it had not been for the sea winds that tempered it. Luckily, the nights were cool, and even in midsummer, the trees and lawns, watered by artificial rain, remained pleasantly green. Every day at noon, the location shown on the dial of the town hall was sent by telegraph to each section of town. On June 17 Standard Island was at latitude seventeen degrees north and longitude one hundred fifty-five degrees west, approaching the tropics.

"We seem to be pulled by the sun," exclaimed Yvernès, "or, if you want it more elegantly, we seem to be towed by the horses of the divine Apollo!"

His observation was as fitting as it was poetic, but it made Sébastien Zorn shrug his shoulders. He did not want to be towed . . . against his will.

"So," he constantly repeated, "we'll see how this adventure ends!"

The quartet rarely missed their daily walk in the park at the time when most people were out. On horseback, on foot, in their carriages, all the notables of Milliard met around the lawns. The stylish ladies were showing off their third outfit of the day, in the same color from the hat to the shoes, and usually of the Indian silk that was very much in fashion that year. They also often wore a shimmering artificial fabric made of cellulose or even an imitation cotton made of processed pine or larch wood.

This prompted Pinchinat to say,

"One day they will make material out of ivy wood for faithful friends and of weeping willow for inconsolable widows!"

In any case, the wealthy women of Milliard City would not have welcomed these fabrics if they had not come from Paris, nor these outfits if they had not been created by the most famous designer of the capital, who once arrogantly proclaimed, "It's the shape that makes the woman."

Once in a while, the king and queen of Malécarlie walked among the elegant crowd. The dethroned royal couple awakened real affection in our musicians. What marvelous thoughts filled their minds when they saw these noble people walking arm in arm . . . ! They were relatively poor compared to the affluent crowd, but one could sense that they were proud and dignified, like philosophers detached from worldly preoccupations. The Americans of Standard Island were in fact very flattered to count a king among their citizens and rendered him the honors due his former position. As for the quartet, they respectfully bowed to Their Majesties when they encountered them on the avenues of the town or the paths of the park. The king and queen were touched by these marks of respect that were so very French. After all, Their Majesties were not more valued than Cyrus Bikerstaff, and maybe even less.

In truth, travelers who fear the sea should adopt this sort of transportation aboard a moving island. They would not have to worry about the vagaries of the ocean or the dreaded squalls. With ten million horsepower in her belly, a Standard Island could never be held back by a lack of wind and would be powerful enough to fight the strongest gales. If collisions were a danger, they would not be for the island, but for the vessels that hurled themselves at full speed or under full sail against her iron sides. But these encounters would hardly have to be feared, thanks to the lights illuminating her harbors, her prow, and her stern, thanks to the electric glow of her aluminum moons that filled the atmosphere at night. As for storms, they were not worth mentioning. The island was capable of calming the fury of the sea.

But when their walks brought Pinchinat and Frascolin to the back or the front of the island, to the Prow or the Stern Battery, they both agreed that these places needed capes, headlands, points, coves, and beaches. These shores were just steel walls held together by millions of bolts and rivets. A painter would yearn for old rocks, as rough as an elephant's skin, and waves caressing the seaweed at high tide! The beauties of nature can never be replaced by the marvels of industry. In spite of his permanent admiration, Yvernès had to agree with them. What was lacking on this artificial island was the stamp of the Creator.

On the evening of June 25, Standard Island crossed the Tropic of Cancer, reaching the torrid zone of the Pacific. At that moment, the quartet performed for the second time in the hall of the casino. It should be noted that, given their initial success, the price of tickets was increased by one-third.

Even so, the room was still too small. The music lovers fought over the seats. Of course, this chamber music was supposed to be excellent for people's health and no one would have doubted its therapeutic qualities. Again, remedies by Mozart, Beethoven, and Haydn as had been determined previously.

It was an immense success for the performers, who would certainly have preferred Parisian bravos, but since these were unavailable, Yvernès, Frascolin, and Pinchinat were satisfied with the hurrahs of the billionaires, while Sébastien Zorn kept on showing his absolute contempt for them.

"What more could we ask for," said Yvernès, "when we enter the tropics . . . ?"

"The tropic of 'concert'!" replied Pinchinat, who fled after this abominable pun.

And when they left the casino, who did they notice among the poor wretches who had not been able to pay three hundred sixty dollars for a seat . . . ? Who but the king and queen of Malécarlie, standing humbly near the door.

IX

~~~~~~~~~

The Hawaiian Archipelago

THERE EXISTS, IN THIS AREA of the Pacific, an undersea mountain range extending for nine hundred leagues that would be visible from the west-northwest to the east-southeast if the three-mile-deep waters that cover it were emptied. Of this mountain chain, only eight summits are visible: Niihau, Kauai, Oahu, Molokai, Lanai, Maui, Kahoolawe, and Hawaii. These eight islands of various sizes form the Hawaiian Archipelago, formerly called the Sandwich Islands. This group of islands extends westward past the tropical zone by only a few rocks and reefs.

Abandoning Sébastien Zorn to his solitary grumbling and letting him wrap himself up in complete indifference toward all natural wonders, like a cello in its case, Pinchinat, Yvernès, and Frascolin exchanged their ideas.

"Well," said one, "I don't mind visiting these Hawaiian Islands! Since we are roaming the Pacific Ocean anyway, the best thing we can do is at least bring home memories!"

"Let me add," answered another, "that the Hawaiian natives will give us a rest from the Pawnee Indians, the Sioux, and the other over-civilized Indians of the Far West. I wouldn't mind meeting true savages . . . cannibals . . ."

"Are the Hawaiians still man eaters . . . ?" asked the third.

"Let's hope so," said Pinchinat seriously. "It was their grandparents who ate Captain Cook, and once their grandfathers tasted this illustrious sailor, how could we imagine that their grandsons would lose their taste for human flesh!"

We must admit that His Highness was speaking a little too irreverently of the famous English sailor who discovered the archipelago in 1778.

What we understood from this conversation was that our musicians hoped that the hazards of their travels would allow them to meet more authentic natives than those found in zoological gardens. Moreover, these savages would be in their own territory, in the very place where they were born. The Parisians were impatient to go there and waited every day for the observatory lookout to report the first sighting of the Hawaiian Islands.

This occurred on the morning of July 6. The news spread immediately throughout the town, and the board at the casino relayed the following telautographic message:

"Hawaiian Group in sight."

True, they were still one hundred fifty miles away, but the highest peaks of the group, those of the island of Hawaii, were more than thirteen thousand feet high and in clear weather were visible at this distance.

Coming from the northeast, Commodore Simcoë was heading for Oahu, with its capital of Honolulu, which is also the capital of the entire archipelago. This island is the third of the group in latitude. Niihau, which is a vast pen for livestock, and Kauai are in the northwest. Oahu is not the largest island of the group, being only six hundred forty-eight square miles, while Hawaii stretches over six thousand five hundred sixty-four square miles. As for the other islands, they comprise only one thousand four hundred seventy-two square miles altogether.

Of course, from the beginning of their trip, the Parisians had formed pleasant relationships with the major officials of Standard Island. All of them, from the governor and the commodore to Colonel Stewart and the chief engineers, Watson and Somwah, had eagerly welcomed them. The musicians often visited the observatory and enjoyed spending hours on the platform of the tower. Thus it is no wonder that, on that very day, Yvernès and Pinchinat, the most inquisitive of the group, went there. Around ten o'clock that morning the elevator brought them "to the top of the mast," as His Highness liked to say.

Commodore Simcoë was already there and, lending his telescope to the two friends, he advised them to aim it at a point in the southwest, between the low clouds in the sky.

"This is Mauna Loa," he said, "or it may be Mauna Kea, two magnificent volcanoes that, in 1852 and 1855, poured out rivers of lava that covered three square miles of the island and whose craters, in 1880, spewed nine million cubic yards of volcanic ash."

"Amazing!" replied Yvernès. "Do you think, Commodore, that we will have the opportunity to witness a spectacle of this kind . . . ?"

"I don't know, Monsieur Yvernès," answered Ethel Simcoë. "Volcanoes do not perform on command . . ."

"Oh! But what if it was just one time, and well-paid . . ." added Pinchinat. "If I were as rich as Mr. Tankerdon and Mr. Coverley, I would order eruptions whenever I felt like it . . ."

"All right, I'll talk to them about that," replied the commodore with a smile, "and I am sure that they will do everything they can to please you."

After that, Pinchinat asked about the population of the archipelago. The commodore told him that, although there were two hundred thousand inhabitants at the beginning of the century, they had, since then, been reduced by half.

"Well, Mr. Simcoë, one hundred thousand savages, that is still a goodly number; and as long as they have remained brave cannibals who haven't lost their appetite, they could make short work of all the Milliardites on Standard Island!"

This was not the first time that Standard Island visited the Hawaiian Archipelago. The year before, she had stopped in this area, attracted by the salubrious climate. Indeed, many sick people came to Hawaii from America, and soon European doctors would also send their patients there, to breathe the healthy air of the Pacific. And why not? Honolulu was only twenty-five days away from Paris, and to fill your lungs with the sort of oxygen that cannot be found anywhere else . . .

Standard Island came within sight of the Hawaiian Group on the morning of July 9. Oahu appeared five miles away, to the southwest. Above it, to the east, rose Diamond Head, an ancient volcano overlooking the rear of the harbor, and another volcanic cone called the Punch Bowl by the English. As the commodore remarked, if this enormous bowl were filled with brandy or gin, John Bull would have no trouble emptying it to the last drop.

They passed between Oahu and Molokai, Standard Island smoothly maneuvering her starboard and larboard propellers like a ship would its rudder. After rounding the southeast cape of Oahu, the vessel stopped about ten cable lengths from the shore, her draft being sizeable. Since the self-propelled island needed to remain at a considerable distance from land in order to keep her from running aground, she was not moored in the strict sense of the term. In other words, they did not use anchors, which would have been worthless in water three hundred feet deep and more. So, with the help of machines that kept working during her entire stay, the island was kept as steady and motionless as the eight main islands of the Hawaiian Archipelago.

The quartet gazed at the mountainous countryside unfolding beneath their eyes. From the ocean, they could only catch glimpses of clumps of trees, copses of orange trees, and other magnificent specimens of the temperate flora. In the west, through a narrow gap in the reefs, they saw a small lake, the Lake of Pearls, a sort of marshy plain pierced by ancient craters.

Oahu looked rather pleasant and, in truth, the cannibals so desired by Pinchinat had no cause for complaint about their surroundings. If they still followed their cannibalistic instincts, His Highness would have nothing more to wish for.

But he suddenly exclaimed,

"Good grief, what is this I see . . . ?"

"What do you see . . . ?" asked Frascolin.

"Over there . . . steeples . . ."

"Yes . . . and towers . . . and the fronts of palaces . . . !" retorted Yvernès.

"They could not have eaten Captain Cook there . . . !"

"We are not in the Hawaiian Islands!" said Sébastien Zorn, shrugging his shoulders. "The commodore took the wrong route . . ."

"He must have!" replied Pinchinat.

But no, Commodore Simcoë did not get lost. This was Oahu indeed, and the sprawling city of several square miles was Honolulu.

There, they had to lower their expectations. How many changes had occurred since the great English navigator had discovered these islands! The missionaries had tried to outdo each other in their dedication and zeal. The Methodists, the Anglicans, the Catholics had rivaled each other; they had civilized the inhabitants and triumphed over the paganism of the ancient Kanakas. Not only was the original language slowly giving way to English, but the islands now had American and Chinese residents—the latter mostly hired by landowners, and from them had sprung a race of half-Chinese people called Hapa-Paké. There were also Portuguese on the islands, hired by the maritime services that ran between the Hawaiian Group and Europe. There were still some native people too, even enough of them to satisfy our four musicians, but they had been decimated by leprosy, an illness imported from China. These natives did not much look like man-eaters.

"Oh local color," exclaimed the first violin, "what hand wiped you from the modern palette?"

Yes! Time, civilization, and progress, which are laws of nature, had almost completely erased this color. Sébastien Zorn and his companions had to admit it, and not without regret, as one of the electric launches of Standard Island, steering past the long line of reefs, brought them to the shores of Oahu.

Between two rows of barriers meeting at an acute angle opened a harbor sheltered from gale winds by a mountain range. Since 1794, the reefs that had protected it against the swell of the open sea had risen by three feet. However, there was still enough water for vessels drawing between eighteen and twenty feet to be moored alongside the wharves.

"What a terrible disappointment . . . !" whispered Pinchinat. "How pitiful to lose so many of one's illusions on a trip . . ."

"That's why people would be better off staying home!" retorted the cellist, shrugging his shoulders.

"Oh, no!" exclaimed Yvernès, the eternal optimist. "What spectacle could be comparable to that of an artificial island visiting the oceanic archipelagos . . . ?"

However, if the moral state of the Hawaiian Islands had regrettably changed, to the great displeasure of our musicians, the same could not be said of the weather. The climate was among the healthiest in this region of the Pacific Ocean, in spite of the fact that the islands were located in an area called the Sea of Heat. Even though the temperature remained high when the trade winds were not blowing from the northeast, even though the opposite trade winds from the south generated violent storms that the natives called kouas, the mean temperature of Honolulu did not go over seventy degrees Fahrenheit. One would have been ill-advised to complain about this on the border of the torrid zone. And indeed, the inhabitants did not complain and, as we mentioned earlier, American patients flocked to the archipelago.

But the further the quartet penetrated the secrets of this archipelago, the faster their illusions fell, like the leaves of trees at the end of autumn. They maintained that they had been deceived, but they should have realized that they brought this deception on themselves.

"It's that Calistus Munbar who tricked us again," affirmed Pinchinat, reminding them that the superintendent had told them that the Hawaiian Islands were the last bastion of indigenous savages in the Pacific.

And when they bitterly reproached him:

"What can I say, my dear friends," he answered with a wink of his right eye. "Everything has changed so much since my last trip that I don't know where I am anymore!"

"What a joker you are!" retorted Pinchinat, playfully patting the superintendent's stomach.

It was certain that if there had been changes, they would have occurred extremely fast. Long ago, the Hawaiian Islands had enjoyed a constitutional monarchy, founded in 1837, with two chambers, one made up of aristocrats, the other of representatives of the people. The first was elected by the landowners, the second by all citizens who could read and write. The aristocrats were elected for six years, the representatives for two. Each chamber had twenty-four members and they deliberated together in the presence of the royal ministry, composed of four counselors to the king.

"So," said Yvernès, "there was a king here, a constitutional monarch, and not a monkey dressed in feathers, to whom foreigners would pay their humble respects . . . !"

"I am sure," said Pinchinat, "that His Majesty did not even have rings in his nose . . . and that he bought his false teeth from the best dentists of the New World!"

"Ah! Civilization . . . civilization!" exclaimed the first violin. "Those Kanakas did not need false teeth to take bites out of their prisoners of war!"

Let us forgive these eccentrics their ways of seeing things! Yes, there had been a king in Honolulu, or at least a queen. Her name was Liliuokalani; she had lost her throne and had fought for the rights of her son, Prince Adey, against the claim to the throne of Hawaii by Princess Kaiulani. In short, for a long time, the archipelago had experienced a series of revolutions, just like the good states of America or Europe that it resembled even in this respect. Could this have brought the efficient intervention of the Hawaiian army and opened a disastrous era of military coups? Probably not, since said army only had two hundred fifty draftees and two hundred fifty volunteers. A regime cannot be overthrown by five hundred men, at least not in the middle of the Pacific.

But the English were there, watching. It is said that England sided with Princess Kaiulani. On the other hand, the Japanese government was ready to make the islands its protectorate and it had partisans among the many coolies employed by the plantations . . .

And what was the American position in all this? Frascolin posed this very question about an expected American intervention to Calistus Munbar.

"The Americans," answered the superintendent, "do not much care about this protectorate. As long as they have a naval station for their ships on the Pacific routes they are satisfied."

And yet, in 1875 King Kaméhaméha, who visited President Grant in Washington, had placed the archipelago under the wing of the United States. But seventeen years later, when Mr. Cleveland decided to reinstate Queen Liliuokalani while at the same time a republican regime was established in the Hawaiian Islands under the presidency of Mr. Sanford Dole, there were violent protests in both countries.

Besides, nothing could have prevented what was probably written in the book of fate concerning countries of ancient or modern origin, and the Hawaiian Archipelago has been a republic since 1894, under the presidency of Mr. Dole.

Standard Island decided to put in at Honolulu for ten days and many of her residents took advantage of this stay to explore the city and its surroundings. The Coverley and Tankerdon families, as well as the principal notables of Milliard City, were brought to the harbor every day. And although this was the second time that the self-propelled island had visited the area, the Hawaiians still showed boundless admiration for this marvel and came in droves to visit her. Cyrus Bikerstaff's police did not easily admit foreigners to Standard Island, though, and they made sure that at night the visitors went home at the appointed time. Thanks to these security measures, it would have been difficult for an intruder to remain on the Jewel of the Pacific without an authorization, which was not easy to obtain. In a word, there were good relations on both sides, but there were no official receptions between the two islands.

The quartet took some very interesting walks. They liked the natives, with their distinctive physiques and their dark faces that were at the same time gentle and proud. And although the Hawaiians were under a republican administration at the time, they may well have regretted their unrestrained independence of the past.

"The air of a country is free," stated one of their proverbs, but they themselves were no longer free.

And indeed, after the conquest of the archipelago by Kaméhaméha and the establishment of the constitutional monarchy in 1837, each island had had its own governor. When the quartet visited them, they were republics and still divided into districts and subdistricts.

"My word," said Pinchinat, "all they need are prefects, subprefects with their deputies, and the Constitution of the Year VIII!"

"All I want is to get out of here!" retorted Sébastien Zorn.

He would have been ill-advised to do so before admiring the principal sites of Oahu. They were splendid, even if the flora was not rich. On the shore, there was an abundance of coconut trees and other palms, breadfruit trees and oil-producing trilobas, castor oil plants, daturas, and indigo plants. In the valleys watered by mountain streams and covered by an invading weed called *menervia*, a good many bushes, such as the chenopodium and *halapepe*, which belong to the asparagus family, were as big as small trees. The forest zone, extending to an altitude of six thousand feet, was covered with woody species, very tall myrtles, enormous docks and creeper shoots mingling with the branches like masses of snakes. As for the crops that could be exported, they were rice, coconut, and sugarcane. There was therefore an important coastal traffic from one island to the other, in order to ship to Honolulu products to be later sent to America.

The fauna were not diverse. Although the Kanakas tended to be absorbed by more advanced people, the animal species did not change.

Only pigs, chickens, and goats were domesticated; there were no wild animals except for a few wild boars. Mosquitoes were a real nuisance. There were many scorpions and a variety of harmless lizards, birds that did not sing, such as the oo—the *Drepanis pacifica* with its black feathers, highlighted by yellow ones. Kaméhaméha's famous cloak, on which nine generations of natives had worked, was made entirely of these yellow feathers.

In the archipelago, the task of men—and it was an extensive task— had been to become civilized, as they had been in the United States, with learned societies, mandatory schools that were awarded a prize at the Exposition of 1878, rich libraries, and newspapers published in English and in Kanaka. Our Parisians should not have been surprised by this, for most of the notables of the archipelago were American and their language was used as commonly as their money. But these notables readily attracted Chinese people from the Celestial Empire to work for them, contrary to what was done in the American West, where they sought to eradicate the "yellow plague."

As was expected, as soon as Standard Island came in sight of the capital of Oahu, small local boats loaded with onlookers started sailing around it. With the magnificent weather and the calm sea, what could have been more pleasant than a jaunt of about twelve miles at a cable length from this steel shore that the customs officers watched so diligently?

Among these excursion boats, one could have noticed a small vessel that continuously sailed the waters of the self-propelled island. It was some sort of Malay ketch with two masts and a square stern. It was manned by ten men or so, under the orders of an energetic captain. The governor, however, did not take offence at this, although their persistence may have seemed suspicious. Indeed, these people kept scrutinizing the entire perimeter of the island, lurking from one port to the other and examining her shore. But after all, even supposing that they had bad intentions, what could their crew have done against a population of ten thousand people? Therefore, the officials of Standard Island did not worry about the maneuvers of this ketch at night or during the day, and they did not report it to the naval authorities of Honolulu.

The quartet said goodbye to Oahu on the morning of July 10. Standard Island got under way at dawn, obeying the impulses of her powerful propellers. She veered south toward the other Hawaiian Islands. She then had to cut diagonally through the east-west equatorial current and counter the northern drift that ran alongside the archipelago.

For the enjoyment of the residents who had gone to the larboard side, Standard Island briskly advanced between the islands of Molokai and Kauai. Above Kauai, one of the smallest islands of the group, rose a six-thousand-foot-high volcano, the Nirhau, which was spewing a few smoky fumes. The foot of the mountain was surrounded by banks of coral dominated by dunes, whose echoes reverberated with a metallic sound when they were violently struck by the surf. As night fell, the vessel was still in this narrow channel, but the residents had nothing to fear under the command of Commodore Simcoë. At the time when the sun disappeared behind the heights of Lanai, the lookouts could not have spotted the ketch that, having left the harbor behind Standard Island, tried to remain in its wake. Anyway, let us say it again: why would they have worried about the presence of this Malay craft?

The next day, when it was light again, the ketch was just a white dot on the northern horizon.

Throughout that day, Standard Island kept traveling between Kahoolawe and Maui. The latter, with Lahaina as its capital, was a port for whalers and the second in size of the Hawaiian Islands. There the Haleahala, or "the house of the sun," rose twelve thousand feet toward the radiant star.

During the next two days, they traveled along the coast of the great Hawaii, whose mountains, as we said before, are the highest of the group. It is in Kealakeacua Bay that Captain Cook, who had first been received as a god by the natives, was killed in 1779, a year after discovering the archipelago that he named the Sandwich Islands in honor of the famous minister of Great Britain. Hilo, one of the main towns of the island on the east coast, could not be detected, but they noticed Kailu on the west coast. This big Hawaii has thirty-six miles of railroad, used mostly to transport exotic products. The quartet could make out the white plumes of its locomotives.

"That's all we needed!" cried Yvernès.

The next day, the Jewel of the Pacific had already left the area when the ketch sailed round the extreme point of Hawaii, dominated by Mauna

Loa, the High Mountain, whose summit was lost among the clouds at an altitude of thirteen thousand feet.

"Robbed," exclaimed Pinchinat. "We were robbed!"

"You're right," answered Yvernès. "We should have come one hundred years earlier. But then we would not have traveled on this marvelous self-propelled island!"

"I don't care! Imagine, finding natives in sport coats and turned-down collars instead of savages in feathers that this sly Calistus Munbar promised us! May God confound him! I miss the time of Captain Cook."

"And what if those cannibals had eaten Your Highness?" asked Frascolin.

"I would have had the consolation of being . . . for once in my life . . . loved for myself alone!"

X

~~~~~~~~~~

Crossing the Line

SINCE JUNE 23, THE SUN had been moving toward the Southern Hemisphere. It was therefore imperative to leave this area where bad weather would soon wreak havoc. The sun, in its apparent journey, was heading for the equinoctial line, which Standard Island should cross in her turn. Beyond, there were pleasant climes where the months, although they are called October, November, December, January, and February, belong to the warm season. The distance between the Hawaiian Archipelago and the Marquesas is about one thousand eight hundred sixty-five miles and Standard Island, being eager to cover it as fast as possible, traveled at her maximum speed.

Polynesia proper is located in this large area of the sea bounded on the north by the equator and on the south by the Tropic of Capricorn. Here, on a surface of two million square miles, are two hundred twenty islands in eleven separate groups; their total length is sixty-two hundred miles and contains thousands of islets. These are the summits of underwater mountains whose chains, running from the northwest to the southeast, extend in almost parallel lines to the Marquesas and to Pitcairn Island.

If we could imagine this vast basin suddenly empty, if the Limping Devil suddenly freed by Cleophas took away all those liquid masses as he did the roofs of Madrid, what extraordinary country would unfold beneath our eyes! What Switzerland, what Norway, what Tibet could possibly equal its grandeur? Most of these underwater mountains are volcanic, but a few are of madreporic origin, made of calcareous or corneous matter secreted in concentric layers by polyps, those tiny animals that possess such a simple organization and such immense reproductive power. Among these islands, the most recent are covered with vegetation only on their peaks; the others, the most ancient, are draped in green from top to bottom even if they are of coralline origin. Therefore, there exists a vast mountainous area buried under the waters of the Pacific Ocean, and Standard Island was traveling among its summits like a balloon between the peaks of the Alps or the Himalayas. Only it was not air, it was water that held her up.

But, just as there are large displacements of atmospheric waves throughout space, there are liquid displacements on the surface of this ocean. The main current flows from east to west and, in the deeper waters, two counter-currents run between June and October when the sun makes its way toward the Tropic of Cancer. Moreover, near Tahiti, four separate kinds of tides can be detected, but since they go in at different times, they neutralize each other and become almost imperceptible. The climate of these diverse archipelagos is variable. The mountainous islands stop the clouds that will pour their rains upon them; the lower islands are drier because their humidity is driven away by constant winds.

It would have been strange for the library of the casino not to have maps of the Pacific Ocean and indeed, it had a complete collection of them. Frascolin, the most serious member of the quartet, often consulted them. Yvernès preferred to indulge in the surprises of the journey and his admiration for the artificial island. He did not want to burden his brain with geographical notions. Pinchinat reflected only on the pleasant and whimsical sides of things. As for Sébastien Zorn, the itinerary did not matter to him, since he was going where he had never intended to go.

Frascolin was therefore the only one studying Polynesia and learning about the principal groups that composed it: the Low Islands, the Marquesas, the Tuamotus, the Societies, the Cook Islands, the Tonga and Samoa Islands, the Austral Islands, Wallis, and Fanning, and also the isolated islands of Niue, Tokelau, Phoenix, Manahiki as well as Easter Island, Salas y Gomez, etc. He knew that in most of these archipelagos, even those under protectorates, the government was always in the hands of powerful chiefs whose influence was never questioned, and the poorer classes were entirely at the mercy of the rich. Moreover, he knew that the natives belonged to different religions: Hinduism, Islam, Protestantism, Catholicism, and that Catholicism was predominant in the islands that belonged to France, owing to the magnificence of its ceremonies. He even knew that the native tongue with its simple alphabet composed of thirteen to seventeen characters was much mixed with English and would ultimately be absorbed by the language of the Anglo-Saxons. Finally, he knew that, in general, from an ethnic point of view, the Polynesian population was decreasing, which was regrettable, for the true Kanaka—the word means man—who was whiter at the equator than in the groups distant from the equinoctial line, was absolutely magnificent. And Polynesia would lose so much by their absorption into foreign races! Yes, Frascolin knew all that and many other things that he had learned in his conversations with Commodore Ethel Simcoë, and when his comrades had questions, he had no trouble answering them.

And so Pinchinat began calling him "the Larousse of the Tropics."

Such were the principal groups among which Standard Island took her wealthy population. This island certainly deserved to be called "the happy island," because everything that could ensure material happiness and, in a certain way, even moral happiness was available there. What a shame that this situation had to run the risk of being troubled by rivalries, jealousies, and discords and by questions of influence and precedence that divided Milliard City into two camps, the Tankerdon camp and the Coverley camp, in addition to the two sections. At any rate, for our musicians, totally indifferent to these matters, the struggle promised to be interesting.

Jem Tankerdon was a Yankee from head to toe, strong-minded and massive, with a large face, a short, reddish beard, and close-cropped hair. The irises of his eyes, still bright in spite of his sixty years, were almost yellow like a dog's; his pupils were alight. He was tall, with a powerful chest and strong limbs. He looked like a trapper, although as far as traps go, he had never set any but those through which he sent millions of pigs to their death in his slaughterhouses in Chicago. He was a violent man who should have become more polished given his position, but he had not received a good early education. He liked to show off his wealth and he was, as they say, rolling in dough. But it seemed that he never had enough, since he, and a few men like him, were thinking of going back into business.

Mrs. Tankerdon was an average American woman. She was good and submissive to her husband, an excellent mother, gentle to her children, predestined to raise a large family, and she never failed to perform her expected functions. When you have two billion dollars to share among your children, why would you not have a dozen of them? And she made them all of sound constitution.

Of this entire tribe, only the eldest son, destined to play a certain role in this story, would attract the attention of the quartet. Walter Tankerdon was a very elegant young man of average intelligence with a pleasant face and demeanor; he took more after his mother than after the head of the family. He was well educated, having visited America and Europe. Though he traveled at times, his habits and tastes always brought him back to the pleasant life on Standard Island. He practiced several sports and was the best among the youth of Milliard City in all the tennis, polo, golf, and croquet competitions. He was not inordinately proud of the fortune he would one day possess and had a good heart. But since there were no poor on Standard Island, he never had a chance to practice charity. In short, it was hoped that his brothers and sisters would take after him. If they were not yet old enough to get married, he, who was almost thirty, must have thought about it. Did he? We will soon see.

There was a striking contrast between the Tankerdon family, the most important in the Larboard section, and the Coverley family, the most prominent in the Starboard section. Nat Coverley was of a more refined nature than his rival. He owed this to the French origin of his ancestors. His fortune had not come from the depths of the earth in the form of petroleum, nor from the smoking guts of pigs. No! It was industrial ventures, railroads, and banking that had made him who he was. Personally, he only wanted to enjoy his wealth in peace—he did not hide this fact—and he would have opposed any attempt to transform the Jewel of the Pacific into an enormous factory or a huge commercial enterprise. Tall and courtly, with a fine head of gray hair, he wore a full chestnut beard streaked with a few silver threads. He had a rather cold disposition and very good manners. He occupied the first rank among the notables of Milliard City who retained the traditions of high society in the southern states. He loved the arts, was a fine connoisseur of music and painting, gladly spoke French, as was the custom among the Starboardites, and kept up with American and European literature. When the opportunity arose, he sprinkled his applause with bravos, while the rough Far West and New England types poured out their hurrahs.

Mrs. Coverley, ten years younger than her husband, had just turned forty and was in excellent health. She was an elegant and well-bred woman belonging to an old half-creole Louisiana family, a good musician and a good pianist; a twentieth-century Reyer would not have disparaged her piano playing. The quartet had many occasions to perform with her in her mansion on Fifteenth Avenue and to compliment her on her artistic talent.

Heaven had not blessed the Coverleys as much as it had blessed the Tankerdons. Three daughters were the only heiresses to an immense fortune that Mr. Coverley did not boast about like his rival. The girls were very pretty and there would be no lack of suitors in the nobility or the banking industry of both worlds to ask for their hands when the time came for them to marry. Besides, these incredible dowries were not rare in America. A few years before, there had been talk of a little Miss Terry who, at two years of age, was already sought after for her seven hundred fifty millions. Let us hope that this child found a husband to her liking and that, to being one of the wealthiest women in the United States, she added being one of the happiest.

The eldest daughter of Mr. and Mrs. Coverley, Diane or Dy as she was familiarly called, was hardly twenty. She was a very pretty young woman who had inherited the physical and moral qualities of both her mother and father. She had beautiful blue eyes and gorgeous light-chestnut hair; her complexion was as fresh as the petals of an opening rose and her features were elegant and gracious. All this explains why she was much admired by the young men of Milliard City, who would probably not give outsiders a chance to conquer this "priceless treasure," to use terms of mathematical precision. There was even reason to think that Mr. Coverley would not consider differences in religion an obstacle to a marriage that would seem to ensure the happiness of his daughter.

In truth, it was regrettable that questions of social rivalry kept apart the two best families of Standard Island. Walter Tankerdon seemed made to measure to become the husband of Dy Coverley.

But this was a union that could not be considered . . . Standard Island should sooner be cut in two, with the Starboardites drifting away on one half and the Larboardites on the other, than such a marriage contract be signed.

"Unless love intervenes!" the superintendent would sometimes say, winking behind his gold pince-nez.

But Walter Tankerdon did not seem attracted to Dy Coverley and neither did she appear fond of him, or at least, even if they liked each other, they were both very reserved and did not awaken the curiosity of the affluent inhabitants of Milliard City.

The self-propelled island continued to head toward the equator, closely following the one hundred sixtieth meridian. Ahead of her extended the thirty-thousand-feet-deep region of the Pacific that is the most devoid of islands and islets. On July 25, during the day, they moved past the Belknap, a twenty-thousand-feet-deep abyss, from which the sounding lines brought up those curious shellfish called zoophytes, made to withstand the pressure of huge masses of water estimated at six hundred atmospheres.

Five days later, Standard Island threaded her way through a group belonging to England, although it is sometimes called the American Islands. Leaving Palmyra and Suncarung to starboard, she came within five miles of Fanning, one of the many guano islands in the region and the most important in the archipelago. These islands were half-submerged peaks, more barren than verdant and from which the United Kingdom had not yet derived much profit. But it had set foot on the area and everyone knows that the large foot of England usually leaves prints that cannot be erased.

Every day, as his comrades walked through the park or the surrounding countryside, Frascolin, much interested by the details of this curious navigation, went to the Prow Battery. There he often met with the commodore. Ethel Simcoë gladly explained to him the phenomena particular to those seas, and when they were of sufficient interest, the second violin did not fail to report them to his companions.

For instance, they could not refrain from showing their admiration for the free spectacle that nature offered them during the night of July 30.

An immense bank of jellyfish covering several square miles had been sighted during the afternoon. The population of Standard Island had not yet encountered such packs of medusas that certain naturalists call *oceanias*. The half-rounded shape of those very elementary animals classifies them within the vegetable kingdom. The fish, as voracious as they are, must regard them as flowers since none of them tries to eat them. The medusas found in the torrid zone of the Pacific are all shaped like multicolored umbrellas, transparent, and bordered with tentacles. They are not longer than an inch. Think of how many billions were needed to form such enormous banks.

And when such huge numbers were mentioned in front of Pinchinat, His Highness replied,

"They should not shock the incredibly rich notables of Standard Island, for billions are everyday fare for them!"

After nightfall, many of the residents moved to the forecastle of the boat that overlooked the Prow Battery. The trams were packed, the electric cars loaded with onlookers. Elegant coaches brought the nabobs from the city. The Coverleys and the Tankerdons stood at a short distance from each other but remained apart. Mr. Jem did not greet Mr. Nat, who did not greet Mr. Jem. All members of the two families were present. Yvernès and Pinchinat enjoyed talking with Mrs. Coverley and her daughter, who always made them feel welcome. Perhaps Walter Tankerdon felt a bit annoyed at not being able to take part in their conversation and perhaps Miss Dy herself would have been happy to chat with him. But heavens, what a scandal this would have caused and what indiscrete hints the *Starboard Chronicle* and the *New Herald* would have printed on their society pages!

When darkness was complete, as much as it can be during these star-studded tropical nights, the Pacific appeared lit to its farthest depths. The immense expanse of water was flooded with phosphorescent glows, illuminated with pink and blue flashes not simply drawn in gleaming lines on the crest of waves but resembling the brightness that countless legions of glowworms would emit. This luminosity became so intense that one could have read by it as by the radiance of a distant aurora borealis. It seemed that the Pacific, having dissolved the fires that the sun poured into it during the day, was sending them back at night in gleaming exhalations.

Soon the prow of Standard Island cut through the mass of medusas, which separated the metallic shore into two branches. In a few hours the self-propelled island was surrounded by a belt of light whose photogenic source was still intact. It looked like a halo, like the circle of light behind saints or the pale nimbus around the head of Christ. This phenomenon lasted until the arrival of dawn, whose first light finally extinguished it.

Six days later, the Jewel of the Pacific reached the imaginary great circle of our globe that, if drawn on a map, would divide the horizon into two equal parts. From this vantage point the dual poles of the celestial sphere could be sighted at the same time: the one in the north lit by the brightness of the North Star, and the other in the south, decorated like a soldier's chest with the Southern Cross. It should be added that, from the various points of this equatorial line, the stars appeared to run in circles perpendicular to the plane of the horizon. If one wanted to enjoy days and nights of perfectly equal length, it is in these areas, in the regions of islands or continents crossed by the equator, that one should settle.

Standard Island had traveled for roughly three hundred seventy-five miles since she had left the Hawaiian Archipelago. It was the second time since her creation that she had passed from one hemisphere to the other, crossing the equinoctial line, going first toward the south and then rallying toward the north. This passage was cause for celebration for the Milliardites. There would be public games in the park, religious ceremonies in the churches, and electric car races around the island. The platform of the observatory would display magnificent fireworks whose rockets and Roman candles would rival the splendor of the stars in the sky.

This was, as you may have guessed, an imitation of the fantastic scenes usually found on ships when they reached the equator, a replica of the baptism on the line. And indeed, that day was chosen to baptize the children born since the departure from Madeleine Bay. There was a similar baptismal ritual for the foreigners who had not yet entered the Southern Hemisphere.

"It's going to be our turn," said Frascolin to his comrades. "We are going to be baptized!"

"Baptized! Well, I'll never!" protested Sébastien Zorn indignantly.

"Oh yes you will, my dear old bass scraper," answered Pinchinat. "They will pour buckets of not even holy water on our heads, seat us on wobbly planks that will topple over, and throw us in tanks full of surprises. Then Old Man Tropic will show up, followed by his buffoons to smear our faces black!"

"If they think that I will submit to the tricks of this masquerade . . . !"

"We'll have to," said Yvernès. "Every country has its customs that guests must submit to . . ."

"Not when they are held against their will!" cried the inflexible head of the Concerting Quartet.

He did not need to worry about this merrymaking that ships had fun with when they crossed the line! He should not have feared the arrival of Old Man Tropic! He and his comrades would get splashed not with seawater but with the best brand of champagne, and they would not be tricked by being shown the equator that had previously been drawn on the lens of a telescope. Such banter could do for simple sailors aboard ships, but not for the grave people of Standard Island.

The celebration took place in the afternoon of August 5. Except for the officers of the customshouse, who always had to be at their posts, all employees enjoyed the day off. All work was suspended in the city and the harbor. The propellers were not activated. The batteries had enough voltage to supply light to the city and transmit electronic messages. But Standard Island herself was not at a standstill. The current carried her toward the dividing line of the world's two hemispheres. Songs and prayers were heard in the Protestant church as well as in Saint Mary's, and the organs poured forth their music. There was a joyous atmosphere throughout the park. Sports were played with gusto. All social classes took part in them. The wealthiest gentlemen, with Walter Tankerdon in their lead, worked wonders in the golf and tennis matches. As soon as the sun fell beneath the horizon, twilight lasting only forty-five minutes, the rockets of the fireworks started flying through space, and a moonless night allowed their splendor to unfold.

In the main room of the casino, the quartet was baptized as expected by Cyrus Bikerstaff himself. The governor offered them foaming champagne that flowed freely, and the musicians drank their fill of Cliquot and Roederer. It would have been in bad taste for Sébastien Zorn to complain about a baptism that in no way could remind him of the salt water he had swallowed in his first days of life.

Thus the Parisians responded to these testimonies of friendship by playing the most beautiful pieces in their repertory: the Seventh Quartet in F major, op. 59, of Beethoven, the Fourth Quartet in C-flat, op. 10, of Mozart, the Fourth Quartet in D minor, op. 17, of Haydn, the Seventh Quartet (*andante*, *scherzo*, *capriccioso*, and *fugue*), op. 81, of Mendelssohn. Yes, they played all these musical marvels in concert and the entrance was free. People pushed at the door and crowded into the room. The musicians had to play their pieces two and even three times and the governor presented them with a gold medal circled with diamonds of great value and engraved with the arms of Milliard City on one side and the following words in French on the other:

This medal is presented to the Concerting Quartet by the company, the municipality, and the citizens of Standard Island.

And if all these honors did not reach the very bottom of the soul of the inflexible cellist, it was undoubtedly because he had a terrible disposition, as his comrades always told him.

"Let's wait for the end!" he simply said, twisting his beard with a feverish hand.

It was at thirty-five minutes past ten in the evening, according to the astronomers of Standard Island, that the self-propelled island would cross the equator. At that precise instant, a salute would be fired by one of the cannons of the Prow Battery. A wire connected this gun to an electric machine set in the middle of the observatory square. There would be enormous pride in store for the notable who received the honor of sending the current that would unleash the formidable detonation!

And on that day, two people were expecting to receive this honor. They were, as you probably guessed, Jem Tankerdon and Nat Coverley. This caused extreme embarrassment to Cyrus Bikerstaff. Previously, there had been difficult negotiations between city hall and the two sections of town. They could not arrive at an agreement. Calistus Munbar himself had intervened at the request of the governor. But in spite of his well-known skills and the resources of his diplomatic mind, the superintendent failed completely. Jem Tankerdon would not give precedence to Nat Coverley, who refused to step aside. A blowup was expected.

And it took no time to explode in full force when the two leaders faced each other in the square.

The machine was set five steps away from them. It needed only the slight push of a fingertip.

The crowd, knowing all about the problems and very excited by these questions of precedence, invaded the gardens.

After the concert, Sébastien Zorn, Yvernès, Frascolin, and Pinchinat also went to the square out of curiosity, in order to observe the various phases of this rivalry. The dispositions of the Larboardites and the Starboardites appeared to portend serious difficulties in the future.

The two notables came forward without even a bow to each other.

"I trust, my dear sir," said Jem Tankerdon, "that you will not deny me the honor . . ."

"This is precisely what I expect of you, my dear sir," answered Nat Coverley.

"I will not suffer this public affront to my person . . ."

"Nor will I to mine . . ."

"We'll see!" cried Jem Tankerdon, taking one step toward the machine.

Nat Coverley took one step forward also. The followers of the two notables started to intervene. Offensive words flew from both camps. Walter Tankerdon was probably ready to stand up for the rights of his father and yet, when he saw Miss Coverley standing a little to the side, he was visibly embarrassed.

As for the governor, although the superintendent stood next to him ready to act as a buffer, he was upset at not being able to combine in a single bouquet the white rose of York and the red rose of Lancaster. Would this deplorable encounter have consequences as regrettable as those suffered by the English aristocracy in the fifteenth century?

But the time was approaching when the prow of Standard Island would cross the equator. Precisely calculated within a quarter of a second of time, the margin of error could not be greater than twenty-five feet. The signal would soon be sent from the observatory.

"I have an idea!" whispered Pinchinat.

"What is it?" asked Yvernès.

"I am going to punch the button of the machine and that will make them agree . . ."

"Don't do that!" said Frascolin, stopping His Highness with a firm hand.

No one knew how this incident would end, when suddenly a detonation was heard. It did not come from the Prow Battery; it was a blast at sea and was distinctly heard.

The crowd stood still.

What was the meaning of this discharge that did not come from a Standard Island gun?

A telegram sent from Starboard Harbor gave them the answer almost instantly.

Two or three miles away, a ship in distress had just signaled its presence and was asking for help.

Fortunate and unexpected diversion! They all forgot to argue in front of the electric button and to salute the crossing of the equator. It was too late anyway. The line had been crossed and the customary greeting remained in the cannon. After all, this was all the better for the honor of the Tankerdon and Coverley families.

The people left the square, and since the trams were no longer running, they quickly walked to Starboard Harbor.

There, following the signal sent from the sea, the officer on duty had taken measures for the rescue. One of the electric launches moored in the harbor had rushed out. At the same time that the crowd arrived, it was bringing back the crew picked up from the disabled ship, which was immediately swallowed by the depths of the Pacific.

This ship was the Malay ketch that had followed Standard Island since its departure from the Hawaiian Archipelago.

XI

~~~~~~~~~~

The Marquesas Islands

ON THE MORNING OF AUGUST 29 the Jewel of the Pacific navigated through the Marquesas Archipelago between latitudes seven degrees, fifty-five minutes, and ten degrees, thirty minutes south and longitudes one hundred forty-one degrees and one hundred forty-three degrees, six minutes west of the Paris meridian. She had covered a distance of two thousand one hundred seventy-five miles since leaving the Hawaiian Islands.

If this group is called Mendana, it is because a Spaniard by this name discovered its southern region in 1595. If it is called the Revolution Islands, it is because Captain Marchand visited its northwest area in 1791. If it is called the Archipelago of Nuku Hiva, it is because Nuku Hiva is the most important of its islands. But then, out of fairness, it should also bear the name of Cook, since this famous navigator traveled through it in 1774.

This last remark was made by Commodore Simcoë to Frascolin, who thought it a most logical observation and added,

"It could also be called the French Archipelago, for we are almost in France in the Marquesas."

Indeed, a Frenchman had the right to look at this group of eleven islands or islets as a squadron of his country moored in the waters of the Pacific, the largest islands being the first-class vessels: Nuku Hiva and Hiva Oa; the medium-sized ones, the cruisers of different sizes: Eiao, Ua Pu, and Ua Huka; the smallest ones, the sloops: Mohotani, Fatu Hiva, and Tahuata; and the islets and atolls the simple escort boats. But all these islands could not move about like Standard Island.

It was on May 1, 1842, that the commander of the naval station in the Pacific, Commodore Dupetit-Thouars, took possession of this archipelago in the name of France. Between one and two thousand leagues separate it from the American coast as well as from New Zealand, Australia, China, the Moluku Islands, and the Philippines. Given these conditions, was the commodore to be praised or blamed? The government praised him, the opposition blamed him. At any rate, France had acquired some island territory where her large fishing boats could find shelter and take on fresh supplies, and if the Panama Canal ever opened, the islands would acquire real commercial importance. This territory would be completed when the Tuamotu and Society Islands would also be acquired or declared protectorates. Since the British influence was widespread in the northwest of this immense ocean, it was good to have the French influence offset it in the southeastern regions.

"But," asked Frascolin of his obliging mentor, "do we have any important military forces there?"

"Until 1859," answered Commodore Simcoë, "there was a detachment of the French navy on Nuku Hiva. Since it was removed, the keeping of the flag has been entrusted to the missionaries, who would not let it come down without a fight."

"And what is the situation now . . . ?"

"On Taiohae, you will find only a minor administrator, a few gendarmes, and soldiers under the command of an officer who also serves as justice of the peace."

"For the lawsuits of the natives?"

"Yes, and of the colonists."

"So there are colonists on Nuku Hiva?"

"Yes . . . about two dozen."

"Not enough for a symphony or even for a harmony; hardly enough for a fanfare!"

Indeed, if the Marquesas Archipelago was one hundred ninety-five miles long and forty-eight miles wide and covered a surface of nine thousand square miles, its population did not even amount to twenty-four thousand natives. That was about one settler for each thousand natives.

Would the Marquesan population increase if an access route were built between the two Americas? The future would tell. But, as for Standard Island, the number of her residents had increased a few days before by the rescue of the Malays of the ketch in the evening of August 5.

There were ten of them and their captain, a vigorous-looking man, as we said earlier. The captain's name was Sarol, and he was about forty years of age. His men were strapping lads, of the race coming from the farthest islands of western Malaysia. Three months earlier, Sarol had led them to Honolulu with a cargo of copra. When Standard Island stopped there for ten days, the arrival of this artificial island aroused their curiosity, as it had in all the other archipelagos. Although they did not visit Standard Island because it was difficult to be admitted on board, let us not forget that their ketch often went out to sea to look at her closer and that they circled around her at a half-cable length. The constant presence of this vessel did not arouse any suspicion and its departure from Honolulu a few hours after Commodore Simcoë's did not arouse any, either. Moreover, was there any reason to be suspicious of a ship of a few hundred tons manned by a few men? Probably not, but then again, perhaps the Milliardites were wrong.

When the cannon blast attracted the attention of the Starboard Harbor officer, the ketch was only two or three miles away. The rescue launch that went to its aid arrived just in time to save the captain and his crew.

These Malays spoke fluent English; this was not surprising for natives of the western Pacific, where, as mentioned before, British predominance had long been established. The Standard Island people thus learned about the accident that had caused their distress. If the launch had arrived a few minutes later, these eleven Malays would have disappeared into the depths of the ocean.

According to these men, twenty-four hours earlier, during the night of August 4, the ketch had been rammed by a fast-traveling steamer. Although Captain Sarol had his lights on, they did not notice him. The collision must have been so minor for the steamer that it probably did not even feel it and continued on its way, unless it chose—something that unfortunately often happened—to proceed as fast as it could in order to avoid unpleasant and costly claims.

But the blow, insignificant for a vessel of heavy tonnage whose iron hull was moving at considerable speed, was disastrous for the Malay ketch. It was cut down just before the mizzenmast, and no one could understand why it had not immediately sunk. It stayed afloat, however, the men clinging to the bulkheads. If the sea had been rough, no one could have held on against the waves sweeping the wreck. Luckily, the current drove the vessel eastward and closer to Standard Island.

But when the commodore talked about this with Captain Sarol, he expressed his surprise that the half-submerged ketch had drifted within sight of Starboard Harbor.

"I don't understand it either," answered the Malay. "Your island must not have traveled very far in the last twenty-four hours."

"That's the only plausible explanation," replied Commodore Simcoë. "But after all, it doesn't matter. We saved you. That's what counts."

And it had been not a minute too soon. The launch was not a quarter of a mile away when the ketch went straight down.

That was the story first told by Captain Sarol to the officer who carried out the rescue, then to Commodore Simcoë, and finally to Governor Cyrus Bikerstaff, after receiving all the assistance that he and his crew seemed to need most urgently.

Next came the question of bringing the captain and his men home. They were sailing toward the New Hebrides when the collision occurred. Standard Island, heading to the southeast, could not modify her itinerary and steer west. So Cyrus Bikerstaff offered to let the shipwrecked sailors get off in Nuku Hiva, where they could wait for a passing freighter bound for the New Hebrides.

The captain and his men looked at each other. They seemed dismayed. The proposal distressed these poor destitute people who had lost all they had along with the ketch and its cargo. If they had to wait on the Marquesas, they might have to stay there for a very long time, and how could they survive?

"Governor," said the captain in an imploring tone, "you saved us and we cannot express how grateful we are to you . . . And yet we would still ask you to ensure better conditions for our return . . ."

"And how could we do this . . . ?" asked Cyrus Bikerstaff.

"In Honolulu they said that Standard Island, after going south, would visit the Marquesas, the Tuamotu and Society Islands, and then head for the west of the Pacific . . ."

"That is correct," said the governor. "And we will probably visit the Fiji Islands before going back to Madeleine Bay."

"The Fiji Islands," replied the captain, "are an English archipelago where we could easily find passage to the New Hebrides, which are not far from them . . . And if you are willing to keep us until then . . ."

"I cannot make any promises," answered the governor. "We are forbidden to take foreigners on board. Let's wait for our arrival in Nuku Hiva. I will contact the Madeleine Bay administration by cable and if they agree, we will bring you to the Fiji Islands, from where you will indeed be more easily brought home."

This is the reason why the Malays were on Standard Island when she arrived in view of the Marquesas on August 29.

This archipelago is located in the path of the trade winds. So are the archipelagos of the Tuamotus and the Societies. The winds ensure a moderate temperature and a salubrious climate to these islands.

Commodore Simcoë arrived in view of the northwestern group early in the morning. He first sighted a sandy islet that the maps called the Coral Atoll, against which the sea, pushed by the currents, lashed incessantly.

Leaving this atoll to port, the lookouts soon caught sight of Fetouou, the first island of the group, which rose sharply from the sea and was circled by vertical cliffs one thousand three hundred fifty feet high. Farther up, they saw Eiao, nineteen hundred feet high. This island appeared barren on their side, but vivid and green on the other, and had two little harbors for small vessels.

Frascolin, Yvernès, and Pinchinat left Sébastien Zorn to his permanent bad mood and settled on the tower with Ethel Simcoë and several of his officers. As could be expected, the name Eiao drove His Highness to utter a few strange onomatopoeias.

"For sure," he said, "the inhabitants of this island are a colony of cats with a tomcat as their leader . . ."

Eiao remained to port. Standard Island did not intend to stop there, and they headed toward the principal island, which had the same name as the group and was going to be temporarily joined with this extraordinary floating island.

On the following day, August 30, our Parisians went back to their lookout post at dawn. The high points of Nuku Hiva had been visible the previous evening. In clear weather, the mountain ranges of this archipelago could be seen as far as sixty miles away because some of its summits stand higher than thirty-nine hundred feet, forming a sort of gigantic backbone along the length of the island.

"You will notice," said Commodore Simcoë to his guests, "the special character of this archipelago. Its summits are singularly bare, which is strange in this zone, but the vegetation that starts about two-thirds up the mountains extends to the bottom of the ravines and gorges and unfolds magnificently onto the white beaches of the coast."

"And yet," remarked Frascolin, "it seems that Nuka Hiva does not follow the general rule, at least in the foliage of the middle zones. They appear bare."

"Because we're arriving from the northwest," answered Commodore Simcoë. "But when we round the south, the contrast will astonish you. Everywhere, there are green plains, forests, and waterfalls a thousand feet tall."

"Hey!" cried Pinchinat, "a waterfall cascading from the top of the Eiffel Tower, that deserves respect . . . ! The Niagara should be jealous . . ."

"Not at all!" answered Frascolin. "It flaunts its width, plunging three thousand feet from the American bank to the Canadian one . . . You know it, Pinchinat, we visited it . . ."

"That's right, and I apologize to the Niagara!" answered His Highness.

On that day, Standard Island floated at the distance of a mile from the shore of Nuku Hiva: it was barren slope after barren slope rising to the central plateau of Tovii, whose rocky cliffs seemed to have no breaks. However, according to Brown, the navigator, there existed good moorings there, and indeed, some were later discovered.

In short, Nuku Hiva, whose name calls to mind such gracious landscapes, looked rather bleak. But, as had been rightly observed by Dumoulin and Desgraz, who accompanied Dumont d'Urville on his travels to the South Pole in Oceania, "All the beauties of nature are confined to the inside of the bays and the grooves formed by the offshoots of the mountain chains rising in the middle of the island." After following this desolate coast beyond the acute angle that it projects to the west, Standard Island, slowing down her portside propellers, slightly modified her direction and went past Tchitchagoff Cape, which had received its name from the Russian navigator Krusenstern. Then the coast ran inward in an elongated semicircle in the middle of which a narrow channel gave access to the harbors of Taioa or Abani, one of the coves of which offered a secure shelter against the mightiest storms of the Pacific.

Commodore Simcoë did not stop there. To the south there were two other bays, that of Anna-Maria or Taiohae in the center and that of Comptroller, the bay of the Taipis, on the other side of Cape Martin, which is situated at the far southeast point of the island. They were going to stop at Taiohae for about two weeks.

A short distance from the shore of Nuka Hiva, the sounding line recorded great depth. They could anchor around the bays where the ocean was still two hundred to two hundred fifty feet deep. So it was easy to haul in very close to Taiohae Bay, which they did on the afternoon of August 31.

As soon as the harbor was in sight, they heard cannon blasts to their right, and coils of smoke rose above the cliffs to the east.

"Hey!" said Pinchinat. "They are firing their cannons to welcome us . . ."

"Not so," answered Commodore Simcoë. "Neither the Tais nor the Hapas, the two principal tribes of the island, possess cannons capable of firing even the simplest salute. What you hear is the roar of the sea rushing into the depths of a cave halfway up Cape Martin, and the smoke is just the spray of the waves hurled back from it."

"I am sorry about that," answered His Highness. "An artillery salute would have been appreciated."

Nuku Hiva Island has several names; they could even be called baptismal names, given it by the godfathers who successively baptized it. It was called Federal Island by Ingraham, Beaux Island by Marchand, Sir Henry Martin Island by Hegert, Adam Island by Roberts, and Madison Island by Porter. It measures seventeen miles from east to west and ten miles from north to south, its circumference being about fifty-four miles. Its climate is healthy. It has the temperature of the intertropical zones tempered by the trade winds.

At this anchorage, Standard Island would not have to fear dangerous winds or torrential rainfalls because she would stop there only between April and October, when the dry winds called *tuatuka* by the natives blow from east to west. The warmest days are in October, the driest ones in November and December. After that, from April to October, the winds blow from the east to the northeast.

The population of the Marquesas, which had been estimated at one hundred thousand by the first explorers, was actually much smaller than that.

Elisée Reclus, who based his findings on reliable documents, estimated that there were no more than six thousand people on the entire archipelago, and it was on Nuku Hiva that most of them lived. If, in the time of Dumont d'Urville, the number of Nuku Hivans could have reached eight thousand, divided into Tais, Hapas, and Taipis, this number had been constantly decreasing. Why did such depopulation occur? From the exterminations of natives by wars, the displacement of the males to the plantations of Peru, the abuse of alcohol, and finally, let us admit it, from all the illnesses brought by the conquest, even when the conquerors belonged to the civilized races.

During this seven-day stop, the Milliardites made many visits to Nuku Hiva. Most of the important Europeans who lived there visited the Milliardites too, the governor having given them free access to Standard Island.

For their part, Sébastien Zorn and his companions made long excursions in Nuku Hiva and the pleasantness of these excursions by far made up for the strain of the walks.

The Bay of Taiohae formed a circle cut by a narrow channel into which Standard Island could not enter, especially since the bay was cut in two by sandy beaches. These beaches were kept apart by a kind of rounded hill with steep slopes where the remains of a fort built by Porter in 1812 could still be seen. It was at this time that Porter conquered the island, and the American camp occupied the eastern beach. But the takeover was not ratified by the federal government.

In place of a city, on the opposite beach, our Parisians found only a small village with the huts of the natives mostly scattered under the trees. But to reach it, they traversed wonderful valleys, such as the valley of Taiohae, that the natives had chosen for their homes! It was a real pleasure to walk among these plantations of coconut and banana trees, these casuarinas, these groves of guava and breadfruit trees, these hibiscuses and so many other species full of overflowing sap. The tourists were received with great hospitality in the huts. In this region where they could have been eaten alive one hundred years earlier, they enjoyed flat cakes made of bananas and the soft part of the *mei*, the breadfruit tree, the yellow flour of the taro, which is sweet when fresh and sour when stale, and the edible roots of the *tacca*. As for the *haua*, a kind of big ray that the natives ate raw, and the fillets of shark that are most appreciated as they begin to decay, our Parisians categorically refused to sample them.

Sometimes Athanase Dorémus accompanied them on their walks. This fellow had visited the archipelago the previous year and acted as their guide. Perhaps he was not very strong in natural history and botany, perhaps he mistook the splendid *Spondias cytherea*, whose fruits resemble apples, for the *Pandanus odoratissimus*, which deserves its superlative designation, or for the casuarina whose wood is as hard as iron, or for the hibiscus whose bark was used by the natives to make clothes, or for the papaya tree, or for the *Gardenia florida* . . . but the quartet did not need the help of his rather questionable science, because the flora of the Marquesas offered them its magnificent ferns, its superb polypodies, its Chinese rosebushes with their red and white flowers, its grasses, its solanaceous plants, among which was the tobacco, its labiates with their violet clusters that are used as ornaments by the young Nuku Hivan beauties, its ten-feet-high castor oil plants, its dracaenas, its sugarcanes, its orange and lemon trees, whose recent importation developed extremely well in this land filled with summer warmth and watered by the many streams running down the mountains.

And one morning, as the quartet walked alongside rapids and past the Tai village to the top of the mountain range, when at their feet the valleys of the Tais, the Taipis, and the Hapas unfolded, they shouted their admiration! If they had had their instruments with them, they could not have resisted the urge to play a lyrical masterpiece in answer to these masterpieces of nature. The performers would probably only have been heard by a few birds! But the *kurukuru* dove that flew over these high places was so lovely, the little *salangane* was so charming, and the phaeton, the regular dweller of the Nuku Hivan gorges, swept the air with such a capricious wing!

Moreover, there were no venomous reptiles in the depths of these forests. The Parisians did not have to worry about the boas that were hardly two feet long and as harmless as grass snakes, nor about the lizards whose light-blue tails blended in with the flowers.

The natives were of an interesting type. Their Asian features revealed a very different ancestry from that of the other Oceanic people. They were of average height, well proportioned, and very muscular, with wide chests. They had delicate hands and feet, oval faces, high foreheads, dark eyes with long lashes, aquiline noses, and regular white teeth. Their complexion was neither red nor black, but rather swarthy like that of Arabs. Their faces were cheerful and gentle.

Tattooing had almost disappeared. It used to be done not by cuts to the skin, but by pinpricks dusted with the charcoal of the *Aleurites triloba*. Lately this art had been replaced by the wearing of cotton fabric brought by missionaries.

"These men are very handsome," said Yvernès, "but perhaps less so than at the time when they wore simple loincloths and long hair and brandished their bows and arrows!"

This observation was made during an excursion to Comptroller Bay with the governor. Cyrus Bikerstaff wanted to bring his guests to this bay that was divided into several harbors like Valetta, and, under English rule, Nuku Hiva would no doubt have become the Malta of the Pacific Ocean. The Hapa tribe was concentrated in this region in the midst of the gorges of a fertile land, with a small river fed by a resounding torrent. This was the main theater of the battle between the American, Porter, and the natives.

Yvernès's remark required an answer and the governor responded, saying,

"You may be right, Monsieur Yvernès, the Marquesans looked more regal with their loincloths, their brightly colored *maros* and pareos, their *ahu* bun, a sort of free-flying scarf, and their *tiputas*, which resembled Mexican ponchos. It is true that modern clothing is not becoming to them. But what do you expect? Decency is a consequence of civilization. As the missionaries work at educating the natives, they encourage them to dress in a less rudimentary way."

"Aren't the missionaries right, commodore?"

"From a moral viewpoint, yes! From a hygienic viewpoint, no! Since the Nuku Hivans and the other islanders began to dress more decently, they have lost their original vigor and their natural cheerfulness, that is certain. They are bored to death and their health has deteriorated. In the past, bronchitis, pneumonia, and tuberculosis were unknown to them . . ."

"And since they do not walk around naked anymore, they catch cold . . . ," cried Pinchinat.

"Yes , indeed! And this has been a serious cause of decline for their race."

"From which I conclude," His Highness went on, "that Adam and Eve, after being driven out of the Garden of Eden, sneezed only after wearing dresses and pants, which in turn has given us, their fallen, degenerate children, diseases of the chest."

"Governor," said Yvernès, "it seemed to us that the women were less beautiful than the men in this archipelago."

"It's also like that in all the others," answered Cyrus Bikerstaff, "and yet, what you see here is the most beautiful type of Oceanic women. But isn't this the way of nature common to all races that still live wild? Isn't it the same in the animal kingdom, where, as far as physical beauty is concerned, males are invariably superior to females?"

"Hey!" cried Pinchinat, "one has to come to the other side of the world to make such observations, and it is something that our pretty Parisian women would never admit!"

There existed only two classes among the Nuku Hivan population, and they were subject to the law of taboo. This law was invented by the strong against the weak, and by the rich against the poor, in order to protect their privileges and their possessions.

The taboo had white for its color, and the lower class did not have the right to touch tabooed objects such as sacred places, funeral monuments, and the houses of chiefs. The priests, sorcerers or *touas*, and *akarkis* or civil chiefs belonged to the tabooed class; most women and poor people were relegated to the lower class. Moreover, it was not only forbidden to touch an object protected by the taboo, but it was even forbidden to look at it.

"And this rule," added Cyrus Bikerstaff, "is so strict in the Tuamotu and Society Islands that I warn you, gentlemen, never to break it."

"Do you hear that, my dear Zorn!" said Frascolin. "Watch your hands! Watch your eyes!"

The cellist simply shrugged his shoulders like a man who has no interest in this sort of thing. On September 5, Standard Island left Taiohae. The island of Ua Uka, the most easterly of the group, was clearly visible. They caught sight of its green summits. It had no beaches, as its perimeter was bordered by steep cliffs. Needless to say, while passing along these islands, Standard Island made sure to proceed slowly because her mass launched at full speed would have caused a tidal wave that would have hurled small craft onto the coast and flooded the beaches. They were only a few cable lengths away from Ua Pu, which offered a striking view, for it was spiked with basaltic needles. Two inlets, one called Possession Bay and the other Bon Accueil Bay, revealed that a Frenchman had baptized them. It is there indeed that Captain Marchand first displayed the French flag.

Farther out, Ethel Simcoë, approaching the second group, headed for Hiva Oa, also called Dominica Island, its Spanish name. The largest island of this archipelago, Hiva Oa, of volcanic origin, measured fifty-six miles around. The quartet could distinctly see its cliffs chiseled in black rock and the waterfalls that came down from its central hills covered with heavy vegetation.

A three-mile-long strait separated this island from Tahuata. Since Standard Island was too big to navigate it, she went around to the west of Tahuata where the Bay of Madre de Dios—Cook's Resolution Bay—had welcomed the first European ships. This island would have been better off standing a little farther away from its rival Hiva Oa. If contact between the two islands had been more difficult, perhaps the tribes would not have gone to war and decimated each other with the gusto they still brought to combat.

After sighting Mohotani to the east, a barren island without shelter or inhabitants, Commodore Simcoë drove toward Fatu Hiva, the old Cook Island. It was just an enormous rock full of tropical birds, a sort of sugarloaf with a circumference of three miles.

This was the last islet of the southeast, and the Milliardites lost sight of it in the afternoon of September 9. In order to follow her itinerary, Standard Island then steered southwest to reach the Tuamotu Archipelago, which she would cross in the middle.

The weather was still good, since the month of September corresponds to the month of March in the Northern Hemisphere.

In the morning of September 11, the Larboard Harbor launch picked up one of the floating buoys, to which a Madeleine Bay cable was attached. The end of this copper wire, completely insulated by a layer of gutta-percha, was connected to the observatory's instruments, and telephone communication was established with the American coast.

The administration of the Standard Island Company was consulted about the shipwrecked crew of the Malay ketch. Would they authorize the governor to bring the Malayan sailors to the vicinity of the Fiji Islands, where their repatriation could be accomplished faster and under less costly conditions?

The response was favorable. Standard Island was even allowed to go west to the New Hebrides and to leave the shipwrecked men there if the notables of Milliard City agreed.

Cyrus Bikerstaff informed Captain Sarol of the decision and Sarol asked the governor to send his warmest thanks to the administrators of Madeleine Bay.

XII

～～～～～～

Three Weeks in the Tuamotus

TO TELL THE TRUTH, THE QUARTET would have been appallingly ungrateful not to thank Calistus Munbar for bringing them, perhaps a bit treacherously, aboard Standard Island. It did not really matter what means the superintendent used to make the Parisian musicians the acclaimed, idolized, and handsomely paid guests of Milliard City. Sébastien Zorn did not stop sulking; you do not change a hedgehog with sharp quills into a cat with soft fur. But Yvernès, Pinchinat, and even Frascolin could not imagine a more delightful existence. An excursion without any danger or strain, across these wonderful Pacific seas! A climate always healthy and almost always even, thanks to Standard Island's changes of location! Moreover, not having to take sides in the rivalry between the two camps, regarded as the musical soul of the island, welcomed by the Tankerdon family and by the most refined families of the Larboard section, welcomed as well by the Coverleys and the most notable people of the Starboard side, treated as honored guests by the governor and his deputies at the town hall, by Commodore Simcoë and his officers at the observatory, by Colonel Stewart and his militia, participating in the festivities at the Protestant church as well as in the ceremonies at Saint Mary's, finding congenial people in both harbors, in the workshops, among the officials and the employees, let us ask any reasonable person how our compatriots could have regretted the time when they traveled from city to city of the Federal Republic, and what man could hate himself enough not to envy them?

"You will kiss my hands!" the superintendent had said when he first met them.

127

And if they had not done this, and would never do it, it was because a man never kisses another man's hands.

One day Athanase Dorémus, the luckiest man in the world, said to them,

"I have been on Standard Island for close to two years now, and I would live here for sixty more if I were told that I still have sixty years to live . . ."

"You certainly are not weary of life, wishing to become a centenarian!" answered Pinchinat.

"Hey, Monsieur Pinchinat, you can be sure that I will reach a hundred! Why would you die on Standard Island?"

"Because people die everywhere . . ."

"Not here, my dear friend, not any more than they do in heaven!"

How would you answer that? Still, once in a while, there were a few ill-advised people who went from life to death even on this enchanted island. And then the steamers would carry their remains to the remote cemeteries of Madeleine Bay. It is indeed written somewhere that one cannot be completely happy in this world.

True, there are always a few dark spots on the horizon. It must even be admitted that these dark spots slowly took the shape of highly electrified clouds on Standard Island and that, before long, they would cause gales, squalls, and storms. This unfortunate rivalry between the Tankerdons and the Coverleys had become troubling and was approaching its acute stage. Supporters rallied round their camps. Would the two factions come to war one day? Was Milliard City threatened by troubles, riots, and revolutions? Would the administration be forceful enough and Governor Bikerstaff strong enough to maintain the peace between the Capulets and the Montagues of a self-propelled island? This remained to be seen. Anything could happen between rivals who seemed to possess boundless self-esteem.

In fact, since the uproar that took place at the crossing of the line, the two Milliardites had become declared enemies. Friends on both sides supported them. No communication remained between the two sections. If Tankerdon and Coverley saw each other in the distance, they avoided each other, and if, by chance, they met, they exchanged threatening gestures and ferocious looks. The news even spread that the former Chicago merchant and a few Larboardites wanted to start a commercial enterprise and that they asked the company for a permit to create a large plant to import one hundred thousand pigs that they would slaughter and salt and then sell to the various archipelagos of the Pacific . . .

After all this, it was easy to believe that the Tankerdon and Coverley mansions had become two powder kegs that a single spark could ignite and make Standard Island explode along with them. But let us not forget that we were dealing with a vessel floating on the deepest of abysses. The truth was that this explosion could be only a "moral" explosion but could still bring serious consequences, since the notables would probably decide to leave the island. This would be a decision that would compromise the future and, no doubt, the financial situation of the Standard Island Company.

All this was fraught with threatening complexities and even material catastrophe. And who knew if the latter was not to be feared . . . ?

Perhaps the authorities of Standard Island should not have let themselves be lulled into a false sense of security. They should have closely watched Captain Sarol and his Malays, whom they had so graciously welcomed after their accident. Not that these people appeared in any way suspicious: they were taciturn, they kept to themselves, they did not engage in close relationships, and they enjoyed a standard of living that they would certainly miss on their wild New Hebrides! So, should the Milliardites have suspected them? Yes and no. Indeed, a more alert observer would have noticed that they never ceased scrutinizing Standard Island. They constantly studied Milliard City, the layout of its avenues, and the location of its palaces and mansions, as if they were attempting to construct an exact map of the place. They were seen in the park and the countryside. They often went to Larboard Harbor or Starboard Harbor to observe the arrival and departure of ships. They took long walks, exploring the shore where the customs officers stood guard day and night. They visited the batteries set in the front and back of the island. But after all, what could have been more natural? How could these Malays, who had nothing to do, make better use of their time than by walking, and why would the islanders have suspected that they were up to something?

Meanwhile, Commodore Simcoë slowly moved toward the southwest. Yvernès, as if his very nature had been transformed since he became a Standard Islander, surrendered to the charms of the voyage. Pinchinat and Frascolin indulged in the same pleasures. How many delightful hours they spent in the casino, waiting for their biweekly concerts and the musical soirées where people fought for pricey seats to hear them! Each morning, thanks to the newspapers of Milliard City that received fresh news through the cables and less important current events through the regular service of steamers, the Parisians learned about all that was of interest on both continents concerning high society, science, art, and politics. And on this last subject, it was clear that the English press of any persuasion never ceased to protest against the existence of this moving island that had chosen the Pacific as the theater of her travels. But such protests were ignored by both Standard Island and Madeleine Bay.

For some weeks now, Sébastien Zorn and his companions had read in the International News column that their disappearance had been mentioned in the American newspapers. The famous quartet, so acclaimed in the states of the Union and so eagerly awaited by those who had not yet had the pleasure of hearing them, could not have vanished without their disappearance making the headlines. San Diego had not seen them on the appointed day, and San Diego had sounded the alarm. A search was conducted, which revealed that the French musicians were aboard the self-propelled island, having been abducted from the coast of South California. Since they had not lodged a complaint about their kidnapping, there had been no diplomatic exchanges between the company and the Federal Republic. When the quartet chose to reappear at the scene of its successes, it would be welcomed.

It is easy to understand that the two violins and the alto imposed silence on the cellist, who would have been happy to cause a declaration of war that would have unleashed a conflict between the new continent and the Jewel of the Pacific!

Besides, our performers had written to France several times since their forced boarding. Their families were reassured and wrote to them often. Their exchange of letters was as regular as the postal service between Paris and New York.

On the morning of September 17, Frascolin, installed in the library of the casino, had the very natural desire to consult the map of the Tuamotu Archipelago, toward which they were heading. As soon as he opened the atlas, as soon as his eyes fell on these regions of the Pacific Ocean, he exclaimed,

"A thousand violin strings! How will Ethel Simcoë ever navigate this chaos . . . ? He will never find his way through this mass of islands and islets . . . ! There are hundreds of them . . . ! Heaps of stones in the middle of a pond . . . ! He will hit bottom, he will run aground, he will scrape his ship on this peak, he will crash on another . . . ! We will all end up stranded in this group of islands, which is more crowded than our Morbihan in Brittany!"

He was right, the reasonable Frascolin. Morbihan has only three hundred sixty-five islands, as many as the days in the year, but on this Tuamotu Archipelago one could easily have counted twice as many. True, the sea that washes them is bound by a belt of coral reefs, the perimeter of which is no less than one thousand nine hundred fifty miles, according to Elisée Reclus.

Nevertheless, examining the map of these isles, one would be amazed that a vessel, and especially one the size of Standard Island, would dare to venture through this archipelago. Situated between the seventeenth and the twenty-eight south parallels and between the one hundred thirty-fourth and one hundred forty-seventh west meridians, the group was made up of about a thousand islands and islets—they have been estimated at seven hundred—from Mata Hiva to Pitcairn.

It is not surprising then that these islands had received various names, including that of the Dangerous Archipelago and the Evil Sea. Thanks to their geographical profusion, which is particular to the Pacific, they were also called the Low Islands, the Tuamotu Islands—which means "the faraway islands"—the Southern Islands, the Islands of the Night, and the Mysterious Lands. As for the designation of Pomotou or Pamautou, which signifies "the surrendered islands," a delegation from the archipelago, convened in 1850 in Papeete, the capital of Tahiti, protested against it, and the French government, deferring to this complaint in 1852, chose from among all the names the one of Tuamotu.

Meanwhile, as dangerous as the navigation appeared to be, Commodore Simcoë did not hesitate. He was so accustomed to those seas that he could be trusted entirely. He maneuvered his island as if she were a dinghy. He made her turn on herself as if he were steering her with paddles. Frascolin should not have worried about Standard Island: the capes of Tuamotu would never scrape her hull of steel.

In the afternoon of the nineteenth, the lookouts at the observatory reported sighting the first summits of the group about twelve miles away. These islands are extremely low. If a few rose about one hundred twenty feet above sea level, seventy-four of them rose by only three feet and would be covered twice a day if the tide were not almost inexistent. The others were just atolls surrounded by totally barren banks of coral, simple reefs following the direction of the archipelago.

Standard Island approached the group from the east in order to reach Anaa Island, which Fakarava replaced as the capital after Anaa was partially destroyed by the terrible cyclone of 1878, which killed a great number of its inhabitants and wreaked havoc as far as Kaukura Island.

They first passed Vahitahi, three miles away. The most minute precautions were taken in this area, the most dangerous of the archipelago, due to the currents and the extensions of reefs to the east. Vahitahi was just a heap of coral surrounded by three wooded islets, the northern one being occupied by the principal village.

The following day they sighted Akiti Island with its reefs carpeted with *prionia*, purslane, yellowy creeping grass, and hairy borage. This island was different from the others, not having an interior lagoon. If it could be seen from a considerable distance, it was because it rose higher above sea level than most of the other islands.

The next day they caught sight of Amanu, another island, a little bigger, whose lagoon communicated with the sea through two channels of its northwest coast.

While the Milliardites were content to sail slowly through the middle of this same archipelago they had visited the previous year, admiring its marvels as they passed, Pinchinat, Frascolin, and Yvernès would have been more than happy to stop in a few places and explore these islands built by polyparies and thus artificial . . . like Standard Island.

"But," remarked Commodore Simcoë, "our island has the power to move . . ."

"Too much power," replied Pinchinat, "as she does not stop anywhere!"

"She will stop at the Hao, Anaa, and Fakarava Islands, gentlemen, and you will have plenty of time to explore them."

Asked about the way these islands had been formed, Ethel Simcoë went along with the most generally accepted theory, explaining that in this portion of the Pacific the ocean floor had gradually sunk approximately one hundred feet. The zoophytes and the polyps had then found, on the submerged summits, a base solid enough for their coral constructions. Little by little, these constructions rose in tiers through the activity of these one-celled animals that cannot work at great depths. They reached the surface and formed this archipelago, the islands of which can be classified into barrier reefs, fringe reefs, and atolls, the Indian name for those having interior lagoons. And then, debris washed up by the waves formed a sort of humus. Seeds arrived on the winds and vegetation grew on these coral rings. Under the influence of the tropical climate, the limestone border sprouted grasses and plants, and soon a few bushes and trees appeared.

"And who knows?" said Yvernès in a rush of prophetic enthusiasm. "Who knows if the continent that was swallowed up by the waters of the Pacific will not reappear one day, rebuilt by these myriads of microscopic animalcules? And then, in these regions that are now crossed by sailing ships and steamers, express trains will run at full speed, linking the old and the new worlds . . ."

"Enough of this nonsense . . . , my dear old Isaiah!" replied the disrespectful Pinchinat.

As Commodore Simcoë had said, on September 23 Standard Island stopped at Hao Island, which she could easily approach in these great depths. Her craft brought a few visitors to the passage on the right, sheltered beneath a curtain of coconut trees. They walked five miles to reach the principal village, set upon a hill. This village had no more than two or three hundred inhabitants, most of them pearl divers employed by Tahitian merchants. There, the pandanus and the *mikimiki* myrtles abounded; they were the earliest trees on a soil that now grew sugarcane, pineapples, taro, *prionia*, tobacco, and above all, coconut trees, in immense groves each containing more than forty thousand coconut palms.

These "miraculous" trees could be said to grow almost without care. Their nuts were the daily fare of the natives, being far superior in nutritive substances to the fruit of the pandanus. With them, they also fattened their pigs, their fowl, and their dogs, whose chops and fillets were particularly appreciated. Moreover, the coconut produced a precious oil. After being grated, reduced to pulp, and dried in the sun, it was pressed with a rather rudimentary device. Cargo ships took loads of this copra to the continent, where the factories processed it in a more productive way.

Hao was not a good place to judge the inhabitants of Tuamotu. There were too few natives there. But the quartet was able to study them more advantageously on Anaa Island, where Standard Island arrived in the morning of September 27.

Anaa's superb forests could only be seen from a short distance. One of the largest islands of the archipelago, it was eighteen miles long and nine miles wide at its coral base.

Rumor has it that in 1878 a cyclone devastated this island and required the moving of the capital of the archipelago to Fakarava. This was true, although beneath the powerful climate of the tropical zone, it could be presumed that the devastation would be repaired in a few years. Indeed, Anaa had become as lively as before and had fifteen hundred inhabitants. However, it was inferior to its rival Fakarava for one important reason: passage between the lagoon and the sea could only be made through a narrow channel filled with whirlpools because of the rising of the water. Conversely, on Fakarava the lagoon had two wide openings, to the north and to the south. However, in spite of the fact that the principal market for coconut oil was moved to this latter island, Anaa was more picturesque and was still the favorite of visitors.

As soon as Standard Island had arrived at Anaa under sunny skies, many Milliardites asked to be transported to land. Sébastien Zorn and his comrades were among the first, the cellist having agreed to take part in the excursion.

First they went to the village of Tuhaora, after studying how this island had been born; its formation was the same as that of all the other islands in the archipelago. Here the limestone border on the width of the ring, so to speak, was between thirteen and sixteen feet, very steep on the sea side and sloping gently on the side of the lagoon, whose circumference was about one hundred miles, as in Rairoa and Fakarava. On this ring were massed thousands of coconut trees, the principal, not to say the only wealth of the island, whose foliage sheltered the huts of the natives.

The village of Tuhaora was crossed by a sandy, dazzling white road. The French administrator of the archipelago no longer lived there because Anaa was no longer its capital. But his house could still be seen, protected by a low wall. Over the barracks of the small garrison entrusted to the care of a navy chief, the French tricolor was floating.

The houses in Tuhaora deserved a special mention. They were no longer huts, but comfortable and salubrious dwellings, adequately furnished, and most of them were built on a coral base. The leaves of the pandanus tree served as their roofs and the precious wood of this tree was used for their doors and windows. Here and there, the houses were surrounded by vegetable gardens that the natives had filled with rich soil and that looked enchanting.

The natives were of a less striking type than the people of the Marquesas, but if their complexion was darker, their faces less expressive, and their disposition less cheerful, they still were beautiful specimens of the population of equatorial Oceania. Moreover, as they were intelligent and hardworking, perhaps they would more easily resist the physical degeneration that threatened the natives of the Pacific.

Their main industry, as Frascolin noticed, was the manufacturing of coconut oil. This explained the considerable quantity of coconut trees planted in the groves of the archipelago. These trees reproduced as easily as the coralline growths on the surface of the atolls. But they had an enemy that the Parisians encountered one day when they lay down on the bank of the interior lake, whose green waters offered a sharp contrast with the blue of the surrounding sea.

At one point, first their attention and then their horror were aroused by a crawling noise in the grass.

What did they see . . . ? A crustacean of enormous proportions. Their initial reaction was to get up, their second to take a closer look at the animal.

"What an ugly thing!" cried Pinchinat.

"It's a crab!" answered Frascolin.

Indeed, it was a crab, the kind called *birgo* by the natives. They were very numerous in these islands. Its front legs formed a pair of strong pincers or shears that it used to crack open the coconuts that were its preferred food. These *birgos* lived in burrows dug deeply between the roots and that they carpeted with coconut fibers. They went looking for fallen nuts mostly at night, and they even climbed the branches of the trees to beat down the nuts. The crab they saw must have been ravenous, as Pinchinat said, to abandon its dark retreat at midday.

The musicians did not disturb the animal because observing it promised to be extremely interesting. The crab noticed a large nut among the bushes. Little by little, it tore away the fibers around the nut with its claws. Then, when the nut was stripped, it attacked the hard shell, hitting and hammering it constantly in the same place. Once an opening was made, the *birgo* removed the inside substance using its back claws, which had very narrow ends.

"It's obvious," observed Yvernès, "that nature created the *birgo* to open coconuts . . ."

"And that it created coconuts to feed the *birgo*," added Frascolin.

"Well, what do you say we thwart the intentions of nature by keeping this crab from eating this nut, and this nut from being eaten by this crab . . . ?" proposed Pinchinat.

"I ask that the crab not be disturbed," said Yvernès. "Let's not give, even to a *birgo*, a negative idea of traveling Parisians!"

They all agreed and, no doubt, the crab gave an angry look to His Highness, then gave a grateful one to the first violin of the Concerting Quartet.

After a stopover of sixty hours at Anaa, Standard Island proceeded north. She entered the main channel through the mass of islands and islets that Commodore Simcoë navigated with complete self-confidence. Of course, under these circumstances Milliard City had been deserted by its inhabitants, who preferred the shore, and especially the vicinity of the Prow Battery. There were always islands, or rather verdant baskets that seemed to float on the surface of the water, to be looked at. It resembled a flower market on one of Holland's canals. Many pirogues tacked about at the approach of the two harbors, but they could not enter them, the agents having received formal orders concerning this.

Many native women came swimming toward the moving island when it closely followed the coral cliffs. If they did not accompany the men in their canoes, it was because these craft were taboo to the Tuamotu's fair sex, who were forbidden to enter them.

On October 4, Standard Island called in at Fakarava, at the entrance of its south passage. Even before the craft were loaded with visitors, the French administrator paid a visit to Starboard Harbor, and the governor gave orders to bring him to the town hall.

Their meeting was very cordial. Cyrus Bikerstaff put on his official face . . . , the one he used in ceremonies of this nature. The administrator, an old officer of the Marine Corps, was not to be outdone. It was impossible to imagine a more serious, more dignified, more respectable, and more stiff encounter.

After the reception, the administrator was authorized to visit Milliard City and Calistus Munbar was asked to show him around. Since they were Frenchmen, the Parisians and Athanase Dorémus wanted to accompany the superintendent. It was a great pleasure for this good man to find himself among compatriots.

The following day, the governor went to Fakarava to return the visit of the old officer, and both retained their awkward composure of the previous day. The quartet went on land, too, and walked toward the residence of the administrator. It was a very simple dwelling occupied by a garrison of twelve former sailors, and on its roof the French flag was floating.

Although, as mentioned before, Fakarava had become the capital of the archipelago, it could not compare with its rival, Anaa. The principal village was not as picturesque beneath the foliage of its trees, and the natives were often on the move. Aside from being employed in the manufacture of coconut oil in Fakarava, they also fished for pearls. The mother-of-pearl trade that developed from this industry required frequent visits to Toau, a neighboring island specially equipped for this endeavor. Intrepid divers, the natives did not hesitate to swim to depths of sixty to ninety feet, since they were accustomed to withstanding such pressure without harm and to holding their breath for more than a minute.

A few of the fishermen were authorized to offer their catch, mother-of-pearl or pearls, to the notables of Milliard City. The affluent ladies of the city were certainly not lacking jewelry. But these natural products in their rough state were not easy to obtain and, as the occasion arose, the fishermen sold their wares at unbelievable prices. As soon as Mrs. Tankerdon bought a very expensive pearl, Mrs. Coverley felt obliged to follow her example. Fortunately, there was no occasion to outbid one another on one unique object, or who knows where the bidding would have stopped. Other families wanted to copy their friends and, as sailors say, the Fakaravians made a good catch.

After about twelve days, on October 13, the Jewel of the Pacific cast off in the early morning. After leaving the capital of the Tuamotus, she reached the western limit of the archipelago. Now Commodore Simcoë no longer had to worry about the mass of islands and islets, the reefs, and the atolls. He left the region of the Evil Sea without any problems. In the open sea extended that portion of the Pacific that, over a space of four degrees, separates the Tuamotus from the Society Islands. Moved by her ten-million-horsepower engines, Standard Island sailed southwest toward the bewitching Tahiti, so poetically celebrated by Bougainville.

XIII

Stopping at Tahiti

THE SOCIETY ISLANDS, ALSO CALLED the Tahitian Archipelago, are located between latitudes fifteen degrees, fifty-two minutes, and seventeen degrees, forty-nine minutes south and longitudes one hundred fifty degrees, eight minutes and one hundred fifty-six degrees west of the Paris meridian. They cover eight hundred fifty square miles.

This archipelago is composed of two groups; the first, the Windward Islands, includes Tahiti or Tahiti Tahaa, Tapamanoa, Eimeo or Moorea, Tetiaora, and Mehetia, which were all French protectorates. The second is the Leeward Islands: Tubuai, Manuae, Huahine, Raiatea, Bora Bora, Tupai, Maupiti, Mopelia, Motu One, and Scilly, which were governed by native monarchs. The English called these islands the Georgian Islands, although Cook, their discoverer, had named them the Society Archipelago in honor of the Royal Society of London. According to the most recent census, this group, located some eight hundred sixty miles from the Marquesas, had but forty thousand inhabitants, natives and foreigners included.

Since Standard Island was arriving from the northeast, Tahiti was the first of the Windward Islands sighted by the crew. It was Tahiti that the lookouts in the observatory saw from a great distance, thanks to the peaks of Mount Maiao, or "the Diadem," rising four thousand feet above sea level.

The crossing had gone smoothly. Aided by the trade winds, Standard Island had traveled these splendid waters above which the sun moved as it descended toward the Tropic of Capricorn. In a little over two months, it would reach the tropic and return toward the equatorial line, and the self-propelled island would have it in her zenith for several weeks of burning heat; then the island would follow it as a dog follows its master, maintaining the prescribed distance.

It was the first time that the Milliardites were to put in at Tahiti. The previous year, their voyage had started too late. They had not gone farther west, and after leaving the Tuamotus, they had turned back toward the equator. And yet the archipelago of the Society Islands is the most beautiful in the Pacific. As they roamed the ocean, our Parisians appreciated more and more the great pleasures of their travel on a vessel free to choose its stops and its climate.

"Yes . . . ! But we'll see how this absurd adventure ends!" invariably concluded Sébastien Zorn.

"May it never end, that's all I ask!" exclaimed Yvernès.

Standard Island arrived in sight of Tahiti at dawn on October 17. The northern shore of the island appeared first. During the night, the lighthouse on Point Venus had been sighted. One day would have sufficed to reach Papeete, Tahiti's capital, located beyond the point, to the northwest. But the council of thirty notables had met under the leadership of the governor. Like any other well-balanced council, it had divided into two camps. One faction, with Jem Tankerdon, wanted to head west; the other, with Nat Coverley, preferred to go east. Cyrus Bikerstaff, possessing the deciding vote in case of a tie, decided that they would reach Papeete by sailing around the south of the island. This decision greatly pleased the quartet, for it allowed them to admire, in all its beauty, the pearl of the Pacific, the New Cythera of Bougainville.

Tahiti covers an area of about four hundred square miles, approximately nine times the surface of Paris. Its population, which in 1875 amounted to seventy-six hundred natives, thirty Frenchmen, and eleven hundred foreigners, now had a total of only seven thousand inhabitants. Its shape was exactly that of an upside-down flask, its body being the principal island, attached to the neck formed by the peninsula of Tatarapu by the narrow isthmus of Taravao.

It was Frascolin who made this comparison while studying the map that detailed the main points of the archipelago, and his comrades found it so accurate that they christened Tahiti the Flask of the Tropics.

Administratively, Tahiti was divided into six sections parceled out into twenty-one districts since the establishment of the protectorate on September 9, 1842. Everyone remembers the difficulties that arose between Admiral Dupetit-Thouars, Queen Pomare, and England at the instigation of that abominable trafficker in Bibles and cotton goods whose name was Pritchard and who was so wittily caricatured in Alphonse Karr's monthly, *Les Guêpes*.

But this is ancient history, no less forgotten than the actions of the just-mentioned Anglo-Saxon.

Standard Island could venture without danger to within a mile of the coast of the Flask of the Tropics. Indeed, this flask sits on a coral base whose foundations descend to the bottom of the ocean. But while approaching, the Milliardite population was able to view its imposing mass, its mountains more generously favored by nature than those of the Hawaiian Isles, its lush summits, its wooded gorges, its peaks rising like the pointed steeples of some gigantic cathedral, and its belt of coconut trees watered by the white foam of the waves on the banks of reefs.

As they followed the western coast throughout the day, the onlookers standing near Starboard Harbor with their binoculars—the Parisians all had theirs, too—took in the thousand details of the shore: the district of Papenoo, whose river ran through a wide valley at the foot of the mountains and flowed into the ocean at a place where there was no reef for several miles; Hitiaa, a very safe port from which millions of oranges were exported to San Francisco; Mahaena, where the conquest of the island ended in 1845 in a terrible battle with the natives.

In the afternoon they arrived just off the narrow isthmus of Taravao. Rounding the peninsula, Commodore Simcoë came close enough for the fertile lands of the Tautira district and the numerous rivers that make it one of the richest places in the archipelago to be admired in all their splendor. Tatarapu, set on its coral base, majestically displayed the rough hills of its extinct craters.

As the sun set on the horizon, the summits turned crimson for the last time, the colors faded and blended into a warm, transparent mist. Soon everything became a confused mass whose exhalations, filled with the fragrance of orange and lemon trees, were carried on the evening breeze. After a very short twilight, the night became dark.

Standard Island then rounded the extreme southeast point of the peninsula, and the next morning at daybreak, she moved up the western coast of the isthmus.

The district of Taravao, intensely cultivated and highly populated, showed its beautiful roads through its orange groves linking it to the district of Papeari. At the highest point, a fort could be seen commanding both sides of the isthmus, protected by a few cannons whose muzzles protruded through narrow apertures like bronze gargoyles. Below was Phaeton Harbor.

"Why does the name of the presumptuous driver of the solar chariot shine on this isthmus?" wondered Yvernès.

The day was spent following, at low speed, the jagged coast of coral substructure that is particular to the west of Tahiti. New districts offered their varied sites: Papeari with its occasional swampy plains, Mataiea with its excellent harbor of Papeuriri, then a wide valley watered by the Vaihiria River, and, in the background, a fifteen-hundred-foot mountain looking like the foot of a washstand supporting a basin with a fifteen-hundred-foot circumference. This ancient crater, probably full of fresh water, did not appear to have any outlet to the sea.

Beyond the district of Ahauraono, where cotton was raised on a large scale, and the district of Papara that was mostly agricultural, Standard Island continued beyond Point Mara, sailing past the wide valley of Paruvia, which was cut off from the Diadem and watered by the Punarun. Beyond Taapuna, Tatao Point, and the mouth of the Faa, Commodore Simcoë steered slightly to the northeast, skillfully avoiding the islet of Motu Ita, and at six in the evening came to a stop before the opening that gave access to the Bay of Papeete.

The channel appeared at the entrance, winding sinuously through the coral reef and bordered by obsolete cannons up to the Point of Farente. Of course, Commodore Simcoë, thanks to his charts, did not need the services of the pilots cruising in their whale boats off the entrance of the channel. One boat came out, however, with a yellow flag at its stern. It was the quarantine boat that called at Starboard Harbor. The laws were strict in Tahiti, and no one could disembark before the island doctor, accompanied by the harbor officer, gave permission to land.

As soon as he reached Starboard Harbor, the doctor made contact with the authorities. It was a mere formality. There were hardly any sick people in Milliard city or the vicinity; in any case, epidemics such as cholera, influenza, and yellow fever were totally unknown there. A clean bill of health was thus given according to custom. But as night, preceded by a very short twilight, fell quickly, the landing was postponed until the next day and Standard Island went to sleep awaiting the morning.

At dawn, shots were heard. It was the Prow Battery sending a twenty-one-gun salute to the group of the Windward Islands and Tahiti, the capital of the French protectorate. At the same time, on the observatory tower the red flag with its golden sun rose and fell three times.

An identical volley was fired in quick succession by the Ambush Battery at the entrance to the main pass into Tahiti.

Starboard Harbor became crowded very early. The trams had brought a considerable number of tourists bound for the capital of the archipelago. Sébastien Zorn and his friends were no doubt among the most impatient. Since the boats of Standard Island were not numerous enough to transport this crowd, the natives were eager to offer their services to cover the six cable lengths separating Standard Island from Tahiti.

But it was appropriate to let the governor set foot first on the island. He needed to have the customary interview with the civil and military authorities of Tahiti and pay the no-less-official visit to the queen.

Thus, around nine o'clock, Cyrus Bikerstaff, his assistants, Barthelemy Ruge and Hubert Harcourt, the three of them all dressed up, the principal notables of both sections, among them Nat Coverley and Jem Tankerdon, Commodore Simcoë and his officers in dazzling dress uniforms, and Colonel Stewart and his escort took their places in the gala launches and headed for the port of Papeete.

Sébastien Zorn, Frascolin, Yvernès, Pinchinat, Athanase Dorémus, and Calistus Munbar took another boat with a group of officials.

Boats and native pirogues followed in procession the officials of Milliard City, duly represented by its governor, its authorities, its notables, two of them rich enough to buy the island of Tahiti and even the entire Society Archipelago, its queen included.

The port of Papeete was excellent and so deep that big ships could anchor there. Three channels led to it: the great northern channel, two hundred feet wide and two hundred sixty feet long, that narrowed at a small entrance marked by buoys; the Tanoa channel on the east; and the Tapuna channel on the west.

The electric launches proceeded majestically alongside the beach, graced by villas and country houses, and the wharves where ships were anchored. The landings took place at the foot of an elegant fountain that served as a watering place and was fed by streams of fresh water from the neighboring mountains, one of which contained the signal station.

Cyrus Bikerstaff and his entourage disembarked amid a great crowd of French, native, and foreign people cheering the Jewel of the Pacific as the most extraordinary marvel ever created by the genius of man.

After the first transports of enthusiasm during the arrival, the cortege moved toward the palace of the governor of Tahiti.

Calistus Munbar, superb in the formal suit he wore only on ceremonial days, invited the quartet to follow him, and they readily accepted his invitation.

The French protectorate comprised not only the islands of Tahiti and Moorea, but also the neighboring isles. The main administrator was a commandant-commissaire, who had under him an organizer who directed the different sections of the military, the navy, colonial and local finances, and the judiciary. The secretary-general of the commandant-commissaire was responsible for the civil affairs of the country. Several minor administrators were established on the islands, in Moorea, at Fakarava in the Tuamotus, at Taiohae in Nuka Hiva, and there was a justice of the peace who also had jurisdiction over the Marquesas. A consulting committee for agriculture and commerce had been formed in 1861 and met once a year at Papeete. The headquarters of the artillery and the engineers were also in Papeete. As for the garrison, it was composed of detachments of the colonial police force, the artillery, and the navy. A curate and a vicar appointed by the government, and nine missionaries scattered among the islands, ensured the practice of the Catholic faith. In truth, the Parisians could believe that they were in France, in a French port, and this was not unpleasant to them.

The villages in the various islands were administered by some sort of native municipal council presided over by a *tavana* assisted by a judge, a *mutoi* chief, and two advisors elected by the inhabitants.

Beneath the shade of beautiful trees, the procession moved toward the government building. Everywhere there were magnificent coconut trees, *miros* with pink leaves, candlenut trees, clumps of orange trees, guava trees, rubber trees, etc. The building arose amid foliage almost as high as its wide roof, brightened by charming mansardes. It looked elegant enough, with its façade revealing a first and second story. The major French officials were assembled there and the colonial police did the honors.

The commandant-commissaire received Cyrus Bikerstaff with an infinite good grace that the governor would certainly not have found in the neighboring English archipelagos. He thanked him for bringing Standard Island into the waters of the archipelago. He hoped that their visit would be repeated annually and regretted that Tahiti could not return the compliment. The meeting lasted half an hour and it was decided that Cyrus Bikerstaff would receive the Tahitian authorities the next day at the town hall.

"Do you intend to remain in Papeete for some length of time?" asked the commandant-commissaire.

"For about two weeks," answered the governor.

"Then you will have the pleasure of seeing the French fleet, which will arrive toward the end of the week."

"We will be happy to do them the honors of our island."

Cyrus Bikerstaff introduced the members of his retinue, his assistants, Commodore Ethel Simcoë, the commander of the army, the various officials, the superintendent of the arts, and the musicians of the Concerting Quartet, who were welcomed as they should have been by a compatriot.

Then there was a slight embarrassment concerning the delegates of the two sections of Milliard City. How could they show the same respect to both Jem Tankerdon and Nat Coverley, those irritating characters who had the right . . .

"By walking them both at the same time," observed Pinchinat, mimicking the famous words of Eugène Scribe.

The difficulty was resolved by the commandant-commissaire himself. Aware of the rivalry between the two well-known Milliardites, he showed such perfect tact filled with so much official correctness, and he acted with so much diplomatic address, that things happened as if they had been regulated by the decree of Messidor. No doubt that on a similar occasion the head of an English protectorate would have arranged things to serve the politics of the United Kingdom. Nothing of the sort happened at the residence of the commandant-commissaire and Cyrus Bikerstaff, enchanted by the welcome he received, went home followed by his retinue.

Needless to say, Sébastien Zorn, Yvernès, Pinchinat, and Frascolin had the intention of letting Athanase Dorémus, who was already out of breath, return to his house on Twenty-Fifth Avenue. As for them, they intended to spend as much time as possible in Papeete, visiting the surrounding areas, touring the main districts, exploring the regions of the peninsula of Tatarapu, in a word, drinking the last drop of this Flask of the Pacific.

Their project was thus decided on and when they communicated it to Calistus Munbar, he entirely agreed. "But," he said to them, "you should wait forty-eight hours before starting your excursion."

"And why not start today . . . ?" asked Yvernès, eager to begin his explorations.

"Because the authorities of Standard Island will pay their respects to the queen, and it would be proper for you to be introduced to Her Majesty and her court."

"How about tomorrow then . . . ?" asked Frascolin.

"Tomorrow the commandant-commissaire of the archipelago will return the visit he received from the authorities of Standard Island and it would be proper . . ."

"For us to be there," answered Pinchinat. "Well, we'll be there, my dear superintendent, we'll be there."

Leaving the seat of government, Cyrus Bikerstaff and his suite walked toward the palace of Her Majesty, a simple promenade under the trees that did not take more than fifteen minutes.

The royal abode was pleasantly located among lush clumps of trees. It was a square construction with two stories whose roof hung over two tiers of verandas, as in a chalet. From the top windows, one could take in large plantations that spread to the city, and even farther away, a stretch of sea. In short, it was a charming dwelling, not luxurious, but comfortable.

The queen had not lost any of her prestige in passing under the rule of the French protectorate. If the flag of France floated on the masts of ships moored in the port of Papeete and anchored in the roadstead, as well as on the civil and military buildings of the city, at least the old colors of the queen, the red and white horizontal stripes with their three-colored canton in the corner, were still displayed on the residence of the monarch.

It was in 1706 that Quiros discovered the island of Tahiti, which he named Sagittaria. Later, Wallis in 1767 and Bougainville in 1768 completed the exploration of this group of islands. When the island was first discovered, Queen Oberea was reigning, and it was after her death that the famous dynasty of the Pomares appeared in the history of Oceania.

Pomare I (1762–80), after reigning as Otoo (the Black Heron), changed his name to Pomare.

His son, Pomare II (1780–1819), gladly welcomed the first English missionaries and converted to the Christian religion ten years later. These were times of dissension and bloody struggles, and the population of the island dropped from one hundred thousand to sixteen thousand souls.

Pomare III, son of the former, reigned from 1819 to 1827, and his sister Aimata, the most famous Pomare, the protégée of the horrible Pritchard, born in 1812, became queen of Tahiti and the neighboring islands. As she had not had children from her first husband, she repudiated him to marry Ariifaaite. From their union was born in 1840 Arione, the heir apparent, who died at age thirty-five. From the following year on, the queen gave four children to her husband, who was the most handsome man in the entire archipelago. One daughter, Teriimaevarna, had been princess of the island of Bora Bora since 1860; Prince Tamatoa, born in 1842, was king of the island of Raiatea and was dethroned by his subjects, who revolted against his brutality; Prince Teriitapunui, born in 1846, was afflicted by a severe limp; and finally, Prince Tuavira, born in 1848, received his education in France.

The reign of Queen Pomare was not entirely tranquil. In 1835 the Catholic missionaries fought with the Protestant ones. First sent home to France, they were brought back by a French expedition in 1838. Four years later, the protectorate of France was accepted by five leaders of the island. Queen Pomare protested, and so did the English. Admiral Dupetit-Thouars deposed the queen in 1843 and expelled Pritchard.

These events provoked the bloody engagements of Mahaena and Rapepa. But after the admiral was practically expelled, Pritchard received an indemnity of twenty-five thousand francs and Admiral Bruat was given the mission of settling the matter.

In 1846 Tahiti gave in and Pomare accepted the protectorate by the treaty of June 19, 1847. She remained queen of Raiatea, Huahine, and Bora Bora islands. There were still more troubles, however. In 1852 a riot overthrew the queen and the republic was proclaimed. Finally, the French government reinstated the monarch, who abandoned three territories: that of Raiatea and Tahaa to her eldest son, that of Huahine to her second son, and that of Bora Bora to her daughter.

During the visit of Standard Island, one of her descendants, Pomare VI, occupied the throne of the archipelago.

The obliging Frascolin continued to justify his nickname of the Larousse of the Pacific, which had been given to him by Pinchinat. Frascolin shared many historical and geographical details with his comrades. He declared that it was important to know something about the people you visited and to whom you talked. Yvernès and Pinchinat replied that he was right to enlighten them concerning the genealogy of the Pomares, but Sébastien Zorn said that "he could not care less."

As for the enthusiastic Yvernès, he immersed himself entirely in the charm of the poetic Tahitian nature. He recalled the enchanting travels of Bougainville and Dumont d'Urville. He did not hide his emotion at the thought that he was going to meet this Majesty of the new Cythera, an authentic Pomare queen, her name alone . . .

"Means 'night of the cough,'" answered Frascolin.

"All right!" cried Pinchinat. "As if you were saying the goddess of influenza or the empress of coryza. Catch that, Yvernès, and don't forget your handkerchief."

Yvernès was angered by the out-of-place remark of this joker; but the others laughed so heartily that the first violin ended up laughing with them.

The reception for the governor of Standard Island, the authorities, and the delegation of notables took place with great pomp and circumstance. The honors were rendered by the *mutoi*, or the police chief, and his native auxiliaries.

Queen Pomare VI was about forty years old. She wore, like her family around her, a pale-pink ceremonial dress, the preferred color of the Tahitians. She received the compliments of Cyrus Bikerstaff with such friendly dignity, if this expression can be used, that a European queen would have approved. She answered graciously, and in correct French, since our language was commonly used in the Society Archipelago. Besides, she had a strong wish to see this Standard Island that was so much talked about throughout the Pacific. She hoped that her stay would not be the last. Jem Tankerdon was particularly well received by her, which was not without bruising Nat Coverley's pride. This was understandable, though, because the royal family was Protestant and Jem Tankerdon was the most notable person of the Protestant section of Milliard City.

The Concerting Quartet was not forgotten during the introductions. The queen was cordial enough to inform its members that she would be delighted to hear them play and to applaud them. They bowed respectfully, affirming that they were at the command of Her Majesty, and the superintendent said that he would make sure that her wish would be answered.

After a meeting that lasted half an hour, the honors rendered the cortege as it entered the royal palace were repeated as it left.

The visitors returned to Papeete. They stopped at the military circle, where the officers had a lunch prepared to honor the governor and the elite of the Milliardite population. Champagne flowed, toast followed toast, and it was six o'clock when the launches left the harbor of Papeete for Starboard Harbor.

And in the evening, when the Parisian musicians were together again in the room of the casino:

"We have a concert ahead," said Frascolin. "What shall we play for Her Majesty . . . ? Will she understand Mozart or Beethoven?"

"We will play Offenbach, Varney, Lecoq, or Audran!" answered Sébastien Zorn.

"Certainly not . . . ! The bamboula will be our choice!" answered Pinchinat, indulging in the characteristic swaying of the hips of this native dance.

XIV

~~~~~~~~~~~~~~~

Parties and More Parties

THE ISLAND OF TAHITI WAS destined to become a regular stop for Standard Island. Every year, before she continued on her way to the Tropic of Capricorn, her inhabitants would spend time in the region of Papeete. Warmly received by the French authorities and by the natives, the Milliardites showed their gratitude by keeping their doors, or rather their ports, wide open. Civilians as well as soldiers from Papeete flocked to the island, exploring her countryside, her park, and her avenues, and it was doubtful that any incident would ever alter this excellent relationship. In truth, at the time of departure, the police had to make sure that the population of Standard Island did not fraudulently increase by the smuggling of a few Tahitians who had not been authorized to live on her floating surface.

In exchange for their friendly treatment, the Milliardites were given full permission to visit any island of the group where Commodore Simcoë might put into port.

In anticipation of their stop at Tahiti, a few rich families thought of renting villas near Papeete, and they reserved them in advance by telegram. They intended to set up house there for a while, as Parisians do in neighborhoods outside Paris, with their servants and horses, in order to live the life of wealthy landowners, of tourists, excursionists, or even hunters, if they are inclined to hunt. In short, they would go on vacation without having anything to fear from this wholesome climate whose temperature varied between fifty-seven and eighty-six degrees Fahrenheit from April to December, the other months of the year being winter in the Southern Hemisphere.

Among the notables who left their mansions on Standard Island for the comfortable dwellings of the Tahitian countryside were the Tanker-dons and the Coverleys. Mr. and Mrs. Tankerdon and their sons and daughters moved the very next day to a picturesque chalet located on the heights of Tatao Point. Mr. and Mrs. Coverley, Miss Diana, and her sisters also replaced their palace on Fifteenth Avenue with a delightful villa hidden beneath the majestic trees of Point Venus. These residences were several miles away from each other and Walter Tankerdon may have found this a bit far. But he could not do anything to bring these two points of the Tahitian shore closer together. Besides, well-kept carriage roads gave direct access to Papeete.

Frascolin pointed out to Calistus Munbar that, since the two families had left, they could not be present during the commandant's visit to the governor.

"True! And it's a good thing, too!" answered the superintendent with a diplomatic wink. Indeed, this would avoid conflicts. If the representative of France went first to the Coverleys, what would the Tankerdons have said; and if he went to the Tankerdons first, what would the Coverleys have said? Cyrus Bikerstaff could only be pleased by their double departure.

"Is there really no reason for hoping that the rivalry of these two families will end . . . ?" asked Frascolin.

"Who knows?" answered Calistus Munbar.

"Perhaps it only depends on the friendly Walter and the charming Diana . . ."

"It doesn't seem, however, that up till now, this heir and this heiress . . . ," observed Yvernès.

"Right . . . !" replied the superintendent. "But one occasion could change things, and, if chance does not make that happen, we will make sure and take the place of chance . . . for the profit of our beloved island!"

And Calistus Munbar turned on his heels with a pirouette that Athanase Dorémus would have applauded and that a seventeenth-century marquis would not have disavowed.

On the afternoon of October 20, the commandant-commissaire, the organizer, the secretary-general, and the major dignitaries of the protectorate landed at Starboard Harbor. They were received by the governor with the honors due their ranks. Artillery salutes were fired from the

Prow and Stern Batteries. Cars decorated with the French and Milliardite colors led the procession to the capital, where the reception rooms of the town hall had been prepared for the meeting. On their way there, the Tahitian dignitaries received a flattering welcome from the population and, on the front steps of the municipal palace, there was an exchange of official speeches that, thankfully, did not last too long.

Then the Tahitians visited the Protestant church, the cathedral, the observatory, the two electric factories, the two harbors, and the park; later they took rides around the coast on streetcars. When they returned, they were served lunch in the main lounge of the casino. It was six o'clock when the commandant-commissaire and his staff reembarked for Papeete amid the thunder of the artillery of Standard Island, taking with them an excellent memory of the reception.

The next morning, October 21, the four Parisians landed at Papeete. They had not invited anyone to accompany them, not even the professor of good manners, whose legs could not withstand such long walks anymore. They were free as air, like schoolchildren on vacation, happy to feel rocks and earth beneath their feet.

First they visited Papeete. The capital of the archipelago was undeniably a fine city. The quartet took real pleasure in loafing and strolling under the beautiful trees that shaded the houses by the beach, the naval storehouses, and the main trade establishments at the rear of the harbor. Then, taking one of the streets that started at the wharf, and where there was an American-style railway, they ventured inside the city.

There, between gardens full of greenery and freshness, the streets were wide and as perfectly straight as the avenues of Milliard City. Even at this early hour, there was a constant coming and going of Europeans and natives. This liveliness, which would be even greater by eight o'clock in the evening, would go on all night long. It must be understood that tropical nights, and especially Tahitian nights, were not made to be spent in bed, even if the beds of Papeete were made of a trellis of ropes and coco fibers, topped by a bedding of banana leaves and mattresses of tufts from the silk-cotton tree, not to mention the nets that protected sleepers from annoying mosquito attacks.

As for the houses, it was easy to distinguish the European dwellings from the Tahitian ones. The first, almost all made of wood, were set a few feet above ground on cement blocks and were as comfortable as possible. The second, rather rare in the city, were scattered here and there under the shade and were made of butt-joined bamboo and covered with mats that kept them clean, well-ventilated, and pleasant.

"And the natives . . . ?"

"The natives . . ." said Frascolin to his comrades. "No more here than in the Hawaiian Islands will we find these brave savages who, before the conquest, dined with pleasure on a human cutlet and reserved for their kings the eyes of a defeated warrior, roasted according to the recipe of Tahitian cuisine!"

"What? So there are no more cannibals in Oceania?" cried Pinchinat. "And we will have traveled thousands of miles without meeting a single one of them!"

"Be patient!" replied the cellist, beating the air with his right hand like the Rodin in *The Mysteries of Paris*, "Be patient! We may still find more of them than we need to satisfy your foolish curiosity!"

He could not have been more right!

The Tahitians probably originate from Malaysia, from the race called Maori. Raiatea, the Holy Island, a charming area washed by the clear waters of the Pacific in the Windward Islands group, was said to be the birthplace of their kings.

Before the arrival of the missionaries, Tahitian society was composed of three groups: the princes, privileged people who were thought to possess the gift of performing miracles; the chiefs or landowners, who were not highly regarded and were oppressed by the princes; and finally, the common people, who did not own land or, if they did, held it only temporarily.

All this changed after the conquest, and even before, under the influence of Anglican and Catholic missionaries. But what did not change was the intelligence of the natives, their lively speech, their cheerful disposition, their unfailing courage, and their physical beauty. The Parisians admired them in the city as well as in the country.

"By Jove!" said one of the Frenchmen. "What handsome boys!"

"And what beautiful girls!" said another.

Yes, these were men taller than average, with reddish skin that looked as if it had been colored by their fiery blood. They had splendid physical features that resembled antique statues, and their faces were gentle and pleasant. They were truly superb, these Maoris, with their big, lively eyes and their rather thick but finely drawn lips. Their tattoos for purposes of war had begun to disappear along with the occasions that had made them necessary.

For sure, the richest natives on the island dressed like Europeans, but they still looked marvelous with their open-neck shirts, their pale-pink jackets, and their trousers falling over their boots. But these did not attract the attention of the quartet. No! To the modern trousers, our tourists preferred the pareo, whose multicolored cotton draped the body from waist to ankle, and instead of top hats or even Panama hats, they admired the *hei*, the headdress common to both sexes, on which flowers and leaves intertwined.

The women were still the poetic and graceful Tahitians of Bougainville. The white petals of the *tiara*, a sort of gardenia, mingled with their black tresses uncoiling on their shoulders; or they wore a light hat made of the outside bark of a coconut bud and "whose sweet name of *reva-reva* seems to come from 'rêverie,'" proclaimed Yvernès. To the charm of this costume, whose colors changed at the slightest movement, as in a kaleidoscope, add their graceful walk, their insouciant attitude, their sweet smiles, their lively looks, and the harmonious sonority of their voices. It is easy to understand that, as soon as someone repeated, "What handsome boys!" the others replied in chorus, "And what pretty girls!"

When the Creator made such marvelous types, would it have been possible for him not to think of giving them an environment worthy of their beauty? And what could he have imagined more delightful than these Tahitian landscapes in which the vegetation is so profuse under the influence of the running streams and the abundant dew of the nights?

During their excursions through the island and the neighboring districts of Papeete, the Parisians never ceased to admire this world of vegetal marvels. Our musicians left the borders of the sea that were more favorable for farming and where the forests were replaced by plantations of lemon and orange trees, by arrowroot plants, sugarcanes, coffee trees, cotton plants, fields of yams, manioc, indigo, sorghum, and tobacco, and they ventured among the thick bushes of the interior, at the foot of mountains whose summits rose above the dome of foliage.

Everywhere, they saw elegant, sturdy coconut trees, *miros* or rosewood trees, and casuarinas or ironwood trees, *tiairi* or candlenut trees, and also *puraus*, *tamanas*, *ahis* or santals, guava trees, mango trees, *taccas* whose roots are edible, and also superb taros, the precious breadfruit trees with their long trunks, smooth and white, and their wide, dark-green leaves, among which nested large fruits with a kind of embossed bark and whose white pulp formed the main food of the natives.

The most common, along with the coconut tree, was the guava tree, which grows almost to the top of mountains and which is called *tuava* in the Tahitian language. They formed thick forests, while the *puraus* formed dreary thickets hard to get through if one was so foolish as to enter their tangled masses.

On the other hand, there were no dangerous animals. The only native quadruped was a sort of pig, a species between the pig and the wild boar. Their horses and cattle had been imported to the island, where they thrived. And so had their sheep and goats. The fauna, including the birds, were thus much less rich than the flora. There were doves and swallows, as on the Hawaiian Islands. No reptiles except for centipedes and scorpions. As for insects, there were wasps and mosquitoes.

The products of Tahiti were mainly cotton and sugarcane, whose cultivation developed largely at the expense of tobacco and coffee; there was also coconut oil, arrowroot, oranges, mother-of-pearl, and pearls.

This was enough to sustain an important trade with America, Australia and New Zealand, with China in Asia, and with France and England in Europe; a trade of three million two hundred thousand francs of imports, offset by four and a half million of exports.

The excursions of the quartet went as far as the Tabaratu Peninsula. A visit to Fort Phaeton allowed them to meet a detachment of marine infantry, who were delighted to welcome their compatriots.

In an inn of the harbor managed by a colonist, Frascolin played the host. To the natives of the neighborhood and the *mutoi* of the district, he served French wine that the innkeeper agreed to sell him at a high price. In return, the locals offered their guests the products of their land: bunches of beautiful yellow bananas from the tree called *fei*, deliciously prepared yams, *maiore*, which is the fruit of the bread tree steamed in a hole filled with hot stones, and finally, a sort of jam with a tart taste, made from the grated nut of the coconut tree, called *taiero*, and preserved in bamboo stems.

Their luncheon was very cheerful. The guests smoked hundreds of cigarettes made of tobacco leaves dried on an open fire and rolled in pandanus leaves. However, instead of imitating the Tahitians, who passed their cigarettes from mouth to mouth after taking a few puffs, the French simply smoked theirs the French way. And when the *mutoi* offered him his cigarette, Pinchinat thanked him with a *mea maitai*, which means "very well"! And his hilarious accent made everyone laugh.

Of course, during their explorations, the hikers could not return to Papeete or Standard Island every evening. But everywhere, in the villages as well as in the scattered houses, with the colonists as well as with the natives, they were always received with much friendship and comfort.

To occupy themselves on November 7, they proposed a hike to Venus Point, an excursion that any tourist worth his salt could not avoid.

At dawn they left, full of energy, and crossed a bridge over the lovely Fantahua River. They went up the valley toward the sound of a deafening cascade, twice as high as Niagara Falls but infinitely narrower, which falls from a height of two hundred forty-five feet with a superb thunder. Following the road alongside Taharahi hill, they arrived at the edge of the sea, on the bluff that Cook had baptized the Cape of the Tree, a name that could be explained in his time by the presence of a lonely tree that had long since died of old age. An avenue planted with magnificent species of trees led from the village of Taharahi to the lighthouse rising at the extreme point of the island.

It was in this place, halfway up a lush hill, that the Coverley family had established its residence. There was thus no serious reason for Walter Tankerdon, whose villa was located far, very far beyond Papeete, to be riding near Point Venus. But the Parisians caught sight of him. The young man was on horseback near the Coverley cottage. He exchanged greetings with the French tourists and asked them if they intended to go back to Papeete in the evening.

"No, Mr. Tankerdon," replied Frascolin. "We have received an invitation from Mrs. Coverley and will probably spend the evening at the villa."

"Then, gentlemen, I will bid you goodbye," replied Walter Tankerdon. And it seemed that the young man's face became darker, although no cloud veiled the sun at that moment. Then he spurred his horse and trotted away after a last look at the white villa amid the trees. And here we must ask: why on earth did his father, the fantastically wealthy Jem Tankerdon, want to be a businessman once again, and why did this man risk sowing discord on Standard Island, which had not been created for business, after all!

"Eh!" said Pinchinat. "Maybe he would have liked to come with us, this charming cavalier."

"Yes," added Frascolin, "and it's obvious that our friend Munbar may be right! Walter goes away very unhappy because he could not see Miss Dy Coverley . . ."

"Doesn't this prove that millions do not bring happiness?" asked the great philosopher Yvernès.

During the delightful hours of the afternoon and evening spent at the cottage with the Coverleys, the quartet enjoyed the same welcome at the villa that they had received at the mansion on Fifteenth Avenue. It was a pleasant get-together agreeably mixed with art. They made excellent music, on the piano of course. Mrs. Coverley played a few new pieces. Miss Dy sang like a true artist, and Yvernès, who had a fine voice, mingled his tenor with the soprano of the young woman.

Without apparent purpose—but maybe with designs of his own—Pinchinat slipped into the conversation the fact that he and his comrades had met Walter Tankerdon riding near the villa. Was this wise on his part, and would it not have been better to keep silent about it . . . ? No, and if the superintendent had been there, he could only have approved of His Highness. A slight smile, almost imperceptible, formed on the lips of Miss Dy, her pretty eyes shone more brightly, and when she started singing again, her voice seemed even more penetrating.

Mrs. Coverley looked at her for an instant and simply said, while Mr. Coverley frowned,

"Are you tired, my child . . . ?"

"No, mother."

"And you, Mr. Yvernès . . . ?"

"Not at all, Madam. Before I was born, I must have been a choirboy in one of the chapels of Paradise!"

The evening drew to a close, and it was almost midnight when Mr.

Coverley thought that it was time to rest. The next day, enchanted by this simple and cordial reception, the quartet went back to Papeete.

The stop at Tahiti would last only one more week. According to the itinerary that had been planned in advance, Standard Island was going to sail southwest again. And probably nothing would have distinguished this final week, during which the four vacationers finished their tours, if a very happy incident had not occurred on November 11.

On that morning, the arrival of the French squadron of the Pacific was announced by the semaphore on the hill behind Papeete.

At eleven o'clock, a heavy cruiser, the *Paris*, escorted by two light cruisers and a launch, called at the harbor.

The usual salutes were exchanged and the rear admiral whose flag was flying on the *Paris* landed with his officers.

After the official artillery salutes were answered by the friendly thunder of the prow and the stern, the rear admiral and the commandant of the Society Islands hastened to pay each other a visit.

It was fortunate for the French ships, their officers, and their crews to have arrived at Tahiti Harbor while Standard Island was still there. This brought a new occasion for receptions and parties. The Jewel of the Pacific was opened to the French sailors, who hastened to visit and admire her marvels. For forty-eight hours, the uniforms of our navy blended with the outfits of the Milliardites.

Cyrus Bikerstaff did the honors at the observatory and the superintendent did the honors at the casino and other quarters entrusted to him.

It is under these circumstances that an idea occurred to the amazing Calistus Munbar, a marvelous idea whose realization was to leave unforgettable memories. And he communicated this idea to the governor, who embraced it after receiving the advice of his council of notables.

Yes! A big party was planned for November 15. Its program would include a gala dinner and a ball offered in the lounges of the town hall. By that time the vacationing Milliardites would have returned, since the departure of Standard Island was to take place two days later.

The important people of both sections would therefore not miss the festival in honor of Queen Pomare VI, the European and native Tahitians, and the French squadron.

Calistus Munbar was charged with organizing the festivities, and they could trust his imagination and his zeal. The quartet offered him their services and it was agreed that a concert would figure among the most attractive features of the program.

As for the invitations, it would be the governor's task to send them out.

First Cyrus Bikerstaff went in person to ask Queen Pomare and the princes and princesses of her court to attend the party, and the queen graciously accepted. He received the same positive answer from the commandant-commissaire, the top-ranking French civil servants, and from the rear admiral and his officers, who all appreciated his kindness.

In short, a total of one thousand invitations was sent. Of course, the thousand guests could not all sit at the municipal table. No! Only about one hundred of them would: the royal persons, the officers of the French squadron, the authorities of the protectorate, the main civil servants, the council of notables, and the high clergy of Standard Island. But there would be banquets in the park, as well as games and fireworks; enough to make the entire population happy.

Needless to say, the king and queen of Malécarlie were not forgotten. But Their Majesties, avoiding all pomp and living apart in their modest dwelling on Thirty-Second Avenue, thanked the governor for an invitation that they regretted they could not accept.

"Oh, the poor monarchs!" said Yvernès.

When the big day arrived, the island put out the French colors mixed with the Tahitian ones and the Milliardite flag.

Queen Pomare and her court, in regal attire, were welcomed aboard at Starboard Harbor to the roar of the double battery. To this thunder responded the cannons of Papeete and of the French fleet.

Around six in the evening, after a stroll through the park, the high society went to the municipal palace, which was magnificently decorated.

What a marvelous sight was offered by its monumental staircase! Each of its steps cost at least ten thousand francs, like those of the Vanderbilt Hotel in New York! And in the splendid dining room, the guests sat down at the banquet tables.

The governor followed the rules of etiquette with perfect tact. There was no cause for conflict between the great rival families of the two sections. Everyone was happy with their seating, among others Miss Dy Coverley, who was sitting across from Walter Tankerdon. This satisfied the young man and woman, for it was better not to seat them any closer together.

It is needless to say that the French musicians had nothing to complain about. By seating them at the head table, the Milliardites gave proof, once again, of their friendship and esteem for their talent.

As for the menu of this memorable meal, studied, mulled over, and put together by the superintendent, it showed that even for its culinary resources, Milliard City had no reason to envy old Europe.

You can judge for yourself by examining this menu, printed in gold on vellum under the care of Calistus Munbar:

Consommé Orleans Style,
Cream Contessa,
Turbot Sauce Mornay,
Sirloin Steaks Napolitan,
Chicken Quenelles Viennese Style,
Mousse of Liver Pate Treviso Style,
Sorbets,
Canapés of Roasted Partridges,
Provençal Salad,
Green Peas English style,
Ice Cream, Fruit Salad, Fruits,
Assorted Cakes,
Parmesan on Savoie bread.
Wines:
Château d'Yquem. Château Margaux. Chambertin. Champagne.
Selection of liqueurs.

Were better combinations for an official menu ever found at the table of the queen of England, the emperor of Russia, the emperor of Germany, or the president of the French Republic? And could the most renowned chefs of both continents have done better?

At nine o'clock, the guests went to the lounges of the casino for the concert. There were four fine pieces on the program, four and not one more:

Fifth Quartet in H major, op. 18, of Beethoven
Second Quartet in D minor, op. 10, of Mozart

Second Quartet in D major, op. 64 (second part), of Haydn
Twelfth Quartet in E-flat of Onslow

The concert was yet another triumph for the Parisian musicians so luckily embarked, no matter what the rebellious cellist would say, on Standard Island.

Meanwhile, Europeans and foreigners took part in the various games installed in the park. Rustic dances started on the lawns and, why not admit it, people danced to the music of accordions, these instruments being much appreciated by the natives of the Society Islands. French sailors also had a weak spot for this instrument with bellows, and as the men on leave from the *Paris* and the other ships of the squadron had come in great numbers, the orchestra was complete and the accordions played loudly. Voices joined in too, and the songs of the sailors mixed with the *himerres* that are the favorite popular tunes of the natives of Oceania.

Besides, the people of Tahiti have a special love for singing and dancing, at which they excel. Several times that evening, they performed the *repauipa*, which can be considered their national dance, the measure of which is kept by the beating of the drums. The choreographers of every origin, natives and strangers, had the time of their lives, thanks to the flowing refreshments offered by the municipality.

At the same time, dances of more sophisticated arrangements and compositions, under the direction of Athanase Dorémus, brought the main families together in the lounges of the town hall. The Milliardite and Tahitian ladies outdid each other with their most elegant outfits, but it should come as no surprise that the former, who were faithful customers of Parisian fashion designers, easily outshone the most elegant European women of the colony. Diamonds sparkled on their heads, their shoulders, and their necks, and it was only for these women that the contest had any interest. But who could have dared to choose between Mrs. Coverley and Mrs. Tankerdon, both of whom were dazzling? Certainly not Cyrus Bikerstaff, always so anxious to maintain a harmonious balance between the two sections of the island.

The queen of Tahiti and her eminent husband were part of the quadrille of honor, along with Cyrus Bikerstaff and Mrs. Coverley, the rear admiral and Mrs. Tankerdon, Commodore Simcoë and the first lady in waiting to the queen. At the same time, other quadrilles were formed in which the couples mingled following their tastes and friendships. The total picture was charming. And yet Sébastien Zorn stayed by himself in an attitude, if not of protest, at least of disdain, like the two grouchy Romans in the famous painting entitled *Décadence*. But Yvernès, Pinchinat, and Frascolin waltzed and danced polkas and mazurkas with the prettiest Tahitians and the most delightful young women of Standard Island. And who knows if that very evening there were not many marriages decided at the end of the ball, which would doubtless have given an increase of work to the civil employees.

Besides, there was general surprise when, in a quadrille, chance gave Walter Tankerdon as partner to Miss Coverley. But was it chance and did not the clever diplomatic superintendent help chance along with one of his crafty combinations? Anyway, it was the event of the evening, perhaps fraught with consequences, if it was a first step toward the reconciliation of the two powerful families.

After the fireworks on the big lawn, the dancing started again in the park and in the town hall, and it lasted until morning.

Such was this marvelous festival, the memory of which would endure throughout the long, happy series of ages that the future, it was hoped, would reserve for Standard Island.

Two days later the stay ended, and at dawn Commodore Simcoë gave orders to get under way. Cannon shots saluted the departure of Standard Island as they had saluted her arrival, and the Jewel of the Pacific returned their salutes.

The direction of the ship was northwest in order to have a look at the other islands of the archipelago, the Windward Group and the Leeward Group.

They sailed along the picturesque shores of Moorea, studded with superb peaks and whose central summit could be clearly seen; Raiatea, the Holy Island that was the cradle of the native royalty, Bora Bora, surmounted by a mountain three thousand feet high, then the islets of Motu-Iti, Mapeta, Tubuai, and Manu, links of the Tahitian chain stretching through the area.

On November 19, at the moment when the sun set on the horizon, the last summits of the archipelago disappeared.

Standard Island then veered southwest, which was the direction recorded by the telegraphic transmitters on the windows of the casino.

If someone had looked at Captain Sarol and his Malays at that moment, he would have been struck by the dark fire in the captain's eyes and the fierce expression on his face as, with a threatening hand, he pointed out to his Malays the direction of the New Hebrides, located thirty-six hundred miles west!

PART TWO

I

~~~~~~~~~~~~

In the Cook Islands

AFTER LEAVING MADELEINE BAY, Standard Island traveled for six months across the Pacific, from archipelago to archipelago. Not a single accident occurred during this fabulous voyage. At this time of year, the surroundings of the equatorial zone are calm and the trade winds blow evenly between the tropics. Besides, whenever a squall or a storm broke out, the solid base supporting Milliard City, its two harbors, its park, and its countryside would not feel the slightest jolt. The squall would go through, the storm would die down. They would hardly be noticed on the surface of the Jewel of the Pacific.

What would have been of greater concern in these circumstances was the monotony of a too-uneventful life. But our Parisians were the first to admit that they experienced nothing of the sort. On this immense desert of ocean, oasis succeeded oasis, such as the groups that they had already visited, the Hawaiian Islands, the Marquesas, the Tuamotus, the Society Islands, and those they would explore before making their way back north: the Cook Islands, the Samoas, the Tonga and Fiji Islands, the New Hebrides, and even other ones, perhaps. So many varied stops, so many anticipated opportunities that would allow them to explore these countries, so interesting for their ethnographic diversity.

As far as the Concerting Quartet was concerned, how could they have thought of complaining, even if they had had time for it? Could they have felt separated from the rest of the world? Wasn't the postal service regular across the two continents? Not only did the petroleum tankers bring their cargos to keep the factories supplied on an almost regular schedule, but never did two weeks go by without steamboats arriving at Starboard Harbor or Larboard Harbor to unload all sorts of freight as well as the mass of information and news that was widely enjoyed by the idle billionaires.

It goes without saying that the compensation promised these musicians was paid with a punctuality confirming the inexhaustible resources of the company. Thousands of dollars found their way into their pockets and quickly piled up there; they would be rich, very rich, by the end of their engagement. Never had performers encountered such luck. They would not regret the "relatively mediocre" results of their tour across the United States of America.

"So," Frascolin said to the cellist one day, "have you given up your prejudices against Standard Island?"

"No," answered Sébastien Zorn.

"And yet," added Pinchinat, "we will have a nice bundle when the tour is over."

"To have a nice bundle is not the only thing that counts; you still have to be sure of taking it with you."

"And you're not sure of this?"

"No."

What could you answer to that? And yet there was nothing to fear concerning the bundle since their salary for each trimester had been sent to America by draft and deposited into the Bank of New York. So we might as well let the stubborn chap stagnate in his groundless mistrust.

Indeed, more than ever, the future seemed assured. It looked as if the rivalries between the two sections had entered a cooling-off period. Cyrus Bikerstaff and his assistants had reason to congratulate themselves. The superintendent had intensified his efforts since "the big event of the ball at the town hall." Yes! Walter Tankerdon had danced with Miss Dy Coverley. Should people have concluded that the relationship between the two families had become less tense? It was certain that Jem Tankerdon and his friends were no longer talking of transforming Standard Island into an industrial and commercial place. Moreover, high society was talking a lot about the ball incident. Some observant people saw a reconciliation in this, maybe even more than a reconciliation, a union that would put an end to dissensions both private and public.

And if these predictions came true, a young man and a young woman, certainly worthy of each other, would see their fondest wishes realized, this we believe we can assert.

There was no doubt that Walter Tankerdon had not remained indifferent to the charms of Miss Dy Coverley. He had thought about her for a year already, but, in view of the situation, he had not entrusted anyone with his secret feelings. Miss Dy had seen into his heart, she had understood him and had been touched by his discretion. She may even have seen clearly into her own heart, and was this heart ready to respond to Walter's? But she did not let any of this show. She remained very reserved, as her dignity and the estrangement between the two families dictated.

However, any observer would have noticed that Walter and Miss Dy never took part in the discussions that sometimes arose in the mansions on Fifteenth and Nineteenth Avenues. When the inflexible Jem Tankerdon indulged in an enraged diatribe against the Coverleys, his son would bow his head, keep silent, and leave the room. When Nat Coverley ranted and raved against the Tankerdons, his daughter would lower her eyes, her pretty face turning pale; she would try to change the subject, but without success. These two characters did not notice a thing; that's the common lot of fathers, whom nature blindfolds. But—at least this is what Calistus Munbar asserted—Mrs. Coverley and Mrs. Tankerdon were not so blind anymore. Mothers have eyes in order to see, and the state of mind of their children was a subject of constant worry for them, since the only possible remedy was out of the question. Basically, they felt that in view of the enmity of the two rivals, in view of their self-esteem being constantly injured by questions of precedence, no reconciliation or union was possible . . . and yet, Walter and Miss Dy loved each other . . . Their mothers had long known it.

More than once already, the young man had been asked to make a choice among the marriageable young women from the Larboard section. There were some charming ones, impeccably brought up, with fortunes almost equal to his, and whose families would have been pleased with such a union. His father constantly urged him to make a choice and so did his mother, although not so pressingly. Walter had always refused, giving as a reason that he felt no inclination toward marriage. But the former Chicago merchant would not accept this as an answer.

When a man possesses hundreds of millions by his marriage, he should not remain single. If his son could not find a young woman to his liking on Standard Island—a young woman of his standing, of course—well, he would have to travel, to roam America or Europe . . . ! With his name, his fortune, let's not even mention his personal charm, his only difficulty would be in making a choice, even if he wanted a princess of imperial or royal blood . . . ! This is what Jem Tankerdon said. Yet every time his father pressured him to marry, Walter refused to look for a wife abroad. And when his mother once said to him,

"My dear child, is there any young woman that you like around here?"

He responded, "Yes, mother!"

But as Mrs. Tankerdon did not inquire further to learn who that young woman was, he did not deem it necessary to name her.

There is no doubt that a similar situation existed in the Coverley family, that the former New Orleans banker wanted to marry his daughter to one of the young men who often came to the mansion, where receptions were very fashionable. If she did not like any of them, well, her mother and father would take her abroad . . . They would visit France, Italy, England . . . Miss Dy answered that she preferred not to leave Standard Island . . . She felt good on Standard Island . . . All she wanted was to stay there . . . Mr. Coverley was rather worried by this reply and its true motive escaped him.

On the other hand, Mrs. Coverley did not question her daughter as directly as Mrs. Tankerdon had questioned Walter, and this is understandable. It is probable that Miss Dy would not have dared to answer as frankly either—even to her mother.

This was where things stood. Once the young people were no longer confused about the nature of their feelings, they exchanged an occasional glance, but they never said a word to each other. If they met, it was in the official rooms of the island, at receptions organized by Cyrus Bikerstaff for events that the important billionaires could not miss if they wanted to retain their status. And in these circumstances, William Tankerdon and Miss Dy Coverley showed total reserve, being in a place where the smallest imprudence on their part could have regrettable consequences . . .

We can thus imagine the effect made by the extraordinary incident that occurred at the governor's ball; people who have a tendency to exaggerate saw it as a scandal and the following day everyone was talking about it. As for what caused this incident, nothing could be simpler. The superintendent had invited Miss Coverley for a dance . . . but he was nowhere to be found when the quadrille started. What a clever man that Munbar was . . . ! Walter Tankerdon offered to take his place and the young woman accepted him as her partner . . .

It is probable and even certain that, after this significant happening in the social life of Milliard City, there were comments in both camps. Mr. Tankerdon must have questioned his son and Mr. Coverley his daughter. But what did Miss Dy answer . . . ? What did Walter say . . . ? Did Mrs. Coverley and Mrs. Tankerdon take part in the discussions, and what had been the result of their intervention . . . ? Despite his acute inquisitiveness and his diplomatic acumen, Calistus Munbar was unable to find out. So, when Frascolin asked him questions about it, he simply answered with a wink of his right eye, which meant nothing since he did not know a thing. What is interesting to note, however, is that since that memorable day, when Walter met Mrs. Coverley and Miss Dy taking their walk, he bowed respectfully and the young woman and her mother returned his greeting.

According to the superintendent, this was "a huge step forward!"

On the morning of November 25, something happened at sea that had nothing to do with the situation of the two most important families of the self-propelled island. At daybreak, the lookouts at the observatory reported seeing several large vessels heading southwest. These ships were advancing in line and maintaining distance among themselves. They could only be from one of the Pacific squadrons.

Commodore Simcoë sent a telegram to the governor, who gave orders to exchange salutes with these warships.

Frascolin, Yvernès, and Pinchinat went up to the observatory tower, wanting to witness this exchange of international courtesy.

The telescopes were trained on the vessels, which were four in number at a distance of five to six miles. There were no flags on their masts and the lookouts could not determine their nationality.

"Does anything indicate to what navy they belong?" Frascolin asked the officer.

"Nothing, "he answered, "but from the way they look, I am inclined to believe that they are British. Besides, in this area you hardly meet anything else than squadrons of English, French, and American ships. Whatever they are, we will know for sure when they come a mile or two closer."

The ships were approaching at a moderate speed and unless they changed course, they would have to pass within a few cable lengths of Standard Island.

Several bystanders went to the forward battery and followed with interest the progress of these warships.

An hour later, the vessels were less than two miles away. They were the old type of cruisers, rigged with three masts; they looked much more imposing than the modern ships that have a single military mast. Curls of smoke coming out of their wide chimneys were driven westward to the extreme limits of the horizon by the breeze.

When they were only a mile and a half away, the officer was able to confirm that they were from the British squadrons of the western Pacific. Some archipelagos located there, such as Tonga, Samoa, and Cook, are British possessions or protectorates.

The officer got his men ready to hoist the flag of Standard Island. It would unfurl fully in the wind, displaying the golden sun of its escutcheon. Everyone was waiting for the salute of the admiral's ship from the squadron.

Ten minutes went by.

"If they are British," remarked Frascolin, "they are none too eager to be polite!"

"What do you expect?" answered Pinchinat. "John Bull usually wears his hat screwed on his head and to unscrew it takes quite an effort."

The officer shrugged his shoulders. "They are British indeed," he said. "I know them, they will not salute."

Indeed, there were no flags hoisted on the first ship to pass honors. The fleet went by, paying no more attention to the self-propelled island than if she had not even existed. And anyway, what right did she have to exist? What right did she have to come and clutter this area of the Pacific? Why would England have paid attention to her, since this nation never stopped protesting against the building of this enormous machine that roamed these seas and cut through the oceans, making pirate attacks more likely . . . ?

The fleet went away like an ill-bred man who refuses to acknowledge acquaintances on the sidewalks of Regent Street or the Strand, and the flag of Standard Island remained at the bottom of the pole.

The way this haughty England, this perfidious Albion, this modern-day Carthage was treated in the city and the harbors is easy to imagine. They made a resolution to never return a British salute if ever there was one—which was impossible to imagine.

"What a difference with our squadron when it arrived in Tahiti!" exclaimed Yvernès.

"That's because the French are always so exquisitely polite!" replied Frascolin.

"*Sostenuta con expressione!*" added His Highness, keeping the beat with his graceful hand.

On the morning of November 29, the lookouts caught sight of the first hills of the Cook Archipelago, situated at latitude twenty degrees south and longitude one hundred sixty degrees west. First called Mangia and Harwey, these islands were later named after Cook, who landed there in 1770. The archipelago consists of the islands of Mangia, Rarotonga, Watim, Mittio, Hervey, Palmerston, Hagemeister, etc. Its population, of Maori origin, had decreased from twenty to twelve thousand souls and was made up of Polynesian Malays converted to Christianity by European missionaries. These islanders were eager to remain independent and had always resisted foreign intrusion. They still believed that they were their own masters, even if they were increasingly subjected to the protective influence—we all know what that means—of the government of British Australia.

The first island of the group was Mangia, the most important and the most heavily populated—actually, it is the capital of the archipelago. The floating island intended to stop there for two weeks.

Was it in this archipelago that Pinchinat would meet real savages—these Robinson Crusoe savages he had unsuccessfully searched for in the Marquesas, the Society Islands, and Nuka-Hiva? Would his Parisian curiosity be finally satisfied? Would he see genuine cannibals tried and true . . . ?

"My dear old Zorn," he said to his pal on that day, "if there are no man-eaters here, then there are man-eaters nowhere!"

"I could answer you that I don't care," replied the old grouch of the quartet, "but instead, I'll ask why you say nowhere?"

"Because an island named 'Mangia' can only be inhabited by cannibals." Pinchinat had just enough time to avoid the punch he deserved for this awful pun. Anyway, whether man-eaters still lived on Mangia or not, His Highness would not have the opportunity to communicate with them.

Indeed, when Standard Island was a mile away from Mangia, a pirogue coming from its harbor arrived at Starboard Harbor pier. It carried the English governor, a simple Protestant pastor who was a worse tyrant on the archipelago than the Mangian chieftains themselves. On this island with a thirty-mile perimeter, inhabited by four thousand people and carefully planted with taro, arrowroot, and yams, it was this reverend who possessed the best land. He was the owner of the most comfortable house in Ouchora, the island's capital, at the foot of a hill bristling with breadfruit trees, coconut trees, mango trees, and all sorts of herbs and plants. He also had a flower garden where coleas, gardenias, and peonies abounded. He owed his power to the native police force, the *mutois*, who formed a squad that the Mangian kings feared. This police forbade people to climb trees, to hunt or fish on Sundays and holidays, to take walks after nine o'clock at night, and to buy consumer products at prices different from those imposed by arbitrary taxes. Infractions were subject to fines paid in piastres—the piastre being worth five francs—that for the most part ended up in the pocket of this unscrupulous minister.

When this fat little man got on board, the harbor officer went toward him and they exchanged salutes.

"In the name of the king and queen of Mangia," said the Englishman, "I present the respects of Their Majesties to His Excellency the governor of Standard Island."

"And I am here to accept them, Your Excellency," answered the officer, "until our governor arrives in person to pay homage . . ."

"His Excellency will be well received," said the pastor, his shifty face exuding shrewdness and greed.

Then he went on in a sugary tone, "There are no health problems on Standard Island, I presume . . . ?

"No, our inhabitants have never been better."

"There could still be a few epidemics, influenza, typhus fever, smallpox . . ."

"Not even a cold, Your Excellency. So please give us a clean bill of health and as soon as we reach your shores, we will communicate with Mangia in the customary way.

"But," retorted the pastor, still hesitant, "if certain epidemics . . ."

"I am telling you again, there are absolutely none."

"Then the inhabitants of Standard Island intend to land . . ."

"Yes . . . as they have recently done in the other groups to the east."

"All right, then," answered the chubby little bureaucrat. "You can be assured that they will be very well received, as long as no epidemics . . ."

"Let me tell you again, there is not the faintest sign of any."

"Let them land, then . . . let them come in large numbers . . . The natives will receive them as well as they can, for the Mangians are hospitable . . . but . . ."

"But what?"

"Their Majesties, in accordance with the council of notables, have decided that on Mangia, as well as on the other islands of the archipelago, the foreigners will have to pay a landing tax . . ."

"A landing tax . . . ?"

"Yes, two piastres . . . It's not much, as you can see . . . two piastres for every person setting foot on the island."

It was obviously the minister who had established this regulation that the king and queen, as well as the council of notables, had readily agreed to. A large part of the money was reserved for His Excellency. Since they had never heard of such a tax on the islands of the eastern Pacific, the harbor officer could not help expressing his surprise:

"Are you serious . . . ?" he asked.

"Absolutely," retorted the minister, "and if you do not pay these two piastres, we cannot let anyone land."

"Very well!" answered the officer.

Then he bowed to His Excellency and went to the telephone office to inform the commodore.

Ethel Simcoë immediately contacted the governor. He asked if the self-propelled island should stop at Mangia, since the formal claims of the Mangian authorities were totally unjustified.

The answer was not long in coming. After discussing the matter with his aides, Cyrus Bikerstaff flatly refused to pay these vexing taxes. Standard Island would not stop at Mangia nor at any of the other islands of the archipelago. The greedy pastor would get nothing out of his proposition and the Milliardites would visit less rapacious natives on the neighboring groups of islands.

An order was thus sent to the engineers to leave at full speed, and this is how Pinchinat was deprived of the pleasure of shaking hands with honorable cannibals—if there were any. But he shouldn't have been too sad! They do not eat each other anymore on Cook's islands—and maybe they regret it!

Standard Island made her way through the wide sound into the string of the four northern islands. Many pirogues appeared; some were well made and rigged with sails, others were simply hollowed out of a tree trunk, but they were manned by daring fishermen who ventured after the whales that are so abundant in these seas.

These islands were very green and fertile and it is easy to understand why England imposed its protectorate on them until it could count them among its possessions in the Pacific. Leaving Mangia, the travelers caught a glimpse of its rocky shores bordered by a circle of coral, its dazzling white houses painted with quicklime extracted from the reefs, and its hills, no more than six hundred feet high, covered with dark tropical greenery.

The next day Commodore Simcoë spotted Rarotonga, with its heavily wooded mountains. Around the center of the island, at an altitude of five thousand feet, the top of a volcano emerged from the foliage of a thick forest. Between those hills, an alabaster building with gothic windows stood out. It was the Protestant church, built in the midst of a forest of mape trees that went down to the shore. These trees were tall, with abundant foliage and twisted trunks. They were crooked, knotted and contorted like the old apple trees of Normandy or the ancient olive trees of Provence.

Perhaps the reverend who directed the Rarotongian consciences was sharing profits with the director of the German Oceanic Company, who had the entire business of the island in his hands, and he had not established a landing tax like his Mangian colleague. Maybe the Milliardites could go pay their respects to the two queens who were sharing the kingdom, one in the village of Arognani and the other in the village of Avarua, without paying a penny. But Cyrus Bikerstaff did not consider it a good idea to land on this island, and he was seconded by the council of notables, whose members were accustomed to being welcomed like kings while traveling. All in all, this was a total loss for the natives, who were dominated by awkward Anglicans, because the people of Standard Island were well heeled and spent generously.

At the end of the day, only the top of the volcano could still be seen, rising like a sword on the horizon. Flocks of seabirds flew over Standard Island and boarded without permit, but when night came they flew swiftly away to the small islands in the north that are constantly beaten by the wind.

There was then a meeting presided over by the governor where a change in the itinerary was proposed. Standard Island was floating through neighborhoods where English influence was dominant. If they went on westward, along the twentieth parallel, as had been decided earlier, they would be heading toward the Tongas and the Fiji Islands. And since what had happened at the Cook Islands was not very encouraging, wouldn't it have been better to head toward New Caledonia and the Loyalty Archipelago, where the Jewel of the Pacific would be received with full French courtesy? Then, after the December solstice, they could return to the equatorial zones. But then they would miss the New Hebrides, where they had agreed to return the shipwrecked sailors of the ketch as well as their captain.

During this discussion about a new itinerary, the Malays appeared very worried, which was understandable since their repatriation would be more difficult if the change was adopted. Captain Sarol could not hide his disappointment and even his anger, and if someone had heard him talking with his men, that person would probably have found the captain's exasperation very suspicious indeed.

"Can you imagine," he said, "letting us off at the Loyalty Islands . . . or in New Caledonia . . . ! While our friends are waiting for us at Erromango . . . ! And our plan that was so well prepared for the New Hebrides . . . ! Will our good luck abandon us . . . ?"

Luckily for these Malays, and unfortunately for Standard Island, the possibility of changing the itinerary was rejected. The notables of Milliard City did not like to alter their habits. The trip would continue according to the initial arrangements made when they left Madeleine Bay. However, in order to replace the two-week stop that was planned for the Cook Islands, they decided to go toward the Samoan Archipelago, sailing northwest before meeting the Tongan Islands.

When this decision was announced, the Malays could not hide their satisfaction . . .

After all, this was totally natural and shouldn't they have been happy that the council of notables did not renounce its plan to repatriate them at the New Hebrides?

II

From Island to Island

IF THE HORIZON OF STANDARD ISLAND seemed calmer since relations between the Starboardites and the Larboardites had become less tense, if this improvement was due to the feelings that Walter Tankerdon and Dy Coverley had for each other, and if the governor and the superintendent had reasons to believe that the future would no longer be jeopardized by internal dissension, the existence of the Jewel of the Pacific was still threatened, and it would be difficult for her to escape the disaster that had long been in the making. The farther she sailed to the west, the closer she came to the region where her destruction was certain. And the perpetrator of this criminal machination was no other than Captain Sarol.

Indeed, it was not chance that had brought the Malays to the Hawaiian Group. The ketch had put in at Honolulu precisely to await the arrival of Standard Island at the time of her annual visit. To follow her as she left, to navigate her waters without raising suspicions, to be picked up as shipwrecked since they could not have been admitted as passengers, and then to steer the island toward the New Hebrides under the pretext of bringing him and his men home, such was indeed the intention of Captain Sarol.

We know how the first part of this plan was carried out. There had been no accident. No ship had collided with the ketch near the equator. It was the Malays themselves who had sunk their vessel, but they did this in such a way as to keep it afloat until help answered their distress signals. Then they let it sink as soon as Standard Island had picked up their crew. This way, their collision would not arouse suspicion. No one would doubt that they were shipwrecked since their vessel had just sunk, and Standard Island would have to give them shelter.

But the governor may not have wanted to keep them on board. Maybe there were rules against letting foreigners reside on Standard Island . . . Maybe the Milliardites would decide to unload them at the nearest archipelago . . . It was a chance to take, and Captain Sarol took it. But after a favorable decision from the company, Standard Island opted to keep the shipwrecked sailors on the island and to bring them to the New Hebrides.

This is how things developed. For four months already, Captain Sarol and his ten Malays had been living in complete freedom on the self-propelled island. They had explored her entirely and learned all her secrets, leaving no stone unturned in their search. Things were going as they wished. For a short while, they feared that the itinerary was going to be modified by the council of notables, and they became worried enough to risk arousing suspicions! Fortunately for their project, the itinerary was not changed. Three months later, Standard Island would arrive in the vicinity of the New Hebrides and there a catastrophe would occur, the likes of which had never been heard of in the history of maritime disasters.

The New Hebrides Archipelago was dangerous for navigators, not only on account of the reefs surrounding its shores and the thunderstorms that constantly spread through it but also because of the natural ferocity of a part of its population. Since the time it was discovered by Quiros in 1706, and after it was explored by Bougainville in 1768 and by Cook in 1773, it had seen many ghastly massacres. Maybe its evil reputation could justify the fears of Sébastien Zorn concerning the end of Standard Island's maritime campaign. Kanakas, Papuans, and Malays mingled there with Australian Blacks, all treacherous and cowardly people who resisted any attempt at civilization. A few islands of this group were real dens of criminals and their inhabitants lived mainly on piracy.

Captain Sarol, a Malay by birth, belonged to this type of plunderers, whalers, sandalwood merchants, and slave traders who, as reported by a navy doctor named Hagon during his travels to the New Hebrides, infested these regions. Daring, enterprising, accustomed to roaming the dangerous archipelagos, knowing his job in and out, and having more than once directed bloody expeditions, this Sarol was no novice, and his crimes had made him infamous in this part of the western Pacific.

A few months earlier, Captain Sarol and his companions, helped by the bloodthirsty population of Erromango Island, one of the New Hebrides, had prepared an attack that would allow them, if successful, to live as honorable people wherever they chose. They knew the reputation of this self-propelled island that, since the previous year, had been traveling through the tropics. They knew what untold wealth this opulent Milliard City contained. But as the island was not supposed to venture too far west, they would have to lure her within sight of that wild Erromango, where everything had been prepared to ensure her complete destruction.

On the other hand, although they would be reinforced by the natives of the neighboring islands, the inhabitants of the New Hebrides had to reckon with their own numerical inferiority and take into account the dense population of Standard Island, not to mention her many means of defense. Therefore, attacking her in the open sea like a simple merchant ship was out of the question, as was boarding her from a flotilla of pirogues. Thanks to the humanitarian feelings that the Malays would have been able to exploit without arousing any suspicion, Standard Island would arrive in the vicinity of Erromango . . . She would drop anchor a few cable lengths from the shore . . . and thousands of natives would invade her by surprise . . . They would drive her onto the rocks . . . She would fall apart . . . She would be open to plundering and killing . . . In truth, this horrible machination had a chance to succeed. In exchange for the hospitality they extended to Captain Sarol and his accomplices, the Milliardites would be heading toward a supreme disaster.

On December 9 Commodore Simcoë reached the hundred seventy-first meridian as it intersects with the fifteenth parallel. Between this meridian and the hundred seventy-fifth one lies the Samoan Group, visited by Bougainville in 1768, by Lapérouse in 1787, and by Edwards in 1791.

Standard Island first caught sight of Rose Island to the northwest; it was an uninhabited island not even worth visiting.

Two days later the island of Manua was sighted, with the two islets of Olosega and Ofu. Manua's highest peak rises twenty-five hundred feet above sea level. Although it contains about two thousand people, it is not the most interesting region of the archipelago, and the governor gave no order to stop there. It was better to stay for two weeks at the islands of Tutuila, Upolu, and Savaii, the most beautiful of this group, which is the most beautiful group of all. And yet Manua has its place in maritime annals. Indeed, on its shores, at Ma-Oma, several companions of Cook perished, at the far end of a bay that has kept its well-justified name of Massacre Bay.

A distance of about sixty miles separates Manua from its neighbor, Tutuila. Standard Island progressed toward it during the night of December 14. On that evening the quartet, who were taking a walk near the Prow Battery, could "smell" Tutuila even though it was still several miles away. The air was filled with the most delightful fragrances.

"This is not an island," cried Pinchinat, "it's Piver's shop, it's Lubin's factory, it's the boutique of a famous *parfumeur* . . ."

"If Your Highness has no objection," retorted Yvernès, "I would prefer you to compare it to a perfume burner."

"A perfume burner if you wish!" answered Pinchinat, who did not want to stifle the poetic outbursts of his comrade.

And indeed, it seemed that perfumed fragrances were carried on the breeze across these admirable waters. They were the emanations of the penetrating scent of the tree to which the Samoan Kanakas have given the name of *moussooi*.

At sunrise Standard Island was coasting along Tutuila, at six cable lengths from its northern shore. This island looked like a basket of greenery, or rather tiered rows of forests unfolding to its highest summits, the tallest being fifty-six hundred feet high. A few islets were sighted before it, Aunuu among others. Hundreds of elegant pirogues manned by vigorous, half-naked natives coordinating their oars with the two-four tempo of a Samoan song hurried to escort the self-propelled island. Each boat had fifty to sixty rowers. This was not an exaggerated number for these long boats that are strong enough to roam the high seas. Our Parisians understood then why the first Europeans gave these islands the name of Archipelago of the Navigators. Its true geographical name is Hamoa or, preferably, Samoa.

Savaii, Upolu, and Tutuila, which spread out from the northwest to the southeast, and Olosega, Ofu, and Manua, located in the southeast, are the principal islands of this group of volcanic origin. The group covers eleven hundred square miles and it has a population of thirty-five thousand six hundred people. The census number given by the first explorer must therefore be reduced by half.

Every one of these islands could enjoy weather as pleasant as that of Standard Island. The temperature remains continuously between seventy-eight and ninety-three degrees Fahrenheit. July and August are the coldest months, with extreme heat in February. From December to April the Samoans are drenched by heavy rain, and it is also the time for storms and hurricanes that often bring disasters.

Trade, mainly with England, and to a lesser extent with America and Germany, amounted to as much as one million eight hundred thousand francs in imports and nine hundred thousand in exports. They exported agricultural products: cotton, whose production increased every year, and copra, the dry nut of the coconut.

Moreover, the population, mostly of Malay-Polynesian origin, numbered only three hundred white residents and a few thousands workers recruited from the Melanesian islands. Starting in 1830, missionaries had converted Samoans to Christianity, but these still retained many of their former religious practices. The majority of the natives were Protestant due to the German and English influence. However, Catholicism had a few thousand converts, and the Marist fathers were doing their best to increase these numbers in order to combat the Anglo-Saxon proselytism.

Standard Island stopped south of Tutuila Island, at the roadstead of Pago Pago. This was the true harbor of the island, whose capital was Leone, situated in the central region. This time there were no difficulties between Governor Cyrus Bikerstaff and the Samoan authorities. They could enter the island freely. It was not on Tutuila but on Upolu that the king of the archipelago resided and it was there that the houses of the Americans and Germans were located. Therefore, there were no official receptions. A few Samoans took advantage of the opportunity afforded them to visit Milliard City and its surroundings. And the Milliardites were assured that the population of the group would give them a cordial welcome.

The harbor was at the head of the bay. The shelter it offered against the winds was wide and excellent and its access easy. Warships often put in there.

It was no surprise that among the first people coming to land that day

were Sébastien Zorn and his comrades, accompanied by the superintendent, who wanted to explore along with them. Calistus Munbar was, as
always, charming and in high spirits. He had heard that an excursion to
Leone had been planned by two or three families of notables. And, as
the Coverleys and the Tankerdons were going to be part of it, maybe
Walter and Miss Dy would be able to see each other, which would not
displease the superintendent.

Walking with the quartet, Calistus Munbar talked about this important event; he was very animated and got carried away, as usual.

"My friends," he kept repeating, "we are watching a comic opera . . .
One lucky incident will bring us to the denouement of this piece . . . A
horse runs away . . . A carriage tips over . . ."

"Brigands attack us . . . !" said Yvernès.

"The excursionists are all massacred . . . !" added Pinchinat.

"And that could very well happen . . . !" growled the cellist in a gloomy
voice, as if he had drawn the dismal sounds from his fourth string.

"No, my friends, no!" cried Calistus Munbar. "Let's not think of a
massacre . . . ! We don't need that . . . ! Just a fortuitous accident where
Walter Tankerdon would be able to save the life of Miss Dy Coverley . . ."

"And with that a little music of Boieldieu or Auber!" added Pinchinat, pretending to turn the crank of a barrel organ with his closed fist.

"So, Mr. Munbar," said Frascolin, "you are still in favor of this
marriage . . . ?"

"Am I in favor of it, my dear Frascolin! I dream about it day and
night . . . ! I am getting cranky over it!"—although it did not really
show—"I am losing weight over it!"—this did not show either—"I
will die if it does not happen . . ."

"Then it will happen, Mr. Superintendent," retorted Yvernès, giving
his voice a prophetic tone, "because God would not want Your Excellency to die . . ."

"He would be the loser indeed!" answered Calistus Munbar.

And they all directed their steps toward a native bar where they had
a few drinks of coconut milk and ate delicious bananas in honor of the
future couple.

The Samoan population strolling through the streets of Pago Pago
and the masses of trees along the harbor were a real feast for the eyes

of our Parisians. The men were taller than average, with a yellowish-brown complexion. Their heads were round, their chests powerful, and their limbs solid with muscles. Their faces were soft and pleasant. Perhaps they had a few too many tattoos on their arms, their torsos, and even their thighs that were only partially covered with grass and leaf skirts. As for their hair, it was supposed to be black, straight or curly, depending on the taste of each native dandy. But they covered it with a layer of white lime so that it looked like a wig.

"Savages à la Louis XV!" noted Pinchinat. "They only need a waistcoat, a sword, knee breeches, stockings, red-heeled shoes, a feathered hat, and a snuffbox to show up at the king's levee at Versailles!"

The Samoan women and girls were as rudimentarily dressed as the men. Their hands and breasts were tattooed; their heads were decorated with gardenias, their necks adorned with necklaces made of red hibiscus, and they justified—at least the young ones—the admiration that had filled the tales of the early navigators. The women were very reserved and even showed a bit of affected prudery, but they were gracious and smiling and they enchanted the quartet with their wishes of *kalofa*— which meant good morning—uttered in sweet, melodious voices.

An excursion, or rather a pilgrimage, that our tourists had wanted to take and that they made the next day gave them the opportunity to cross the island from coast to coast. A local carriage brought them to the opposite shore, to França Bay, whose name brings back a memory of France. There, on a white coral monument, was fixed a bronze plaque bearing in engraved letters the unforgettable names of Commander Langle, naturalist Lamanon, and nine sailors—the companions of Lapérouse—who were massacred at this location on December 11, 1787.

Sébastien Zorn and his comrades returned to Pago Pago by the interior of the island. What admirable masses of trees intertwined with lianas they encountered: coconut trees, wild banana trees, and numerous species used in furniture making! In the countryside there were fields of taro, sugarcane, and cotton, as well as coffee and cinnamon trees. Everywhere, orange, guava, mango, and avocado trees abounded. There were also creeping plants, orchids, and gigantic ferns. An incredibly diversified flora had sprung from this rich soil that a damp, warm climate fertilized. As for the Samoan fauna, amounting to a few birds and reptiles more or less harmless, they only had a small rat to represent the native mammals of the rodent family.

Four days later, on December 18, Standard Island left Tutuila and the "fortuitous accident" so ardently wished for by the superintendent had not yet happened. Yet it was obvious that the relations between the two rival families were continuing to improve.

There were hardly thirty-six miles between Tutuila and Upolu. On the morning of the following day, Commodore Simcoë passed a quarter of a mile away from the shores of the three consecutive atolls of Nuntua, Samusu, and Salafuta that defended the island like three freestanding forts. He maneuvered very skillfully and moored his vessel at Apia in the afternoon.

Upolu, with a population of sixteen thousand people, was the most important island of the archipelago. It is there that Germany, America, and England built the residences of their representatives who formed a sort of council for the protection of their people. The king of the group "reigned" in his court at Malinuu, at the easternmost point of Apia.

Upolu looked very much like Tutuila; a mass of mountains, dominated by the peak of Mission Mount and forming a sort of backbone down the entire length of the island. These inactive ancient volcanoes were now covered up to their craters with thick forests. At the foot of these mountains, plains and fields reached the beds of alluvial deposits on the shore where vegetation grew in the luxuriant disorder of the tropics.

The next day Governor Cyrus Bikerstaff, his two aides, and a few notables landed at the harbor of Apia. They were expected to pay an official visit to the representatives of Germany, England, and America, this composite municipality that regulated the administrative services of the archipelago.

While Cyrus Bikerstaff and his group went to pay their respects to these residents, Sébastien Zorn, Frascolin, Yvernès, and Pinchinat, who had come ashore with them, occupied their time visiting the city.

At first they were struck by the contrast between the European houses where the merchants practiced their trades and the huts of the old Kanaka villages that the natives stubbornly kept as their lodgings. These dwellings were comfortable, salubrious, and in a word, charming. They were scattered on the banks of the Apia River, and their low roofs were sheltered by the elegant umbrellas of the palm trees.

The harbor was very lively. It was the busiest of the group, and the Commercial Company of Hamburg kept a flotilla there that sailed between the Samoas and the neighboring islands.

However, if the triple English, American, and German association had the greatest influence in this archipelago, France was represented by Catholic missionaries, whose honesty, devotion, and zeal gave it a good reputation among the Samoan population. A true feeling of satisfaction and even of deep emotion gripped our musicians at the sight of the little mission church, which did not have the puritan severity of the Protestant churches, and of a schoolhouse that flew the tricolor flag.

They made their way there and a few minutes later were welcomed into the French mission. The Marists received the *falanis*—which is the name given by Samoans to foreigners—with a patriotic embrace. Three fathers lived there, serving the mission. Two others were on Savaii, and several nuns lived on other islands.

It was such a pleasure to talk with the father superior, who was elderly and had lived in the Samoan Islands for many years. He was so ecstatic to welcome compatriots, especially musicians from his country! The conversation was interrupted by refreshing drinks made according to the mission's own recipe.

"First and foremost, my dear sons," said the old man, "don't think for a moment that the islands of our archipelago are wild. You will not find natives practicing cannibalism here . . ."

"We have hardly met any until now," remarked Frascolin.

"A fact that we deeply regret," added Pinchinat.

"What do you mean . . . deeply regret . . . ?"

"Please, Father, excuse this confession of an inquisitive Parisian! It's out of my love for local color!"

"Oh!" said Sébastien Zorn. "We are not yet at the end of our campaign, and maybe we'll see more of those man-eaters begged for by our comrade than we would desire . . ."

"This is possible," answered the father superior. "Near the western islands, in the New Hebrides and the Solomon Islands, navigators must venture with extreme prudence. But in Tahiti and the Marquesas, as well as in the Society Islands and Samoa, civilization has made remarkable progress. I know that the massacre of Lapérouse's companions has given the Samoans the reputation of being ferocious adepts of cannibalistic practices. But they have changed so much since, thanks to the influence of Christianity! Today's natives are a civilized people, enjoying a European-style government, with two chambers as in Europe, and revolutions . . ."

"Just like in Europe . . . ?" asked Yvernès.

"Yes, my dear son, just like in Europe. The Samoans are not exempt from political dissensions!"

"We know this, on Standard Island," answered Pinchinat, "because what do we not know on this island blessed by the gods! We even believed that we were arriving in the middle of a dynastic war between two royal families . . ."

"Indeed, my friends, there was a struggle between King Tupua, who is a descendant of the ancient kings of the archipelago and whom we support with all our influence, and King Malietoa, backed by the English and Germans. A lot of blood was shed, especially in the great battle of December 1887. These kings saw themselves successively recognized and deposed, and finally Malietoa was declared king by the three powers, according to the measures stated by the Berlin court . . . Berlin, imagine!"

And the old missionary could not refrain from making a convulsive gesture as this name came out of his mouth.

"You see," he said, "until now the German influence has prevailed in the Samoan Islands. Nine-tenths of the cultivated lands are in the hands of Germans. In the vicinity of Apia, in Suluafata, they have received a very important concession from the government, close to a harbor that could bring supplies to their warships. Rapid-fire arms were introduced by them. But all this will perhaps come to an end someday . . ."

"To the advantage of France . . . ?" asked Frascolin.

"No . . . to the advantage of the United Kingdom!"

"Oh!" said Yvernès. " England or Germany, either one . . ."

"No, my dear friend," answered the father superior, "there is a notable difference . . ."

"But what of King Malietoa . . . ?" asked Yvernès.

"Well, King Malietoa was once again deposed, and do you know who the candidate was who would have had the greatest chance of succeed-ing him . . . ? It was an Englishman, one of the most important charac-ters of the archipelago, a simple novelist . . ."

"A novelist . . . ?"

"Yes . . . Robert Louis Stevenson, the author of *Treasure Island* and the *Arabian Nights*."

"See where literature can lead you!" cried Yvernès.

"What an example for our French novelists to follow!" retorted Pinchi-nat. "Imagine! Zola I, the former king of Samoa . . . recognized by the British government, sitting on the throne of the Tupuas and the Malietoas, and his dynasty following that of the native rulers . . . ! What a dream!"

The conversation ended after the father superior had mentioned sev-eral details concerning the culture of the Samoans. He added that if the majority of them belonged to the Wesleyan religion, Catholicism was making progress every day. The church of the mission was already too small for their services, and the school would need to be enlarged soon. The father was very happy about this, and his guests were happy for him.

The stop at Upolu Island lasted three days. The missionaries came to repay their visit to the French musicians. They were shown around Milliard City, which filled them with wonder. And why not add that in the casino hall, the Concerting Quartet entertained the father and his colleagues with a few selections from their repertoire? The dear old man was moved to tears because he loved classical music and, to his great regret, he had never had a chance to enjoy any during the festi-vals of Upolu.

The day before they left, Sébastien Zorn, Frascolin, Pinchinat, and Yvernès, accompanied this time by the professor of dance, charm, and good manners, went to take leave of the Marist missionaries. The good-byes were touching on both sides. They were the goodbyes of people who had known each other for a few days and would never see each other again. The old man blessed them and hugged them, and they left deeply moved.

The following day, December 23, Commodore Simcoë got underway at dawn, and Standard Island traveled in the middle of a procession of pirogues that would escort her to Savaii, the next island.

This island was separated from Upolu by a strait of only twenty to twenty-five miles. But since Opia Harbor was located on the northern shore, they had to sail along the coast all day before reaching the strait.

According to the governor's itinerary, they were not going to go around Savaii but would pass between it and Upolu in order to reach the Tonga Archipelago from the southwest. As a result, Standard Island advanced at a very moderate pace, as she did not want to enter the strait flanked by the two little islands of Apolinia and Manono during the night.

At dawn the next day, Commodore Simcoë maneuvered between these two islets. One of them, Apolinia, had no more than a hundred fifty inhabitants, and the other, Manono, a thousand. These natives had a well-deserved reputation for being the bravest and most honest Samoans in the entire archipelago.

From there, Savaii could be admired in all its splendor. Solid granite cliffs protected it from the attacks of a sea that the hurricanes, tornadoes, and cyclones of the winter season made even more threatening. This island was covered with thick forests dominated by an ancient volcano four thousand feet high. Sparkling villages were visible beneath a dome of gigantic palm trees. Savaii was watered by turbulent cascades and pitted with deep caverns from which the assaults from the sea escaped in violent echoes.

And if legends are to be believed, this island was the very cradle of the Polynesian races, whose eleven thousand natives were of the purest type. At that time its name was Savaïki, the famous Eden of the Maori gods.

Standard Island moved slowly away from it and lost sight of its last summits on the evening of December 24.

III

~~~~~~~~~~

Concert at the Court

ON DECEMBER 21, AFTER STOPPING at the Tropic of Capricorn, the sun, in its apparent movement, started to travel north again. It abandoned these regions to the bad weather of winter and brought summer back to the Northern Hemisphere.

Standard Island was only ten degrees away from this tropic. Sailing to the islands of Tonga Tabu, she would reach the extreme latitude set by her itinerary and would then start back on her northern route in the most favorable climatic conditions. In truth, she could not avoid a period of extreme heat when the sun would be in the zenith; but this heat would be tempered by the sea breeze and would subside as the sun distanced itself from the earth.

Between the Samoan Islands and the principal island of Tonga Tabu, there are eight degrees or about five hundred sixty miles. There was no reason to go fast. The self-propelled island cruised on a sea that was always serene and as calm as its atmosphere, which is hardly ever troubled by rare, sudden storms. The vessel needed to reach Tonga Tabu by the first days of January, to stop there for a week, and then head for the Fiji Islands. From there, Standard Island would steer back toward the New Hebrides, where she would deposit the Malay crew. Then, heading northeast, she would regain the latitude of Madeleine Bay, and her second voyage would come to an end.

Thus life went on in Milliard City without trouble. It was the typical existence of a big American or European city, in constant communication with the new continent by means of the steamers or the telegraphic cables, the usual visits among the families, the visible attempts at reconciliation between the two rival sections, the walks, the games, and the concerts of the quartet still in great demand with the music lovers.

When Christmas came, that holiday so dear to Protestants and Catholics alike, it was celebrated with great pomp at the churches, as well as in the palaces, the mansions, and the neighboring houses of the commercial quarters. This solemnity would render the island festive for the entire week starting on December 24 and ending January 1.

In the meantime, the Standard Island press, the *Starboard Chronicle* and the *New Herald*, kept their readers informed on local and international news. One particular item published simultaneously by both newspapers elicited a great number of comments.

Indeed, the December 26 issue informed the public that the king of Malécarlie had gone to the city hall, where he was granted an audience by the governor. What was the purpose of His Majesty's visit . . . ? What was its object . . . ? All sorts of rumors went around and they would soon have come to the wildest assumptions if the papers had not published specific information on the subject the following day.

The king of Malécarlie had asked for a position at the Standard Island Observatory and the highest administration had readily agreed to his request.

"Good gracious," exclaimed Pinchinat, "you have to live in Milliard City to witness such things . . . ! A monarch looking into a telescope and watching the stars in the sky . . . !"

"It's a star of the earth communicating with his brothers in the heavens . . . ," retorted Yvernès. The news was true and here is why His Majesty felt compelled to seek this position.

The king of Malécarlie had been a good king, and the princess, his wife, had been a good queen. They did all the good that enlightened liberal minds could do in one of the moderate-sized states of Europe. They did not claim their dynasty to be of divine origin, even if it was one of the oldest in Europe. The king had a solid knowledge of the sciences and he loved the arts, especially music. A learned man and a philosopher, he was not blind concerning the future of European monarchies. Consequently, he was always prepared to leave his kingdom as soon as his people no longer wanted him. Since he had no direct heir, he would do no harm to his family when the moment seemed right for him to abandon his throne and lay aside his crown.

This moment had come three years earlier. But there had been no revolution in the kingdom of Malécarlie, at least no bloody revolution. The contract had been broken by mutual agreement between His Majesty and his subjects. The king became simply a man, and his subjects became citizens. He left with no more ado than a traveler buying a ticket at the local railroad station and allowed one regime to be replaced by another.

Still robust at sixty, the king had a better constitution, perhaps, than the one his former kingdom was trying to acquire. But the queen's health was rather frail and required an environment with no sudden temperature changes. It was difficult to find such even climates anywhere except on Standard Island. Elsewhere you would have to wear yourself out pursuing beautiful weather across the latitudes. It thus appeared that Standard Island offered all the advantages one could desire, since the richest nabobs of the United States had made it their adopted city.

This is why, as soon as the self-propelled island was built, the king and queen of Malécarlie decided to go live in Milliard City. They received the authorization to do so as long as they agreed to live as common citizens without any particular distinctions or privileges. It was clear that Their Majesties did not desire a different life. A small house with a garden opening on the big park on the Starboard section of Thirty-Ninth Avenue was leased to them. That was where the two monarchs lived, keeping to themselves, taking absolutely no part in the disputes and intrigues of the rival sections, and satisfied with their modest existence. The king kept busy studying the stars, a subject that he always had been extremely interested in. The queen, a devout Catholic, lived an almost cloistered life, not even having the opportunity to do charity work, since there were no poor on this Jewel of the Pacific.

Such was the story of the former rulers of Malécarlie, a tale that the superintendent told our musicians. And he added that these sovereigns were the finest people one could meet, although they had relatively meager resources.

The quartet was very moved by this royal decline, accepted philosophically and with calm resignation. They felt a respectful sympathy toward the deposed monarchs. Rather than taking refuge in France, the country of exiled kings, Their Majesties had chosen Standard Island, like affluent people who choose Nice or Corfu, for reasons of health. Of course, they were not exiles, they had not been driven out of their kingdom, they could have stayed, they could return and reclaim their rights as citizens. But they did not consider doing this. They liked their peaceful existence and obeyed the laws and rules of the self-propelled island.

It was absolutely true that the king and queen of Malécarlie were not rich compared to the majority of the Milliardites, and especially considering the cost of living in Milliard City. What could one do with a yearly income of two hundred fifty thousand francs when it cost fifty thousand francs to lease a modest house? And the former monarchs were already not very wealthy compared to the emperors and kings of Europe, who themselves would not have cut much of a figure alongside the Goulds, the Vanderbilts, the Rothschilds, the Astors, the Makays, and the other gods of finance. Although their life was devoid of luxuries, and they bought only the bare necessities, they were still in a difficult situation. But the health of the queen was so much better on Standard Island that the king could not think of leaving. He wanted to increase his income by his work, and when a position became available at the observatory—a very highly paid position—he went to the governor to ask for it. Cyrus Bikerstaff, after consulting the high administration of Madeleine Bay by telegram, appointed the monarch to the post, and this is why the newspapers had announced that the king of Malécarlie had just become the astronomer of Standard Island.

What gossip this would have caused in any other country! Here they talked about it for two days and then forgot about it. It seemed entirely normal that a king would look for work in order to be able to continue his peaceful existence in Milliard City. The king was a scientist; they would benefit from his knowledge. This was all very honorable. If he discovered a new celestial body, planet, comet, or star, it would be named for him and take its rightful place among the mythological names that filled the official directories.

Walking through the park, Sébastien Zorn, Pinchinat, Yvernès, and Frascolin discussed the incident. That morning they had seen the king going to his office but they were not yet Americanized enough to accept this rather extraordinary situation. So they talked about it and Frasco-lin reported,

"I've heard that if the king had not been an excellent astronomer, he could have given music lessons."

"A king looking for work!" cried Pinchinat.

"That's right, and if you consider how much his students would have paid for his lessons . . ."

"Indeed, he is supposed to be a very good musician," remarked Yvernès.

"I am not surprised that he is crazy about music," retorted the cellist; "during our concerts we saw him standing at the door of the casino for want of money to pay for seats for the queen and for himself."

"Eh! fiddlers! I have an idea!" said Pinchinat.

"An idea from His Highness," retorted the cellist, "it must be a weird idea!"

"Weird or not, my dear old Sébastien," replied Pinchinat, "I am sure that you will approve it."

"Let's hear Pinchinat's idea," said Frascolin.

"It's to give a concert to Their Majesties, to them alone, in their living room. And to play for them the most beautiful pieces in our repertoire."

"Eh!" said Sébastien Zorn. "Your idea is not bad."

"Heavens! My head is full of ideas like that, and when I shake it . . ."

"It jingles like a bell!" added Yvernès.

"My dear Pinchinat," said Frascolin, "let's just make do with your proposal today. I am sure that we will make this good king and his good queen very happy."

"Tomorrow we will write them to ask for an audience," said Sébas-tien Zorn.

"Better than that!" answered Pinchinat. "Let's go to the king's house with our instruments this very evening, like a group of musicians com-ing to play an aubade."

"You mean a serenade," replied Yvernès, "since it will be in the evening."

"Yes, my exacting first violin, you're right. But let's not argue over words . . . ! Are we going . . . ?"

"Yes, let's go." This was truly an excellent idea. The king, who loved music, would of course be touched by the thoughtful attention of the French musicians and delighted to hear them play. So, at nightfall, the Concerting Quartet, carrying three violin cases and one cello case, left the casino and headed for Thirty-Ninth Avenue, located at the end of the Starboard section. The house was very simple. In front of it was a small courtyard with a green lawn. The outbuildings were on one side, the stables, which were not in use, on the other. The house itself had only two floors. There were steps that led to the first floor, and the second floor had a window and a sloping roof. To the left and the right, two magnificent elm trees shaded the double path leading to the garden. Beneath the trees of this garden, which was no larger than five acres, there was a lawn. This cottage could not be compared with the mansions of the Coverleys, the Tankerdons, and other notables of Milliard City. It was the retreat of a wise man who lived away from the world, a learned man, a philosopher. Abdalonymus, leaving the throne of the kings of Sidon, would have been satisfied with this abode.

The king had only one manservant and the queen but one chambermaid. An American cook completed the staff employed by these deposed monarchs, who had once been treated as equals by the emperors of the old continent.

Frascolin pressed an electric button. The manservant opened the gate. Frascolin explained that his comrades and himself, all French musicians, wished to pay homage to His Majesty and asked to be received.

The servant let them in, and they waited at the bottom of some steps. The servant returned almost instantly and informed them that the king would gladly see them. They were led into the foyer, where they left their instruments, and then into the parlor, which Their Majesties promptly entered.

That was the entire ceremony surrounding their reception.

The musicians bowed respectfully to the king and queen.

The queen was soberly dressed in dark clothes. The gray curls of her luxuriant hair, the only ornament on her head, lent great charm to her pale face and her melancholy eyes. She went to sit in an armchair near a window opening on the garden, beyond which the trees of the park could be seen.

The king stood, greeted his visitors, and invited them to explain what had brought them to his home, here in the farthest corner of Milliard City.

The four musicians felt moved in the presence of this monarch whose entire being was marked by undeniable dignity. Beneath almost black eyebrows, the king's eyes were lively; they had the penetrating look of a learned man. His white beard spread wide and silky on his chest. His charming smile tempered the serious aspect of his face and made him well liked by everyone who came in contact with him.

Frascolin started speaking, and his voice trembled a little:

"We thank Your Majesty," he said, "for granting this audience to musicians who wish to pay you their respects."

"The queen and I thank you, gentlemen, and we are touched by your visit. It seems that you brought a little of the fine atmosphere of your France to this island where we hope to spend our last years in peace. Gentlemen, you are not unknown to a man who, although he works in the sciences, passionately loves music, to which you have given such a good name in the artistic world. We know of your success in Europe and America. We joined in the applause that welcomed the Concerting Quartet to Standard Island, even if it was from afar. Thus we have only one regret, and it is not to have heard you yet as you should be heard."

The king invited his guests to sit down. Then he moved next to the fireplace; on the mantel sat a magnificent bust of the still-young queen by Franquetti.

To begin, Frascolin simply replied to the king's last statement.

"Your Majesty is correct," he said "and the regret you express is indeed justified by the kind of music that we play. Chamber music, these quartets of the masters of classical music, requires an intimacy that cannot exist among a large audience. Its needs the tranquil atmosphere of a sanctuary."

"Yes, gentlemen," said the queen, "this music should be listened to as you would listen to music from heaven, and it needs a sanctuary indeed."

"Then may the king and the queen allow us to transform their parlor into a sanctuary for one hour," said Yvernès, "and to be heard by Their Majesties alone . . . ?"

Even before Yvernès could finish his sentence, an excited look appeared on the sovereigns' faces.

"Gentlemen," answered the king, "you wish . . . you really had such a wonderful thought?"

"It was the object of our visit . . ."

"Ah!" said the king, extending a hand of friendship to them. "This is typical of French musicians, whose hearts are as big as their talent . . . ! I thank you in the name of the queen and in my own name, gentlemen . . . ! Nothing could please us more!"

And while the servant was asked to bring the instruments and arrange the parlor for this improvised concert, the king and the queen invited their guests to accompany them to the garden. There they talked about music as only artists could, in complete abandon.

The king expressed his enthusiasm for this art as a man completely enthralled by it and who understood all of its beauties. To the surprise of his guests, he showed a deep knowledge of the composers he would hear in a few moments . . . He extolled the naïve but inventive genius of Haydn. He reminded them of the words of one critic concerning Mendelssohn, the outstanding composer of chamber music, who expressed his ideas in the language of Beethoven . . . The king admired the exquisite sensitivity of Weber and his chivalrous mind that placed him in a category by himself . . . ! He called Beethoven the prince of instrumental music, whose symphonies possess a soul . . . who was able to put the creations of his genius on a par, in grandeur and worth, with the masterpieces of poetry, sculpture, and architecture. The king saw him as the sublime star that went out, during its last sunset, with the *Choral* Symphony, in which the voices of the instruments mix so intimately with the human voices!

"And yet he could not keep time when he danced!"

It is easy to imagine this ill-timed remark coming from old Pinchinat.

"That's right," answered the king with a smile, "and it proves, gentlemen, that the ear is not the essential organ for the musician. It is with his heart, only with his heart that he hears! And didn't Beethoven confirm this with the incomparable symphony I talked to you about, that he composed when his deafness did not allow him to perceive sounds anymore?"

After speaking of Haydn, Weber, Mendelssohn, and Beethoven, His Majesty spoke of Mozart with stirring eloquence.

"Ah! Gentlemen," he said, " my delight runs over! For so long now, I have had to refrain from baring my soul like this! You are the first artists to understand me since I arrived on Standard Island! Mozart . . . ! Mozart . . . ! One of your dramatic composers from the end of the nineteenth century, whom I consider the greatest, wrote admirable things about Mozart! I read his work, and nothing could erase it from my memory! He talked about the ease with which Mozart gave each note its special function of precision and intonation without disrupting the style or character of the musical phrase . . . He said that Mozart joined emotional truth and the perfection of plastic beauty . . . Isn't Mozart the only one who unlocked with such constant assurance the musical form of all feelings, of all nuances of passion and character, that is to say of everything that encompasses the human drama? Mozart is not a king—after all, what's a king worth today?" added His Majesty, shaking his head. "I'll say that he is a god since we still believe that God exists . . . ! He is the God of Music!"

What could not be translated, what could not be expressed, was the ardor with which His Majesty expressed his admiration. And when the queen and he came back to the parlor, where the musicians followed him, he picked up a booklet laying on the table. This booklet, which he had probably read over and over again, bore this title: *Don Juan by Mozart*. He opened it and read these few lines from the pen of the master who best understood and loved Mozart, the illustrious Gounod: "O Mozart! Divine Mozart! Only those who do not understand you do not adore you! You, constant truth! You, perfect beauty! You, inexhaustible charmer! You, always deep and clear! You, complete humanity and, at the same time, the simplicity of a child! You who felt everything and expressed everything in a musical sentence that has never been and will never be surpassed!"

Then Sébastien Zorn and his companions picked up their instruments and, with the glow of the electric bulb pouring soft lighting into the parlor, played the first piece that they had chosen for this concert.

It was the Second Quartet in A Minor, op. 13, of Mendelssohn, which brought infinite delight to the audience.

After this quartet, they performed the Third in C Major, op. 75, of Haydn, which is *The Austrian Hymn*, which they executed with incomparable mastery. Never had the performers come closer to perfection than in the privacy of the sanctuary where our musicians had only two dethroned monarchs to listen to them.

And when they finished this hymn that confirmed the genius of the composer, they played the Sixth Quartet in A-flat, op. 18, of Beethoven, that *Malinconia*, so infinitely sad and powerful that the eyes of Their Majesties filled with tears.

Then came the admirable Fugue in C Minor of Mozart, so perfect and so devoid of scholastic pedantry, and so natural that it seemed to flow like clear water or drift through the leaves like the breeze. Finally, they played one of the most admirable quartets by this divine composer, the Tenth in D Major, op. 35, thus ending an unforgettable evening, which was better than any that the nabobs of Milliard City had ever experienced.

And the French musicians did not tire of performing these admirable works since the king and queen did not tire of listening to them.

But at eleven o'clock, His Majesty said,

"We thank you, gentlemen, and our thanks come from the bottom of our hearts! Thanks to the perfection of your performance, we just experienced an artistic enjoyment that we will never forget! It made us feel so marvelous . . ."

"If the king wishes, we still could . . ." said Yvernès.

"Thank you, once again, gentlemen, thank you. We do not want to take advantage of your kindness! It is late, and also . . . tonight . . . I am on duty . . ."

This expression from the mouth of a king brought the musicians back to reality. In front of a monarch speaking like this to them, they felt almost embarrassed . . . They lowered their heads . . .

"Yes! Gentlemen," added the king in a lively tone, "I am the astronomer of the Standard Island Observatory . . . and," he added with emotion, "inspector of the stars . . . the shooting stars . . . ?"

IV

~~~~~~~~~~

British Ultimatum

DURING THIS LAST WEEK OF the year, devoted to the joys of Christmas, many invitations to dinners, evenings, and official receptions were sent out. A banquet offered by the governor to the principal residents of Milliard City and accepted by the Starboardite and Larboardite notables revealed a sort of softening between the two sections of the city. The Tankerdons and the Coverleys sat at the same table. On January 1 there would be an exchange of greeting cards between the mansion on Nineteenth Avenue and that on Fifteenth Avenue. Walter Tankerdon even received an invitation to one of Mrs. Coverley's concerts. The welcome extended to him by the lady of the house appeared to be a good sign. But this did not really mean that close ties had been established between the two parties. They were still a long way from that, even if Calistus Munbar, always brimming with enthusiasm, kept saying to anyone willing to listen, "It's done, my friends, it's done!"

Meanwhile, the self-propelled island continued her peaceful navigation toward the archipelago of Tonga Tabu. It seemed that nothing could hinder her travel when, during the night of December 31, a rather unexpected meteorological phenomenon occurred.

Between two and three o'clock in the morning, distant shots were heard. At first, the lookouts did not pay much attention to them. They did not think that it was a naval battle, unless it was between ships of those South American republics that were always at war. After all, why would Standard Island, an independent entity at peace with both worlds, have been worried?

However, these blasts coming from the west of the Pacific continued until dawn and could not be mistaken for the full and regular rumble of far-off artillery.

Commodore Simcoë, alerted by one of his officers, scrutinized the horizon from the top of the observatory tower. There was not the faintest glow on the large area of sea stretching beneath his eyes. However, the sky did not have its usual aspect. Reflections of flames colored it to the very zenith. The atmosphere appeared foggy although the weather was beautiful, and no sudden drop in the barometer indicated a change in the atmosphere.

At dawn, the early risers of Milliard City received a strange surprise. Not only did the blasts continue, but the air was mixed with a red and black mist, a sort of impalpable dust that started to fall like rain. It looked like a shower of sooty molecules. In a few moments, the streets of the city and the roofs of the houses were covered with particles whose shades of crimson, madder, light red, and scarlet mixed with black slag.

Everyone was outside except, of course, for Athanase Dorémus, who never got up before eleven after going to bed at eight the night before. The quartet had sprung out of bed and rushed to the observatory, where the commodore, his officers, his astronomers, and, as can be expected, the new royal employee were trying to comprehend the nature of this phenomenon.

"It's too bad," remarked Pinchinat, "that this red substance is not a liquid, and that this liquid is not a shower of Pomard or Château Lafitte!"

"Boozer!" answered Sébastien Zorn.

But what precisely could have been the cause of this phenomenon? There have been many instances of these showers of dust made of a mixture of silica, albumin, chromium, and iron oxide. At the beginning of the century, Calabria and the Abruzzo region were inundated by these rains, in which the superstitious insisted on seeing drops of blood while it was nothing more than cobalt chloride, as in Blankenberghe in 1819. Molecules of soot and coals from distant fires are sometimes carried over to other places. There were showers of soot in Fernambouc in 1820, yellow showers in Orléans in 1829, and in 1836, in the Low Pyrenees, there were showers of pollen from the pine trees in bloom.

Where could this dust mixed with scoriae have come from? The air seemed saturated with it as it fell in thick, reddish masses on Standard Island and the surrounding sea.

The king of Malécarlie was of the opinion that this substance came from a volcano in the islands to the west. His colleagues agreed with him. They picked up handfuls of the slag, which was warmer than the surrounding atmosphere and had not cooled during its passage through the skies. A very violent eruption would explain the irregular detonations that were still being heard. These regions were indeed sprinkled with craters, some still active, others extinct but capable of flaring up under certain subterranean conditions. There were even new volcanoes that a geological explosion occasionally brought up from the depths of the ocean, and the force of their projection was often extraordinary.

And indeed, was it not in the middle of this Tonga Archipelago that Standard Island was fast approaching that, a few years earlier, the Tufua Mountain had covered an area of forty square miles with its eruptions? The blasts of the volcano were heard for many hours as far as one hundred twenty-five miles away.

And in August 1883 the eruption of Krakatoa devastated the area of the isles of Java and Sumatra next to the Strait of the Sound, destroying entire villages, leaving numerous victims, causing earthquakes, dirtying the soil with compact mud, making the sea rise in incredible swells, polluting the atmosphere with sulfurous fumes, and putting ships in distress.

The Milliardites began to wonder if their self-propelled island was not risking danger of the same sort.

Commodore Simcoë was worried because the navigation threatened to become very difficult. After he gave the order to reduce speed, Standard Island advanced extremely slowly.

Fear gripped the Milliardite population. Was Sébastien Zorn's dire prediction concerning the ending of their campaign about to come true . . . ?

Around noon, they were in complete darkness. The people had left their houses, which would not withstand the pressure if the metal hulk of their island was lifted by Plutonian forces. The danger would be no less frightening if the sea went over the framework of the shore and flooded the countryside.

Governor Cyrus Bikerstaff and Commodore Simcoë went to the Prow Battery with a group of residents. Officers were sent to both harbors and ordered to stay put. The engineers were ready to send the self-propelled island on its way if it had to flee in the opposite direction. The problem was that the navigation became more and more difficult as it became darker and darker.

Around three o'clock in the afternoon, the islanders could hardly see ten feet in front of themselves. There was not the faintest bit of light, since the mass of cinders had absorbed the rays of the sun. What was most to fear was that Standard Island, overloaded with the weight of the slag fallen on its surface, could not keep its waterline above the ocean level.

Standard Island was not a ship that could be made lighter by jettisoning its merchandise or by dumping ballast . . . What could the inhabitants do but wait and put their trust in the strength of the vessel?

Evening came, or rather night, but they noticed it only by the hands on the clocks. It was totally dark. The electric moons could not be kept standing beneath the showers of scoriae. They had to lay them down. The artificial lighting of the houses and streets, which had been functioning all day, would be used as long as the problem lasted.

Night came, and the situation did not change. The detonations, however, appeared less frequent and less violent. The fury of the eruptions began to wane and the showers of cinder, carried away to the south by a strong breeze, began to die down.

The Milliardites, their minds a little more at ease, returned to their houses, hoping that the next day Standard Island would be back to normal and that she would simply require a long and thorough cleaning.

So much for that! What a sad first day of the year for the Jewel of the Pacific, and how close Milliard City had come to sharing the fate of Pompeii or Herculaneum! Although Standard Island was not located at the foot of Mount Vesuvius, her navigation still exposed her to many of those volcanoes that are so numerous in the submarine regions of the Pacific.

The governor, his adjuncts, and the council of notables decided to stay at the town hall. The lookouts on the tower watched for any change that might occur on the horizon or the zenith. In order to maintain her southwest course, the self-propelled island forged ahead, but at the reduced speed of two to three miles per hour. When daylight came back, or at least when darkness lifted, she would again sail toward the Tonga

Archipelago. There the Milliardites would learn on which island in this part of the ocean such a violent eruption had occurred.

In any case, it was obvious, as night progressed, that the disturbance was growing weaker.

Around three in the morning, there was another incident that brought new fear to the residents of Milliard City.

Standard Island suddenly received a shock whose impact was felt throughout the compartments of her hull. The jolt was not strong enough, though, to rattle the houses or put the engines out of commission. The propellers kept driving the vessel along. However, there was no doubt that the front of the island had struck something.

What happened . . . ? Had Standard Island hit bottom . . . ? Certainly not, since she continued to advance . . . Had she run up against a reef . . . ? In the midst of this darkness, had there been a collision with a ship that had not seen her lights while crossing her path . . . ? Had this collision caused great damage to the vessel, maybe not enough to jeopardize her safety, but enough to require major repairs at its next stop . . . ?

Cyrus Bikerstaff and Commodore Simcoë reached the Prow Battery with great difficulty, tramping over thick layers of scoriae and ashes.

There, the customs officers told them that a collision had indeed occurred. A large ship, a steamer sailing from west to east, was hit by the prow of Standard Island. The collision had caused no damage to the self-propelled island, but it may have been different for the steamer . . . The officers saw it only as they collided . . . They heard cries, but only for an instant . . . The officer in charge and his men ran to the front of the battery, but they did not see or hear anything else . . . Did the ship sink instantly . . . ? This assumption was, unfortunately, very plausible.

As for Standard Island, the engineers reported that the collision had not caused any serious damage. Her bulk was so massive that if she brushed past another vessel, even at a low speed, any powerful ship, even a first-class battleship, would risk being lost with all hands. This was probably what had happened.

As for the nationality of this ship, the officer in charge thought he heard orders being given in a rough voice, in those roars peculiar to the British navy. He could not, however, swear to it.

This was a very serious case that could entail very serious consequences. What would the United Kingdom say . . . ? An English ship is a part of England, and everyone knows that Great Britain does not let a portion of itself be amputated without retaliating . . . Standard Island could expect enormous protests and claims . . .

This is how the New Year started. On that day, Commodore Simcoë could not scan the sea before ten in the morning. The air was still blurry with vapors, although the wind got cooler and began to stop the shower of ashes. Finally, on the horizon, the sun broke through the fog.

Milliard City, its park, its countryside, its factories, and its harbors were in terrible shape! What a task the cleaning would be! But after all, this was the job of the maintenance department. It was just a question of time and money. And the Milliardites had plenty of both.

They put the most urgent matters first. The engineers went to the Prow Battery, on the side of the shore where the collision had taken place. The damage there was insignificant. The solid steel hull had not suffered anything worse than would a nail driven through a piece of wood, which, in this case, was the ship they collided with.

On the sea, there was no debris or wreckage. From the top of the observatory tower, the most powerful telescopes did not notice anything suspicious even if, since the collision, Standard Island had not moved more than two miles.

The Standard Island administration decided to pursue its investigations out of humanitarian concerns.

The governor consulted Commodore Simcoë. Orders were given to the engineers to stop the engines and to the electric launches of both harbors to scour the sea.

Their search of an area of five to six square miles did not produce any results. It appeared certain that the ship, punctured below its waterline, had sunk without leaving a trace.

Then Commodore Simcoë gave the order to sail on at normal speed. At noon, the observatory indicated that Standard Island was one hundred fifty miles southwest of Samoa.

Meanwhile, the lookouts were ordered to scan the horizon with extreme care.

Around five at night, they reported thick smoke from the southeast.

Was this smoke coming from the last eruptions of the volcano that had so deeply disturbed the area? This was hardly possible since the maps did not indicate any island or islet nearby. Had a new crater emerged from the oceanic depths . . . ?

No; it was indeed obvious that the smoke was coming closer to Standard Island.

An hour afterward, three ships were sighted advancing at high speed.

Half an hour later, the lookouts realized that these were battleships. One more hour passed until Standard Island could be absolutely sure of their nationality. It was the British squadron that, five weeks earlier, had refused to show its colors as it crossed Standard Island's bow.

At nightfall, these ships were not more than four miles away from the Prow Battery. Were they going to pass it and continue on their way? Probably not; the lookouts saw that their lights were not moving.

"These ships must want to communicate with us," said Commodore Simcoë to the governor.

"Let's wait and see," answered Cyrus Bikerstaff. But what would the governor have said to the commander of the squadron if this man had come to make a claim about the recent collision? Indeed, this may well have been his intention; perhaps the crew of the ship that was struck was able to get away in lifeboats and was picked up by another ship. In the end, the governor would still have to decide what to do when he learned what these ships wanted.

And they learned it in the early morning of the following day.

As the sun rose in the sky, the rear admiral's pennant flew from the mizzenmast of the lead cruiser, which was now two miles away and slowly approaching Larboard Harbor. A small boat was launched and set out for the port.

Fifteen minutes later, the governor received the following dispatch:

"Captain Turner of the cruiser *Herald*, chief of staff of Admiral Sir Edward Collinson, requests to be taken immediately to the governor of Standard Island."

As soon as Cyrus Bikerstaff was informed of the request, he authorized the harbor officer to let the Englishman on board and answered that he would be awaiting Captain Turner at the town hall.

After ten more minutes, a car put at the disposal of the chief of staff, who was accompanied by a lieutenant, brought the two Englishmen in front of the municipal palace.

The governor received them immediately in the room adjoining his office.

The customary greetings were exchanged, very stiffly from both sides.

Then, deliberately pronouncing his words as if he were reciting a work of literature, Captain Turner expressed himself in one single, endless sentence:

"I have the honor of bringing to the attention of His Excellency the governor of Standard Island at this moment situated at one hundred seventy-seven degrees, thirteen minutes east of the meridian of Greenwich and at sixteen degrees, fifty-four minutes south latitude, that during the night of December 31, the steamer *Glen* of Glasgow Harbor, of thirty-five hundred tons, loaded with a cargo of wheat, indigo, rice, and wine of considerable worth, was struck by Standard Island, belonging to the Standard Island Company Limited, whose headquarters are at Madeleine Bay, Southern California, even though the steamer had its running lights on, the white at its mizzenmast, the green on its starboard side, and the red on its port side, and that after disengaging itself after the collision, the steamer was met the next day, thirty-five miles away from the scene of the accident, as it was about to sink due to a hole in its port side, and that it did indeed sink after it fortunately succeeded in putting its captain, its officers, and its crew on board the *Herald*, cruiser of the first class of His British Majesty, navigating under the flag of Rear Admiral Sir Edward Collinson, who reported this fact to His Excellency Cyrus Bikerstaff, requesting him to acknowledge the responsibility of the Standard Island Company Limited under the warranty of the residents of the aforesaid Standard Island, to the owners of the aforesaid *Glen*, whose hull, machinery, and cargo were estimated at a value of one million two hundred thousand pounds sterling or six million dollars, which sum shall be delivered into the hands of the aforesaid Admiral Collinson, failing which it will be obtained by force, if needed, from the aforesaid Standard Island."

A sentence of several hundred words with a handful of commas and not a single period! But it said everything and allowed no way out! Would the governor accept the claim of Sir Edward Collinson as to the responsibility of the Standard Island Company and his estimate of one million two hundred thousand pounds sterling to be paid to the steamer *Glen* of Glasgow?

Cyrus Bikerstaff answered with the usual arguments concerning a collision:

The weather was very bad on account of a volcanic eruption that seemed to have occurred in the west. If the *Glen* had its lights on, so did Standard Island. Neither of them could have seen the other. So no one could be blamed. In a case like this, according to maritime law, each party must pay for its own repairs, so there was no ground for claim or blame.

The reply of Captain Turner:

His Excellency would probably have been right if this had been about two vessels sailing under ordinary conditions. The *Glen* was one of those, but it was obvious that Standard Island was not. She could not be regarded as a ship. She constituted a permanent danger to all vessels as she moved her enormous mass along maritime routes; she was rather an island, or at least an islet, or a reef that moved, never allowing her location to be definitively placed upon a map. England had constantly protested against this obstacle that had no permanent position on the ocean, and Standard Island would always be held responsible for accidents caused by her very nature, etc., etc.

It was evident that Captain Turner's arguments were logical. And Cyrus Bikerstaff felt that they were fair. But he could not make a decision on his own. The claim would be brought before the authorities and he could only acknowledge receiving it from Admiral Sir Edward Collinson. Fortunately, there had been no loss of lives.

"That was fortunate indeed," answered Captain Turner, "but there was the loss of a ship, and millions of dollars were swallowed up because of Standard Island. Will the governor then agree to pay Admiral Sir Edward Collinson the sum representing the total value of the *Glen* and its cargo?"

How could the governor have agreed to such a payment . . . ? After all, Standard Island herself should have been enough of a guarantee . . .

She was there in case damages needed to be paid for, if the courts ruled, after an expert assessment, that she had caused the accident and determined the amount of the loss.

"Is this your Excellency's last word . . . ?" asked Captain Turner.

"Yes, it is," answered Cyrus Bikerstaff, "because it is not for me to decide if the company was responsible or not."

There was a new exchange of salutations, even stiffer than before, between the governor and the English captain. The latter was brought back to Larboard Harbor by car. He then took his steam launch and returned to the *Herald*.

When the council of notables heard the negative response of Cyrus Bikerstaff, they approved it, as did the entire population of Standard Island. The Milliardites could not accept the insolent, imperious demands of His British Majesty's representatives.

This matter settled, Commodore Simcoë ordered the self-propelled island to proceed at full speed.

But if Admiral Collinson had persisted, could Standard Island have evaded his claim? His ships were much faster than Standard Island. And if he backed up his complaint with naval gunfire, would Standard Island have fired back? No doubt, the batteries of the island were powerful enough to vie with the Armstrongs possessed by the cruisers of the British fleet. But the area open to English fire was much larger . . . What would become of the women and children if it was impossible to find shelter . . . ? All the English rounds would reach their objectives, while the batteries of the prow and the stern would waste at least fifty percent of their shells on a narrow, moving target . . . !

So they had to wait and see what Admiral Sir Edward Collinson would decide.

They did not have to wait for long.

At nine forty-five, a blank shot was fired from the central turret of the *Herald* at the same time that the flag of the United Kingdom was hoisted to the top of the mast.

The council of notables immediately convened to discuss the situation in the meeting room of the town hall under the presidency of the governor and his assistants. This time, Jem Tankerdon and Nat Coverley shared the same opinion. These Americans, being practical men, did not think of trying to resist, a decision that could have brought a loss of people and possessions.

A second cannon blast was heard. This time, a shell whistled by, aimed at a point in the sea half a cable length from Standard Island. It exploded with incredible violence, raising enormous masses of water.

By order of the governor, Commodore Simcoë lowered the flag that had been raised in response to the *Herald*. Captain Turner returned to Larboard Harbor. There he received IOUs signed by Cyrus Bikerstaff and endorsed by the principal notables for the sum of one million two hundred thousand pounds sterling.

Three hours later, the last traces of smoke from the British fleet disappeared in the east, and Standard Island resumed her voyage toward the Tonga Archipelago.

V

~~~~~~~~

The Taboo at Tonga Tabu

"AND NEXT," ASKED YVERNÈS, "will we stop at the main islands of Tonga Tabu?"

"Yes, my dear friend!" answered Calistus Munbar. "You will have a chance to get acquainted with this archipelago that you may call the Hapai Archipelago, or even the Friends Archipelago, as it was christened by Captain Cook when he was so well received by the natives."

"And we will probably be better treated there than we were at the Cook Islands," said Pinchinat.

"Probably, yes."

"Will we visit all the islands of that group . . . ?" asked Frascolin.

"Of course not, there are at least a hundred fifty of them . . ."

"And later, where shall we go . . . ?" Yvernès wanted to know.

"Later we will go to the Fiji Islands, and then to the New Hebrides, and after we bring the Malays home, we will come back to Madeleine Bay, where our travels will end."

"Will Standard Island call at several places in the Tonga Archipelago?" asked Frascolin.

"Only at Vavao and Tonga Tabu," replied the superintendent, "but you will not find the true savages of your dreams at those islands either, my dear Pinchinat!"

"I guess there are none left, even in the western Pacific!" replied His Highness.

"Oh yes, there are still a considerable number of them in the New Hebrides and the Solomon Islands. But at Tonga, the subjects of King George I are rather civilized, and I will add that their women are charming. I would, however, warn you against marrying one of those ravishing Tongan beauties."

"And why is that . . . ?"

"Because marriages between foreigners and natives are usually unhappy. Incompatibility of character!"

"That's a shame!" cried Pinchinat. "Our old fiddler Zorn had planned to get himself a wife on Tonga Tabu."

"Me?" retorted the cellist, shrugging his shoulders. "Neither on Tonga Tabu nor anywhere else, you can be sure of that, you silly joker!"

"Our orchestra leader is a sage," retorted Pinchinat. "You see, my dear Calistus, but first, may I call you Eucalistus, since I find you so congenial . . . ?"

"You certainly may, Pinchinat!"

"Well, my dear Eucalistus, a man does not scrape away at the fiddle for forty years without becoming a philosopher, and philosophy teaches us that the only way to be happy in marriage is to stay unmarried."

On the morning of January 6, the heights of Vavao were sighted on the horizon. It was the most important island of the northern group. This group was very different from the other two, Hapai and Tonga Tabu, because of its volcanic origin. These three groups are located between the seventeenth and the twenty-second degrees south and the one hundred seventy-sixth and one hundred seventy-eighth degrees west. They cover a surface of nine hundred fifty square miles shared by one hundred fifty islands with a total population of sixty thousand people.

Tasman's ships sailed there in 1643 and those of Cook in 1773, during his second voyage across the Pacific in search of new lands. After the overthrow of the Finare-Finare dynasty and the creation of a federal state in 1797, a civil war decimated the population of the archipelago. It was then that Methodist missionaries arrived on these isles and brought much success to this ambitious sect of the Anglican religion. At the time our story unfolds, King George I was the undisputed monarch of this kingdom, which was a British protectorate until . . . These few dots at the end of the preceding sentence are there to leave the future open, as British protectors too often do for their overseas protégés.

The navigation was rather difficult among this maze of islands and islets planted with coconut trees, through which Standard Island had to tread her way in order to reach Nu Ofa, the capital of the Vavao Group.

Valvao was volcanic, and as such was subject to earthquakes. To deal with the problem, the natives had built houses without using a single nail. Braided rush and boards of coconut tree wood were used for the walls, and their oval roofs were supported by pillars or tree trunks. These dwellings were very fresh and clean. This sort of landscape particularly attracted the attention of our musicians, who were at the Prow Battery while Standard Island passed through the canals bordered by Kanaka villages. Here and there, a few European houses flew the flags of Germany and England.

But if part of this island was volcanic, it was not from its volcanoes that the horrible eruptions of scoriae and cinder were thrown onto the South Pacific. Unlike Standard Island, the Tongans had not been in the dark for forty-eight hours. The western breeze had sent the clouds of eruptive debris in the opposite direction. It was more than probable that the crater that spewed out these ashes belonged to an isolated island in the east, or to a recently formed volcano between Samoa and Tonga.

The stop of Standard Island at Vavao lasted only eight days. This island merited a visit even if, several years earlier, it had been devastated by a terrible cyclone that brought down the little church of the French Marists and destroyed many of the native dwellings. However, the countryside was still very attractive, with its numerous villages bordered by orange trees, its fertile plains, its fields of sugarcane and sweet potatoes, its clumps of banana, mulberry, breadfruit, and sandalwood trees. Pigs and poultry were the only domesticated animals, and the only birds were pigeons by the thousands and parrots with colorful feathers and a noisy cackle.

As for reptiles, there were just a few harmless snakes and pretty green lizards that could be mistaken for fallen leaves.

The superintendent had not exaggerated the beauty of the native type common to the Malay race of the various archipelagos of the Central Pacific. These were superb men, tall, if sometimes a bit stout, but with an admirable bearing and a noble appearance. They had a proud look in their eyes. Their skin color varied from dark copper to olive. The women were graceful and well proportioned. Their hands and feet were so delicately shaped and so small that they made the German and English women of the European colony green with envy. The main occupation of the native women was the making of mats, baskets, and material similar to Tahitian cloth, but their fingers were not deformed by the process. It was easy to spot the perfection of the Tongan beauty at first sight. Neither the odious trousers nor the ridiculous trains added to dresses had yet been adopted by the island's trendsetters. The men wore a simple loincloth or a belt; the women, who were at the same time charming and reserved, had on blouses and short skirts decorated with fine, dry bark. Both sexes kept their hair well groomed. The young women smartly piled their tresses high upon their heads, maintaining them there with a mesh of coconut fibers that they used as a comb.

But all these attributes were not enough for the grouchy Sébastien Zorn to put aside his prejudices. He would not get married, either in Vavao or Tonga Tabu or anywhere else under the sun.

It was always a pleasure, though, for Zorn and his comrades to land on these archipelagos. They certainly liked Standard Island, but they still enjoyed setting foot on terra firma. Real mountains, real countryside, real rivers allowed them to take a rest from artificial streams and fake shores. Only a Calistus Munbar would proclaim that the Jewel of the Pacific was superior to nature's creations.

Although the regular residence of King George was not on Vavao, he still owned a palace, or should we say a lovely abode, at Nu Ofa, where he often stayed. But it was on the island of Tonga Tabu that stood the real royal palace and the houses of the English residents.

Standard Island was to make her last stop almost exactly at the Tropic of Capricorn, the extreme point that she would reach during her voyage through the Southern Hemisphere.

For two entire days after their departure from Vavao, the Milliardites enjoyed an exciting voyage. They lost sight of one island only to catch a glimpse of another. These islands, all of volcanic origin, had emerged in a burst of Plutonian forces. In this respect, the southern group was very similar to the central one of Hapai. The maps of these parts of the ocean were very precisely detailed and allowed Commodore Simcoë to venture safely among the canals of this maze from Hapai to Tonga Tabu. Besides, he would not have been lacking in pilots if he had needed their services. A great number of boats sailed along the coasts of these islands. Most of them were schooners displaying the German colors and used for coastal navigation, while the big merchant ships served to export cotton, copra, coffee, and corn, the principal products of the archipelago. And not just the pilot boats would have been eager to come if Ethel Simcoë had needed them, but even the crews of the double-rigged pirogues that could carry up to two hundred men would have been happy to help. Yes! Hundreds of natives would have come running at the first call; what a godsend this would have been for them if the price of the piloting was based on the tonnage of Standard Island! Imagine, two hundred fifty-nine million tons! But Commodore Simcoë, being familiar with the area, did not require their help. He trusted only himself and the worth of his officers, who obeyed his orders with absolute precision.

Tonga Tabu was sighted on the morning of January 9, when Standard Island was only three to five miles away. This island was of very low height. It had not been formed by a geological explosion; it had not risen from the depths of the ocean like so many islands that were set in place after they came to take a breath at the surface of the ocean. Tonga Tabu had been built, little by little, by animalcules constructing their coral layers.

And what an enterprise this had been! A circumference of sixty-two miles, an area of two hundred seventy to three hundred square miles on which twenty thousand people were living!

Commodore Simcoë stopped in front of Maofuga Harbor. Communication was immediately established between the stationary island and the moving one, sister of the mythological Latone! What a difference between this archipelago and the Marquesas, the Tuamotus and the Society Archipelago! Here the English influence was dominant and, approving of this domination, King George I would not be eager to welcome these American Milliardites.

However, the quartet found a small French center in Maofuga. The bishop of Oceania resided there, but he was on a pastoral tour of the various islands at the time. The center also housed the Catholic mission, the nunnery, and the school for boys and girls. No need to say that the Parisians were warmly received by their countrymen. The director of the mission offered to lodge them, so they did not have to stay at the

"House for Foreign Visitors." Their excursions would bring them to two other important places: Nakualofa, the capital of King George's states, and the village of Mua, with its four hundred residents being Catholic.

When Tasman discovered Tonga Tabu, he called it Amsterdam; this name cannot really be justified by the houses made of pandanus leaves and coconut fibers. There are indeed many European-style dwellings, but its indigenous name fits this island much better.

Maofuga Harbor was on the northern coast. If Standard Island had stopped a few more miles to the west, Nakualofa, with its royal palace and its gardens, would have been displayed in front of the Milliardites. If, on the other hand, Commodore Simcoë had headed farther east, he would have encountered a bay that cut rather deeply into the shore and at the rear of which the village of Mua stood. But he did not do any of this because his vessel would have risked running aground among the hundreds of islets whose passages were only wide enough for medium-size boats. So the self-propelled island had to remain in front of Maofuga during her entire stop.

A small group of Milliardites went ashore at this port, but only a few wished to venture into the interior of the island. It was a charming place, though, and it deserved the praise that Elisée Reclus had showered it with. It is true that the temperature was very high and the weather stormy. There were indeed extremely heavy rains that could dampen the enthusiasm of the travelers. You had to have tourist fever to want to explore the interior. This was, however, what Frascolin, Pinchinat, and Yvernès did. As for the cellist, it was impossible to convince him to leave his comfortable room in the casino just before nightfall when the sea breeze was cooling the shores of Maofuga. The superintendent himself apologized for not joining the three enthusiasts.

"I would melt along the way!" he told them.

"Well, we would bring you back in a bottle!" answered His Highness.

This engaging perspective could not convince Calistus Munbar, who preferred to maintain his solid state.

Luckily for the Milliardites, the sun had already been moving toward the Northern Hemisphere for the past three weeks. Standard Island would therefore be able to stay at a distance from this white-hot furnace and enjoy a normal temperature.

Thus, on the following day, the three friends left Maofuga at dawn and walked toward the capital of the island. It was hot indeed but the heat was bearable beneath the shade of the coconut trees, the *leki-lekis*, and the *toui-touis* or candle trees, the cocas whose red and black fruits formed clusters of dazzling precious stones.

Around noon, the capital finally appeared in all its floral splendor, an expression that described it perfectly at this time of the year. The king's palace seemed to emerge from a gigantic bouquet of greenery. There was a striking contrast between the huts of the natives, all in bloom, and the very British houses that belonged to the Protestant missionaries. But the influence of these Wesleyan ministers had been considerable and the Tongans, after massacring a certain number of them, adopted their beliefs, although they never totally renounced the practices of their Kanaka religion. For them, the high priest was superior to the king. In the teachings of their bizarre cosmogony, both good and bad spirits played important roles. Christianity would not easily replace the taboos that they still revered, and when they wished to break them, it could not be done without expiatory ceremonies in which human lives were sometimes sacrificed.

Let us mention that, according to the accounts of certain explorers—and especially in those of Aylie Marin in his travels of 1882—Nakualofa was still just a half-civilized area.

Frascolin, Pinchinat, and Yvernès did not have the slightest desire to throw themselves at King George's feet. This last expression should not be taken in its metaphorical sense since it was the custom to kiss the feet of this monarch. And our Parisians were very happy with their decision when they caught a glimpse of the *tui*, as His Majesty was called, wearing a sort of white shirt and a short skirt made of local cloth tied around his waist. The kissing of his feet would certainly have been one of the most unpleasant memories of their voyage.

"You can see," remarked Pinchinat, "that there are not many waterways in this country."

Indeed, in Tonga Tabu and Vavao, as in the other islands of the archipelago, the maps showed no streams or lagoons. Rainwater collected in cisterns was all that nature had to offer the natives, and the subjects of George I used it as sparingly, as did their monarch.

At the end of the day, the three tourists returned exhausted to the port of Maofuga. They were happy to regain their apartment in the casino of Standard Island. To the skeptical Sébastien Zorn they asserted that their excursion had been most interesting, but even the poetic incitements of Yvernès did not convince the cellist to accompany them to the village of Mua the next day.

The trip promised to be long and tiring. The excursionists could easily have avoided this toil by using one of the electric launches that Cyrus Bikerstaff would have gladly put at their disposal. But they thought that the interior of this strange land was worth exploring, so they started on foot for the Bay of Mua, following the coral beach bordered by islets that seemed to contain all the coconut trees of Oceania.

In the late afternoon they arrived at Mua, where they would spend the night. There they found an ideal place for Frenchmen to stay: the residence of the Catholic missionaries. The father superior welcomed his guests with a genuine pleasure that reminded them of the warm reception by the Marists in Samoa. What a wonderful evening! What interesting conversations they had concerning France rather than the Tongan colony. It was not without a certain nostalgia that these religious men reflected upon their native country so far away! But their regrets were compensated by the good they did in these islands. It was gratifying to see themselves respected by all these people whom they had shielded from the influence of the Anglican pastors and converted to the Catholic faith. Their success was such that the Methodists had to create a sort of annex to the village of Mua in order to provide for the Wesleyan preachers.

The father superior proudly showed his guests the buildings of the mission, the house that had been built free of charge by the natives of Mua, and the beautiful little church, a creation of Tongan architects that their French counterparts would not have disavowed.

During the evening, they strolled around the village and walked to the ancient tombs of Tui Tonga, where shale and coral mingled in a charming primitive art. They even visited an antique plantation of *meas* and banyans, or monstrous fig trees, with their roots intertwining like snakes and whose circumference sometimes exceeds two hundred feet. Frascolin measured them and, after recording their girth in his notebook, asked the father superior to confirm in writing that his figures were correct. How could anyone doubt, after this, that such a phenomenal tree exists?

After a good supper and an excellent night spent in the most comfortable bedrooms of the mission, the three Parisians were served a satisfying breakfast and bid hearty farewells to the missionaries of Mua. They were back on Standard Island as the bells in the town hall's belfry struck five o'clock. This time our three travelers did not need metaphorical amplifications to convince Sébastien Zorn that their trip would leave them with unforgettable memories.

The next day Cyrus Bikerstaff was visited by Captain Sarol. The object of his visit:

A certain number of Malays—about a hundred—had been recruited in the New Hebrides and brought to Tonga Tabu to clear land. Such recruiting had been indispensable because of the nonchalance, one could even say the laziness, of the native Tongans, who lived from day to day. The Malays had recently completed their work and were waiting for the first opportunity to return to their archipelago. Would the governor allow them passage on Standard Island? This was the request that Captain Sarol came to make. Five or six weeks later, Standard Island would arrive in Erromango and the transportation of these natives would cost the municipality of Standard Island very little. It would not have been generous to refuse these good people a service that was so easy to give. Thus the governor gave the authorization and was thanked by Captain Sarol and the Marists of Tonga Tabu, who had recruited the Malays.

Who would have suspected that Captain Sarol was in fact gathering accomplices, that the New Hebrideans would help him when he needed it, and that he should congratulate himself for having met them on Tonga Tabu and brought them to Standard Island?

But this was the last day the Milliardites would spend on the archipelago. Their departure was set for the following day.

In the afternoon they were going to attend one of those half-civil, half-religious festivities in which the natives participate with such extraordinary enthusiasm.

The program of those entertainments, which the Tongans are as fond of as their counterparts in Samoa and the Marquesas, included various dance numbers. Since this was of interest to our Parisians, they went ashore around three o'clock.

The superintendent accompanied them, and this time Athanase Dorémus was happy to join them. The presence of a professor of dance and charm was certainly suited to this sort of entertainment. Sébastien Zorn decided to follow his comrades; he probably wanted to hear Tongan music rather than watch the choreographic frolics of the populace.

When they arrived on site, the festivities were in full swing. The kava liquor extracted from the dry roots of the pepper plants was making the rounds in gourds and was running down the throats of a hundred dancers, men and women, young men and girls, the latter adorned with the long hair that they must wear untied until their wedding day.

The orchestra was very simple. Their instruments were flutes called *fanghu fanghu* and a dozen *nafas*, or drums, on which they pounded vigorously and "even in time," as Pinchinat remarked.

Evidently, the very proper Athanase Dorémus could feel only the utmost contempt for dances that were not quadrilles, polkas, mazurkas, or waltzes from the French school. Therefore he did not refrain from shrugging his shoulders, while Yvernès, for his part, found these dances quite original.

First the natives executed seated dances that consisted of simple postures, gestures, pantomimes, and a swinging of the body to a slow, sad rhythm that produced a strange effect.

After this swinging came the standing dances in which the Tongans abandon themselves to the full passion of their temperament, now making graceful passes, then showing the fury of the warrior on the warpath.

The quartet watched this spectacle as artists, wondering what these natives would do if they were aroused by the intoxicating music of Parisian ballrooms.

And then Pinchinat, it was his idea indeed, proposed to his comrades to send for their instruments in the casino and give these ballet dancers the most boisterous six-eights and the most awesome two-fours of Lecoq, Audran, and Offenbach.

His proposal was accepted and Calistus Munbar thought the effect produced would be fantastic.

Half an hour later, the instruments having arrived, the ball began.

The natives were extremely surprised but extremely pleased when they heard the cello and the three violins playing this ultra-French music with the utmost enthusiasm. They were deeply moved by this sort of music. It has long been recognized that popular dances are instinctive and learned without lessons, no matter what Athanase Dorémus may have thought. The Tongans, men as well as women, rivaled with each other, doing splits, swinging their hips, and pirouetting when Sébastien Zorn, Yvernès, Frascolin, and Pinchinat launched into the boisterous rhythms of *Orpheus in the Underworld*. The superintendent himself was overwhelmed and engaged in a frenzied quadrille, while Athanase Doré-mus buried his face in his hands in front of such horrors. At the height of this cacophony, mixed with the nasal sound of flutes and the sono-rous beat of drums, the fury of the dancers reached an intensity beyond control, and one wonders where it would have ended if an incident had not occurred that put a stop to this diabolical revelry.

A Tongan, a big, strong man, marveling at the sounds that the cel-list drew from his instrument, hurled himself upon the cello, grabbed it, took it away, and fled, screaming,

"Taboo . . . taboo . . ."

So the cello was taboo! Nobody could touch it without committing sacrilege! The high priest, King George, the dignitaries of his court, and the entire population would revolt if this sacred custom was violated . . .

But Sébastien Zorn was not concerned by this. He loved his cello, a masterpiece constructed by Gand and Bernardel. He ran after the thief. His comrades followed immediately. The natives started to run too. It was a general exodus.

But the Tongan ran so quickly that they had to abandon their pursuit. In a few minutes, he was far away . . . very far away!

Worn out, Sébastien Zorn and the others returned toward Calis-tus Munbar, who was still out of breath. To say that the cellist was in a state of indescribable furor would hardly be enough. He was foam-ing with rage, he was choking! Taboo or not, his instrument had to be returned to him! Even if Standard Island had to declare war to Tonga Tabu—had wars not begun for less serious causes?—the cello had to be restored to its owner.

Fortunately, the island authorities intervened. One hour later, they apprehended the native and forced him to return the instrument to its owner. But the restitution did not occur without trouble, and they came close to the point when an ultimatum from the governor would perhaps have aroused the religious passions of the entire archipelago concerning the question of taboo.

The breaking of the taboo had to be done in the proper fashion, according to the *fata* cult. Following custom, a considerable number of pigs were slaughtered and braised in a hole filled with hot stones, yams, taros, and the fruit of the *macore*, and then they were eaten, to the extreme satisfaction of Tongan stomachs.

As for the cello, which had been somewhat mistreated in the scuffle, Sébastien Zorn simply had to tune it up, after making sure that the native incantations had not made it lose any of its positive attributes.

VI

~~~~~~~~~~

A Collection of Wild Animals

LEAVING TONGA TABU, STANDARD ISLAND headed northwest toward the Fiji Archipelago. She started to sail away from the tropics, following the sun, which was making its way to the equator. She did not need to hurry. Only six hundred miles separated the floating island from the Fiji Group, so Commodore Simcoë kept her at a slow speed.

The breeze was variable, but the winds were unimportant to this powerful vessel. If violent storms sometimes occurred suddenly at the limit of the twenty-third parallel, the Jewel of the Pacific did not even think of worrying. The electricity saturating the atmosphere was absorbed by the numerous rods protecting the buildings and houses. As for rains, even torrential ones brought on by the stormy clouds were more than welcome. The park and the countryside became verdant under these heavy showers that were, in fact, rare. Thus life went on in the most pleasant way, amid parties, concerts, and receptions. Contacts between the two sections were frequent and it looked as if, from now on, nothing could threaten the security of the future.

Cyrus Bikerstaff had no reason to regret giving passage to the New Hebrideans taken on board at Captain Sarol's request. These natives tried to make themselves useful. They did farm work, as they had done in the Tongan countryside. Sarol and his Malays hardly left them during the day, and at nightfall they returned to the two harbors, where the authorities had assigned them quarters. There were no complaints against them. Maybe this was the right moment to try and convert these good people. They had not yet adopted the Christian beliefs; in fact, a large segment of the New Hebrides population was against those beliefs in spite of the efforts of the Anglican and Catholic missionaries. The clergy of Standard Island had thought of taking advantage of this opportunity, but the governor had refused to authorize any attempts of this nature.

These New Hebrideans, whose ages varied between twenty-four and forty years, were of average height. They had a darker complexion than the Malays and were of a less pleasing type than the Tongan and Samoan natives, but they were extremely resilient. They carefully kept the little money they had earned working for the Marists of Tonga Tabu and did not even think of spending it on alcoholic drinks, which would not have been readily sold to them anyway. Moreover, since they had no expenses, they were probably happier than they had ever been in their primitive archipelago.

And yet, because of Captain Sarol, these natives and their New Hebridean countrymen would become accomplices in a destructive plot that would soon be put into action. Then all their natural ferocity would reappear. Were they not, after all, the descendants of the murderers who gave such a fearsome reputation to the people of this part of the Pacific?

In the meantime, the Milliardites went on with their day-to-day lives, thinking that nothing could compromise their existences, where everything was so logically anticipated and so wisely organized. The quartet still reaped success upon success. People never tired of listening to them and applauding them as they interpreted the entire works of Mozart, Beethoven, Haydn, and Mendelssohn. In addition to the regular concerts at the casino, Mrs. Coverley held musical evenings that were very well attended. The king and queen of Malécarlie honored them several times with their presence. The Tankerdons had not yet paid a visit to the Fifteenth Avenue mansion, but Walter had become a regular at its concerts. Everyone believed that his marriage with Miss Dy would definitely occur in the near future. People talked about it openly in the Starboardite and Larboardite parlors. They even named the possible witnesses of the future engaged couple. The only thing missing was the authorization by the two heads of family. If only something would happen that would force Jem Tankerdon and Nat Coverley to give their assent . . .

This impatiently expected occurrence would not be long in coming. But it would bring a peril that would gravely threaten the very safety of Standard Island.

On the afternoon of January 16, about midway between Tonga and

Fiji, a ship was sighted to the southeast. It seemed to be headed for Starboard Harbor and looked like a steamer of between seven and eight hundred tons. There was no flag flying from its mast and it did not show its colors, even when it was within a mile of Standard Island.

What was the nationality of this steamer? The lookouts at the observatory could not identify its shape. Since it did not even honor the detested Standard Island with a salute, it was probably an English vessel.

Anyway, the said ship did not try to reach one of the harbors. It seemed anxious to go on its way and would probably soon be out of sight.

Night came, a very dark and moonless night. The sky was covered with high clouds that looked like the fluffy cloth that absorbs light but does not let its rays come through. There was no wind. The water and the air were absolutely calm. There was deep silence and total darkness.

Around eleven o'clock, the weather changed. A storm was coming. Streaks of lightning cut across the sky until past midnight; rumblings of thunder were heard, but not a drop of rain fell.

Perhaps these rumblings from some distant storm kept the customs officers on duty at the Prow Battery from hearing the bizarre whistles and howls disturbing this part of the shore of the island. These were not bolts of lightning or the crash of thunder. This strange phenomenon, whatever its cause, occurred only between two and three in the morning.

The following day at dawn, troubling news poured into the outer parts of the city. The guards watching the flocks grazing in the meadows had suddenly become panic-stricken and ran in every direction, some toward the harbors, others toward the gates of Milliard City.

But there had been another, much more serious incident: a number of sheep, about fifty of them, had been devoured during the night, and their bloody remains were scattered around the Prow Battery. Dozens of cows, does, and deer that were kept in the enclosed meadows of the park, and about twenty horses, had suffered the same fate . . .

These animals had obviously been attacked by wild beasts . . . What sort of wild beasts . . . ? Lions, tigers, panthers, hyenas . . . ? This was unthinkable. Had a single one of these carnivores ever been seen on Standard Island . . . ? Could they possibly have come from the sea . . . ? Besides, was the Jewel of the Pacific located near India, Africa, or Malaysia, whose fauna possessed this sort of ferocious beasts . . . ?

No! Standard Island was not near the mouth of the Amazon or the Nile, and yet, around seven in the morning, two women found in the town hall square had been pursued by an enormous alligator that, after reaching the banks of the Serpentine River, had disappeared into the water. At the same time, the shaking of the grass alongside the river betrayed the presence of other saurian creatures wriggling through the water.

Imagine the effect of this incredible news! One hour later, the lookouts caught sight of several pairs of tigers, lions, and panthers leaping through the countryside; sheep that were fleeing toward the Prow Battery were killed by two enormous tigers. Domestic animals came running from every direction, terrified by the roaring of the beasts. Workers who had been called to the fields at dawn were also running. The first streetcar for Larboard Harbor had just enough time to take shelter in its garage. Three lions had chased after it and had come within a hundred feet of it.

It was evident that Standard Island had been invaded by packs of big cats that would soon take over Milliard City unless serious precautionary measures were taken immediately.

It was Athanase Dorémus who informed our musicians of the situation. The professor of charm and good manners, who had gone out earlier than usual, did not dare to return to his house. He took refuge in the casino, from which no human power could extract him.

"Come on . . . ! Your lions and tigers are nothing but rumors," cried Pinchinat, "and your alligators are simply jokes!"

But the evidence had to be accepted. The municipality gave orders to close the gates of the city and to refuse entry to the two harbors and the customshouses. At the same time, the streetcar service was stopped and it was forbidden to walk through the park or the countryside until all the dangers from this inexplicable invasion were eliminated.

And at the very moment when the agents closed the end of First Avenue on the side of the observatory square, a pair of tigers leaped from fifty paces away, with fiery eyes and bloody mouths. A few seconds later, these ferocious animals would have been inside the gates.

On the town hall side the same precautions were taken, and Milliard City no longer had to fear an attack.

What an event this was, what fodder for the papers, what great news items for the *Starboard Chronicle*, the *New Herald*, and the other Standard Island dailies.

But in truth, the terror was at its peak. The mansions and houses were securely locked up. The buildings in the commercial quarters closed their shutters. Not a single door stayed open. Alarmed faces appeared at second-floor windows. In the streets, only military units under the command of Colonel Stewart, and police detachments under the orders of their officers, could be seen.

Cyrus Bikerstaff and his deputies, Barthelemy Ruge and Hubley Harcourt, who had rushed to the government building at the first warning, settled into the administration office. Through the telegraphs of both ports, the batteries, and the shore posts, the municipality received the most alarming news. There were wild cats everywhere . . . hundreds of them . . . said the telegrams; fear may have added a zero to many to these numbers, but it was certain that lions, tigers, panthers, and even caimans were running all over the countryside.

What had happened, then . . . ? Had a menagerie broken out of its cages and taken refuge on Standard Island . . . ? But where would this menagerie have come from . . . ? What ship might have brought it . . . ? Was it the steamer they had seen the previous day . . . ? And if it was, what had become of this ship . . . ? Did it draw alongside Standard Island's shore at night . . . ? Were these wild cats able to land on the lower part of the coast near the mouth of the Serpentine River, after swimming away from the steamer . . . ? And did the vessel sink after that . . . ? And yet, as far as the lookouts could see, as far as Commodore Simcoë's telescope could scan the waters, no debris was floating on the surface of the sea, and Standard Island had hardly moved since the previous day . . . ! Moreover, if the ship had sunk, would its crew not have sought refuge on Standard Island, since the carnivores were able to do so . . . ?

The telephone of the town hall questioned the various posts about this, and the various posts answered that there had been no collision or shipwreck. This could not have eluded the guards on duty, even on a dark night. Evidently, of all the speculations, this one was the least acceptable.

"It's a mystery . . . a mystery . . . !" Yvernès kept repeating.

He and his comrades were gathered at the casino, where Athanase

Dorémus was going to share their breakfast and maybe, if he had to, their lunch and their six o'clock dinner.

"Well," said Pinchinat, nibbling on the chocolate newspaper that he dunked into his steaming coffee, "I give up . . . Whatever this means, Mr. Dorémus, let's eat before we are eaten ourselves . . ."

"Who knows . . . ?" replied Sébastien Zorn. "And by lions, tigers, or cannibals, what difference does it make . . . ?"

"I would prefer cannibals . . . !" answered His Highness. "To each his own, right . . . ?"

He was laughing, this perpetual joker, but the professor of charm and good manners did not laugh. He was scared to death and certainly did not feel like playing games.

At eight in the morning, the council of notables, summoned to the town hall, did not hesitate to answer the call of the governor. There was no one in the avenues and the streets, except the squads of militia and the police going to their assigned locations.

The council, presided over by Cyrus Bikerstaff, immediately began its deliberations.

"Gentlemen," said the governor, "you all know the cause of the well-justified panic that has taken hold of the population of Standard Island. Last night, our island was invaded by a pack of carnivores and saurians. The most urgent thing to do is to destroy these animals, and, no doubt, we will accomplish this. But our constituents will have to accept the measures that we were forced to take. Although traffic is still allowed through Milliard City, whose gates have been closed, it is forbidden to enter the park and the countryside. Consequently, until the ban is lifted, nobody can go from the city to the two harbors or the Prow or Stern Batteries."

Once these measures were approved, the council began to discuss what means to use to destroy the fearful animals terrorizing Standard Island.

"Our militia and our sailors," the governor continued, "are going to organize battues in the various areas of the island. We ask those of you who are experienced hunters to join them, to direct their moves, and to try to avoid, as much as possible, any real catastrophe . . ."

"I hunted in India and in America for years," said Jem Tankerdon, "so I am no novice. I am ready to help, and my eldest son will come with me."

"We thank the honorable Mr. Jem Tankerdon," answered Cyrus Bikerstaff, "and for my part, I will follow his example. At the same time as Colonel Stewart's militia, a squad of sailors will work under the command of Commodore Simcoë, and their ranks are open to you, gentlemen!"

Nat Coverley proposed his services just as Jem Tankerdon had, and, in the end, all the notables who were still young enough hastened to offer their aid. Rapid-firing and far-reaching arms were plentiful in Milliard City. There was no doubt, then, that Standard Island, thanks to everyone's dedication and courage, would soon be rid of this fearsome scourge. But, as Cyrus Bikerstaff repeated, the essential was not to incur any fatalities.

"As for these wild beasts, whose number we cannot predict, they must be destroyed as soon as possible. If we allow them to adapt to the environment and multiply, we will jeopardize the security of our island."

"There are probably not that many . . . ," remarked one of the notables.

"Indeed, they could only come from a ship transporting a menagerie," answered the governor, "a vessel coming from India, the Philippines, or the Sunda Islands and going to some business in Hamburg, where these animals are often sold."

That was indeed the location of the main market for wild animals, whose going prices reached twelve thousand francs for elephants, twenty-seven thousand for giraffes, twenty-five thousand for hippopotamuses, five thousand for lions, four thousand for tigers, and two thousand for jaguars; rather interesting prices, and ones that were on the rise, while the value of snakes was going down. And when a council member observed that the menagerie at hand may have included a few snakes as well, the governor replied that no one had reported any reptiles. Besides, even if lions and alligators had been able to swim their way to the mouth of the Serpentine River, snakes could not have done it.

Cyrus Bikerstaff went on, saying,

"Therefore, I believe that we don't have to fear the presence of boas, rattlers, cobras, vipers, or other members of this species. But let's not waste time, gentlemen, and before looking for the cause of this invasion by ferocious animals, let's destroy them. They are here, but they must not remain here."

Nothing could have been wiser or better put. The meeting of the notables was about to break up, in order for them to take part in the battues with the help of Standard Island's most skillful hunters, when Hubley Harcourt asked for permission to make an observation.

They granted it to him, and here is what the honorable deputy felt was his duty to tell the council:

"Gentlemen, I am not trying to postpone the work we have decided on. Our most urgent task is to begin the hunt. However, allow me to share with you an idea that came to me. Maybe it would furnish a very plausible explanation for the presence of these wild beasts on Standard Island."

Hubley Harcourt belonged to an old family from the West Indies that had been Americanized, having settled in Louisiana. He was highly respected in Milliard City. He had a very serious mind, was extremely reserved, never spoke without thinking, and used his words sparingly. Everyone valued his opinion. Therefore, the governor invited him to speak his piece, and he did so with impeccable logic:

"Honorable gentlemen, a ship was spotted by our lookouts yesterday afternoon. This ship did not reveal its nationality, probably because it did not want it to be known. And, in my opinion, there is no doubt that this ship was transporting a cargo of animals . . ."

"That is quite evident," responded Nat Coverley.

"Well, gentlemen, if some of you believe that the invasion of Standard Island was due to an accident at sea . . . I, for one, do not believe it!"

"But then," cried Jem Tankerdon, who thought he was beginning to see the light through Hubley Harcourt's words, "would it have been willingly . . . deliberately . . . with premeditation . . . ?"

"Oh!" exclaimed the council.

"I am convinced of this," asserted the deputy in a strong voice, "and this plot can only be the work of our eternal enemy, this John Bull who would use any means to destroy Standard Island."

"Oh!" went the council again.

"Having no right to demand that our island be destroyed, they wanted to make her uninhabitable. That is why this collection of jaguars, tigers, panthers, and alligators was thrown on our island, at night, by the steamer!"

"Oh!" went the council for the third time.

But if at first their "oh" was doubtful, it had now become assertive.

Yes, it must have been vengeance by these dastardly English, who would go to any end to maintain their maritime supremacy! Yes, this vessel had been hired to perform this criminal act; then, its attack perpetrated, it disappeared. Yes, the government of the United Kingdom would not hesitate to sacrifice a few thousand pounds in order to render Standard Island uninhabitable for its people.

And Hubley Harcourt added,

"If I came to this conclusion, if my suspicions were changed into certitudes, it is because I remembered a similar incident, a scheme carried out in almost the same way, which England was never able to wash its hands of."

"And yet, you'd think they'd have enough water!" said one of the notables.

"But salt water does not really wash!" answered another.

"No more than the ocean could have washed the blood from the hand of Lady Macbeth!" cried a third. And these respectable councillors talked this way even before Hubley Harcourt told them about the incident he was alluding to:

"Honorable gentlemen," he continued, "when England was forced to abandon the West Indies to France, it wanted to leave a trace of its passage, and what a trace it left! Until then, there had never been a single snake on Guadeloupe or Martinique and, after the departure of the Anglo-Saxon colony, Martinique was infested with them. It was John Bull's vengeance! Before clearing out, they had released hundreds of reptiles on the land they lost, and since then, these ugly animals have multiplied ad infinitum and caused great damage to the French colonists!"

This accusation against England, which was never refuted, made Hubley Harcourt's explanation very plausible. But should we believe that John Bull had wanted to render the self-propelled island uninhabitable, and even that he had tried to do the same thing to the French West Indies . . . ? None of these facts was ever proven. However, the Milliardite population accepted them as true.

"Well," exclaimed Jem Tankerdon, "if the French did not succeed in ridding Martinique of the vipers that the English had left there in their place, the Milliardites . . ."

Here a thunder of hurrahs broke out at the comparison concocted by our fiery fellow.

". . . will succeed in ridding Standard Island of the wildcats that England set loose on their land."

There was a second round of applause that stopped only to start again, more loudly, after Jem Tankerdon added,

"To our posts, gentlemen, and let us not forget while we are tracking down these lions, jaguars, tigers, and caimans, that it is the English whom we are truly hunting!"

On that note, the meeting broke up.

One hour later, when the principal newspapers published a word-for-word account of this meeting, when people learned whose hands had opened the cages of this floating menagerie, when they read who was responsible for the invasion by this multitude of wild animals, a cry of indignation rose out of every chest, and England was cursed, along with its children and grandchildren, until its abhorred name would ultimately be erased from the memory of the world!

VII

~~~~~~~~~

The Hunt

THE ANIMALS THAT HAD INVADED the island had to be completely destroyed. If a single pair of those fearsome saurian or carnivorous beasts had escaped, the future safety of Standard Island would have been compromised forever. This pair would have multiplied and the Milliardites might as well have lived in the forests of India or the jungles of Africa. After building a vessel out of steel, after launching it on the vast expanses of the Pacific Ocean without ever landing on unsafe shores or archipelagos, after taking all the necessary precautions to avoid epidemics and invasions, suddenly . . . in one night . . . Actually, the Standard Island Company should not have hesitated to bring proceedings against the United Kingdom at an international tribunal, and to claim huge damages! Were not the people's rights horrifyingly violated here? They certainly were, and if it were ever proved . . .

But, as the council of notables had decided, in the meantime they had to attend to the more urgent task.

First they rejected the request of a few terrified families who asked to take shelter on the steamers anchored in the harbors and flee Standard Island. After all, these vessels could not have carried everyone.

No, flee they would not! The islanders would hunt down those animals released by the English; they would destroy them, and the Jewel of the Pacific would soon regain her customary serenity.

They got to work immediately. A few did not hesitate to propose extreme measures such as bringing the sea onto the self-propelled island or spreading fire throughout the woods in the park, the plains, and the fields, in order to drown or burn all the wild animals. But since this would not have worked against amphibians, it was preferable to proceed with well-organized hunts.

And this is what they did.

It is worth mentioning here that Captain Sarol, his Malays, and the New Hebrideans had offered their services and that the governor had eagerly accepted their help. These good people wanted to show their gratitude for what had been done for them. In fact, Captain Sarol mostly feared that this incident would cut the voyage short, that the Milliardites and their families would want to abandon Standard Island, and that they would force the administration to return directly to Madeleine Bay, which would completely destroy his plans.

The quartet proved up to the task and worthy of their nationality. Nobody could say that the four Frenchmen had not put themselves on the line; they were exposed to great dangers. They took their orders from Calistus Munbar, who, if you believed him, had seen far worse and shrugged his shoulders to show his contempt for those lions, tigers, panthers, and other harmless beasts. Perhaps he had been an animal trainer, this grandson of Barnum, or at least, the director of a traveling menagerie.

The hunt started in the morning and was successful from the very beginning.

The first day, two crocodiles made the mistake of venturing out of the Serpentine River and, as everyone knows, saurians are fearsome in the water, but less so on land because they cannot easily turn around. Captain Sarol and his Malays attacked them courageously and ridded the park of them, although one of his men was wounded in the process.

In the meantime, ten more crocodiles were reported; that was presumably their total number. They were very large animals, twelve to fifteen feet in length, and thus very dangerous. Since they had taken refuge in the river, sailors stood ready to use those explosive bullets that can blow up the hardest of shells.

In other areas, teams of hunters had scattered throughout the countryside. One of the lions was killed by Jem Tankerdon, who was right to say that he was no novice. He had regained the cool and the skills he had learned as a hunter in the Far West. The big cat was gorgeous, worth five or six thousand francs. A steel bullet had pierced its heart as it leaped toward the quartet and its group, and Pinchinat claimed that "he felt the sweep of its tail as it ran past him!"

In the afternoon, one of the militiamen was bitten on his shoulder during an attack, and the governor brought down an absolutely beautiful lioness. These animals that John Bull had hoped would propagate had been stopped in their desire to have offspring.

The day ended only after a few tigers fell under the fire of Commodore Simcoë, who commanded a detachment of sailors, one of whom was gravely wounded by the claws of a beast and had to be carried back to Starboard Harbor. According to the reports, those ferocious big cats seemed the most numerous among the carnivores that had found their way to the self-propelled island.

As night fell, the wild animals retreated to the woods adjoining the Prow Battery, from where the hunters intended to dislodge them at dawn.

From evening until the following morning, frightening roars never stopped bringing terror to the women and children of Milliard City. Their fear never abated, and would it ever? Indeed, how could they truly be assured that Standard Island had completely destroyed this vanguard of the British Army? Understandably, protests against perfidious Albion unraveled like an endless stream among all classes of the Milliardites.

At dawn the hunt resumed. On orders from the governor, and with the assent of Commodore Simcoë, Colonel Stewart prepared to use artillery against the remaining carnivores, so as to flush them out of their lairs. Two cannons from Starboard Harbor, the kind that work like Hotchkiss guns, firing volleys of iron bullets, were brought to the Prow Battery.

At this location the streetcar going toward the observatory crossed thickets of elm trees. It was there that several of the beasts had spent the night. A few heads of lions and tigers with sparkling eyes appeared amid the lower branches. The sailors, the militiamen, and the hunters, led by Jem and Walter Tankerdon, Nat Coverley, and Hubley Harcourt, positioned themselves to the left of these trees, waiting for the ferocious beasts that the cannons had not eliminated.

At the signal of Commodore Simcoë, the two cannons fired simultaneously. Horrifying roars followed. Evidently, several carnivores had been hit. The others, about twenty of them, leaped, and as they passed the quartet, were met by a volley of shots that killed two of them. But at that very moment, an enormous tiger pounced on the group, and Frascolin, struck by its careening body, rolled ten feet on the ground.

His comrades ran to his help. He was almost unconscious but he quickly came to. He had only received a shock . . . but what a shock!

Meanwhile, other men were hunting down the caimans in the waters of the Serpentine River, but how could the Standard Island population ever be sure that they were free of these voracious amphibians? Fortunately, Deputy Hubley Harcourt had the clever idea of closing the sluice gates of the Serpentine River, and the hunters found themselves in a better position to successfully attack the saurian beasts.

The only victim they lost was a magnificent dog that belonged to Nat Coverley. Caught by an alligator, the poor animal was cut in two with one single snap. But a dozen of these saurian beasts succumbed to the shots of the militiamen and Standard Island was probably freed for good of these fearful amphibians.

The day had been good. Six lions, eight tigers, five jaguars, and nine panthers, male and female, had been killed.

When evening came, the quartet, including Frascolin, who had recovered from his shock, went and sat in the casino's restaurant.

"I'd like to believe that we are at the end of our troubles," said Yvernès.

"Unless this steamer, being a second Noah's ark, carried all the animals of the creation . . . ," answered Pinchinat.

This was rather improbable and Athanase Dorémus felt confident enough to return to his home on Twenty-Fifth Avenue. There, in his barricaded house, he found his old servant devastated at the thought that all that was left of her old master was probably a few bloody remains.

The next night was quiet enough. Only a few distant howls were heard coming from the Larboard Harbor side. It was believed that a general hunt through the countryside the following day would destroy the remaining beasts.

The teams of hunters regrouped at dawn. Needless to say, Standard Island had not moved for the last twenty-four hours, her entire operating staff being engaged in the common task.

Squads of twenty men armed with rapid-fire rifles were ordered to crisscross the entire island. Colonel Stewart no longer thought it necessary to use the cannons against the wild beasts, now that they had dispersed. Thirteen of these animals, cornered near the Prow Battery, were felled by bullets. But the hunters had to rescue, with much difficulty, two customs officers from the neighboring post, who, knocked down by a tiger and a panther, had been seriously wounded.

The last hunt brought to fifty-three the number of animals destroyed since the first hunt the day before.

It was four in the morning. Cyrus Bikerstaff and Commodore Simcoë, Jem Tankerdon and his son, Nat Coverley and the two deputies, as well as a few notables escorted by a detachment of the militia walked toward the town hall, where the council was waiting for the reports from the two harbors and the Prow and Stern Batteries.

As they were approaching and were only one hundred feet from the administrative building, violent cries were heard. An entire group of people, including women and children, clearly in a panic, was fleeing along First Avenue.

Immediately, the governor, Commodore Simcoë, and their comrades ran toward the square, whose gate should have been locked . . . But due to inexplicable negligence, this gate was open, and it was obvious that one of the big cats, the last one, perhaps, had run through it.

Nat Coverley and Walter Tankerdon, who arrived first, rushed into the square.

Suddenly, three steps from where Nat Coverley stood, Walter was knocked down by an enormous tiger.

Nat Coverley, who had no time to slip a cartridge into his rifle, drew his hunting knife from his belt and came to the rescue of Walter at the very moment when the claws of the beast raked the young man's shoulder.

Walter was saved, but the tiger turned around and attacked Nat Coverley.

He stabbed the animal with his knife but could not reach its heart and fell backward.

The tiger stepped back, roaring, its jaws wide open, its tongue covered with blood.

A blast was heard . . .

It was Jem Tankerdon who had fired.

There was a second blast . . .

The bullet of his rifle exploded in the tiger's body.

They helped Walter to his feet, his shoulder badly torn.

As for Nat Coverley, although he was not wounded, he had never been so close to death. He got up and, walking toward Jem Tankerdon, said in a deep voice,

"You saved my life . . . Thank you!"

"Thank you! You saved my son . . . ," answered Jem Tankerdon.

And they shook hands to show their gratitude, which could very well end up in a sincere friendship.

Walter was immediately transported to the mansion on Nineteenth Avenue, where his family had taken refuge, while Nat Coverley, on the arm of Cyrus Bikerstaff, returned to his house. As for the tiger, the superintendent offered to put its magnificent fur to good use. The superb animal was to be stuffed by the best taxidermist and placed in the museum of natural history of Milliard City with this inscription:

Offered by the United Kingdom of Great Britain and Ireland to Standard Island, forever grateful.

If the attack had indeed come from England, a wittier vengeance could not have been found. At least this was the opinion of Pinchinat, who was a good judge in such matters.

We should not be surprised that the very next day Mrs. Tankerdon visited Mrs. Coverley to thank her for the service rendered to Walter and that Mrs. Coverley visited Mrs. Tankerdon to thank her for the service rendered to her husband. We shall even say that Miss Dy wanted to accompany her mother, and was it not natural for both of them to ask how the injured young man was doing?

Well, everything was for the best, and Standard Island, rid of her fearsome visitors, resumed her voyage toward the Fiji Archipelago in complete safety.

VIII

~~~~~~

The Fiji Islands and Their Inhabitants

"HOW MANY DID YOU SAY . . . ?" asked Pinchinat.

"Two hundred fifty-five, my friends," answered Frascolin. "Yes . . . there are two hundred fifty-five islands and islets in the Fiji Archipelago."

"Why would that be of interest to us," asked Pinchinat, "as long as the Jewel of the Pacific does not make two hundred fifty-five stops?"

"You will never master geography!" declared Frascolin.

"But you, you know it too well!" retorted His Highness.

This was how the second violin was usually received when he wanted to enlighten his recalcitrant comrades.

However, Sébastien Zorn, who listened more readily to Frascolin than the others, followed him to the map in the casino where the exact position of Standard Island was displayed every day. It was easy to follow the itinerary of the ship since her departure from Madeleine Bay. Her route formed a large S whose lower curve ended at the Fiji Group.

Frascolin showed the cellist the profusion of islands discovered by Tasman in 1643. The archipelago was spread between the sixteenth and the twentieth parallels south, and between the hundred seventy-fourth meridian west and the hundred seventy-ninth meridian east.

"So, we are going to steer this bulky contraption along a road strewn with hundreds of stones?" said Sébastien Zorn.

"Yes, my old string companion," answered Frascolin, "and if you watch carefully . . ."

"And with your mouth closed . . . ," added Pinchinat.

"Why is that . . . ?"

"Because as the proverb says, 'If you keep your mouth shut, bugs won't fly in.'"

"What bug are you talking about here?"

"The one that's bugging you now as you rant and rave about Standard Island."

Sébastien Zorn shrugged his shoulders contemptuously and went back to Frascolin:

"What were you saying . . . ?"

"I was saying that in order to reach the two large islands of Viti Levu and Vanua Levu, there are three passages that cross the eastern group: the Nanuku, the Lakemba, and the Oneata passages . . ."

"You forgot the passage where we'll smash into a thousand pieces," cried Sébastien Zorn. "That's how we'll end up . . . ! How can anyone navigate such seas with an entire city full of people . . . ? It is against the laws of nature!"

"The bug!" retorted Pinchinat! "Here it is, Zorn's bug . . . here it is again!"

Indeed, here again were the unfortunate predictions that the stubborn cellist refused to abandon.

In truth, in this region of the Pacific, the first group of the Fiji Islands formed a sort of barrier to ships coming from the east. But, not to worry, the passages were wide enough for Commodore Simcoë to venture through with his floating island. He did not even need the routes recorded by Frascolin. Among these islands, the most important ones, in addition to the two Levus situated in the west, were Ono, Ngaloa, Kandavu, etc.

A sea was enclosed between these summits that rose from the depths of the ocean, the Sea of Koro, and if this archipelago, sighted by Cook and visited by Bligh in 1789 and Wilson in 1792, was known in great detail, it was thanks to the noteworthy travels of Dumont d'Urville in 1828 and 1833, those of the American Wilkes in 1839 and of the English Erskine in 1853, and also because of the Herald Expedition with its captain named Durham. And if Commodore Simcoë was able to chart an accurate course for their travel, it was thanks to the excellent mapping of the sea by maritime cartographers.

The commodore did not hesitate for a moment. Coming from the southeast, he entered the Vulanga passage, leaving to port the island of the same name. This island was shaped like a dented pancake served on a coral tray. The next day Standard Island reached the interior sea, protected against the heavy swells of the ocean by submarine mountain ranges.

However, the fear of the ferocious animals that had probably been brought by the British had not completely disappeared. The Milliardites were still on the alert. Endless searches were organized through the woods, fields, and waters. No traces of wild beasts were found, though. No roaring was heard day or night. At first, a few nervous people refused to leave the city and to venture into the park or the country. They dreaded that the steamer might have let loose a cargo of snakes, as had happened on Martinique, and that the thickets were infested. A reward was offered to anyone who caught a few of these reptiles. They would be paid the reptiles' weight in gold, or their length in inches, and if they were the size of boas, that would make a hefty sum! But since the searches did not bring any results, the residents felt reassured. Once again, Standard Island was totally safe. Far from making any gains, the perpetrators of this dirty trick simply lost their animals.

The most positive result of all this was the total reconciliation that had occurred between the two sections of the city. Since the Walter-Coverley episode and the Coverley-Tankerdon episode, the Starboardite and Larboardite families had visited each other, invited each other over, and received each other. It had been reception after reception and party after party. Every evening there were balls and concerts at the houses of the principal notables, and more particularly at the mansions on Nineteenth and Fifteenth Avenues. The Concerting Quartet could hardly keep up with this, and the enthusiasm they aroused, far from waning, became even more intense.

One morning, great news spread throughout the city as Standard Island churned the tranquil surface of the Sea of Koro with her powerful propellers. Mr. Jem Tankerdon had paid an official visit to the mansion of Mr. Nat Coverley to ask for the hand of Miss Dy Coverley, his daughter, for his son, Walter Tankerdon. And Mr. Coverley had agreed to give the hand of Miss Dy Coverley, his daughter, to Walter Tankerdon, the son of Mr. Jem Tankerdon. The amount of the dowry never came into question. It was to be two hundred million for each of the young spouses.

"They will have enough to live on, even in Europe!" remarked Pinchinat judiciously.

Congratulations from everywhere were sent to both families. Governor Cyrus Bikerstaff did not hide his great satisfaction. Thanks to this marriage, the rivalry that looked so menacing for the future of Standard Island had disappeared. The king and queen of Malécarlie were among the first to send their congratulations and best wishes to the young couple. Calling cards printed in gold on aluminum filled the mailboxes of the mansions. The newspapers published article upon article about the festivities to come, such as had never been seen in Milliard City or anywhere else in the world. Telegrams were sent to France to buy wedding presents. The most modern stores, the famous millinery and tailor shops, the jewelers and artistic craftsmen received the most incredible orders. A special steamer leaving from Marseille was to travel by Suez and the Indian Ocean to bring these marvels of French industry to Standard Island. The wedding was set for five weeks later, on February 27. The merchants of Milliard City were also to benefit from the affair. Their stock would be bought as wedding gifts, and the money spent by the nabobs of Standard Island would be enough to create fortunes.

Superintendent Calistus Munbar was the chosen organizer of these parties. His personal feelings at the announcement of the marriage of Walter Tankerdon and Miss Dy Coverley would be hard to describe. Everyone knew how he had hoped and worked for it. It was a dream come true, and since the municipality had given him carte blanche, you could be sure that he would be up to the task and would organize an absolutely marvelous festival.

Commodore Simcoë sent a note to the newspapers to let them know that on the date chosen for the wedding, the self-propelled island would be in the part of the sea that lay between the Fiji Islands and the New Hebrides. But first she was going to stop for about ten days at Viti Levu, and this would be the only stop she would make in the middle of this huge archipelago.

The sailing was delightful. Numerous whales were playing on the surface of the ocean, and the water squirting out of their blowholes made the sea look like an immense fountain of Neptune. Compared to this, the fountains of Versailles were mere children's toys, remarked Yvernès.

Then hundreds of huge sharks appeared and escorted Standard Island as they would a sailing ship.

This portion of the Pacific formed the boundary of Polynesia and bordered Melanesia, where the archipelago of the New Hebrides was located. It was crossed by the one hundred eightieth degree of longitude, which is the conventional line traced by the meridian dividing this immense ocean into two halves. When they reached this meridian, sailors coming from the east had to remove one day from their calendar and, conversely, those coming from the west had to add one day to it. Without this precaution, the dates would no longer match. The year before, Standard Island had had no need to make this adjustment since she did not travel west beyond this meridian. But this time, she had to conform to the rule since she came from the east, and January 22 became January 23.

Of the two hundred fifty islands forming the Fiji Archipelago, only about one hundred were inhabited. It was a sparsely populated region, the total number of people being approximately one hundred twenty-eight thousand for an area of eighty-one hundred square miles.

None of these islets, which were fragments of atolls or summits of underwater mountains surrounded by a coral belt, had a surface larger than fifty-eight square miles. This insular domain was nothing but a political division of Australasia ruled by the British Crown since 1874, which meant that England had simply annexed it to its colonial empire. If the Fijians had finally decided to accept the British protectorate, it was because in 1859 they had been threatened by a Tongan invasion that the United Kingdom prevented through the intervention of the infamous Pritchard, the Pritchard we met on Tahiti. The archipelago was then divided into seventeen districts administered by native chiefs who more or less belonged to the family of the last King Thakumbau.

"It's obvious that the natives are becoming extinct," said Commodore Simcoë, who was conversing with Frascolin, "and I wonder if this is due to the English system. Will the Fiji Islands meet with the same fate as Tasmania? I don't know. The colony is not doing well, the population is not increasing, and what proves this is the smaller number of women compared to men."

"This is indeed an indication of the approaching extinction of a race," answered Frascolin. "In Europe there already are a few states threatened by this disparity."

"Anyway, here," the commodore went on, "the natives are nothing but slaves, just like those of the neighboring islands, who are recruited by the planters to clear the land. Moreover, sickness decimates them; smallpox alone killed more than ten thousand in 1875. And yet this Fiji Archipelago is an admirable region, as you will see for yourself! In the center of the islands, it is very hot, but on the shores the climate is moderate and the land is very fertile in fruits and vegetables, in coconut and banana trees, etc. You only have to harvest the sweet potatoes, the taros, and the nourishing core of the palm tree that produces sago . . ."

"Sago!" exclaimed Frascolin. "That reminds me of our Swiss Family Robinson!"

"As for the pigs and chickens," continued Commodore Simcoë, "these animals have multiplied incredibly fast after being imported. Life is easy here. Unfortunately, the natives are rather lazy, they love their *farniente*, although they are very intelligent and witty."

"And when they are so witty . . . ," said Frascolin.

"Children do not live long!" continued Commodore Simcoë, repeating one of Casimir Delavigne's famous sayings.

In fact, all these natives, Polynesians, Melanasians, and others, were very much like children.

Advancing toward Viti Levu, Standard Island passed several smaller islands, among which were Vanua Vatu, Moala, and Ngan, but they did not stop.

From everywhere, circling the shores of Standard Island, appeared flotillas of long pirogues with bamboo outriggers that maintained the boats' balance and stabilized their cargo. They sailed around, moving gracefully, but they did not attempt to enter Starboard Harbor or Larboard Harbor. They probably would not have been allowed to, since the Fijians had a rather bad reputation. These natives had become Christian, though. Since European missionaries had settled in Lecumba in 1835, almost all Fijians had become Wesleyan Protestants; there were also a few thousand Catholics. But the Fijians had practiced cannibalism for so long before that they had perhaps not completely lost their taste for human flesh. Moreover, it was a question of religion. Their gods loved blood. Benevolence was looked upon as a weakness and even as a sin among those people. To eat an enemy was to honor him. They would cook the man they despised, but they would not eat him. Children were the main dish at feasts, and, not so long ago, King Thakumbau liked to sit under a tree, each branch of which held a human limb reserved for the royal table. Sometimes an entire tribe was devoured; this happened to the Nulocas, on Viti Levu near Namosi. Only a few women were spared, and one of them lived until 1880.

Frankly, if Pinchinat did not meet any grandsons of cannibals who had retained the customs of their grandfathers on these islands, he would have to forever relinquish his desire to find vestiges of local color in the archipelagos of the Pacific.

The western group of the Fiji Islands was made up of two large isles, Viti Levu and Vanua Levu, and two medium-sized ones, Kandavu and Taveuni. The Wassava Islands and the passage of the Round Island that Commodore Simcoë had to take to head toward the New Hebrides were located more to the northwest.

On the afternoon of January 25, the heights of Viti Levu were sighted on the horizon. This mountainous island was the largest of the entire archipelago. It was one-third larger than Corsica and had an area of six hundred thirty-five square miles.

Its summits were four and five thousand feet above sea level. These were inactive volcanoes, or at least they were so at the time, but when they woke up, they were generally in a very bad mood.

Viti Levu was linked to its neighbor, Vanua Levu, by an underwater barrier of reefs that were probably above sea level in earlier times. Standard Island could sail over it without danger. Moreover, in the north of Viti Levu, the depth of the water was estimated at about fifteen hundred feet and in the south, at between fifteen hundred and six thousand feet.

In the past, Levuka, on the island of Ovalau to the east of Viti Levu, was the capital of the archipelago. Its trading posts, founded by English companies, may still have been more important than those of Suva, the present capital, located on Viti Levu. But the harbor of Viti Levu offered serious advantages to ships, being located at the southeast extremity of the island between two deltas that watered its shores. The port of call for steamers doing business with the Fiji Group was located in Ngaloa

Bay, south of Kandavu Island, which was the closest to New Zealand, Australia, the French islands of New Caledonia, and the Loyalties.

Standard Island stopped at the mouth of Suva Harbor. The formalities were completed the same day and they were given permission to land. Since these visits could only benefit the colonists and the natives, the Milliardites could expect to be very well received, even if it was more out of interest than genuine kindness. Let us not forget that the Fiji Islands were under the control of the English Crown and that the relationship was always tense between the Foreign Office and the administration of the Standard Island Company, which wanted to keep its independence at any price.

The following day, January 26, the merchants of Standard Island who wanted to buy or sell went on land in the early morning. The tourists, with our Parisians among them, disembarked soon after. Although Pinchinat and Yvernès enjoyed kidding Frascolin, Commodore Simcoë's distinguished student, about his ethno-geographico-boredom-inducing studies, as His Highness called them, they still availed themselves of his knowledge. The second violin always had informative answers to the questions of his comrades about the natives of Viti Levu, their customs, and their activities, and Sébastien Zorn himself did not refrain from occasionally asking for his explanations. But first, when Pinchinat learned that not long ago, the area had been the main region where cannibalism was practiced, he could not keep from sighing and said,

"Yes, but we come too late and you will see that these Fijians, spoiled by civilization, now prefer chicken fricassee and pigs' feet Sainte-Menehould style."

"Cannibal!" yelled Frascolin. "You deserve to have been a featured dish at the table of King Thakumbau . . ."

"Hey! Hey! A Pinchinat steak with Bordelaise sauce . . ."

"Come," retorted Sébastien Zorn, "if we waste our time on pointless recriminations . . ."

"We will not progress forward!" cried Pinchinat. "This is the sort of phrase you like, isn't it, my old violoncelluloidist! Well then, forward, march!"

The town of Suva, built to the right of a small bay, offered scattered houses on the side of a green hill. It had wharves for the mooring of ships and streets with plank sidewalks, just like the beaches of our best seaside resorts. The wooden houses, with only one story and sometimes, but rarely, two, were pleasant and clean. On the periphery, the native dwellings showed their gables turned up in the shape of horns and decorated with shells. Their roofs were very strong and could sustain the winter rains that were torrential from May to October. In fact, Frascolin, who was an expert in statistics, said that in March 1871 the town of Mbua, located in the east of the island, received fifteen inches of rain in thirty-eight days.

Viti Levu, just like the other islands of the archipelago, had a varied climate, and its vegetation differed from one shore to the other. On the side exposed to the trade winds of the southeast, the air was humid and magnificent forests covered the area. On the other side there were immense savannas fit for cultivation. However, certain trees had begun to die out; the sandalwood, for example, had almost completely disappeared, as well as the *dakua*, a pine particular to the Fiji Group.

During their walks, the quartet had noticed that the flora of the island was of tropical luxuriance. Everywhere were forests of coconut and palm trees, their trunks covered with parasite orchids, clumps of casuarinas, pandanus, acacias, tree ferns, and, in the swampy areas, numerous mangroves, whose roots meandered above the ground. But the cultivation of cotton and tea did not give the results that the wonderful climate had caused people to expect. In fact, the soil of Viti Levu, clayey and yellowish, as in the entire group, was formed by volcanic ash, to which decomposition had given some productive qualities.

The fauna were no more varied than in the other areas of the Pacific; there were about forty kinds of birds, parakeets and canaries used to the climate, bats, legions of rats, nonvenomous reptiles whose flesh was much appreciated by the natives, lizards in the thousands, and repulsive cockroaches as voracious as cannibals. But there were no wild animals, which provoked this joke from Pinchinat:

"Cyrus Bikerstaff, our governor, should have kept a few pairs of lions, tigers, panthers, and crocodiles and brought these carnivorous beasts to the Fiji Archipelago . . . It would be a restitution, since they belonged to England."

The natives, who were of mixed Polynesian and Melanesian descent, included many beautiful specimens but less remarkable than those on Samoa and the Marquesas. The men's complexion was coppery, almost black, their head covered with very thick hair. Many of them were of mixed race, very tall and strong. Their clothing was rather rudimentary, most often a simple loincloth or a blanket of *masi*, the native material made from a special kind of mulberry tree that also produced paper. The fabric first obtained was perfectly white, but the Fijians knew how to dye it in bright colors, and it was much in demand throughout the eastern Pacific. These men were not against wearing old European cast-offs from the secondhand shops of the United Kingdom and Germany. They were fine fodder for jokes by a Parisian, these Fijians cramped in shapeless trousers, ancient vests, or even a black coat that, after many phases of decadence, ended up on the back of a Viti Levu native.

"One could write a novel about one of these coats!" exclaimed Yvernès.

"A novel with a sad ending!" replied Pinchinat.

The women wore *masi* skirts and loose blouses that covered them not very decently, in spite of the Wesleyan sermons. They were rather good-looking, and when young could pass for pretty. But they had the appalling habit—as did the men—of plastering lime on their black hair, which then became a sort of chalky hat, in order to preserve them from sunstroke!

And like their husbands and brothers, they smoked the native tobacco that smelled like burned hay. When their cigarettes were not being chewed between their lips, they slipped them into their earlobes, in the place where in Europe it is most common to find circles of diamonds and pearls.

In general, these women were reduced to the condition of slaves and burdened with the heaviest household tasks. Not so long ago, after accepting her husband's laziness for years, a wife was strangled on his tomb.

Several times during the three days they roamed around Suva, our tourists tried to visit native huts; but they were repulsed, not by the lack of hospitality of their owners but by the abominable odor. They could not endure the smell of these natives anointed with coconut oil, their close proximity to pigs, chickens, dogs, and cats in these foul-smelling straw huts, and the suffocating smoke released by burning the resin of the *dammana* for light . . . Besides, if they had sat in a Fijian home, in order to be polite they would have had to accept dipping their lips in the bowl of kava, the traditional Fijian drink. While this spiced kava, extracted from the dried-up roots of the pepper tree, was not pleasing to European palates, the manner in which it was prepared was still worse. It would have caused the most insurmountable repugnance. They did not grind their pepper, but they chewed it and ground it between their teeth and spat it into a bowl of water. Then they offered it to you with a savage insistence that did not allow for refusal. You were finally supposed to thank them with the following words that were very much in use in the archipelago: "E mana ndina," which meant *amen*.

Moreover, let us not forget the cockroaches swarming inside the huts, the white ants that devoured them, and the millions of mosquitoes on the walls, the floors, and in the clothes of the natives.

It was no wonder that His Highness, imitating those English clowns pretending to speak French, kept exclaiming "moustique," the French equivalent of "mosquito," with the most hilarious English accent, every time he noticed another swarm of those annoying insects.

Neither he nor his comrades could muster the courage to enter the Fijian huts and because of this their ethnological studies would remain incomplete. The learned Frascolin himself abstained, which would forever leave a gap in his travel memoirs.

IX

~~~~~~~~~~

A Casus Belli

WHILE OUR MUSICIANS SPENT THEIR time taking walks and trying to educate themselves about the customs of the archipelago, a few notables from Standard Island chose to meet with the native authorities of the area. The *papalangis*, as foreigners were called in these islands, did not have to fear being badly received.

The European authorities were represented by a main governor, who was also the general consul of England for these western groups that were more or less well-run protectorates of the United Kingdom. Cyrus Bikerstaff did not think that he owed this governor an official visit. Two or three times, they had had a chance to glare at each other, but this was the extent of their relations.

As for the German consul, who was also one of the principal business-men of the area, Cyrus Bikerstaff only exchanged calling cards with him.

During the stay, the Tankerdons and the Coverleys had organized excursions around Suva and in the forests that covered its highest peaks.

The superintendent made a very pertinent remark about this to his friends from the quartet:

"If our Milliardites are so fond of exploring these mountains," he said, "it is because our Standard Island does not have any hills . . . She is too flat, too uniform . . . But I hope that someday we will build an artificial mountain on our island that will rival the highest summits of the Pacific. Meanwhile, every time they have a chance, our citizens are eager to climb a few hundred feet in order to breathe the pure and invigorating air of the open spaces . . . It fills a need of human nature . . ."

"That's a great idea," said Pinchinat, "but let me give you some advice, my dear Eucalistus! When you build your mountain of steel or aluminum, don't forget to put a lovely volcano inside it . . . a volcano with lots of fireworks and huge explosions . . ."

"And why not, my witty friend . . . ?" answered Calistus Munbar.

"Why not indeed . . . ? That's exactly what I was thinking," replied His Highness.

Of course, Walter Tankerdon and Miss Dy Coverley took part in those excursions arm in arm.

On Viti Levu, they made sure to visit the curiosities of the capital, the *mbure-kalu* or temples of spirits, and also the building where political meetings were held. These constructions, raised on a base of dry stones, were made of plaited bamboo, with beams covered by some sort of vegetal lacework and boards strategically placed to support the thatched roofs. The tourists also visited the hospital, which proved to be very sanitary, and the botanic gardens shaped like an amphitheater at the rear of the town. Their walks often lasted till evening and they came back, lantern in hand, as in the good old days. "In the Fiji Islands, the town councils have not yet established gas meters and incandescent, arc, or acetylene lamps, but this will come under the enlightened protectorate of Great Britain!" Calistus Munbar said sarcastically.

And what were Captain Sarol, his Malays, and the New Hebrideans who were taken aboard on the Samoan Islands doing during this stay? Nothing other than that which they usually did. They did not go ashore because they already knew Viti Levu and the neighboring isles; some of them had sailed along these coasts before and others had worked for the planters. They much preferred to stay on Standard Island, which they constantly explored, never tiring of visiting the city, the harbors, the park, the countryside, and the Stern and Prow Batteries. A few weeks later, thanks to the kindness of the company and Governor Bikerstaff, these good people would land in their own country after staying on the self-propelled island for five months . . .

Once in a while our musicians talked with Sarol, who was very intelligent and spoke English fluently. Sarol spoke enthusiastically of the New Hebrides, their indigenous population, their eating customs, and their cuisine. This was a subject of particular interest to His Highness. Indeed, Pinchinat's secret ambition was to discover a new dish, the recipe for which he would communicate to the gastronomic societies of old Europe.

On January 30 Sébastien Zorn and his comrades, using one of the electric launches of Starboard Harbor that the governor had put at their disposal, sailed up the Rewa, one of the main rivers of the island. The captain of the launch, one engineer, and two sailors were on board, as well as a Fijian pilot. They had asked Athanase Dorémus to accompany them, but he refused. The professor of good manners and charm had lost his taste for adventure . . . Besides, while he was away, a new student might come to see him, and he preferred not to leave the studio of the casino.

At six in the morning, the boat, well armed and stocked with food, since it would only return to Starboard Harbor in the evening, left the Bay of Suva and sailed along the shore toward the Bay of Rewa.

There were a lot of reefs and sharks in these areas, so they had to watch out for both.

"Phooey!" said Pinchinat. "Your sharks are not even saltwater cannibals anymore . . . ! The English missionaries must have converted them to Christianity like they did the Fijians . . . ! I bet that these animals have lost their taste for human flesh . . ."

"Don't be too sure of that," answered the pilot, "and don't trust the Fijians of the interior, either."

Pinchinat simply shrugged his shoulders. He thought that they were pulling his leg with these tales of so-called cannibals who did not even eat human flesh on feast days.

The pilot was thoroughly familiar with the bay and the course of the Rewa. On this important river, which was also called Wai Levu, the tide could be felt for a distance of twenty-eight miles, and the boats could go as far as fifty miles upstream.

The width of the Rewa exceeded six hundred feet at its mouth. It flowed between sandy banks, low on the left side and steep on the right, where banana trees and coconut trees stood out on a wide stretch of greenery. The name of the river was actually Rewa, using the double word, which is very common among the Pacific tribes. Was this not, as Yvernès pointed out, an imitation of the childish pronunciations found in *papa, mama, dada, bonbon*, etc.? And in fact, these natives were still very much children!

The real Rewa was formed by the confluence of the Wai Levu (the Great Water) and the Wai Manu, and its principal mouth was called Wai Ni Ki.

After rounding the delta, the launch ran past the village of Kamba, half hidden among flowers. They did not stop there because they did not want to lose the tide, nor did they did stop in the village of Naitasiri. Besides, this village had just been declared "taboo," as well as its houses, its trees, its inhabitants, and even the waters of the Rewa touching its beaches. The natives would not have allowed anyone to set foot on this land. The taboo may not have been a particularly respectable custom, but it was a highly respected one, as Sébastien Zorn had already learned, and the excursionists accepted it.

As they sailed alongside Naitasiri, the pilot invited them to look at a tall tree, a *tavala*, which rose from the bank.

"Why is this tree of special interest . . . ?" asked Frascolin.

"For no other reason than its bark is marked with notches from its roots to its branches," answered the pilot. "These notches indicate the number of human bodies that were cooked here and then eaten . . ."

"Like the notches the baker makes on his loaves of dough," remarked Pinchinat, shrugging his shoulders to show his incredulity.

He was wrong, however. The Fiji Islands had always been known as the land of cannibalism, and, we must repeat, these practices were not entirely abandoned. The love of good food would keep them alive for a long time among the tribes of the interior. Yes, the love of good food, since, according to the Fijians, nothing could compare to the taste and tenderness of human flesh, which is far superior to beef. If the pilot was to be believed, there had been a chief by the name of Ra-Undrenudu, who had large stones set on his land, and when he died, these stones numbered eight hundred twenty-two.

"And do you know what these stones stood for . . . ?"

"We could never guess," answered Yvernès, "even if we applied all our knowledge as musicians to it."

"They stood for the number of human bodies this chief had eaten!"

"All by himself . . . ?"

"Yes, all by himself!"

"He sure was a big eater!" replied Pinchinat simply. He had formed his own opinion about these "Fijian jokes."

Around eleven o'clock, a bell rang on the right bank. The village of Naililii, made up of a few straw huts, appeared beneath the shade of coconut and banana trees. There was a Catholic mission in this village. The tourists wanted to stop for an hour, long enough to shake hands with the missionary, a compatriot. The pilot saw no reason to refuse, and the launch was moored to a tree stump.

Sébastien Zorn and his comrades landed, and they had not walked for two minutes before they met the father superior of the mission.

He was a man of about fifty, with a pleasant and energetic face. Very happy to see Frenchmen, he brought them to his hut in the middle of the village, which contained about a hundred Fijians. He insisted that his guests sample a few of the local refreshments. Let us not worry, it was not the repulsive kava but a sort of drink or rather a broth with a good enough taste obtained by cooking *cyreae*, the shellfish that was abundantly found on the beaches of the Rewa.

This missionary devoted himself, body and soul, to the propagation of Catholicism, and it was not easy because he had to contend with a Wesleyan pastor who gave him a real challenge in the neighborhood. He was, however, very satisfied with the results he had obtained but admitted that he had a hard time tearing his faithful away from the love of *bukalo*, that is to say, human flesh.

"And since you are going to explore the interior of the island, my dear compatriots," he added, "be careful and stay on your guard."

"Do you hear that, Pinchinat?" said Sébastien Zorn.

They left a few minutes before the bell of the little church rang the noon angelus. On their way, they met a few pirogues carrying cargos of bananas. This was the local currency that the tax collector extracted from the natives. The shores were still bordered with laurels, acacias, lemon trees, and cacti with bright red flowers. Above those, banana and coconut trees displayed their towering branches laden with bunches of fruit. All this foliage stretched back to the mountains dominated by the peak of the Mbugge Levu.

In these woods stood one or two European factories, which seemed out of place given the wild nature of the country. They were sugar factories, equipped with all the modern machinery, and their products, as a traveler named Mr. Verschnur had said, "could be advantageously compared with the sugars of the West Indies and other colonies."

Around one o'clock, the boat reached the end of its voyage on the Rewa. Two hours later the ebb tide would begin, and they would take advantage of it for their return downstream. This trip would be quick because the tide ebbed fast. The excursionists would be back at Starboard Harbor by ten in the evening.

Therefore they had time to spend in this place, and how could they have put it to better use than by visiting the village of Tampoo, whose first huts could be sighted half a mile away? They agreed to leave the engineer and the two sailors to guard the launch, while the pilot would guide his passengers to the village, where the ancient customs had been preserved in their total Fijian purity. In this portion of the island, the missionaries had wasted their efforts and their sermons. Sorcerers still reigned and witchcraft was still practiced, especially that which was called Vaka Ndran ni Kan Tacka, which is to say, "the incantation practiced by the leaves." The people adored the Katoavus, gods whose existence had no beginning and would have no end. These gods liked special sacrifices that the governor general was powerless to prevent or even to punish.

Perhaps the tourists would have been well advised not to venture among these dubious tribes. But our musicians, curious like all Parisians, insisted on it, and the pilot agreed to accompany them, advising them not to stray from the group.

As they entered Tampoo, made up of about one hundred straw huts, they first came across women, true savages, wearing a simple piece of cloth knotted around their hips. They showed no surprise at the sight of these foreigners disturbing their work. These visits did not bother them anymore since the archipelago had become an English protectorate.

These women were busy preparing the *curcuma*, roots preserved in pits that had been lined with grass and banana leaves; these roots were taken out, grilled, scraped, and then pressed into baskets lined with ferns. The juice that came out was poured into bamboo stems. This juice served as a food as well as an ointment and, as such, was very popular.

The little group entered the village. There was no welcome from the natives, who did not hurry to greet the visitors or to offer them hospitality. The exterior aspect of the huts was not in the least attractive. The smell coming out of them, mostly of rancid coconut oil, made the quartet happy that the laws of hospitality were so poorly observed there.

However, when they arrived in front of the cottage of the chief, a tall Fijian with a savage look and a ferocious face, he came toward them with an escort of natives. His hair, all white with lime, was frizzy. He was dressed in his ceremonial garb, a striped shirt, a belt around his waist, an old tapestry slipper on his left foot, and—one wonders how Pinchinat did not burst out laughing—he wore an antique blue coat with gold buttons, patched in several places and whose uneven tails flapped against his calves.

But advancing toward the group of *papalangis*, the chief stumbled on a stump, lost his balance, and fell to the ground.

Immediately, following the etiquette of *baie muri*, his entire entourage stumbled in turn and fell respectfully to the ground, "in order to take their share of the ridicule of this fall."

This was explained by the pilot, and Pinchinat approved of this formality as no more laughable, at least in his opinion, than many in use at European courts.

In the meantime, as everyone had gotten back on their feet, the chief and the pilot exchanged a few words in the Fijian language, of which the quartet did not understand a word. The only purpose of these sentences translated by the pilot was to find out why the foreigners had come to the village of Tampoo. They responded that they simply wanted to visit the village and take a walk around it, and, after a brief exchange, they were authorized to do so.

The chief showed neither pleasure nor displeasure concerning this arrival of tourists in Tampoo and simply signaled the natives to return to their straw huts.

"They don't look very mean after all!" remarked Pinchinat.

"Yet this is not a good reason to be careless!" replied Frascolin.

For an entire hour, the musicians walked about the village without being at all bothered by the natives. The chief with his blue coat had returned to his hut, and it was obvious that the inhabitants felt only deep indifference toward the visitors.

After wandering through the streets of Tampoo for two hours without any straw hut ever opening its door to welcome them, Sébastien Zorn, Yvernès, Pinchinat, Frascolin, and the pilot headed toward the ruins of temples, some sort of abandoned, dilapidated cottages close to the home of one of the local sorcerers.

This sorcerer, standing at his front door, gave them a disturbing look, and his gestures seemed to indicate that he was casting an evil spell upon them.

Frascolin tried to talk to him using the pilot as an interpreter, but the sorcerer put on such a forbidding look and such a threatening attitude that they had to abandon all hope of getting a word out of this Fijian porcupine.

At this time, and in spite of the recommendations that he had received, Pinchinat moved away from the group and crossed a thick clump of banana trees set out in terraces on the side of a hill.

When Sébastien Zorn, Yvernès, and Frascolin, rebuked by the hostility of the sorcerer, got ready to leave Tampoo, they did not see their comrade anywhere.

The moment had come, however, to return to the launch. The water was already retreating, and they would need the few hours the ebb lasted to sail down the Rewa.

Frascolin, worried by not seeing Pinchinat, called out his name in a loud voice but there was no reply.

"Where could he be . . . ?" asked Sébastien Zorn.

"I don't know . . . ," replied Yvernès.

"Has any of you seen where your friend went . . . ?" asked the pilot.

But no one had seen him! "He must have gone back to the launch by the path to the village . . . ," said Frascolin.

"He was wrong if he did," replied the pilot. "But let's not waste any time. Let's try to catch up with him."

They started on their way, very anxious. Pinchinat always did crazy things, and to consider as fairy tales the ferocity of these natives who had remained so obstinately wild could have exposed him to very real dangers.

Crossing Tampoo, the pilot noted with anxiety that there was not a single native in sight anymore. The doors of all the huts were shut. There was no longer a crowd in front of the chief's home. The women who had been busy preparing the *curcuma* had disappeared. The village looked as if it had been abandoned in the last hour.

The little group walked even faster. They called their missing friend several times, but the missing friend did not answer. Had he perhaps returned to the shore where the launch had been moored . . . ? Would the launch no longer be where they had left it, with the engineer and the two sailors . . . ?

They still had a few hundred feet to go. They hurried on and, as soon as they had gone through the trees, they saw the launch and the three men at their posts.

"Our comrade . . . ?" shouted Frascolin.

"Is he not with you . . . ?" asked the engineer.

"No . . . we haven't seen him for half an hour . . ."

"He did not come back here . . . ?" inquired Yvernès.

"No."

What became of this careless fellow? The pilot did not conceal his extreme anxiety.

"We must return to the village," said Sébastien Zorn. "We cannot abandon Pinchinat . . ." One of the sailors was left in charge of the launch although it may have been dangerous to do so. But it was better to go back to Tampoo in numbers and well armed this time. Even if they had to search every hut, they would not leave the village and return to Standard Island before finding Pinchinat.

They went back along the path to Tampoo. The same silence still reigned in the village and around it. Where had all the people gone? There was not a sound in the streets and the huts were empty.

Unfortunately, they could no longer have any doubt . . . Pinchinat had ventured into the forest of banana trees . . . he had been seized . . . he had been dragged away . . . where . . . ? It was only too easy to imagine the fate that these cannibals whom he had mocked had in store for him . . . ! Searching around Tampoo would not produce any result . . . How could one find a trail in the middle of these woods, through this brush that only the Fijians knew . . . ? Besides, did not the tourists also have to fear that the Fijians would try to seize the boat guarded by a single sailor . . . ? If this misfortune occurred, all hope of saving Pinchinat would be lost, and the safety of his companions would be compromised as well.

The despair of Frascolin, Yvernès, and Sébastien Zorn was impossible to describe. What could they do . . . ? The pilot and the engineer did not know what to do either.

Then Frascolin, who had kept his composure, said,

"Let's go back to Standard Island . . ."

"Without our comrade . . . ?" cried Yvernès.

"How could you even think of that . . . ?" added Sébastien Zorn.

"I don't see what else we can do," replied Frascolin. "The governor of Standard Island must be informed . . . The authorities of Viti Levu must also be alerted and ordered into action . . ."

"Yes . . . let's leave," advised the pilot. "If we want to take advantage of the tide, we don't have a minute to lose!"

"This is the only way to save Pinchinat," cried Frascolin, "if it's not too late already!" It was the only way indeed.

They left Tampoo, terrified that they would not find the launch where they had left it. It was in vain that they all shouted the name of Pinchinat! Perhaps if the pilot and his companions had been less upset, they would have seen among the bushes a few of those fierce Fijians watching their departure.

The launch had not been disturbed. The sailor had not seen anyone lurking about on the shores of the Rewa.

It was with very heavy hearts that Sébastien Zorn, Frascolin, and Yvernès decided to get into the boat . . . They hesitated . . . They called again . . . But they had to leave, said Frascolin. He was right to say it, and they were right to do it.

The engineer started the engines, and the launch, helped by the tide, went down the Rewa incredibly fast.

At six o'clock, they sailed around the western point of the delta. Half an hour later, they moored at the pier of Starboard Harbor.

Fifteen minutes later, Frascolin and his two comrades took the tram to Milliard City and went to the town hall.

As soon as he learned of the mishap, Cyrus Bikerstaff headed for

Suva, where he asked for an interview with the governor general of the archipelago. This was granted to him.

When the representative of the queen learned what had happened in Tampoo, he agreed that it was a very serious matter . . . This Frenchman was at the mercy of one of the tribes of the interior that rejected all authority . . .

"Unfortunately," he added, "we cannot do anything before tomorrow; our launches cannot go up to Tampoo against the tide of the Rewa. Besides, we will have to go in large numbers, and the best way would be to go through the brush . . ."

"All right," answered Cyrus Bikerstaff, "but it's not tomorrow, it's today, at this very instant, that we must go . . ."

"I do not have the necessary personnel at my disposal," replied the governor.

"But we have them, Sir," retorted Cyrus Bikerstaff. "Take the necessary measures to have our men accompanied by a few soldiers from your army and under the command of one of your officers who knows the country well . . ."

"Excuse me, Sir," replied His Excellency curtly. "I am not used to . . ."

"Excuse me too," said Cyrus Bikerstaff, " but I am warning you that if you do not act immediately, if our friend, our companion is not returned to us, the responsibility will be yours, and . . ."

"And . . . ?" asked the governor in a haughty tone.

"The batteries of Standard Island will totally destroy Suva, your capital, with all its foreign properties, English or German!"

This was a formal ultimatum, and the governor had no choice but to accept it. The few cannons of the island were no match for the artillery of Standard Island. Thus the governor agreed, but we must admit that it would have been better for him to have shown more goodwill in the name of humanity.

Half an hour later, a hundred men, soldiers and sailors, disembarked on Suva under the command of Commodore Simcoë, who wanted to lead the operation himself. The superintendent, Sébastien Zorn, Yvernès, and Frascolin were at his side. A squad of police from Viti Levu accompanied them.

The expedition marched directly through the brush, rounding the bay of the Rewa under the direction of the pilot, who knew the difficult regions of the interior. They took the shortest way, at a rapid pace, to reach Tampoo as quickly as possible.

They did not need to go to the village. Around a minute past midnight, the column was ordered to halt.

In the depths of an almost impenetrable thicket, they saw the glare of a fire. It was, without any doubt, a gathering of the natives of Tampoo, the village being within half an hour's walk to the east.

Commodore Simcoë, the pilot, Calistus Munbar, and the three Parisians went forward.

They had not walked a hundred paces before they stopped, frozen.

Across from the glowing fire, surrounded by an agitated crowd of men and women, Pinchinat, half-naked, was tied to a tree . . . and the Fijian chief was running toward him with an ax in his hand . . .

"Forward, march!" cried Commodore Simcoë to his sailors and his soldiers.

The natives were very rightly surprised and terrified. The detachment did not spare them shots and blows. The place emptied in a flash and the entire crowd disappeared among the trees . . .

Pinchinat, untied from the tree, fell into the arms of his friend Frascolin.

The joy felt by these musicians, these brothers, could not be expressed; it was, however, mixed with a few tears and well-deserved reproaches.

"But, what got into you, you fool, leaving us like that . . . ?" said the cellist.

"Call me a fool as much as you want, my dear old Sébastien," replied Pinchinat, "but do not overwhelm an alto as scantily dressed as I am now . . . Pass me my clothes so that I can present myself to the authorities in more acceptable attire."

They found his clothes at the bottom of a tree. He took them back, keeping completely cool. Only then, when he was "presentable," did he go shake hands with Commodore Simcoë and the superintendent.

"Well," said Calistus Munbar, "do you believe now that the Fijians are real cannibals . . . ?"

"They are not such great cannibals, after all, these sons of bitches," replied His Highness. "I am not even missing an arm or a leg."

"You're still the same wicked eccentric!" cried Frascolin.

"And do you know what bothered me most when I was human game ready for the roasting pit . . . ?" asked Pinchinat.

"I don't have the slightest idea!" replied Yvernès.

"Well, it was not to be a quick snack for these natives . . . ! No! It was to be devoured by a savage in a suit . . . in a blue suit with gold buttons . . . with an umbrella under his arm . . . a horrible British umbrella . . . !"

X

~~~~~~

Change of Owners

THE DEPARTURE OF STANDARD ISLAND was set for February 2. The day before, having ended their excursions, the tourists returned to Milliard City. Pinchinat's adventure had made an enormous splash. The entire population of the Jewel of the Pacific rallied around His Highness, the Concerting Quartet being held in such high esteem by everyone. The council of notables entirely approved of Governor Cyrus Bikerstaff's forceful conduct. The newspapers congratulated him profusely and Pinchinat became the celebrity of the day. Imagine! An alto ending his musical career in the stomach of a Fijian . . . ! His Highness readily agreed that the natives of Viti Levu had not completely renounced their cannibalistic tastes. After all, according to them, human flesh was so good, and that darned Pinchinat was so appetizing!

Standard Island left at dawn, heading for the New Hebrides. This detour would bring the vessel ten degrees or about six hundred miles west of its normal route; but it could not be avoided since Captain Sarol and his comrades were to be dropped at the New Hebrides. The Milliardites did not regret this delay, however. They were glad to help these good people who had shown so much courage in the fight against the wild animals. Besides, the New Hebrideans seemed so happy to be repatriated in this way after their long absence and the Milliardites would have the opportunity to visit a group of islands that they had never seen before.

They sailed slowly on purpose. It was indeed between the Fiji Islands and the New Hebrides, at latitude nineteen degrees, thirteen minutes south and longitude one hundred seventy degrees, thirty-five minutes east, that the steamer sent from Marseille at the expense of the Tankerdon and Coverley families was to meet Standard Island.

Needless to say, the wedding of Walter and Miss Dy was more than ever on everyone's mind. How could they have thought of anything else? Calistus Munbar did not have a minute to himself. He was preparing and combining the various elements of a festival that would never be forgotten in the entire history of Standard Island. No one would be surprised if he lost weight in the process.

Standard Island sailed at a speed not exceeding twelve to fifteen miles per twenty-four hours. She soon arrived within sight of Viti, whose superb banks were bordered with luxuriant dark-green forests. She spent three days on these calm waters, sailing from Wanara Island to Round Island. The passage that is also called the Round on the maps was wide open to the Jewel of the Pacific, which engaged in it easily. A large number of whales, startled and panic-stricken, struck her steel hull, which shook beneath their blows. But the iron compartments of the boat were solid and there was no damage.

On the afternoon of the sixth, the last peaks of the Fiji Islands finally disappeared below the horizon. At this moment, Commodore Simcoë left Polynesia and entered the Melanesian region of the Pacific.

During the three following days, Standard Island continued drifting toward the west after reaching the nineteenth degree of latitude. On February 10 she was located in the area where the European steamer they expected was to meet her. This point, marked on all the maps of Milliard City, was known by all the inhabitants. The lookouts at the observatory were on alert. Hundreds of telescopes scanned the horizon and, when the ship was spotted . . . the entire population was waiting . . . Did this not seem like the prologue of the drama eagerly awaited by the people and whose denouement would bring the wedding of Walter Tankerdon and Miss Dy Coverley . . . ?

Standard Island just had to stay put, bracing herself against the currents of these seas squeezed between the archipelagos. Commodore Simcoë gave the necessary orders, and his officers made sure that they were carried out.

"Our situation is decidedly most interesting!" said Yvernès on that day.

This was during the two-hour siesta that he and his comrades usually took after their midday meal.

"Yes," replied Frascolin, "and we will not have to regret our cruise on board Standard Island . . . whatever our friend Zorn might think . . ."

"And despite his eternal sour notes . . . ," quipped the eternal joker Pinchinat. "Thank God they do not show up in his music!"

"Yes, perhaps we'll have nothing to regret . . . especially when the cruise is over," retorted the cellist, "and the fourth-trimester salary that we so well deserve is in our pockets . . ."

"Hey!" said Yvernès. "We already had three trimesters paid by the company since we came aboard, and I much admire Frascolin, our worthy accountant, for sending this considerable sum to the New York bank."

Indeed, the worthy accountant had thought it wise to send this money, through the bankers of Milliard City, to one of the dependable savings banks of the Union. He did not do this out of mistrust, but only because a bank on dry land seemed to offer more security than one floating on the fifteen to eighteen thousand feet of water that is commonly found in the Pacific.

It was during this conversation, among the scented wreaths of smoke from cigars and pipes, that Yvernès made the following observation:

"The wedding festivities promise to be splendid, my friends. Our superintendent is not sparing his imagination or his pains. There will be showers of dollars, and I am certain that the fountains of Milliard City will flow with the finest wines. However, do you know what will be missing from this ceremony . . . ?"

"A cataract of liquid gold flowing onto rocks of diamonds!" cried Pinchinat.

"No," replied Yvernès, "a cantata . . ."

"A cantata . . . ?" inquired Frascolin.

"Of course," said Yvernès. "There will be music; we'll play the most popular pieces for the circumstances . . . but if there is no cantata, no nuptial song, no epithalamium in honor of the young couple . . ."

"Why not, Yvernès?" said Frascolin. "If you feel up to the task of rhyming a dozen lines of verse of unequal length, Sébastien Zorn, who is a seasoned composer, will be happy to put your poem to music . . ."

"What an excellent idea!" exclaimed Pinchinat. "Do you agree, you grumpy old grouch . . . ? Something truly matrimonial, with plenty of *spiccato*, *allegro*, *molto agitato*, and a frenzied *coda* . . . at five dollars a note."

"No . . . free this time . . . ," retorted Frascolin. "It will be the contribution of the Concerting Quartet to the notable nabobs of Standard Island."

It was thus decided, and the cellist declared himself ready to pray to the God of Music for inspiration if the God of Poetry would pour his light onto Yvernès's heart.

From this noble collaboration would issue the Cantata of Cantatas, in imitation of the Song of Songs, in honor of the union of the Tankerdons and Coverleys.

On the afternoon of the tenth, the news spread that a large steamer was in sight, coming from the northeast. Its nationality could not be ascertained because it was still a dozen miles away when the fog of twilight darkened the sea.

The steamer seemed to be sailing at full speed and everyone was certain that it was coming straight toward Standard Island. It probably wanted only to berth alongside the next day at sunrise.

The news produced an indescribable effect. The women were all aflutter at the thought of the marvels of jewelry, fashion, and art objects brought by this ship that had been transformed into an enormous wedding basket of five to six hundred horsepower!

They had made no mistake; this boat flying the flag of the Standard Island Company was definitely bound for Standard Island. Indeed, in the early morning, it drew close to the pier of Starboard Harbor.

But suddenly more news was transmitted to Milliard City by telephone: the flag of this vessel had been lowered to half-mast.

What had happened? An accident . . . a death on board . . . ? This would have been a sad presage for the marriage that was to assure the future of Standard Island.

But it was something quite different. The boat in question was not the one expected, and it did not come from Europe. It came from the American shores, from Madeleine Bay, precisely. Besides, the steamer loaded with the nuptial riches was not at all late. The wedding date was set for February 27, and it was only the eleventh. The steamer still had plenty of time to arrive.

What did this vessel want, then . . . ? What news was it bringing . . . ? Why was its flag at half-mast . . . ? Why did the company send it to this area of the New Hebrides, where they knew it would meet Standard Island . . . ?

Was it bringing an extremely pressing and important communication to the Milliardites . . . ?

Yes, and they would soon learn about it.

The steamer had hardly come alongside when a passenger disembarked.

It was one of the main agents of the company, who refused to answer the questions of the numerous and impatient crowd that had converged on the Starboard Harbor pier.

A tram was ready to leave and, without wasting an instant, the agent jumped onto one of its cars.

Ten minutes later, having arrived at the town hall, he urgently requested an audience with the governor, and this audience was readily granted to him.

Cyrus Bikerstaff received the agent in his office with the door closed.

Less than fifteen minutes later, each one of the thirty council notables was called by telephone and ordered to go immediately to the town hall.

Meanwhile, minds were racing in the harbors and in the city, and curiosity was replaced by the deepest apprehension.

At seven forty, the council met under the direction of the governor, assisted by his two aides. The agent then made the following declaration:

"On January 23, the Standard Island Company Limited went bankrupt, and Mr. William T. Pomering was appointed its liquidator with full powers to act in the best interests of said company."

Mr. William T. Pomering, who had been delegated these functions, was the agent sitting in front of them.

The news spread and, in truth, it did not provoke the effect it would have produced in Europe. What did you expect? Standard Island was "a detached piece of that great region called the United States of America," as Pinchinat said. And a bankruptcy was not going to surprise Americans, and even less catch them off guard . . . Was this not a natural phase of business, an acceptable and accepted incident . . . ? Thus the Milliardites examined the case with their usual calm. The company had gone under . . . okay. This could happen to the most honorable corporation . . . Were its liabilities considerable . . . ? Very much so, as the assessment of the liquidator showed: five hundred million dollars, or two billion five hundred million francs . . . And what could have caused this bankruptcy . . . ? Speculations, wild speculations if you want to call them that since they went sour, but they might have succeeded . . . It was a huge project for the building of a new city in Arkansas on land that had suddenly been swallowed up in an earthquake that could not have been foreseen. After all, it was not the company's fault, and if the lands went down, why should one be surprised if the stockholders went down at the same time . . . ? As solid as Europe seemed, it could happen there one day, too . . . Nothing of the sort was to be feared for Standard Island, and didn't this incident victoriously demonstrate her superiority over the continental lands and terrestrial islands . . . ?

The essential was to act. The total assets of the company were, at the time, equal to the value of the self-propelled island, her hull, factories, hotels, houses, countryside, and flotilla, in other words, everything that the floating device designed by engineer William Tersen carried, everything connected to it, and in addition, the buildings on Madeleine Bay. Would it be the right thing to do then to form a new company that could buy the entire island as a whole in a friendly agreement or at auction . . . ? Yes . . . There was no hesitation on this point and the proceeds of the sale would be applied to pay the company's debts . . . But in forming this company, would the Milliardites need the help of foreign capital . . . ? Were they not wealthy enough to buy Standard Island for themselves with their own resources . . . ? Would it not be preferable for them to become the owners of this Jewel of the Pacific instead of the mere tenants that they were . . . ? Wouldn't their administration be as good as that of the failed company . . . ?

It was no secret that there were billions in the wallets of the council of notables. And thus they made the decision to buy Standard Island as soon as possible. Did the liquidator have the power to carry out the transaction . . . ? He did. Indeed, if the company had any chance to quickly find the money needed for its liquidation, it would be in the pockets of the notables of Milliard City, a few of whom already were among its wealthiest stockholders. Now that the rivalry between the two principal families and the two sections of town had died down, the transaction would be very easy. Among the Anglo-Saxons of the United States, business is done quickly. The funds were gathered immediately. According to the council of notables, it was not even necessary to tap the public. Jem Tankerdon, Nat Coverley, and a few others offered four hundred million dollars. There was not even any discussion as to the price . . . It was to take or to leave . . . and the liquidator took it.

The council of notables got together at eight thirteen in the meeting room of the town hall. When their meeting broke up, at nine forty-seven, Standard Island had become the property of the two super-rich Milliardites and a few of their friends under the name of Jem Tankerdon, Nat Coverley and Co.

If news of the recent failure of the company had brought practically no worry to the population of Standard Island, the news of its acquisition by the main notables triggered no particular anxiety either. They found it very natural, and if a larger sum had been needed, the funds would have been available in no time at all. It was deeply satisfying for these Milliardites to feel that they were at home, or at least that they no longer depended on an outside company. And so the Jewel of the Pacific, represented by all her classes, employees, agents, officers, militiamen, and sailors, went to thank the two heads of families who had so well understood the general welfare.

On that day, a meeting took place in the middle of the park, where the changes were accepted and followed by a triple volley of applause. They immediately named delegates who were sent to the Coverley and Tankerdon mansions.

The delegation was graciously received and left with the assurance that nothing would be changed regarding the rules and customs of Standard Island. The administration would stay the same! All the public employees would keep their positions and all the other employees their jobs.

It could not have been otherwise!

The results from all this were that Commodore Ethel Simcoë remained in charge of maritime services, having command of the movements of Standard Island, following the itineraries decided on by the council of notables. It would be the same for Colonel Stewart and his command of the militia. The same also for the observatory, whose services were unchanged; the king of Malécarlie did not risk losing his position as astronomer. In a word, no one lost the position he had previously held, in the two harbors, the electrical facilities, or the administration of the city. Even Athanase Dorémus was not relieved of his useless functions, although his students persisted in not attending his lessons of dance, good manners, and charm.

There was of course no change in the contract signed with the Concerting Quartet, who, until the end of the voyage, would continue to receive the incredible remuneration that had been promised them at the time of their engagement.

"Those people are amazing!" said Frascolin when he learned that everyone was pleased with the deal that had been made.

"It's because their millions are flowing!" replied Pinchinat.

"We could perhaps have taken advantage of the change of ownership to break our contract . . . ," remarked Sébastien Zorn, who wanted to stick to his absurd prejudices against Standard Island.

"Break our contract!" cried His Highness. "Don't even think about it!"

And with his left hand whose fingers moved as if he were furiously playing his instrument, he threatened the cellist with a powerful punch.

However, a change had to take place in the position of the governor. Cyrus Bikerstaff, being the direct representative of the Standard Island Company, felt that he had to relinquish his post. Under the present circumstances, his decision seemed logical. Thus his resignation was accepted, but under the most honorable conditions. His two aides, Barthelemy Ruge and Hubley Harcourt, half-ruined by the failure of the company, of which they were major shareholders, intended to leave the self-propelled island on one of the next steamers.

Cyrus Bikerstaff agreed to remain as head of the city government until the end of the voyage.

This is how the important financial transformation of the ownership of Standard Island took place, without discussion, problems, or rivalries. The transaction was accomplished so wisely and so quickly that the liquidator was able to leave on the same day, taking with him the signatures of the main buyers and the guarantee of the council of notables.

As for that remarkable character named Calistus Munbar, the superintendent of fine arts and entertainment on the incomparable Jewel of the Pacific, he was simply confirmed in his responsibilities, wages, and benefits, and surely the Milliardites could never have found a worthy successor to this irreplaceable man.

"Well," remarked Frascolin, "everything is for the best, the future of Standard Island is secure, there is nothing more to fear . . ."

"We shall see!" muttered the cellist.

These were the conditions under which the wedding of Walter Tankerdon and Miss Dy was to take place. The two families were now united by monetary interests, which, in America as anywhere else, create the most solid social bonds. It assured the prosperity of all the citizens of the island. Now that Standard Island belonged to the principal Milliardites, she seemed more independent than before, and more in charge of her own destiny! Before, a cable had kept her moored to Madeleine Bay in the United States, but now she had broken that cable!

And now was the time to celebrate!

We do not need to dwell on the joy of the celebrations in question, to express the inexpressible, to depict the happiness radiating around them. The fiancés spent all their time together. What could have been seen as a marriage of convenience was, in truth, a love match. Interest played no part in the affection Walter and Miss Dy felt for each other. These two young people possessed qualities that would ensure them a lifetime of happiness. Walter's soul was made of gold, and the soul of Miss Dy was made of the same substance, in a metaphorical sense, of course, and not in the literal sense of their millions. They were made for each other; these rather banal words were never so true. They were counting the days and the hours separating them from February 27, the date that they were so eagerly awaiting. They only regretted that Standard Island was not sailing toward the one hundred eightieth degree of longitude, because, coming from the west, she would have had to erase twenty-four hours from her calendar. The happiness of the future couple would have been advanced by one day. But they could do nothing about that; it was in sight of the New Hebrides that the ceremony was to take place and they simply had to accept this.

But the ship loaded with the marvels of Europe and all the wedding presents had not arrived yet. These were luxuries that the two fiancés would have gladly done without; they did not need this royal lavishness. They gave each other their love; they wanted nothing more.

But the families, the friends, and the inhabitants of Standard Island wanted this ceremony to be one of exceptional brilliance. Their telescopes were constantly scrutinizing the eastern horizon. Jem Tankerdon and Nat Coverley even promised a large prize to the person who would first sight this steamer whose propellers could never turn fast enough for the impatient public.

Meanwhile, the program of festivities was carefully planned. It included games, receptions, the double ceremonies at the Protestant and Catholic churches, the gala evening at the town hall, and the festival in the park. Calistus Munbar kept an eye on everything; he was everywhere, he spared no effort, to the point of ruining his health. It could not be otherwise. His temperament drove him, and he could no more be stopped than could a train at full speed.

The cantata was ready. Yvernès, the poet, and Sébastien Zorn, the musician, proved worthy of each other. The cantata would be sung by the chorus of an Orphic Society that had been founded for this very purpose. When the music exploded in the observatory square, electrically illuminated for the night, the effect would be fantastic.

Next, the young couple would appear before the civil officer, and later, at midnight, the religious ceremony would take place amid the bright, festive lights of Milliard City.

At last the awaited ship was sighted on the horizon. It was one of the lookouts of Starboard Harbor who won the prize that amounted to an impressive number of dollars.

It was nine o'clock on the morning of February 19 when the ship passed the harbor's jetty, and the landing began immediately.

There is no need to give a detailed cataloging of the jewelry, the dresses, the latest fashions, and the art objects that composed this nuptial cargo. It is enough to say that the display of these objects in the large rooms of the Coverley mansion was an unparalleled success. The entire population of Milliard City wanted to admire these marvels. Most of the Milliardites, who were immensely wealthy, could certainly have afforded to buy such magnificent items, but they were ecstatic about the artistic qualities of these objects. Moreover, the foreign women who may have wanted to know what some of these articles were could find out by referring to the *Starboard Chronicle* or the *New Herald* of February 21 and 22. If they were still not completely satisfied, it is because absolute satisfaction does not exist in this world.

"Gosh," said Yvernès simply when he came out of the showrooms of Fifteenth Avenue with his three comrades.

"'Gosh' seems to me the right expression," observed Pinchinat. "It would make one want to marry Miss Dy without a dowry . . . for herself alone!"

As for the engaged couple, they paid only vague attention to this stockpile of artistic and fashion masterpieces.

Meanwhile, after the steamer's arrival, Standard Island headed west again in order to reach the New Hebrides. If one of the islands of the group had been sighted before the twenty-seventh, Captain Sarol would have disembarked with his companions, and Standard Island would have started on her return voyage.

The navigation of the western Pacific was expected to be easy because the Malay captain knew the region well. At the request of Commodore Simcoë, who had asked for his help, he settled into the observatory tower. When the first land appeared, he was to sail close to Erromango Island, one of the easternmost islands of the group; this would allow Standard Island to avoid the treacherous reefs of the New Hebrides.

Was it just by chance, or did Captain Sarol make a point of sailing slowly because he hoped to participate in the wedding festival? Whatever the reason, the first islands appeared only on the morning of February 27, the very day set for the marriage ceremony.

But it did not really matter. The marriage of Walter Tankerdon and Miss Dy Coverley would be just as happy if it were celebrated in view of the New Hebrides, and if the brave Malays—as they seemed to imply— would find great pleasure in taking part in the festival, they would be welcome to it.

Standard Island first encountered a few islets, and after sailing around them as Captain Sarol advised, she headed for Erromango, leaving the heights of Tanna Island to the south.

In this area, Sébastien Zorn, Frascolin, Pinchinat, and Yvernès were not very far—three hundred miles at the most—from the French possessions of this part of the Pacific, the Loyalty Islands and New Caledonia, with its prison located half a world away from France. The interior of Erromango had very thick forests and many hills, with large expanses of arable land in the valleys. Commodore Simcoë dropped anchor within a mile of the eastern coast of Cook Bay. It would have been dangerous to come closer because the coral reefs could be seen just above the water half a mile into the ocean. Moreover, Governor Bikerstaff had never intended to stop at this island or at any other of this archipelago. After the festivities, the Malays were to disembark and Standard Island was to sail back toward the equator to return to Madeleine Bay.

It was one o'clock in the afternoon when Standard Island came to a halt.

The authorities gave the order for everyone to stop working: civil servants, employees, sailors, and militia men all had the time off, except for the customs officers who were on duty along the coast.

The weather was beautiful, cooled by the sea breeze. According to the well-known expression, "the sun shone down on them."

"Really, this lofty disk seems to be at the beck and call of these rich people!" cried Pinchinat. "If they ordered it to prolong the day, like Joshua did a long time ago, it would do so! Oh! The power of money!"

We will not elaborate on the various acts of the sensational program created by the superintendent of entertainment of Milliard City. From three in the afternoon, all the residents, those from the country as well as those from the city and the harbors, flocked to the park alongside the banks of the Serpentine River. The notables mixed familiarly with the ordinary people. Sports were played with great enthusiasm; perhaps the value of the prizes had something to do with this. There were dances in the open air. The most brilliant ball took place in one of the large halls of the casino, where the young men and women tried to outdo each other in grace and vivacity. Yvernès and Pinchinat took part in these dances and were second to none; they danced with the prettiest Milliardites of Standard Island. His Highness had never been more charming, never had he shown such wit, never had he had so much success. It is not surprising that, after a whirlwind waltz, when his partner said to him, "I am dissolving into water, Monsieur," he answered, "But it's the waters of Vals, Miss, the waters of excitation!"

Frascolin, who was listening, blushed to the roots of his hair, and Yvernès, who overheard Pinchinat too, feared that lighting from the heavens would explode upon the head of the indelicate chap.

All the Coverleys and Tankerdons were there and Miss Dy's graceful sisters seemed very happy for her. Miss Dy was walking on the arm of Walter, which was totally acceptable among the citizens of liberated America. People applauded the lovely couple, they congratulated them, they offered them flowers and compliments that were received with perfect affability.

During the following hours, abundant refreshments maintained the high spirits of the guests.

When night fell, the park was aglow with light from aluminum moons. The sun had wisely disappeared below the horizon! He would have been humiliated to witness these artificial illuminations that rendered the night as bright as day.

The cantata was sung between ten and eleven o'clock with such success that neither the poet nor the composer could believe it. And at that moment, the cellist may very well have felt his unfair prejudice against the Jewel of the Pacific finally disappear . . .

At the stroke of eleven, the long wedding procession advanced toward the town hall. Walter Tankerdon and Miss Dy Coverley walked amid their families. The whole population accompanied them along First Avenue.

Governor Cyrus Bikerstaff was waiting in the grand lounge of the town hall. The most beautiful of all weddings in which he had officiated during his long administrative career was about to take place . . .

But suddenly cries exploded from the Larboard section.

The procession stopped abruptly.

Almost immediately, along with cries that became louder, detonations were heard in the distance.

Moments later, several customs officers—a few of whom were wounded—ran into the square of the town hall.

Anxiety was at its height. The irrational terror that is born of unknown danger tore through the crowd.

Cyrus Bikerstaff appeared on the porch of the town hall, followed by Commodore Simcoë, Colonel Stewart, and the notables who had just joined them.

To the questions aimed at them, the customs officers replied that Standard Island had just been invaded by a band of three or four thousand New Hebrideans, with Captain Sarol as their leader.

XI

~~~~~~~~~

Offense and Defense

SUCH WAS THE START OF the vile conspiracy prepared by Captain Sarol, with the collaboration of the Malays rescued with him on Standard Island, the New Hebrideans taken on board at Samoa, and the natives of Erromango and the neighboring islands. What would be its outcome? This could not be predicted, given the conditions in which this sudden violent aggression took place.

The New Hebridean Group was made up of one hundred fifty islands under the general protection of England but depending geographically on Australia. However, as in the case of the Solomon Islands located in the northwest of the same area, the question of protectorate was a subject of discord between France and the United Kingdom. Moreover, the United States was not happy to see European colonies established in the middle of an ocean that it hoped to claim as its alone in the foreseeable future. By taking possession of these various groups of islands, Great Britain was trying to form the supply stations that it would need in case the Australian colonies refused to recognize the supremacy of the Foreign Office.

The population of the New Hebrides was made up of blacks and Malays of Kanaka origin. But the dispositions of these natives, their temperaments and their instincts, were different in the northern and southern islands, and thus this archipelago could be seen as divided into two distinct groups.

In the northern group, in Santo Island and Saint Philip Bay, for example, their physical type was more refined, with a lighter complexion and straighter hair. The men, stocky and strong, gentle and peaceful, never attacked the European trading posts or vessels. The same situation existed in Vate or Sandwich Island, where several villages flourished. Among these was Porta Villa, the capital of the archipelago, also called Franceville, where our colonists took advantage of the fertile soil, the rich pastures, the fields suitable for cultivation, the land ideal for raising coffee, bananas, and coconuts, and where the copra industry was thriving. The customs of this group of natives had completely changed since the arrival of the Europeans. Their moral and intellectual levels had increased. Thanks to the efforts of the missionaries, the cannibalism that used to be so rampant no longer existed. Unfortunately, the Kanaka race was in decline and was obviously going to disappear, to the detriment of this northern group that had been transformed through contact with the European civilization.

But regrets of this sort would have been totally out of place in the southern islands of the archipelago. Thus it was not without reason that Captain Sarol had chosen the southern group to organize his criminal attack on Standard Island. On these islands, the natives had remained true Papuans, relegated to the bottom of the human scale, in Tanna as well as in Erromango. Concerning this last island in particular, a former sandalwood merchant had rightly told Dr. Hayen, "If this island could talk, it would tell things horrible enough to make your hair stand on end!"

Indeed, these Kanakas of inferior origin had not been improved by the infusion of Polynesian blood as had those in the northern islands. The Anglican missionaries—five of whom had been murdered since 1839—had converted only half of the twenty-five hundred inhabitants of Erromango to Christianity. The other half remained pagan. Moreover, converts or not, they were still the same ferocious people who deserved their sinister reputation, although they were shorter and less robust than the natives of Santo Island or Sandwich Island. Tourists who ventured through this southern group had to be on guard against the constant possibility of attack.

The following are but a few examples:

About fifty years ago, pirates attacked the brig *Aurore* and France made them pay dearly. In 1869 the missionary Gordon was bludgeoned to death. In 1875 the crew of a British vessel was treacherously attacked and murdered and then devoured by the cannibals. In 1894, in the neighboring Louisiade Archipelago, at Rossel Island, a French merchant and his workmen, as well as the captain of a Chinese ship and his crew, perished beneath the blows of these cannibals. Finally, the English cruiser *Royalist* was compelled to go on a campaign to punish these savages for having murdered a large number of Europeans. And when these stories were told, Pinchinat, who had recently escaped from the terrible molars of the Fijians, no longer shrugged his shoulders.

Such was the population from which Captain Sarol had recruited his accomplices. He had promised them that, together, they would sack the opulent Jewel of the Pacific and not spare even one of her inhabitants. Some of the natives who were watching the approaching vessel from the coast of Erromango came from the neighboring islands that were set apart only by narrow passages. They came mostly from the island of Tanna, which was only thirty-five miles south. From there also came the robust savages of the Wanissi district who went around almost completely naked and fiercely worshipped the god Teapolo, plus the natives of Plage Noire and of Sangalli, the most fearsome and most feared people of the archipelago.

But while the northern group was relatively less brutish, it did not mean that these natives would not be of help to Captain Sarol. To the north of Sandwich Island was Api Island, with its eighteen thousand inhabitants who ate their prisoners. Their victims' chests were given to the young people, their arms and thighs to the adults, and their innards to the dogs and pigs. There was also Paama Island, whose tribes were as fierce as the natives of Api. There was Mallicolo Island, with its Kanaka cannibals. And finally there was Aurora Island, the worst one of the archipelago, where not a single white man had ever established his residence and where, a few years before, the entire crew of a French boat had been massacred. It was from these various islands that Captain Sarol recruited his reinforcements.

As soon as Standard Island appeared, as soon as she was only a few cable lengths from Erromango, Captain Sarol sent the signal awaited by the natives.

Within a few minutes, three or four thousand savages were able to reach Standard Island, stepping on the rocks at the water level.

The danger was most serious, because these New Hebrideans, once unleashed upon Milliard City, would not back down from any sort of attack or violence. They had the advantage of surprise and were armed not only with long spears tipped with bones that caused dangerous wounds and arrows capped with vegetable poison but also with Snyder rifles, which were much in use on the archipelago.

At the start of the attack that had been long in the making—for it was Sarol who was leading the assailants—the militia, the sailors, the civil employees, and all the able-bodied men on Standard Island were sent into combat.

Cyrus Bikerstaff, Commodore Simcoë, and Colonel Stewart remained calm. The king of Malécarlie offered his services, too, for although he no longer had the strength of a young man, his courage was still intact. The natives were on the side of Larboard Harbor, where the port officer was trying to organize resistance. But it was obvious that the gangs of savages would soon hurl themselves upon the city.

To begin with, orders were given to lock the gates of the fence surrounding Milliard City, where almost the entire population had gathered for the wedding festivities. That the countryside and the park would be trampled was to be expected. That the two harbors and the electric plants would be wrecked was also to be feared. That the Prow and Stern Batteries would be destroyed could not be avoided. The greatest misfortune would be that the artillery of Standard Island would be used to ravage the city, and it was not impossible that the Malays knew how to use it . . .

First of all, on the recommendation of the king of Malécarlie, most of the women and children were sheltered in the town hall.

This vast municipal building was shrouded in darkness, as was the entire island, for the electric generators had stopped functioning when the engineers had to flee the attackers.

Meanwhile, Commodore Simcoë ordered that the arms stored in the town hall be distributed to the militia and the sailors, and there was plenty of ammunition to go around. Leaving Miss Dy with Mrs. Tankerdon and Mrs. Coverley, Walter came to join the group made up of Jem Tankerdon, Nat Coverley, Calistus Munbar, Pinchinat, Yvernès, Frascolin, and Sébastien Zorn.

"Well . . . it seems things had to end up like this . . . !" murmured the cellist.

"But it has not ended yet!" cried the superintendent. "It certainly has not ended yet, and our beloved Standard Island is not going to succumb to a handful of Kanakas!"

Well spoken, Calistus Munbar! The anger that consumed you at the thought of these New Hebrideans interrupting such a well-organized festival was understandable! Yes, you had to hope that they would be driven back. But unfortunately, if they were not superior in number, they had the advantage of being the assailants.

In the meantime, shots continued to be heard far away, coming from the direction of the two harbors. Captain Sarol had begun by stopping the propellers to keep Standard Island from drifting away from Erromango, where his operations were based.

The governor, the king of Malécarlie, Commodore Simcoë, and Colonel Stewart, who had formed a defense committee, first thought of counterattacking. But this would have meant sacrificing many of the defenders whom they sorely needed. They could not hope for more mercy from these natives than from the wild animals that had invaded them two weeks earlier. Moreover, would these savages not have tried to run Standard Island aground on the rocks of Erromango in order to plunder her later . . . ?

An hour later, the assailants arrived at the gates of Milliard City. They tried to tear the gates down, but the gates held. They tried to climb them, but the Milliardites repulsed them with gunfire.

As they had not been able to take Milliard City by surprise, the savages could not hope to force an entry in total darkness. Therefore, Captain Sarol brought them back to the park and the countryside, where they waited for daybreak.

Between four and five in the morning the first light of dawn appeared in the east. The militia and the sailors, under the command of Commodore Simcoë and Colonel Stewart, leaving half of their men at the town hall, assembled in Observatory Square, thinking that Captain Sarol might try to force open the gates on that side. Indeed, as no help could have come from the outside, they absolutely had to keep the savages from entering the town.

The quartet followed the defenders whose officers led them toward the end of First Avenue.

"To think that we escaped the cannibals on the Fiji Islands and that now we have to defend our own cutlets against the cannibals from the New Hebrides . . . ," cried Pinchinat.

"By Jove, they will not eat us whole!" answered Yvernès.

"And I will resist to my last shred, like the hero of Labiche!" he added. Sébastien Zorn remained silent. Everyone knew what he thought of their adventure, but this would not keep him from doing his duty.

As soon as it became day, shots were exchanged through the gates of the square. The enclosure of the observatory was courageously defended. There were victims on both sides. In the camp of the Milliardites, Jem Tankerdon sustained a slight shoulder wound, but he would not abandon his post. Nat Coverley and Walter were among the most dangerously exposed fighters. The king of Malécarlie, defying the shots from the Snyder rifles, tried to hit Captain Sarol, who was leading his savages.

In truth, there were too many assailants! Every fighter from Erromango, Tanna, and the neighboring islands was attacking Milliard City. There was one fortunate circumstance, however, and Commodore Simcoë took notice of it: Standard Island, instead of moving with the current toward the coast of Erromango, was drifting in the direction of the northern archipelago, although it would have been better if she had gone out to sea.

Yet time went by. The savages redoubled their efforts, and the defenders could not hold them back in spite of their courageous resistance. Around ten o'clock, the gates were torn down. Faced with the screaming hordes that were invading the square, Commodore Simcoë was forced to retreat to the town hall, which would have to be defended like a fortress.

Retreating, the militia and the sailors lost ground step by step. Perhaps they could hope that the New Hebrideans, having forced the gates, would scatter through the various quarters of the city, driven by their instinct for plunder. It would have given the Milliardites some advantage . . .

Vain hope! Captain Sarol would not let the natives leave First Avenue. It was from there that they would reach the town hall and crush the last efforts of the besieged. Once Captain Sarol had captured the town hall, his victory would be assured and the hour of massacre and looting would begin.

"Clearly, there are too many of them!" said Frascolin, whose arm had just been grazed by a spear.

The arrows were raining down and so were the bullets as the defenders retreated farther and farther.

Around two o'clock, they had been forced back to the square of the town hall. Each camp already had about fifty casualties, and at least two or three times as many wounded. Before the municipal palace could be invaded by the savages, the defenders ran to it, closed its doors, and made the women and children take refuge in the inside apartments where they would be sheltered from the projectiles. Next, Cyrus Bikerstaff, the king of Malécarlie, Commodore Simcoë, Colonel Stewart, Jem Tankerdon, Nat Coverley, their friends, the militia, and the sailors posted themselves at the windows and the firing started again with renewed violence.

"We must hold here," said the governor. "It is our last chance. May God grant a miracle to save us all!"

The order to attack was immediately given by Captain Sarol, who felt certain that he would win the battle even if the task proved very arduous. Indeed, the doors of the town hall were solid and it would have been difficult to break them down without the help of cannons. The savages attacked them with axes, and the gunfire from the windows made them lose many men. But this did not stop their leader, and yet, if he had been killed, perhaps everything would have changed . . .

Two hours went by and the town hall still resisted. Bullets were decimating the assailants, but their number was constantly renewed. The best marksmen, Jem Tankerdon and Colonel Stewart, tried in vain to hit Captain Sarol. While many of his people fell around him, he seemed invulnerable.

Bu it was not Sarol whom the bullet of a Snyder rifle reached on the central balcony in the middle of the heaviest gunfire. It was Cyrus Bikerstaff, who was hit in the middle of his chest. He fell and could pronounce only a few indistinct words. Blood was pouring out of his mouth. They brought him to the back room, where he soon expired. And so perished the first governor of Standard Island, who had been a skillful administrator and a great and honest man.

The assault continued with redoubled fury. The doors were about to give in beneath the axes of the savages. How could the defenders keep the last fortress of Standard Island from falling? How could they save the women, the children, and all the people who were inside from a general massacre?

The king of Malécarlie, Ethel Simcoë, and Colonel Stewart debated then if it would not be wise to flee through the back doors of the palace. But where could they find safety . . . ? At the Prow Battery . . . ? But would they be able to reach it . . . ? In one of the harbors . . . ? But hadn't the savages already taken them . . . ? And their numerous wounded, would they abandon them . . . ?

At that moment something very fortunate happened that would reverse the situation.

The king of Malécarlie appeared on the balcony, ignoring the bullets and arrows that rained around him. He raised his rifle and fired at Captain Sarol at the very moment when one of the doors was opening to the assailants.

Captain Sarol fell dead on the spot.

The Malays, stunned by the loss of their leader, drew back, taking his body with them, and ran back toward the gates of the square.

Almost at the same time, shouts were heard at the top of First Avenue, where the shooting became louder.

What was happening . . . ? Had the defenders of the harbors and their batteries regained the advantage . . . ? Had they run toward the city . . . ? Were they trying to overtake the savages from the rear, in spite of their own small number . . . ?

"Isn't the firing getting louder near the observatory . . . ?" asked Colonel Stewart.

"It's probably reinforcements coming for these scoundrels!" answered Commodore Simcoë.

"I don't think so," observed the king of Malécarlie. "These shots cannot be explained . . ."

"Indeed . . . ! This is something new," cried Pinchinat, "and it is going to help us . . ."

"Look . . . look!" cried Calistus Munbar. "All the rascals are starting to run away . . ."

"Let's go, my friends," said the king of Malécarlie, "let's chase these devils out of our city . . . Hurry up . . . !"

The officers, the militia, and the sailors went down to the first floor and ran out the main door.

The square was being abandoned by a crowd of fleeing savages, some of them running along First Avenue and the others running through the neighboring streets.

What could have caused such a swift and unexpected change . . . ? Was it the disappearance of Captain Sarol and the lack of leadership that followed . . . ? Was it possible that the assailants, who were so superior in number, were so discouraged by the death of their leader, and this at the very moment the town hall was about to be invaded . . . ?

Led by Commodore Simcoë and Colonel Stewart, about two hundred members of the navy and the militia accompanied by Jem and Walter Tankerdon, Nat Coverley, Frascolin, and his comrades went down First Avenue, pursuing the fleeing savages, who never even turned around to fire off a final bullet or arrow and dropped their Snyder rifles along with their bows and arrows.

"Forward . . . ! Forward . . . !" cried Commodore Simcoë in a booming voice.

However, as they approached the observatory, the firing became louder and it was evident that the fighting was very fierce . . .

Had some help come to Standard Island . . . ? But what sort of help, and from where . . . ? Anyway, the assailants were fleeing in every direction, seized by an incomprehensible panic. Were they being attacked by reinforcements that came from Larboard Harbor . . . ?

Yes . . . a thousand New Hebrideans had invaded Standard Island under the command of the French colonists from Sandwich Island. The quartet was greeted in their national language when they met their courageous compatriots! Following are the circumstances that brought about this unexpected, we could even say quasi-miraculous, intervention.

During the previous night and since daybreak, Standard Island had constantly drifted toward Sandwich Island, where, as we must recall, a prosperous French colony had been established. And when the colonists heard of the attack made by Captain Sarol, they decided, along with a thousand devoted natives, to rush to the aid of the self-propelled island. But to bring them there, the small vessels of Sandwich Island were inadequate . . .

You can imagine the joy of these good colonists when, in the morning, Standard Island, pushed by the current, moved closer and closer to their land. The colonists leaped into their boats, followed by the natives, most of them swimming behind them, and landed at Larboard Harbor . . .

In an instant, they were joined by the men of the Stern and Prow Batteries who had remained in the harbors. Together they ran toward Milliard City, crossing the countryside and the park. Thanks to this diversion, the town hall did not fall into the hands of the savages, who had already been badly shaken by the death of Captain Sarol.

Two hours later, the New Hebridean bands, pursued from every direction, tried to save themselves by jumping into the sea in order to reach Sandwich Island, and most of them drowned beneath the bullets of the militia.

After that, Standard Island had nothing more to fear: she was saved from plunder, massacre, and total annihilation.

One would think that the outcome of this terrible affair would have produced public displays of joy and thanksgiving . . . But no! These Americans are always so amazing! It seemed that the final result did not surprise them . . . that they had been expecting it . . . And yet the attempt of Captain Sarol had come so close to causing a dreadful disaster!

However, we may be allowed to believe that the main owners of Standard Island congratulated themselves privately for having been able to keep their two-billion-dollar property, especially at the moment when the marriage of Walter Tankerdon and Miss Dy Coverley was going to assure its future.

When the two fiancés saw each other again, they fell in each other's arms, and no one considered their conduct improper. After all, they should have been married twenty-four hours earlier . . .

You will not find an example of the ultra-American reserve in the welcome our Parisian musicians gave to the French colonists of Sandwich Island, though. The Concerting Quartet received warm handshakes and congratulations from their compatriots. Even though the bullets had spared the Parisians, they did their duty gallantly, our two violins, our alto, and our cello! As for the excellent Athanase Dorémus, who quietly stayed in the casino room, he had been waiting for a student who persisted in not coming, but could we reproach him for that . . . ?

The superintendent reacted differently from the others. As thoroughly Yankee as he was, he was still wild with joy. What could you expect? The blood of the famous Barnum was coursing through his veins, and we should gladly accept the fact that the descendant of such an ancestor was not as reserved as his North American compatriots!

After the battle was over, the king and queen of Malécarlie went back to their home on Thirty-Seventh Street, and the council of notables went to thank the king for his courage and his devotion to the common cause.

Standard Island was thus safe and sound. Its defense had been costly: Cyrus Bikerstaff killed at the height of the battle, sixty militiamen and sailors hit by bullets and arrows, and about as many among the civil servants, employees, and merchants who had fought so bravely. The entire population took part in the public mourning, and the Jewel of the Pacific would never forget it.

Besides, the Milliardites, accustomed to acting quickly in any circumstances, would restore order in no time. After a stop of a few days at Sandwich Island, any trace of the bloody battle would have disappeared.

In the meantime, there was complete agreement on the military command of the island being given to Commodore Simcoë. Because of this, there was no competition and no problem. Neither Mr. Jem Tankerdon nor Mr. Nat Coverley wanted to take this away from him. Later, an election would resolve the important business of choosing a new governor for Standard Island.

The following day, an impressive ceremony called the population to the quays of Starboard Harbor.

The corpses of the Malays and the natives were thrown into the sea. It would not be the same for the citizens killed defending the island. Their bodies were piously gathered and brought to the church and the cathedral, where they received due honors. Governor Cyrus Bikerstaff as well as the humblest among them were honored with the same prayers and the same grief.

Then the funeral cargo was entrusted to one of the rapid steamers of Standard Island, and the vessel departed for Madeleine Bay, carrying the precious remains to Christian soil.

XII

~~~~~~~~~~

Taking the Helm, Starboard or Larboard?

STANDARD ISLAND HAD LEFT THE Sandwich Island region on March 3. Before their departure, the Milliardites had expressed their heartfelt gratitude to the French colony and its native allies. These were friends whom they would see again; they were brothers whom Sébastien Zorn and his comrades left on this island of the New Hebrides Group that would, from now on, figure on the annual itinerary of Standard Island.

Under Commodore Simcoë's direction, the repairs had been quickly made. Besides, the damage was slight. The electric generators were intact. With the petroleum they had left, their machines could run for several weeks. Moreover, the self-propelled island would soon reach the area of the Pacific where her underwater cables would allow her to be in contact with Madeleine Bay. People were therefore reassured that the voyage would end without any further complications. In less than four months, Standard Island would be back on the American coast.

"Let's hope so," said Sébastien Zorn while the superintendent was as usual getting carried away about the future of his marvelous seafaring machine.

"But," observed Calistus Munbar, "what a lesson we were given . . . ! Those Malays who seemed so helpful and that Captain Sarol, no one would have suspected them . . . ! For sure, this is the last time that Standard Island will ever give shelter to strangers . . ."

"Even if a shipwreck puts them in your path?" asked Pinchinat.

"My dear friend, I don't believe in shipwrecks or shipwrecked people anymore!"

But although Commodore Simcoë was still commander of the self-propelled island, he was not its governor. Since Cyrus Bikerstaff's death,

Milliard City had had no mayor and, as we know, his former aides had not kept their posts. Thus Standard Island needed a new governor.

As long as the government offices no longer existed, Walter Tankerdon and Miss Coverley could not be married. This was a predicament that would not have come about had it not been for the machinations of that rascal Sarol! And not only the future spouses, but all the notables of Milliard City and the entire population wanted this wedding to take place as soon as possible. It was one of the most reliable assurances for the future. They had to hurry because Walter Tankerdon was already planning to board one of the Starboard Harbor steamers and head with both families to the nearest archipelago, where a mayor could celebrate the wedding . . . ! After all, there were mayors on Samoa, on Tonga, and on the Marquesas Islands, and if they sailed at full speed, in less than a week . . .

The more experienced people talked sense into the impatient young man . . . They started to prepare for the election . . . In a few days, a new governor would be chosen . . . The first act of his administration would be to perform with great pomp the marriage ceremony that had been awaited for so long. The previous program of festivities would resume . . . We need a mayor . . . we need a mayor . . . ! This was the cry from every mouth . . . !

"Let's hope that this election will not reignite old rivalries that were never completely extinct!" observed Frascolin.

"It won't," thought Calistus Munbar, and he was determined to do all he could to bring the matter to a good end.

"Anyway," he said "aren't our lovers here . . . ? You will agree with me, I think, that vanity has no chance to win over love!"

Standard Island kept advancing northeast toward the point where the twelfth parallel south crosses the one hundred seventy-fifth meridian west. It was in this area that the last cablegrams sent before the stop at the New Hebrides had asked the supply ships from Madeleine Bay to rendezvous with the self-propelled island. But Commodore Simcoë was not particularly concerned about their arrival. Since the island had enough provisions for more than a month, there was no cause for worry. But foreign news was in short supply. The *Starboard Chronicle* deplored the scarcity of political news, and the *New Herald* was upset . . . But what did it matter! Standard Island was a little world unto herself, and why should she be concerned about what was happening in the rest of the earthly sphere . . . ? Were people dying to hear about politics . . . ? They would soon experience enough politics on their own territory . . . too much perhaps!

Indeed, the electoral period had started. The thirty members of the council of notables, with an equal number of Larboardites and Starboardites, were hard at work. It was readily evident that the choice of the new governor would provoke serious discussion, since Jem Tankerdon and Nat Coverley were to be on opposite sides.

A few days were spent preparing for the contest. From the very outset, it was obvious that the council would not come to an easy agreement, given the egotism of both candidates. A muted anxiety pervaded the city and the harbors. Agents from both sections tried to initiate a popular movement that would bring pressure on the notables. Time went by and it did not seem that an agreement would be reached. Should it not have been feared that Jem Tankerdon and the main Larboardites would want to impose their ideas that had been rebuked earlier by the main Starboardites, that they would again consider their unfortunate project of transforming Standard Island into an industrial and commercial island . . . ? This would never be accepted by the other faction! At times the Coverley party seemed about to prevail, and at other times the Tankerdon camp looked as if they had the upper hand. This caused bitter recriminations and ugly exchanges between the two camps, an iciness that Walter and Miss Dy did not even want to recognize. All this political rubbish was of no concern to them.

There was, however, one very simple solution, at least from an administrative point of view; they could have decided that the two contenders would, each in their turn, act as governor, one for the first six months of the year and the other for the next six, or even each man for one year at a time, if this seemed preferable. Then there would be no further rivalry, and the agreement would satisfy both parties. But common sense never stands a chance of being adopted in this world, and although Standard Island was independent of the terrestrial continents, she was still under the influence of all the passions of sublunar humanity!

"Here," said Frascolin one day to his comrades, "are the problems that I feared . . ."

"And what do we care about these quarrels!" answered Pinchinat. "What harm could come to us from them . . . ! In a few months we will be back at Madeleine Bay, our commitment will expire, and we will all be on solid ground again . . . with a cozy little million in our pockets . . ."

"If another catastrophe does not occur before that!" retorted the inflexible Sébastien Zorn. Can a floating machine of this sort ever be sure of its future . . . ? After the attack by the English ship, came the invasion of the wild beasts; and after the wild beasts, the invasion of the New Hebrideans . . . and after the savages, the . . ."

"Will you be quiet, o bird of ill omen!" cried Yvernès. "Be quiet or we will padlock your beak!"

Yet there were ample reasons to regret that the Tankerdon-Coverley marriage had not been celebrated on the chosen date. If the families had been joined by this new tie, perhaps the tension would have been reduced . . . The young couple would have played a more efficient role . . . But after all, this unrest could not last much longer, as the election was to take place on March 15.

At this point Commodore Simcoë tried to reconcile the two opposing camps, but he was told to mind his own business. He had the island to steer, and he should concentrate on that . . . ! He had the reefs to avoid, and he should concentrate on that . . . ! Politics was none of his business.

Commodore Simcoë had learned his lesson.

Even religious passions entered the dispute and the clergy, perhaps wrongly, took a bigger part in it than they should have. The church and the cathedral, the pastor and the bishop, had always been such good friends!

As for the newspapers, they too entered the arena. The *New Herald* fought for the Tankerdons and the *Starboard Chronicle* for the Coverleys. The ink flowed, and it was even feared that it would soon mix with blood . . . ! Good heavens! Had not the virgin ground of Standard Island already been soaked in blood during the fight against the savages of the New Hebrides . . . !

In truth, most people of Standard Island were interested in the young couple whose love story had been interrupted in its first chapter. But what could they have done to assure their happiness? Exchanges between the two sections of Milliard City had already come to an end. There were no more receptions, no more invitations, no more musical evenings! If this continued, the Concerting Quartet's instruments would mildew in their cases, and our musicians would earn their enormous salaries with their hands in their pockets.

The superintendent was sick with worry, although he did not want to admit it. He felt that his position was false because he had to use all his intelligence not to displease anyone, which is the surest way to displease everyone.

By March 12, Standard Island had advanced quite a way toward the equator, but not enough to meet the ships from Madeleine Bay. It would not be long before they did, but the elections would take place before that, as they were fixed for the fifteenth.

Meanwhile, the Larboardites and the Starboardites were constantly examining their chances of success. It always came down to projections of a tie. No majority would be possible unless a few voters broke away from one side or the other. But the voters held to their opinions like the teeth to the jaw of a tiger.

Then a brilliant idea emerged. It seemed to have sprung forth at the same time from the minds of all those who were not going to be consulted. This idea was simple, it was good, it would put an end to the rivalries. The candidates themselves would probably accept this just solution.

Why not offer the government of Standard Island to the king of Malécarlie? This former monarch was a wise person, a big and strong mind. His tolerance and philosophy would be the best guarantees against future problems. He knew men because he had observed them at close range. He knew that he would encounter their weaknesses and their ingratitude. He was no longer ruled by ambition and would never try to substitute his personal power to the democratic institutions of the self-propelled island. He would simply be the chairman of the board of the new Tankerdon-Coverley Company, Incorporated.

A significant group of merchants and civil employees of Milliard City, accompanied by a considerable number of officers and sailors from both harbors, decided to present this proposal, as their wish, to their royal fellow citizen.

Their Majesties received the delegation in the downstairs living room of their house on Thirty-Ninth Street. They listened kindly to the people but adamantly rejected their offer. The deposed rulers thought of their past and confronted their memories.

"I thank you, gentlemen," said the king. "We are touched by your request, but we are happy as we are, and we hope that, from now on, nothing will interfere with our future. Believe me, we have lost all illusions of any monarchy to come! I know that I am just a simple astronomer in the observatory of Standard Island and I do not wish for anything more."

There was no good reason to persist after such a formal refusal, and the delegation left.

In the final days prior to the vote, the people became even more agitated and could not agree on anything. The supporters of Jem Tankerdon and Nat Coverley avoided meeting each other in the streets. People no longer walked from one section to the other. Neither the Starboardites nor the Larboardites crossed First Avenue. Milliard City was now made up of two hostile cities. The only character who still ran from one side to the other, agitated, crushed, exhausted, sweating blood, wearing himself out with his good advice, repulsed by one and all, was the despairing superintendent Calistus Munbar. Two or three times a day, he ran aground, like a rudderless ship, in the rooms of the casino where the quartet showered him with useless words of comfort.

As for Commodore Simcoë, he simply did what he had been hired for. He kept the self-propelled island on her required course. Since he despised politics, he would accept anyone who was proposed as governor. His officers and those of Colonel Stewart showed as little interest as he did in the question that made everyone else boil with anger. It was not on Standard Island that military rebellions had to be feared.

In the meantime, the council of notables, in permanent session at the town hall, kept discussing and disputing. They started to argue about the personalities of the candidates. The police were forced to be on the alert because, from morning to night, a crowd giving out seditious cries gathered in front of the municipal palace.

On the other hand, a deplorable bit of news suddenly went around; Walter Tankerdon had called at the Coverley mansion the day before and had not been received. The two fiancés had been forbidden to see each other and, since the marriage had not been celebrated before the attack of the New Hebridean bands, who would have dared say that it would ever take place . . . ?

March 15 finally arrived. The election was scheduled to take place in the main room of the town hall. A turbulent crowd filled the square as the Roman population did, centuries ago, in front of the Quirinal Palace, when the conclave carried out the elevation of a pope to the throne of Saint Peter.

What would be the outcome of these extreme deliberations? The predictions still showed an equal division of the votes. If all the Starboardites stayed faithful to Nat Coverley and all the Larboardites to Jem Tankerdon, what would happen . . . ?

The big day finally arrived. Between one and three o'clock, normal life seemed at a standstill on Standard Island. Five to six thousand people moved about beneath the windows of the municipal building. They were waiting for the results of the notables' votes, and this vote would immediately be communicated by phone to the two sections and the two harbors.

The first round took place at thirty-five minutes past one.

Both candidates received the same number of votes.

One hour later there was a second ballot that brought no change to the first results.

At thirty-five minutes past three, the third and last round took place.

Here again, neither of the two candidates received half of the votes plus one.

The council then broke up, which was a wise decision. Its members were so exasperated that they might have come to blows if they had stayed in session. As they crossed the square to go back to the Tankerdon mansion, or to the Coverley palace, the crowd greeted them with the most unpleasant grumblings.

It was still imperative to find a solution to this untenable situation, which could not be allowed to continue even for a few more hours. This state of affairs was simply too harmful to the interests of Standard Island.

"Just between us," said Pinchinat, after he and his comrades had learned the result of the three rounds of voting from the superintendent, "I believe that there is a very simple way to solve the problem."

"And what is it . . . ?" asked Calistus Munbar, lifting his arms in despair to the sky. "What is it . . . ?"

"Cut the island in the middle, like a pancake, and let the two halves sail wherever they want, each with the governor of its choice."

"Cut our island in half . . . !" cried the superintendent as if Pinchinat had proposed to cut off one of his limbs.

"The problem would be solved with a cold chisel, a hammer, and a monkey wrench that would remove the bolts," added His Highness, "and there would be two floating islands instead of one on the surface of the Pacific Ocean!"

Pinchinat could never be serious, even when circumstances were so grave!

However, although his advice would not be followed, at least in a material sense, if hammers and monkey wrenches would not be used, if no removing of bolts on First Avenue would cut off the Prow Battery from the Stern Battery, from a moral point of view, the separation did take place. The Larboardites and Starboardites were becoming strangers to one another, as if they had been three hundred miles apart. Indeed, the thirty notables then decided to vote separately in each section, since they had not been able to come to an agreement. Jem Tankerdon was immediately elected governor of his side of the island, which he would govern as he saw fit. As for Nat Coverley, he was of course chosen as governor of his own portion that he would govern as he wanted. Each section would keep its harbor, its ships, its officers, its sailors, its militia, its civil employees, its merchants, its electric plant, its machines, its motors, its engineers, its stokers, and both sections would be self-sufficient.

This was all well and good, but how could Commodore Simcoë satisfy both sections at the same time, and how could Superintendent Calistus Munbar fulfill his functions to everyone's satisfaction?

Concerning the latter, the question was not important because his position would become irrelevant. How could people think of pleasures and festivals when a civil war was threatening Standard Island? Because, indeed, a reconciliation had become impossible.

The following incident proved the gravity of the situation: on March 17 the newspapers had announced the final breakup of the engagement of Walter Tankerdon and Miss Dy Coverley.

Yes! Their engagement was broken, in spite of their prayers and supplications. In spite of what Calistus Munbar had once proclaimed, love did not win! But wait a minute! Walter Tankerdon and Miss Dy would not go their separate ways . . . They would rather abandon their families . . . they would get married abroad . . . they would find someplace in the world where they could be happy, without so many millions being an obstacle to their desires!

However, after Jem Tankerdon and Nat Coverley had been chosen, nothing had changed regarding the itinerary of Standard Island. Commodore Simcoë still headed northeast, as had been planned. Once they reached Madeleine Bay, many Milliardites, tired of the current state of affairs, would perhaps return to the continent to try and regain the peace and quiet that the Jewel of the Pacific no longer offered them. The self-propelled island might even be completely abandoned . . . And then she would be sold, auctioned off, or reduced to scrap iron; she might even be melted down!

So be it, but the five thousand miles she still had to cover would take about five months of travel. During this voyage, couldn't the course of the self-propelled island be imperiled by the whim or stubbornness of the two leaders? Indeed, the spirit of revolt had infiltrated the very souls of the people. Would the Starboardites and Larboardites come to blows, would they start shooting at each other, would they soak the steel roads of Milliard City with their blood . . . ?

No! The parties would probably not go that far . . . ! They would not see another civil war, not between north and south, of course, but between the Larboard and Starboard sections of Standard Island . . . But the downfall had arrived and was threatening to provoke a catastrophe.

On the morning of March 19, Commodore Simcoë was in his office at the observatory, awaiting the first report of the day concerning the location of the island. According to his calculations, Standard Island could not have been far from the region where she was to meet the supply ships. The lookouts at the top of the tower where scouring a vast area of the sea in order to signal the steamers as soon as they appeared on the horizon. Next to the commodore stood the king of Malécarlie, Colonel Stewart, Sébastien Zorn, Pinchinat, Frascolin, Yvernès, and a number of officers and civil servants, all people who could be called neutral since they did not participate in the internal dissension. For them, the essential point was to reach, as soon as possible, Madeleine Bay, where this deplorable situation would come to an end.

At that moment, two rings were heard, and two orders were transmitted to the commodore by phone. These orders came from the town hall where Jem Tankerdon, in the right wing, and Nat Coverley, in the left, had met with their principal supporters. It was from these locations that they administered Standard Island, giving, as can be imagined, absolutely contradictory orders.

And that same morning, the two governors had not agreed on the itinerary that Ethel Simcoë should follow, a subject that required agreement. Nat Coverley had decided that Standard Island should sail northeast in order to stop at the Gilbert Archipelago. But Jem Tankerdon, persisting in his project to create commercial relations, resolved to go southwest to the Australian region.

That is where the two rivals stood, and their friends swore to back them up.

When he received the two orders that had been sent simultaneously to the observatory, the commodore said,

"This is what I feared . . ."

"And, in the public interest, it cannot go on!" added the king of Malécarlie.

"What will you decide?" asked Frascolin.

"By Jove," cried Pinchinat, "I'd be interested to know how you are going to maneuver, Mr. Simcoë."

"Certainly not well!" observed Sébastien Zorn.

"Let us first inform Jem Tankerdon and Nat Coverley that their orders cannot be carried out, since they contradict each other," answered the commodore. " Besides, it is better for Standard Island to stay in place and wait for the ships that are going to meet with her in this region."

This very wise response was immediately transmitted to the town hall.

An hour went by without any new communications being sent to the observatory. No doubt each governor had decided against changing his itinerary for the opposite one.

Suddenly, a peculiar vibration was felt coming from the hull of Standard Island . . . What did this vibration mean . . . ? That Jem Tankerdon's and Nat Coverley's stubbornness knew no limits.

They all looked at each other inquisitively.

"What is the matter . . . ? What is the matter . . . ?"

"The matter is," answered Commodore Simcoë, shrugging his shoulders, "that Jem Tankerdon sent his orders directly to Mr. Watson, the Larboard Harbor engineer, while Nat Coverley sent conflicting orders to Mr. Somwah, the Starboard Harbor engineer. One gave orders to go ahead to the northeast, and the other to back down to the southwest. The result is that Standard Island is turning on its center, and this gyration will last as long as the whims of those two obstinate characters last!"

"Well!" cried Pinchinat, "it all had to end in a waltz . . . ! The waltz of the pigheaded . . . ! Athanase Dorémus should resign . . . ! The Milliardites no longer need his lessons . . . !"

Perhaps this absurd situation, which was comical in a way, could have made people laugh. But unfortunately, this double maneuver was extremely dangerous, as Commodore Simcoë remarked. Pulled in opposite directions by the strength of her ten million horsepower, Standard Island was in danger of falling to pieces.

Indeed, the engines were working at full capacity: the propellers were turning at maximum speed, and this could be felt in the shuddering of the steel base. Imagine a team of horses pulling with all their might, one forward, and the other one backward, and you will have an idea of what was happening.

Then, as the movement grew stronger, Standard Island began to revolve on her center. The park and the countryside turned in concentric circles, and the points of the shore located on their circumference moved at a speed of ten to twelve miles an hour.

There was no way Commodore Simcoë could reason with the engineers whose maneuvers provoked these gyrations. He had no authority over them. They were driven by the same passions as the Larboardites and the Starboardites. Faithful servants of their bosses, Watson and Somwah would compete to the bitter end, machine against machine, generator against generator . . .

And then something happened that should have calmed their minds and softened their hearts.

Due to the rotation of Standard Island, many Milliardites, especially the women, started to feel totally out of sorts. Inside their houses, especially in those which, farthest from the center, received a stronger gyrating movement, people felt terribly nauseous.

When they were confronted with this wild, hilarious result, Yvernès, Pinchinat, and Frascolin burst into laughter, even as the situation was becoming more and more critical. And indeed, the Jewel of the Pacific was threatened with a material destruction that would equal to and even be greater than her moral destruction.

As for Sébastien Zorn, under the influence of this constant turning, he became pale, "as pale as the white flag of surrender," Pinchinat said, and he felt sick to his stomach; would this bad joke never end . . . ? To be a prisoner on this huge, turning table that cannot even reveal the secrets of the future . . .

During an endless week, Standard Island never stopped revolving on her center, which was in Milliard City. That is why the city was always full of people looking for relief from their nausea, since the constant turning was not felt as strongly in this area of Standard Island. The king of Malécarlie, Commodore Simcoë, and Colonel Stewart all tried to intercede with the two powers sharing the municipal palace, but to no avail . . . Neither one nor the other was willing to give in. Cyrus Bikerstaff himself, if he could have come back, would have seen his efforts fail against their ultra-American tenacity.

And, adding to the misfortune, the sky had been so constantly covered with clouds that it had been impossible to determine the position of the ship. Commodore Simcoë no longer knew the exact location of Standard Island. Pulled in opposite directions by her powerful propellers, the ship trembled through the steel of her base. No one wanted to go back inside their houses. The park was crammed with people. They were camping outside. Cries of "Hurrah for Tankerdon!" rose on one side, of "Hurrah for Coverley!" on the other. Eyes were flashing, fists were threatening. Would the civil war begin with the worst excesses now that the population was nearing the paroxysm of panic . . . ?

As matters stood, both camps refused to see the approaching danger. They would not give in, even if the Jewel of the Pacific burst into a thousand pieces. She would continue to turn until the time when, for lack of power, the generators would stop activating the propellers . . .

In the middle of this general exasperation that he did not share, Walter Tankerdon felt a deep distress, not for himself, but for Miss Dy Coverley. He feared that a sudden breaking up might annihilate Milliard City. For the past week, he had not been allowed to see the young woman who was his fiancée and should have been his wife. Despairing, he begged his father again and again not to persist in this deplorable maneuver . . . but Jem Tankerdon sent him away without even listening to him . . .

Then, during the night of March 27, taking advantage of the dark, Walter Tankerdon tried to join the young woman. He wanted to be with her if a disaster happened. After slipping through the people crowding First Avenue, he entered the rival section in order to reach the Coverley mansion . . .

Just before daybreak, a powerful explosion rattled the atmosphere to the very heavens. Pushed beyond their limits, the larboard boilers had blown up along with the buildings in which they were located. And, as the source of electricity had suddenly stopped on that side, half of Standard Island was plunged into the deepest darkness . . .

XIII

~~~~~~~~

The Last Word by Pinchinat

WHILE THE ENGINES OF LARBOARD Harbor were now out of order following the explosion of the boilers, those of Starboard Harbor were still intact. But, in truth, Standard Island had completely lost her capacity to move forward. Left with only her starboard propellers functioning, she would continue to turn around and around, unable to steam straight ahead.

Thus this accident only made the situation worse. Indeed, as long as Standard Island still possessed her two sets of engines that could work together, all that was needed to put an end to the dire situation was an agreement between the Tankerdon and the Coverley camps. The motors would have resumed their normal work of moving in the same direction, and the ship would have been heading toward Madeleine Bay only a few days late.

Now things were different. Even if an agreement were reached, it was impossible to sail. Commodore Simcoë no longer had at his disposal the necessary propulsive force to leave this faraway region.

And if at least Standard Island had stayed in place during this last week, if the awaited steamers had been able to meet with her, it would perhaps have been possible to return to the Northern Hemisphere . . .

But this was now out of the question, and on that day, a sextant sighting enabled them to notice that Standard Island had moved south during her lengthy gyration. She had drifted from the twelfth to the seventeenth parallel.

And indeed, between the New Hebrides and the Fiji Group, there are currents caused by the narrows between the two archipelagos that spread southeast. As long as her motors worked together, Standard Island was able to easily push back these currents. But from the moment she started rotating, she was irresistibly swept away toward the Tropic of Capricorn.

Once this became obvious, Commodore Simcoë did not hide the gravity of the situation from all the good people who could be called neutral. Here is what he told them:

"We have been swept five degrees south. But I cannot do with Standard Island what a captain can do with a steamer that has lost its engines. Our island has no sails that would allow us to use the wind, and we are at the mercy of the currents. Where will they push us? I don't know. As for the steamers coming from Madeleine Bay, they are vainly looking for us in the area we had agreed upon, but it is toward the least populous region of the Pacific that we are now drifting at a speed of eight to ten miles an hour!"

With these few sentences, Ethel Simcoë had given a clear picture of the circumstances the Milliardites were facing and that he was helpless to change. Standard Island was like an enormous wreck left to the whims of the currents. If they pushed her north, she would head up north. And if they shifted south, she would go south, perhaps to the extreme limits of the Antarctic sea. And then . . .

Very soon, the population of Milliard City and the harbors learned where things stood. They clearly felt that extreme danger was coming and, faced with this new peril, minds became calmer, which is very human. They no longer thought of coming to blows in a fratricidal war, and, if hatred was still strong, at least it would not erupt into violence. Little by little, everyone went back to their section, their neighborhood, and their house. Jem Tankerdon and Nat Coverley stopped fighting over who should command. And then, on the suggestion of the two governors themselves, the council of notables opted for the only decision acceptable under the circumstances: they handed over all their power to Commodore Simcoë, the only leader to whom, from then on, the rescue of Standard Island would be entrusted.

Ethel Simcoë readily accepted this charge. He was counting on the devotion of his friends, his officers, and his people. But what could he do on board this vast floating machine with an area of ten and a half square miles that had become impossible to steer since it no longer had its two sets of engines at its disposal . . . ? And after all, were there not reasons to recognize this disaster as a condemnation of Standard Island, which had been regarded until then as the masterpiece of naval construction, since her mishap had made her a plaything of the winds and the waves . . . ?

True, this accident had not been caused by nature; the Jewel of the Pacific, from her very beginning, had always successfully stood up to hurricanes, storms, and cyclones. It was the internal dissensions, the rivalries of billionaires, the fanatical stubbornness of some to sail south and of others to travel north, that had brought about the disaster. It was the immeasurable stupidity of human beings that had made the boilers of Larboard Harbor explode . . . !

But what is the use of criticizing? What they needed to do first was to determine the damage to Larboard Harbor. Commodore Simcoë gathered his officers and his engineers. The king of Malécarlie joined them. This royal philosopher was certainly not surprised that human passions had brought about such a catastrophe!

The appointed group visited the area where the electrical plant had stood with its machinery. The explosion of the steam-making machines, which had been grossly overheated, had destroyed everything and killed two technicians and six stokers. The damages were just as serious to the plant where the electricity for the various services of that half of the island was generated. Luckily, the dynamos at Starboard Harbor kept working, and as Pinchinat remarked,

"We'll get away with seeing out of one eye!"

"All right," answered Frascolin, "but we have also lost a leg, and the one we have left will not be of much use!"

One-eyed and lame, that was too much.

The result of the investigation was that since Standard Island was beyond repair, it would be impossible to stop her drift toward the south. The ship would first have to escape the current that was pulling her beyond the Tropic of Capricorn.

Once the external damage was known, the steel compartments of the hull needed to be inspected. They, too, may have been compromised by the gyrating movement that shook them so violently during those eight days . . . Did the metal panels separate, did the rivets come loose . . . ? If there were leaks, how could they be repaired . . . ?

The engineers conducted a second inspection. The report they made to Commodore Simcoë was very alarming. In many places, the shaking had cracked the panels and broken the joints. Thousands of bolts had snapped and tears had appeared. Some of the compartments were already filled with water. But since the waterline had not moved, the integrity of the metal floor was not seriously threatened, and the new owners of Standard Island had nothing to fear for their property. It was at the Stern Battery that the cracks were the most numerous. As for Larboard Harbor, one of its piers had been engulfed by the explosion . . . But the Prow Harbor was intact and its wharves offered complete security to vessels against the swells of the ocean.

Meanwhile, orders were given to immediately repair all that could be repaired. It was important to reassure the population concerning its security. It was enough and even too much already that Standard Island, missing its larboard engines, could not head for the nearest land, and for this there was no remedy.

Also, the important questions of hunger and thirst remained to be dealt with . . . Would the reserves be sufficient for one month, for two months . . . ?

Following are the estimates given by Commodore Simcoë:

Regarding the water, there would be no problem. If one of the distilleries had been destroyed by the explosion, the other continued to function and could meet all their needs.

Regarding the food, the situation was less certain. All things considered, the provisions would not last more than two weeks, unless severe rationing was imposed on the ten thousand residents of the island. Except for their fruits and vegetables, everything came from the outside, as we know, and the outside . . . where was it . . . ? How far was the nearest land, and how could it be reached . . . ?

Thus Commodore Simcoë had to opt for rationing, no matter what deplorable effects this decision could have. That same evening, the telephone and telautographic lines spread the calamitous news.

Following this, terror spread throughout Milliard City and both harbors with a premonition of even worse catastrophes to come. Would the specter of famine, to use a familiar but striking image, soon appear on the horizon, since there was no way to replenish the stocks . . . ? Indeed, Commodore Simcoë did not possess a single vessel to send to the American continent . . . Fate had sent his last steamer to sea three weeks earlier, carrying the bodies of Cyrus Bikerstaff and the defenders who had been killed during the battle against Erromango. The Milliardites had not suspected then that questions of vanity would put Standard Island in a worse position than when she was invaded by the New Hebridean bands!

Frankly, what was the use of possessing billions of dollars, of being as rich as the Rothschilds, Mackays, Astors, Vanderbilts, and Goulds, if no riches could ward off famine . . . ! These nabobs must have had most of their fortunes securely stashed in the banks of the old and the new continents! But who knew if the day were not coming when a million could not provide them with a pound of meat or bread . . . !

After all, the fault lay in their absurd dissensions, their stupid rivalries, and their desire to seize power! They were the guilty ones, the Tankerdons and the Coverleys; they were the cause of all this trouble! They had better watch out for retaliation, for the rage of the officers, the civil servants, the employees, the merchants, and the entire population that they had put into such danger! What excesses would these people commit when they were tortured by hunger?

These reproaches were never addressed to Walter Tankerdon or Miss Dy Coverley; the blame deserved by their families did not reach them. The young couple was not responsible for the disaster! They were the link that was to assure the future of the two sections and they were not the ones who broke it!

For two days, due to poor atmospheric conditions, no sextant sighting could be taken, and the position of Standard Island could not be determined with any certainty.

On March 31, at dawn, the sky was clear enough and the fog from the ocean began to dissipate. It seemed that a fairly accurate altitude could be recorded.

The measurement was feverishly awaited. Several hundred residents gathered at the Prow Battery. Walter Tankerdon was among them. But neither his father nor any of the notables who could have been so rightly accused of bringing about this state of affairs had left their houses, where they were confined by the public indignation.

A little before noon, the observers were getting ready to shoot the sun. Two sextants, one in the hands of the king of Malécarlie and the other held by Commodore Simcoë, were directed toward the horizon.

As soon as the altitude was taken, they made their calculations with the necessary corrections, and the result was: latitude twenty-nine degrees, seventeen minutes south.

Around two o'clock, a second sextant sighting was taken under the same favorable conditions. It indicated longitude one hundred seventy-nine degrees, thirty-two minutes east.

This meant that since Standard Island had been caught in this gyrating folly, the currents had made her drift about a thousand miles southeast.

When they looked at their position on the map, here is what they found:

The nearest islands, located at least a hundred miles from them, formed the Kermadeck Group, a mass of sterile rocks with almost no people or resources, and anyway, how could they reach it . . . ?

Three hundred miles to the south was New Zealand, but how could they get there when the currents were making them drift toward the open sea? Fifteen hundred miles to the west was Australia. A few thousand miles to the east was South America, more specifically Chile. Beyond New Zealand were the Antarctic ocean and the desert. Was it on the South Pole that Standard Island was going to wreck . . . ? Was it there that explorers would one day find the remains of an entire population who had died of misery and starvation . . . ?

Commodore Simcoë was going to carefully study the currents of these seas. But what if the currents never changed, what if they never met opposing currents and if one of those formidable storms that often develop in the regions around the poles broke out . . . ?

This sort of news was just what was needed to provoke terror. People became more and more angry against the authors of their trouble, the evil nabobs of Milliard City who were responsible for this situation. The influence of the king of Malécarlie, the energy of Commodore Simcoë and Colonel Stewart, the devotion of the officers, the authority of the militia on the sailors and the soldiers were all sorely needed to avoid an uprising.

The day passed without any change. Everyone had to submit to the rationing of food and make do with the bare necessities, the very rich as well as those who were not as well off.

Meanwhile, lookouts were posted and carefully watched the horizon. If a ship appeared, they would signal it immediately, and perhaps it would be possible for the broken communications to be restored. Unfortunately, the self-propelled island had drifted outside the usual maritime routes, and there were few vessels that crossed the area neighboring the Antarctic sea. And in the panicked imaginations of the passengers arose the specter of the South Pole, lit by the ruddy gleams of the volcanoes named Erebus and Terror!

Finally, a positive incident occurred during the night of April 3. The north wind that had blown so violently during the past few days suddenly subsided. A dead calm followed and the breeze suddenly turned southeast in one of these atmospheric whims that are so frequent during the period of the equinox.

Commodore Simcoë began to hope again. Standard Island needed only to be pushed back westward a hundred miles for the countercurrent to bring her closer to Australia or New Zealand. In any case, her sailing toward the polar sea seemed stopped, and ships could possibly be encountered near the vast territory of Australasia.

At sunrise, the breeze from the southeast was already strong. Standard Island definitely felt its force. Her high structures, the observatory, the town hall, the church, and the cathedral, caught some of the wind. The buildings acted as sails aboard this enormous ship of four hundred thirty-two million tons!

Although clouds rapidly crossed the sky, the sun appeared from time to time, and a good sighting could probably be taken.

Indeed, twice they were able to capture the sun between the clouds.

The calculations showed that Standard Island had gone two degrees toward the northwest since the day before.

It would have been hard to maintain that Standard Island was simply pushed by the wind. It had to be concluded that she had entered one of those eddies that divide the great currents of the Pacific. If she had had the good fortune of meeting the northwest current, her chances of being saved would have improved. But, by God, this needed to happen quickly; indeed, the rationing had already become more severe. The provisions were diminishing at a worrisome rate, as ten thousand residents had to be fed!

When the last measurement was communicated to the ports and the city, people quieted down a little. Everyone knows how quickly a crowd can go from one feeling to another, from despair to hope. That is what happened. These people, very different from the miserable masses piled up in the big cities of the continents, should have been and were, indeed, less subject to panic; they were more thoughtful and patient. But given the threat of famine, anything could happen . . .

During the morning, the wind became cooler. The barometer fell slowly. The sea swelled in long powerful waves, proving that there had been great disturbances in the southeast. Standard Island, which had been invincible in the past, could no longer endure these enormous rollers. A few houses shook alarmingly from top to bottom, and objects tumbled down inside them. It felt like an earthquake. This phenomenon, new for the Milliardites, caused deep worry.

Commodore Simcoë and his people settled permanently in the observatory, where all services were concentrated. The jolts felt in the edifice made them very concerned and they were forced to recognize the extreme seriousness of the situation.

"It's obvious," said the commodore, "that the base of Standard Island has been damaged . . . Her compartments are coming undone . . . Her hull no longer has the sturdiness that made it so strong . . ."

"And may God spare her any violent storm," added the king of Malécarlie, "because she would no longer possess the strength to resist!"

So it was, and the people no longer trusted the artificial groundwork of the ship . . . They felt that her base would betray her . . . It would have been a hundred times better to be wrecked on the rocks of the Antarctic lands . . . ! To fear at any instant that Standard Island might break apart and be engulfed in the midst of the abysses of the Pacific that no sounding line had ever even been able to measure, this was what even the most valiant hearts could not imagine without trembling.

It was impossible to deny that new damages had occurred in some of the compartments. Partitions had caved in, and gaps had caused the riveting of the steel panels to break. In the park, alongside the Serpentine River and on the surface of the outer streets of the city, irregular bucklings caused by the dislocation of the base could be seen. Several buildings were already leaning and if they fell, they would break the substructure supporting their base! As for the leaks, they could not be stopped. It was absolutely certain that the sea had invaded several parts of the subsoil of the island, because the waterline had changed. On almost the entire periphery, in the two ports as well as in the Prow and Stern Batteries, the waterline had sunk one foot, and if it sank even lower, the waves would invade the shore. If the base of Standard Island were compromised, her sinking would be only a few hours away.

Commodore Simcoë wanted to keep this situation from the people because it could have started a panic and perhaps even worse! To what excesses would people go against the authors of such a debacle! The inhabitants could not try to save themselves by fleeing like the passengers of a ship, they could not jump into a lifeboat, they could not build a raft where a crew usually takes refuge, hoping to be picked up at sea . . . No! This raft was Standard Island herself, and she was ready to sink . . . !

From hour to hour during that day Commodore Simcoë kept track of the changes in the waterline. The level of Standard Island continued to go down. This meant that the infiltration of seawater through the compartments was continuing; it was slow, but constant and unstoppable.

At the same time the weather was getting worse. The sky had a wan reddish and coppery glow. The barometer fell more quickly. The atmosphere seemed to announce an approaching storm. Behind the gathering mist, the horizon had shrunk so much that it seemed to end at the shore of Standard Island.

When evening came, terrifying gusts of wind raged. Under the violence of the swells, compartments cracked, joints broke, and steel panels were torn apart. Everywhere, metallic creaks could be heard. The avenues of the city and the lawns of the park were ready to burst . . . And as night approached, Milliard City was abandoned for the countryside, which offered more safety because it was less covered with heavy buildings. The entire population wandered between the two ports and the Stern and Prow Batteries.

Around nine o'clock, a deep tremor shook Standard Island to her foundations. The factory at Starboard Harbor, which supplied the electric light, had just collapsed into the ocean. The darkness was so deep that the sea and the sky were invisible.

Soon a new trembling of the ground announced that dwellings were starting to fall down like houses of cards. A few hours later, there would be nothing left of the superstructure of Standard Island.

"Gentlemen," said Commodore Simcoë," we cannot stay at the observatory any longer. It will fall at any minute. Let's go into the country where we'll wait for the end of the storm . . ."

"It's a cyclone," answered the king of Malécarlie, who showed the barometer that had fallen to 713 millimeters.

And indeed Standard Island had been caught in one of these cyclonic movements that act like condensers. These circling storms, made up of a mass of water gyrating around an almost vertical axis, develop from west to east, passing along the south of the Southern Hemisphere. A cyclone is the storm that causes the most disasters, and, in order to survive it, one needs to reach its center, which is relatively calm, or at least the right side of its path, the half circle that is manageable and shielded from the fury of the waves. But this maneuver was impossible to make due to the lack of engines. This time it was no longer human stupidity or the foolish stubbornness of her leaders that was dragging down Standard Island, it was a tremendous typhoon that was finally going to annihilate her.

The king of Malécarlie, Commodore Simcoë, Colonel Stewart, Sébastien Zorn and his comrades, the astronomers, and the officers had abandoned the observatory, where they were no longer safe. Just in time! They had hardly walked two hundred steps when the high tower fell with a dreadful crash, made a huge hole in the ground of the square, and disappeared in the abyss.

An instant later, the entire structure was just a heap of ruins.

However, the quartet wanted to go up First Avenue and run into the casino, where their musical instruments were, in order to possibly save them. The casino was still standing; they were able to reach it; they went up to their rooms and took the two violins, the viola, and the cello to the park, where they sought shelter.

Several thousand people from both sections were gathered there.

The Tankerdon and Coverley families were there, and it was perhaps fortunate for them that in the midst of this darkness, they could not see or recognize one another.

Walter was lucky enough, however, to join Miss Dy Coverley. He would try to save her at the moment of supreme catastrophe. He would try to hang on to some piece of wreckage with her . . . The young woman sensed that the young man was near her, and she let out this cry:

"Ah! Walter . . . !"

"Dy . . . my dear Dy . . . Here I am . . . ! I will never leave you again . . ."

As for our Parisians, they did not want to be separated either . . . They stayed together. Frascolin did not lose his cool. Yvernès was very nervous. Pinchinat was ironically resigned. As for Sébastien Zorn, he kept repeating to Athanase Dorémus, who had finally decided to join his compatriots, "I predicted that it would end up badly . . . ! I predicted it!"

"Enough of your tremolos in the minor key, my old Isaiah," cried His Highness, "save your penitential psalms!"

Around midnight, the cyclone became more violent. The converging winds raised monstrous waves and hurled them against Standard Island. Where would this battle of the elements carry her . . . ? Would she be destroyed against some reefs . . . Would she break apart in the middle of the ocean . . . ?

Her hull had holes everywhere and her joints were cracking all over. The buildings, the church, the cathedral, and the town hall had collapsed because of the enormous wounds through which the sea gushed forth in gigantic sprays. Not a trace of these magnificent edifices remained. So many treasures, paintings, statues, and objets d'art were lost forever! People would no longer see anything of the superb Milliard City when daylight came, if daylight did come for them and they were not swallowed up along with Standard Island.

Indeed, the sea was starting to invade the park and the country where the subsoil had resisted. The waterline had lowered again. The surface of the island was now at the level of the sea and the cyclone hurled the raging waves of the ocean over her.

There was no shelter or refuge left anywhere. The Prow Battery, at the mercy of the wind, offered no protection against the breaking waves or the gusts of wind that stung like a hail of bullets. The compartments burst open and the damage spread with a roar more powerful than the most violent thunder . . . The final catastrophe was near . . .

Around three in the morning, the park was cut in two along a three-mile length of the Serpentine River, and thick sheets of water started flowing through this crevice. People had to flee as quickly as possible, and they escaped into the countryside. Some ran toward the harbors, others toward the batteries. Families became separated and mothers looked in vain for their children, while the unbridled waters swept the surface of Standard Island like a huge tidal wave.

Walter Tankerdon, who had not left the side of Miss Dy, tried to drag her toward Starboard Harbor, but she did not have the strength to follow him. He picked up her almost unconscious body and carried her in his arms. He ran through the terrifying cries of the crowd in the middle of the horrible darkness.

At five in the morning, a new resounding ripping was heard in the east. A chunk of about half a square mile had just broken off Standard Island . . .

It was Starboard Harbor, with its factories, its machinery, and its stores, that was drifting away . . .

Under the increasing blows of the cyclone at the peak of its strength, Standard Island was tossed about like a wreck . . . Her hull fell to pieces . . . Her compartments burst, and a few people, swept away by the waves, disappeared into the depths of the ocean.

"First the crackup of the company," cried Pinchinat, "and now the smashup of the self-propelled island." And this sentence summarized the situation.

Indeed, only a few pieces of the marvelous Standard Island remained, and they resembled the scattered fragments of a broken comet that were floating, not in space, but on the surface of the immense Pacific Ocean.

XIV

<div style="text-align:center">~~~~~~~~~~~</div>

Denouement

AT FIRST LIGHT, THIS IS what an observer standing a few hundred feet above the area of the disaster would have seen: three fragments of Standard Island, each with an area of about five to seven and a half acres floating on the sea, and a dozen smaller ones at a distance of about ten cable lengths from each other.

The cyclone started to die down with the first glow of day. Its center moved about thirty miles toward the east, with the speed common to these major atmospheric disturbances. Yet the ocean that had been so terribly choppy was still rough, and the wreckage—both large and small pieces—was tossed about like ships on a raging sea.

The portion of Standard Island that was most heavily damaged was the base of Milliard City. It had totally sunk under the weight of the buildings. Not a single trace of the monuments and mansions that lined the main avenues of the two sections remained! The separation between the Larboardites and the Starboardites had never been greater, and they certainly had not dreamed that it would have happened this way!

Were there a substantial number of victims . . . ? There were reasons to believe so, although the population had sought refuge early enough in the countryside, where the ground was less likely to break up.

And now were they satisfied, these Coverleys and these Tankerdons, with the results brought about by their evil rivalries . . . ! Neither of them would ever serve as governor . . . ! Milliard City had been swallowed up by the sea, and with her the enormous sum that they had paid for her . . . ! But let's not pity their fate! They still had enough millions in American and European banks to provide them with their daily bread throughout their old age!

The largest fragment of the island was made up of the area of the countryside that had been located between the observatory and the Prow Battery. On its surface of about seven and a half acres, three thousand shipwrecked people—if we may call them by that name—were crammed together. The second fragment, somewhat smaller, had kept a few of its buildings that were close to Larboard Harbor: the port with several supply stores and one of the cisterns of potable water. As for the electric plant and the buildings containing the machinery and the boilers, they had disappeared when the furnaces exploded. This second fragment served as a refuge for two thousand inhabitants. They would perhaps have been able to establish communication with the first wreck if all the launches of Larboard Harbor had not been destroyed.

As for Starboard Harbor, it must be remembered that this portion of Standard Island had violently broken away from the rest of the ship around three in the morning. It had probably sunk, for as far as the eye could see, there was no sign of it on the ocean.

In addition to the first two fragments, a third one with an area of about ten to twelve acres was floating nearby; it comprised the part of the countryside that had been next to the Stern Battery and had about four thousand people on it.

And there were a dozen more pieces measuring about one thousand square feet each, where the rest of the population saved from the disaster was gathered.

That was all that remained of the Jewel of the Pacific!

The number of dead would have been estimated at several hundred. And yet, thank heaven! Standard Island had not been totally engulfed by the waters of the Pacific!

But since they were far from land, how could these fragments ever reach any shore on the Pacific . . . ? Were not these shipwrecked people destined to die of hunger . . . ? Would not one single witness survive this disaster that had no precedent in maritime necrology . . . ?

Yet there was no need to despair. These drifting fragments carried energetic men who would do anything to save everyone, and they would succeed.

It was on the fragment that had been adjacent to the Prow Battery that Commodore Simcoë, the king and queen of Malécarlie, the observatory personnel, Colonel Stewart, a few of his officers, some of the notables of Milliard City and the members of the clergy, as well as an important part of the population, were gathered.

It was there, too, that the Coverley and Tankerdon families were, overcome by the terrible responsibility that rested on their leaders. And were they not already distressed enough by the disappearance of Walter and Miss Dy . . . ? Could one of the other fragments have picked them up . . . ? Was there hope of ever seeing them again . . . ?

The members of the Concerting Quartet were all there, along with their instruments. To use a well-known expression, "only death could have parted them"! Frascolin was considering the situation with his usual cool, and he had not lost all hope. Confronted with such a disaster, Yvernès, who always looked at the unusual side of things, exclaimed,

"Who could have imagined a more grandiose finish!"

As for Sébastien Zorn, he was beside himself. He could not find comfort in the fact that he had been the prophet predicting the woes of Standard Island like Jeremiah had predicted those of Zion. He was hungry and he had caught a cold. He was shaken by violent coughing fits. And the incorrigible Pinchinat, with his priceless French accent, exclaimed, taking "fits" for "fifths,"

"You're wrong, my dear old Zorn, don't you know that two consecutive fits are forbidden in harmony?"

The cellist would have strangled His Highness if he had been strong enough to do so, but he was too weak . . .

And what was Calistus Munbar doing in the meantime . . . ? Well, the superintendent was sublime . . . simply sublime! He refused to despair about the safety of the people or the state of Standard Island . . . He was certain that they would go back to land and that Standard Island would be repaired . . . Her remains were in good shape, and it could not be said that the elements had gotten the better of this masterpiece of naval architecture!

What was certain was that danger was no longer imminent. All that could sink during the cyclone had already gone down with Milliard City: its monuments, its mansions, its houses, its fabrics, its batteries, the entire superstructure with its enormous weight. At that moment, the fragments were in good condition, the waterline had risen considerably, and the waves were no longer sweeping over their surfaces.

There was thus a significant respite, a tangible amelioration, and, as the threat of immediate sinking was dismissed, most people felt in better spirits. Their minds were calmer and only the women and the children, who could not be rational, were unable to control their fears.

And what happened to Athanase Dorémus . . . ? At the beginning of the breakup, the professor of charm, dance, and good manners was carried away on one of the pieces of the ship, with his old servant. But a current had brought him back to the fragment where his compatriots from the quartet were.

Meanwhile, Commodore Simcoë, like the captain of a disabled ship, had begun his work, aided by his devoted personnel . . . First he studied whether it would be possible to bring together the fragments that were floating apart. If this proved impossible, how would they be able to communicate with each other? This last problem was soon solved, since several launches in Larboard Harbor were intact. By sending them from one fragment to the next, Commodore Simcoë would learn what resources they still had, how much potable water and food were left.

But would he be able to determine the position of this flotilla of wrecks, its latitude and longitude . . . ?

No! They no longer had the necessary instruments to take these measurements, and so they could not determine if they were close to a continent or an island.

Around nine in the morning, Commodore Simcoë and two of his officers boarded a launch that Larboard Harbor had just sent him. This boat allowed him to visit the different fragments. The following is what he found out during his survey.

The distilleries of Larboard Harbor had been destroyed, but the cistern still contained a two-week supply of potable water, provided that it was used very sparingly. The reserves of the harbor stores could feed the shipwrecked people for about as long.

It was thus absolutely necessary for the shipwrecked people to land at some point on the Pacific coast within two weeks at the most.

To a certain point, this information was reassuring. However, Commodore Simcoë now realized that that terrible night had left several hundred victims. As for the Tankerdon and Coverley families, their grief was inexpressible. Neither Walter nor Miss Dy were found on the fragments visited by the launch. At the time of the catastrophe, the young man had been walking toward Starboard Harbor, carrying his unconscious fiancée in his arms, and nothing of this part of Standard Island had been left on the surface of the Pacific.

In the afternoon, the wind becoming weaker and weaker by the hour, the sea fell and the fragments hardly moved under the undulations of the swells. Thanks to Larboard Harbor's launches, Commodore Simcoë was able to feed the people, allocating to them only what was strictly necessary in order not to starve to death.

Communications became easier and faster. The various fragments, obeying the laws of attraction like pieces of cork floating on the surface of a basin full of water, began to draw closer. And how could this not have seemed like a good sign to the trusting Calistus Munbar, who already foresaw the reconstruction of his Jewel of the Pacific . . . ?

The night passed in total darkness. The time had long gone when the avenues of Milliard City, the streets of the commercial quarters, the lawns in the park, the fields, and the meadows shone under the electric lights, when the aluminum moons abundantly poured their blinding brightness onto the surface of Standard Island!

In the midst of the darkness, a few fragments struck each other. These shocks could not have been avoided, but, luckily, they were not strong enough to cause serious damage.

At daybreak, it was noticed that the wrecks had moved much closer to each other but were floating together on the peaceful sea without colliding. With a few strokes of their oars, people could go from one wreck to the other. Commodore Simcoë could easily control the distribution of food and drinkable water. This was the main concern, but the shipwrecked people understood and resigned themselves.

The launches carried several families. They went to search for their loved ones whom they had not seen yet. There was great joy among those who found each other again; they no longer thought of the dangers threatening them. But what grief for those who looked in vain for the missing.

It was of course very fortunate that the sea had become calm again. It was perhaps regrettable, though, that the wind had not continued blowing from the southeast. It would have helped the current, which runs toward the Australian coast in this part of the Pacific.

By order of Commodore Simcoë, lookouts were posted so as to be able to observe the entire perimeter of the horizon. If a ship appeared, they would immediately send signals. But very few vessels sail in these faraway regions, especially during the time of the year when equinoctial storms rage.

The chance of sighting a ribbon of smoke or a sail on the horizon was thus slight . . . And yet, around two in the afternoon, Commodore Simcoë received the following communication from one of the lookouts:

"Something has been spotted to the northeast, and although no hull can be seen, it is certain that a ship is passing near Standard Island."

This news caused extraordinary excitement. The king of Malécarlie, Commodore Simcoë, the officers, the engineers, all of them went to the side where this ship had been sighted. The order was given to attract the ship's attention by raising flags at the ends of spars and by simultaneous detonations of the firearms they still had. If night fell before their signals were perceived, they would light a fire on the first fragment. In the dark, it would be visible from a great distance and impossible to miss.

They did not have to wait until night. The mass in question was visibly approaching. Thick smoke poured from its top and it was obvious that it was trying to reach the fragments of Standard Island.

The telescopes did not lose sight of it, even though its hull was not much higher than sea level and it did not have any masts or sails.

"My friends," exclaimed Commodore Simcoë, "I believe I am right . . . ! It is a fragment of our island . . . and it can only be Starboard Harbor, which drifted into the high seas, pushed by the currents . . . ! I suppose that Mr. Somwah was able to repair his engines, and he is coming toward us!"

Demonstrations bordering on folly welcomed the news. The safety of all now seemed assured! It was as if a vital part of Standard Island was returning to her with this portion of Starboard Harbor!

Indeed, everything had happened as Commodore Simcoë had supposed. After the tearing, Starboard Harbor, caught by a countercurrent, had been pushed toward the northeast. When day had come, Mr. Somwah, the port officer, had made repairs to the engines, which had been only slightly damaged, and then returned to the scene of the sinking, bringing back with him several hundred more survivors.

Three hours later, Starboard Harbor was only one cable length away from the flotilla . . . What transports of joy, what enthusiastic shouts welcomed its arrival . . . ! Walter Tankerdon and Miss Dy Coverley, who had found refuge on it, were there, next to each other . . .

Now that Starboard Harbor had arrived with reserves of food and water, the Milliardites felt that they would be saved. The reserves contained enough fuel to make the engines and dynamos turn the propellers for a few days. The five-million horsepower of Starboard Harbor would allow them to reach the nearest land. This land was New Zealand, according to the observations made by the port officer.

But the problem was now to find room for thousands of people on Starboard Harbor, whose surface was no larger than sixty-five hundred to seventy-five hundred square feet. Would they have to look for help fifty miles away . . . ?

No, this voyage would have taken too long, and they did not have that much time. There was not a day to lose, if they wanted to save the people from the horrors of famine.

"There is a better way," said the king of Malécarlie. "The fragments of Starboard Harbor and of the Stern and the Prow Batteries can carry all the survivors of Standard Island. Let's attach these three fragments with strong chains, one behind the other, like barges behind a tugboat. And then Starboard Harbor will take the lead with its five-million horsepower and bring us to New Zealand!"

The advice was excellent; it was practical and had every chance of success. Confidence was restored to the hearts of the people as if they were already in sight of a port.

The rest of the day was spent fastening the chains that were found in the storehouses of Starboard Harbor. Commodore Simcoë estimated that, under in these conditions, the floating string of fragments could cover between eight and ten miles in twenty-four hours. Thus in five days, and aided by the currents, they would travel the fifty miles that separated them from New Zealand. And they were confident that their provisions would last them until that date. The rationing was, however, strictly enforced as a precaution against delays.

When the preparations were complete, Starboard Harbor took the lead of the string of fragments around seven in the evening. Moved by the power of its propellers, the fragments in tow advanced slowly on the dead calm of the ocean.

The next day at dawn, the lookouts had lost sight of the wreckage of Standard Island.

No particular incident occurred during April 4, 5, 6, 7, and 8. The weather was favorable, the swell could hardly be felt, and the trip was made under excellent conditions.

Around eight in the morning on April 9, land was sighted on the port side, a high land that could be seen from a great distance.

After sightings were taken with the instruments that had been saved by Starboard Harbor, there was absolutely no doubt about the identity of this land.

It was the point of Ika Na Mawi, the large northern island of New Zealand.

One more day and night passed and the next day, April 10, in the morning, Starboard Harbor ran aground at a cable length from the shore in Ravaraki Bay.

What satisfaction, what safety all these people felt, having real earth under their feet instead of the artificial soil of Standard Island! But yet, how many years would this solid naval construction have lasted if human passions, stronger than the winds and the sea, had not brought about its destruction!

The shipwrecked people were very well received by the New Zealanders, who were eager to provide them with everything they needed.

As soon as they arrived in Auckland, the capital city of Ika Na Mawi, the wedding of Walter Tankerdon and Miss Dy Coverley was finally celebrated with all the pomp appropriate for the circumstances. The Concerting Quartet was heard for the last time during this ceremony attended by all the Milliardites. This marriage would be a happy union and it was regrettable for the common interest of the people that it did not take place earlier! Now the young couple would probably have no more than a one-million yearly income each . . .

"But," as Pinchinat said, "everything seemed to indicate that they would still find happiness in spite of their mediocre fortune!"

As for the Tankerdons, the Coverleys, and the other notables, they intended to go back to America, where they would not have to argue about the government of a self-propelled island.

Commodore Simcoë, Colonel Stewart, and their officers, the observatory personnel, and even the superintendent Calistus Munbar had the same intention, but the latter did not renounce, however, his idea of building another artificial island.

The king and queen of Malécarlie did not keep secret their regret for Standard Island, where they had hoped to end their days in peace . . . ! Let's hope that these monarchs found a place on earth where they could spend their final years sheltered from political dissension!

And the Concerting Quartet . . . ?

Well, the Concerting Quartet, in spite of all that Sébastien Zorn might have said, did not get a bad deal; and if the cellist was still angry at Calistus Munbar for taking him aboard against his will, he would have been a very ungrateful fellow.

Indeed, from May 25 of the preceding year until April 10, eleven months went by during which they lived the lavish life that we have heard about. They received the four trimesters of their salary. Three of those were held by banks in San Francisco and New York and would be paid to them as soon as they signed for them.

After the marriage ceremony in Auckland, Sébastien Zorn, Yvernès, Frascolin, and Pinchinat said goodbye to their friends, including Athanase Dorémus. Then they boarded a steamer for San Diego.

When, on May 3, they arrived in this capital city of Southern California, their first task was to apologize through the newspapers for having failed to keep their appointment eleven months earlier and to express their regrets for having left people waiting.

"Gentlemen, we would have waited for you twenty years longer!" was the response they received from the kind director of musical evenings in San Diego.

He could not have been more obliging or gracious. The only way to acknowledge so much courtesy was to give the concert that had been advertised so long ago!

And in front of a public as numerous as it was enthusiastic, the Quartet in F Major from Mozart's op. 9 gave these virtuosos who had escaped the wreck of Standard Island one of the greatest successes of their artistic careers.

This is how the story of this ninth marvel of the world, this incomparable Jewel of the Pacific, ended! All is well that ends well, says the proverb, but all is bad that ends badly, and was this not the case of Standard Island . . . ?

But it has not ended yet! Standard Island will be rebuilt one of these days, if Calistus Munbar is to be believed.

And yet—this cannot be repeated too many times—is creating an artificial island, an island that travels on the surface of the seas, not going beyond the limits assigned to human genius, and has man, who does not control the winds or the sea, not been forbidden to usurp so recklessly the power of the Creator . . . ?

IN THE BISON FRONTIERS OF IMAGINATION SERIES

Gullivar of Mars
By Edwin L. Arnold
Introduced by Richard A. Lupoff
Afterword by Gary Hoppenstand

A Journey in Other Worlds:
A Romance of the Future
By John Jacob Astor
Introduced by S. M. Stirling

Queen of Atlantis
By Pierre Benoit
Afterword by Hugo Frey

The Wonder
By J. D. Beresford
Introduced by Jack L. Chalker

Voices of Vision: Creators of Science
Fiction and Fantasy Speak
By Jayme Lynn Blaschke

The Man with the Strange Head and
Other Early Science Fiction Stories
By Miles J. Breuer
Edited and introduced by
Michael R. Page

At the Earth's Core
By Edgar Rice Burroughs
Introduced by Gregory A. Benford
Afterword by Phillip R. Burger

Back to the Stone Age
By Edgar Rice Burroughs
Introduced by Gary Dunham

Beyond Thirty
By Edgar Rice Burroughs
Introduced by David Brin
Essays by Phillip R. Burger and
Richard A. Lupoff

The Eternal Savage:
Nu of the Niocene
By Edgar Rice Burroughs
Introduced by Tom Deitz

Land of Terror
By Edgar Rice Burroughs
Introduced by Anne Harris

The Land That Time Forgot
By Edgar Rice Burroughs
Introduced by Mike Resnick

Lost on Venus
By Edgar Rice Burroughs
Introduced by Kevin J. Anderson

The Moon Maid:
Complete and Restored
By Edgar Rice Burroughs
Introduced by Terry Bisson

Pellucidar
By Edgar Rice Burroughs
Introduced by Jack McDevitt
Afterword by Phillip R. Burger

Pirates of Venus
By Edgar Rice Burroughs
Introduced by F. Paul Wilson
Afterword by Phillip R. Burger

Savage Pellucidar
By Edgar Rice Burroughs
Introduced by Harry Turtledove

Tanar of Pellucidar
By Edgar Rice Burroughs
Introduced by Paul Cook

Tarzan at the Earth's Core
By Edgar Rice Burroughs
Introduced by Sean McMullen

Under the Moons of Mars
By Edgar Rice Burroughs
Introduced by James P. Hogan

The Absolute at Large
By Karel Čapek
Introduced by Stephen Baxter

The Girl in the Golden Atom
By Ray Cummings
Introduced by Jack Williamson

The Poison Belt: Being an Account of Another Amazing Adventure of Professor Challenger
By Sir Arthur Conan Doyle
Introduced by Katya Reimann

Tarzan Alive
By Philip José Farmer
New foreword by Win Scott Eckert
Introduced by Mike Resnick

The Circus of Dr. Lao
By Charles G. Finney
Foreword by John Marco
Introduced by Michael Martone

Omega: The Last Days of the World
By Camille Flammarion
Introduced by Robert Silverberg

Ralph 124C 41+
By Hugo Gernsback
Introduced by Jack Williamson

Perfect Murders
By Horace L. Gold
Introduced by E. J. Gold

The Journey of Niels Klim to the World Underground
By Ludvig Holberg
Introduced and edited by
James I. McNelis Jr.
Preface by Peter Fitting

The Lost Continent: The Story of Atlantis
By C. J. Cutcliffe Hyne
Introduced by Harry Turtledove
Afterword by Gary Hoppenstand

The Great Romance: A Rediscovered Utopian Adventure
By The Inhabitant
Edited by Dominic Alessio

Mizora: A World of Women
By Mary E. Bradley Lane
Introduced by Joan Saberhagen

Prisoner of the Vampires of Mars
By Gustave Le Rouge
Translated by David Beus
and Brian Evenson
Introduced by William Ambler

A Voyage to Arcturus
By David Lindsay
Introduced by John Clute

Before Adam
By Jack London
Introduced by Dennis L. McKiernan

Fantastic Tales
By Jack London
Edited by Dale L. Walker

Master of Adventure: The Worlds of Edgar Rice Burroughs
By Richard A. Lupoff
With an introduction to the Bison
Books edition by the author
Foreword by Michael Moorcock
Preface by Henry Hardy Heins
With an essay by Phillip R. Burger

The Year 3000: A Dream
By Paolo Mantegazza
Edited and introduced by
Nicoletta Pireddu
Translated by David Jacobson